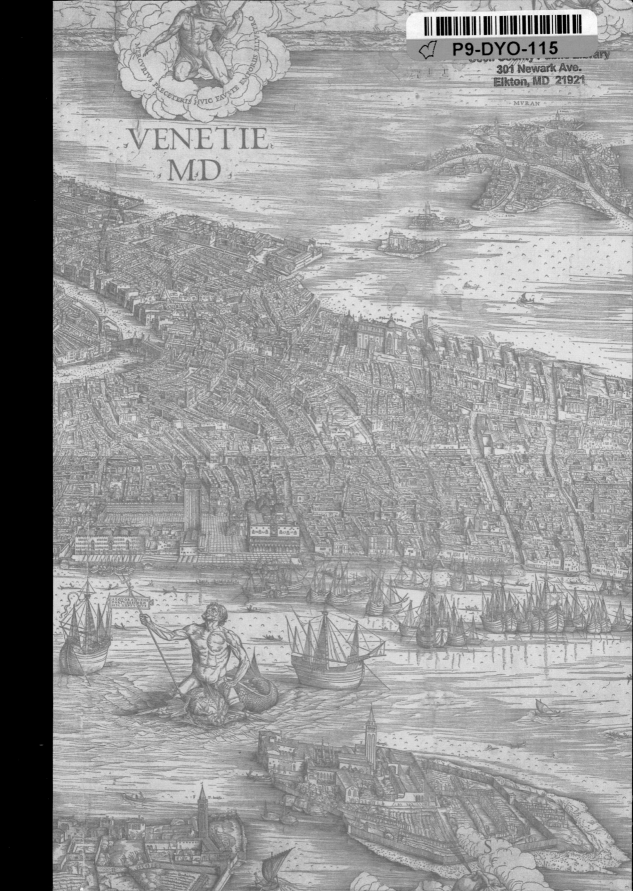

VENETIE
MD

MERCVRIVS PRECETERIS HVIC FAVSTE EMPORIIS ILLVSTRO

MVRAN

ALEQVORA TVENS PORTVS QVÆ IACET HIC NEPTVNVS

IAGO

A Novel

David Snodin

Henry Holt and Company • New York

Henry Holt and Company, LLC
Publishers since 1866
175 Fifth Avenue
New York, New York 10010
www.henryholt.com

Henry Holt® and ⬛ *® are registered trademarks of Henry Holt and Company, LLC.*

Library of Congress Cataloging-in-Publication Data

Snodin, David.
  Iago : a novel / David Snodin.
      p.   cm.
  Includes bibliographical references.
  ISBN 978-0-8050-9370-4
  1. Brothers—Fiction.   2. Murder—Investigation—Fiction.   3. Iago (Fictitious character)—
Fiction.   4. Cyprus—History—Venetian rule, 1474–1570—Fiction.   I. Title.
  PR6119.N63124 2011
  823'.92—dc22   2011017830

Henry Holt books are available for special promotions and premiums.
For details contact: Director, Special Markets.

First Edition 2011

Designed by Meryl Sussman Levavi

Printed in the United States of America

1 2 3 4 5 6 7 8 9 10

This is a work of fiction, inspired by another work of fiction, which was probably inspired by a still earlier piece of fiction, one of a set of Italian stories, which some claim may have been in its turn inspired by certain events that took place in Venice in the early sixteenth century. Diligent research has not enlightened me as to what these events actually were or if they ever occurred, but that is why I have set my novel in Venice and Cyprus in the early sixteenth century. I hope readers will indulge me in the liberties taken by my imagination, such as it is, just as they can pardon my matchless muse William Shakespeare for the many liberties he took with his own source and with history, for the sake of telling a good story. All comparisons between William Shakespeare and me end there.

Part

I

1. *The Castle*

On a disconcertingly mild February afternoon, some fifteen hundred and twenty years after Christ, two lords of Venice and a Florentine labored up a peak in the string of mountains that dominates much of the northern coast of the island of Cyprus. To the south a never-ending flatland, thickly forested, glimmered under a cloudless sky. Their destination remained far above them; they could not see it yet, because the peak was forested too.

Neither of the Signors had made so precipitous a trek in their long lives, though one was a soldier of great experience. They were wearing thick cloaks, as they would have in their home city, a thousand leagues north, so were hot and irritable. They had ridden hard for the best part of three hours to the base of the mountain, had endured an almost inedible lunch at an inn, and, because the trail could not accommodate horses, they had been offered a couple of bony, malodorous mules. They regretted declining them.

In strong contrast to their darkening humor, the Florentine seemed sprightly. His ascent was less arduous than theirs, not on account of his youth but because he was being carried by a pair of burly retainers in a chair strapped between two poles, for he had only one leg. The lords of Venice, fifty-seven and sixty-five years of age respectively, but with both legs intact, envied him. The ease of his passage, not to mention his high spirits, made him, in their opinion, less than endearing.

"Half a century old, Signors," the young man proclaimed, pointing upward, "but still sturdy and impregnable. Built by the lords of Byzantium as a protection against Arab incursion and subsequently expanded by the Lusignan kings, it was once called the Castle of the Lion, for it was besieged by the English Crusader King Richard. But today it is more commonly referred to as Buffavento, a shortening of *Buffa di Vento*."

As if in affirmation, a sudden and surprising gust of cold air almost toppled one of the Venetians, propelling his hat down the craggy path. A fortunately placed soldier, one of many following the party at a respectful distance, hurried to return it.

The Florentine laughed, annoying the briefly hatless Venetian still more. "Along with the other hill castles on the island, it is no longer thought to serve any strategic function—except as a place from which to espy invaders from the sea. But the steepness of the surrounding cliffs and this path being the only means of access make it an excellent place of confinement."

"Which is why you've put the murderer here," said Graziano Stornello, the elder of the two nobles. He'd been rather affronted by the young man's presumption that he knew nothing of history. He knew a fair amount—especially about military history and, indeed, the building of castles.

"Certainly," the Florentine replied.

"It's not very . . . convenient though, is it?" puffed the other Venetian, Graziano Stornello's younger brother Lodovico (who had briefly lost his hat). "Wouldn't it be more sensible to keep him closer to hand?"

The Florentine motioned to his bearers to stop awhile. "You must understand, Signors, that this is no ordinary villain. He is like a . . . like a . . . a pestilence, a . . . foul infection, an insidious contagion that cannot be felt until it is too late. He is a danger to all who come near him."

"I only meant," gasped Lodovico Stornello as they trudged on, "that for the purposes of interrogation it seems quite remote."

"Interrogation has proved futile thus far, though we continue to make efforts . . ." The Florentine raised an eyebrow. "The man has refused to speak a word since he was arrested."

The lords glanced at each other.

"Not a word?" asked Graziano Stornello.

"Not one."

The patricians allowed themselves to hang back as the Florentine was transported farther up the path and around yet another bend, not least because they needed to rest their aching legs.

"I think this criminal he talks of should come back to Venice with me," Graziano Stornello said quietly.

"I concur," his brother replied. "He should be placed in the hands of the *interroganti* and subjected to *proper* inquisitorial methods. They've probably only tickled him here."

"A contagion . . ." Graziano Stornello mused. "That's an interesting way of describing a man. And if he is indeed a danger to all who come close to him, as the young fellow claims, then I think the sooner he is removed from this volatile land the better."

"I don't suppose they even have the *strappado* here!" exclaimed Lodovico Stornello.

Graziano Stornello laid a hand on his kinsman's shoulder. "That's a shortcoming you will be able to remedy, I'm sure, when you're governor."

"Not much farther, lords!" the young Florentine shouted from above. They could see him waving through the trees.

"Arrogant pup," Lodovico Stornello muttered. "Didn't like him from the moment we landed. Swanking about as if he owns the place."

"Technically he does," Graziano Stornello said. "Until it's formally handed over to you. I shall perform the ceremony tonight."

Lodovico Stornello gazed south. There was good hunting to be had, apparently, in the vast forest beneath him. He saw mountains beyond it—loftier still than the range within which they stood, judging by the clouds that covered their peaks. And in the far distance a city sparkled: the capital, Nicosia. He would no doubt have a palazzo there. Indeed, he might have any number of palazzi. But then he shivered in the icy wind. "I'm not sure I want it."

They'd traveled for a month over rough seas to reach this colony, and Lodovico Stornello, who was generally forthright in his opinions, had not once vacillated during the voyage. This sudden hesitation was unsettling. "It produces fruit of many excellent varieties," Graziano

Stornello ventured. "You said yourself the wine we had last night was more than passable."

"But, as *you* admitted, it's . . . volatile . . . full of rebels . . ."

"Most outposts of the empire are, brother. They don't like us being here."

Graziano Stornello, a veteran of many conflicts and currently invested with the title of Captain-General of the Sea, understood that his sibling was in need, at that moment, of dedicated encouragement.

Toward the end of the previous year, reports had reached Venice that Cyprus, a perennially bothersome colony, had become yet more unmanageable. A new governor had been dispatched to rid it of the menace from the Ottoman—whose lands were less than a hundred leagues across the water. This he had managed to do. His second task had been to quell the natural insubordination of the island's unruly inhabitants. In this endeavor he had singularly failed. More disturbing still, the Venetian garrison itself had become riotous and disobedient. And the Ottoman Turks, alert to the disarray, were prodding once more at a precariously accessible coastline with their caïques and skiffs. Farther out to sea, bigger ships had been spotted. The place was, as ever, full of spies and agitators.

And so it was that the Serene Republic had decreed that Lodovico Stornello should take the governor's place. Graziano Stornello was to oversee the handover and to ensure, as a respected commander, that it was as swift and unruffled as possible. It had been his intention to conduct the ritual of conferral upon landing the previous morning, but circumstances had not allowed it.

To the Signors' astonishment, Cyprus was now under the command of the young Florentine. The governor whom Lodovico Stornello was there to replace had been murdered some three weeks earlier. Among the killer's other victims had been the governor's young wife. Niece to the two lords, daughter to their brother, Brabantio Stornello, her name was Desdemona.

But Graziano Stornello had lobbied hard for Lodovico Stornello's advancement. He decided, as they both surveyed the vista below them, to appeal to his mercantile instincts. "You could raze those thousands of acres of forest and plant anything you liked. We always have need of grain. Or exotic fruits—oranges, why not? Why must Venice go to Persia for her oranges? We are but three hundred leagues from Persia here, and almost as far south as they are. Why must we trade with the infidel for oranges? There's a fortune to be made here."

"I already have a fortune," Lodovico Stornello said smugly. He was indeed one of the richest men in Venice and had managed to become so without straying too far from the Rialto. Recently, however, he'd started to be tempted by more than the power of money. He had other brothers besides Graziano and Brabantio—ten in all—most of whom enjoyed positions of weight in the republic. Although Lodovico Stornello was a member of the Great Council, as were all the patricians in Venice, he'd grown a bit envious of his more politically engaged relatives, of their confidence and influence. Some had sway over men's lives.

"Agreed, brother, you have enriched yourself beyond anything I could contemplate," said Graziano Stornello. "But a shrewd and ruthless plutocrat such as yourself will always have a taste for further opportunity."

"Ruthless? Am I ruthless?"

"As unrelenting in business as I am sure you will be in the governance of this land."

"Yes, I suppose it does need an uncompromising approach," Lodovico Stornello mused. "A firm hand," he added, with a slight clench of a fist.

Graziano Stornello again patted the other's shoulder. "This young pup of a Florentine, as you so correctly call him, has evidently been far too moderate since his *entirely unapproved* accession to the governorship. And the previous governor, the Moor, was probably too lenient also."

"The Moor, yes . . . Brabantio always mistrusted him. What can have possessed the Doge and the Council to give command of this territory to a man with skin as black as night?"

Graziano Stornello did not elaborate on the color of the Moor's skin. He had in fact been an advocate of the Moor's appointment; he had always and only judged him as a warrior. So he changed the subject. "Brabantio won't take his daughter's death well, I think."

"It'll probably kill him. He's been sick for months."

Neither of the Signors had any real regard for their brother Braban-tio and had not felt any particular sorrow upon learning of the death of a niece they had rarely met, but they were, finally and most importantly, Stornelli. So Graziano Stornello said, "I think it behooves us, as Stor-nelli, to . . . sort this place out once and for all?"

"For the sake of a murdered niece, yes," said Lodovico Stornello.

"So that, dear Lodovico, is your mission."

"Yes, my mission," the younger lord repeated. "But what about the damned Turks?"

"The Turks, brother, are my problem, not yours." Graziano Stornello paused. "And you could be home within the year."

"I could?"

"Sooner, perhaps, if you're properly steadfast."

"Steadfast, yes . . ."

"And Venice, I'm confident, would be boundless in her gratitude."

"Boundless, yes . . ."

"Are you bolstered, brother?"

"I am," said Lodovico Stornello.

"That's good. Now let's go and meet the extraordinary devil who may well have been the cause of this whole upheaval."

They resumed their ascent, scuffing their fine shoes on the ever-steeper path.

The edifice they at last reached seemed piled upon itself on the mountain's summit, with level upon level of buttresses and battlements and many separate boxlike buildings. It appeared rather delicate in its way, despite having withstood five hundred years or so of high, batter-ing winds and a substantial number of sieges.

"Welcome to one of the most invincible fortresses in Christendom!" the Florentine exclaimed proudly.

"Invincible from within as well as without, we hope," said Graziano Stornello.

"There are guards posted at every corner of the trail, as you saw. You will witness for yourselves that the rest of the castle is encircled by cliffs."

The gate tower was a square, thick-walled, two-storey structure. The double doors were massive, a foot thick at least, and as they passed through them, Graziano Stornello noted that they could be secured from within by two sturdy ten-foot beams, currently resting against a wall, and with little evidence of having been moved for some time.

The guards in the tower did not look alert. The arrival of no less a personage than the Governor of Cyprus, let alone two illustrious members of the Venetian Signory, appeared to have no impact on them.

A small courtyard gave onto a steep flight of steps leading up to the rest of the castle. Even if an invading force were to overwhelm the main entrance, it would remain an easy target from above. Graziano Stornello peered over the low wall that would be the only means of escape and saw a drop of about three thousand feet, with nothing to break the fall.

The two lords ascended steps so vertiginous that the Florentine had to be lifted from his chair and carried up by one of his brawny soldiers. The Signors felt pleasingly nimble by comparison.

The lower ward of the castle was a cluster of buildings around a central enclosure—a hall, sleeping quarters, latrines, a bathhouse, a grain store, and a small chapel. Some of the doors could be reached directly, but others only by more steps or ladders. The space must have once bustled with life, but today its few occupants were asleep or dozing. Protected from the wind, the air was once again warm here, even sultry. Mangy dogs sniffed at one another, and chickens clucked. Despite the stench of urine and decomposing food, Graziano Stornello detected the scent of spices, which reminded him of the infidel *souks* he had known on his travels. He saw women, too, whom by the darkness of their skin he presumed to be local girls, prostitutes probably, for he knew of the island's reputation for lasciviousness.

"So where's our prisoner?" Lodovico Stornello asked brusquely, looking in vain for evidence of a door that might lead to a dungeon.

"I'm afraid you'll have to climb a bit farther still," said the Florentine.

The lords stared aloft, considering it an odd notion to have to clamber up again. They'd expected to be led down a dank flight of stairs to some airless, lightless chamber more suited to incarceration.

The upper section of the castle was yet another jumble of parapets and redoubts and lookout towers, all connected by still more steps, some of which hung precariously over the crags.

"Are all the prisoners kept up here?" Lodovico Stornello asked, puffing with the effort of almost vertical ascent.

"There is but one prisoner," the Florentine responded.

Graziano Stornello, though surprised, was also reassured. "So you keep the fellow in isolation. Good . . . good . . ."

"Even those assigned to watch the Mantuan never enter his cell," said the Florentine. "Only his interrogators are permitted to approach him. And I would advise you too, lords, to venture into his presence with caution—"

"The Mantuan?" Lodovico Stornello snapped.

"He's from Mantua?" Graziano Stornello echoed.

"Originally, or so he claims."

"He's not a Turk, then."

"No, Signor Lodovico, he is not a Turk, although he has traveled to Constantinople and other infidel lands."

"So he could be a spy, or some damned agitator."

"Are there any interrogators with him now?" Graziano Stornello inquired.

"They come and they go," said the Florentine. "You will be able to see for yourselves, lords, for that is where he is held."

They had reached the very top of the castle, the apex of the mountain indeed. The young man from Florence, still at a level below theirs, was pointing up to a small white box, the only structure to have been erected at this lofty altitude. It seemed to dangle hazardously over a plunging rock. It once must have been the castle's highest lookout point. There were windows indicative of that function on three of the walls. The murderer of the governor and his wife, and by report several others besides, was evidently not being consigned to the darkness he surely deserved.

The door to the little building was open. "As I said, Signors," said the Florentine, who was being carried up the final steps, "approach with care."

With some impatience, they entered.

Graziano Stornello walked to a window on the northern wall. It was not barred, or curtained, but open to the elements. He looked out and down. There was nothing between him and a ragged coastline, thousands of feet below. The sea seemed infinite and almost white under a blasting sun. Thoughts of home assaulted him, as they always do when a Venetian sailor stares at the ocean. He moved to the other two windows. There was the same abrupt plunge from both.

Aside from a narrow pallet bed, a table with a flagon and some playing cards upon it, and three or four chairs, one of which was on its side, the room was empty.

2. A Patrician's Funeral

Brabantio Stornello had been a philanthropist. Much of his wealth, inherited and accrued from his trading, had gone to good causes, notably toward the welfare of those far less advantaged than he. He would never mention—let alone boast about—his munificence, but many thousands of poor Venetians had reason to be grateful to him.

Typically for such a reticent individual, he had left instructions that when his time on earth was over he should be buried in the unexceptional Chiesa di San Rocco, set on the other side of the Campo San Rocco from the far larger church of the Frari—the imposing resting place of many great patricians and war heroes and senators and even three or four Doges, to say nothing of a number of Stornelli.

The church was also only a short walk from his own palazzo—so perhaps he'd hoped that any procession from home to final entombment would be a brief and unceremonious affair.

But Brabantio Stornello had also been a procurator of St. Mark's—one of only nine, in the sole gift of the Doge, who therefore had to attend the funeral, and the supreme leader's participation in the proceedings ensured that, however unassuming the interment, the preamble would be as ostentatious as possible.

Shortly after morning prayers, the bells of the Campanile di San Marco began to toll, two strokes at a time, signifying the passing of a great one. On the other side of town, at the palazzo, those of the Stornello family who were in Venice gathered in their mourning mantles to present their condolences, individually, to the widow and her three surviving daughters. Nobody who knew of the absence of Brabantio Stornello's fourth child—and most did—could fail to be moved; his fifteen-year-old daughter had perished as a consequence of some as-yet-unspecified ailment in Cyprus less than a month previously. The report of her passing and that of her husband, the governor of that land, had reached Venice a week earlier. Some were saying—though nobody even whispered it here—that the terrible news had been too much for Brabantio Stornello, who had died of a broken heart.

Once condolences had been offered and received, the Stornelli processed to the nearby Chiesa di San Rocco, where Brabantio Stornello's body had lain overnight. They walked four abreast, led by Alfredo Stornello, who as Archbishop of Treviso was the most senior cleric in the family, and three local priests, singing out prayers. Isabella Stornello and her daughters followed. The procurator lay in his open coffin, apparently composed and at peace, dressed in the habit of the Scuola di San Rocco—a golden cloak and a black velvet cap, with spurs on his boots and a sheathed sword at his side—for he was a knight of that charitable order. The Stornelli shuffled by him in a long line, bending their knees and crossing themselves. A good hour passed before everybody could be packed into the small church. The Most Reverend Patriarch of Venice Antonio Contarini offered up more prayers, and the coffin was lifted by four elderly fellow knights of the *scuola* and two of the Stornello brothers—the oldest present, Vincenzo Stornello, in his seventy-first year, and the youngest, Fabrizio Stornello, still a relatively sprightly fifty-two—and carried out, shakily but successfully, to a carriage for the onward journey to the Piazza San Marco.

By now a sizable crowd had assembled, some out of curiosity, some out of self-interest, but many from the less salubrious parts of the city to demonstrate their genuine sorrow.

There were senators too, members of the *Collegio,* and the Great Council, and the *Zonta,* and the Council of Ten, and the city's *Avogadori,* and sea captains and land captains, and bureaucrats and magistrates and inquisitors and hardheaded bankers and merchants, and clerical men. It seemed most of the nobility, the *ottimati,* had turned up, from all the ancient families: the Contarinis, the Corners, the Dandoli, the Malipieri, the Barbarini, the Grimanis, the Grittis, the Vendramins, the Loredans, the Morosini and the Mocenigi, the Veniers. For this day at least, the clans of Venice—often at one another's throats in matters of business and ambition, and their younger members through adolescent intemperance and a taste for violence—were at peace, united, if briefly, in mourning.

Carnival, at its height in this month of February, had been put on hold for the duration. On the route to the Piazza San Marco, the shops and even the taverns were shut. Some sixty monks from the Scuola della Misericordia joined the procession, flagellating themselves, along with about a hundred Jesuits calling out for Jesus's mercy. Well over a thousand torches spat and flickered in the gloomy morning air.

In the great piazza, the bells went on tolling as the coffin was lifted from its carriage and laid upon a catafalque in the immense church. Doge Grimani, approaching his ninetieth year and bent almost double, appeared, along with several dignitaries with whom he had been in conference: a visiting cardinal and a papal nuncio, a German prince on a mission from the Emperor, a French count on a similar one from the King of France, and the Duke of Urbino's son Guidobaldo della Rovere, accompanied by an uncle because he was not yet ten years old.

Doge Grimani made obeisance to the deceased—lengthily because of his great age—and then proffered his hoarse and barely audible condolences to the late procurator's widow. Following more prayers conducted by the patriarch, the coffin was hoisted up again, this time by eight sturdy members of the ducal guard, carried out of the basilica, and raised three times above their heads in front of the portico (a tradition accorded only to the procurators of St. Mark's). Each lift was greeted by a collective ululation from the assembled crowd, and Brabantio Stornello's body began its stately return journey. Many in the populace craned over the heads in front of them, or out of windows and from balconies, or from the rooftops and awnings onto which they had clambered. They had not had much sight of Doge Grimani recently. Most were saying he had become too old and too ill even to walk, and the luxuriously draped *portantina* in which he sat was heavily curtained. Nevertheless, some of those closest began to approach the conveyance, with pleas and petitions of various sorts, and had to be pushed back by the ducal guard.

Now there was a shout of "God save the Procurator Stornello!" Someone else yelled, "God save *il nobiluomo benevolo!*" and both cries were taken up by the multitude. Perhaps Isabella Stornello obtained some consolation from such evidence of public support for her late husband, but if she did she gave no indication of it, remaining somber and stoic. Then another in the throng yelled, "God save his daughter!" and that was echoed too, even more volubly. And, louder still, a chant began, following the full course of the procession, as more and more people cried out the name of Brabantio Stornello's youngest child—"Desdemona! Desdemona! Desdemona!"—over and over and over again. The sixteen-year-old Caterina Stornello, sister of Desdemona, stumbled slightly when she heard the sound, and the tears again coursed down her face.

The resonant reverberation of this single, sad appellation appeared to take the other Stornelli, and many of the *ottimati*, by surprise. The illustrious ones began to look anxious. The ducal guard grasped the hilts of their swords. Some became somewhat rougher than they perhaps needed to be, and a few individuals in the throng were shoved, and punched, and even beaten about the head. Some were pushed so forcibly that they sprawled painfully on the stony ground.

One of these unfortunates was a Stornello, even though, wearing black, he should have been readily identified as an official mourner. Sadly, none of his relatives noticed as his buttocks hit the cobbles or heard him emit a little yelp, because he had lagged behind. "I'm family!" he'd protested as he brushed the detritus of the street off his clothes, and the guard, after some self-important bristling and sneering, let him pass. He heard snickering as he moved off, which he thought predictable. He was a *nobiluomo*, after all, and such discomfiture was bound to provoke amusement among those less privileged.

He was not, however, a very significant Stornello. His was a paltry branch on the great Stornello tree. He was still a boy, really, with little knowledge of the world, having not yet reached his sixteenth year. He was by no means handsome, or well built, but skinny and with a delicate frame. His face might have been deemed pretty if he'd been a girl. He had a full mouth and a small nose. His hair, unusually for a Stornello, was the color of pale straw and hung down, if not very lustrously, to his shoulders, as was the fashion with sons of the nobility. His eyes were his most notable attribute—or so his mother had liked to coo when she was alive. They were large and green-blue, with long pale lashes. If people cared to look into them, and few did, they would have discerned a keen and watchful intelligence.

It was Gentile Stornello's sharp curiosity in all that was going on around him that had caused him to dawdle and to find himself at some distance from the main part of the procession. He had, almost from the start of the proceedings, been observing the progress of a beggar, a scrawny old man in stinking rags, with no legs and a monkey on his shoulder. The wretch had scraped himself along the ground, pushing himself forward with his fists, for the entire duration of the parade, with a surprisingly cheery expression on his pitted, toothless face. He'd made quite a lot of money for his efforts, perhaps three hundred *soldi*. But he'd eventually been stopped by a soldier, who had kicked him and struck him on the back of the neck with his sheathed sword. Gentile Stornello was pondering on the lives and fates of such desperately penurious people when he'd heard the chanting of the crowd.

He'd been as astonished as the rest of his kinsmen. He had not known Desdemona well; they had spoken only two or three times. If he remembered her at all it was as a demure, unexceptional girl. And yet the people of Venice were now calling out her name as they might for a hero returning from the wars or a saint on a saint's day.

Once he'd been permitted to move on, it still took him a good twenty minutes to join the principal mourners, by which time his uncle's corpse was waiting at the bottom of the steps of the small church that was to be its final place of rest.

But the Doge and his party had been delayed, and nobody could enter the church before the Doge, not even the late Brabantio Stornello. So Gentile Stornello, being of an observational bent, took advantage of the hiatus by devoting his attention to his great family, concentrating mostly on his uncles, seven of whom were present. They did not meet too frequently like this and presumably had much to discuss.

3. My Family

As we stand in the Campo San Rocco waiting for the Doge, and as I watch my uncles, I feel a large rough hand on my shoulder and hear a gruff, familiar voice. "Thought we'd lost you."

It's my brother Benvenuto. He towers over me. He's a tall and broad young man with an open, amiable face. Whenever I see him, which isn't often as he's mostly away in the wars, I'm somehow surprised that we *are* brothers. We couldn't be more different—in temperament, in interests, in appearance. He's a simple, generally cheerful, and unquestioning soul, and a soldier, of course. I'm more the scholarly sort, by nature a thinker and doubter, and I don't have a soldierly bone in my body. He's handsome in his way, and I don't think anybody could call me that. Whenever I'm in his company, I feel so very small and puny. "I got a bit lost in the crowd . . ."

"Head in the clouds again?"

I decide not to tell him of my encounter with the ducal guard and that I was pushed to the ground and that my backside still aches, because he will either laugh at me or, in his impulsive way, he will try to find the guard and push *him* to the ground and probably thrash him a bit too—and, while that is something I'd dearly like to see, I'm not sure it would be fitting on such a solemn day as this.

"God, this is *boring*," he grumbles.

"It's a funeral," I say. "What did you expect?"

"But how much *longer* is it going to go on for?"

"Oh, another few hours, I don't doubt. There's a liturgy to come, a Communion, an oration, I suppose, and then our uncle has to be put into his tomb."

"God!" he mutters, and then: "Promise me something, brother. If I get killed, will you make sure that I'm not sent off to heaven in such a long and tedious way?"

"Don't say that!"

"Soldiers do get killed in wars, you know."

"Don't say it anyway."

"Why not?"

"Because it's a fateful thing to say."

"I thought you didn't believe in fate."

"I don't, but I don't think you should tempt it anyway."

He laughs and gives me a friendly cuff about the head. "You're a complicated mite, aren't you?" Then he announces in a low growl, "I believe in fate; I believe there's a battlefield somewhere with my name on it."

I can only react with a shudder. We're not very close, but I'm always delighted to see him. He's right. Soldiers do get killed in the wars. Some of my cousins have been killed. Why should he be spared? So every time he returns to Venice I'm overjoyed that he's still alive.

He guffaws again and grasps me around the shoulders. "Or maybe there isn't. Maybe I'll become a feeble and toothless old sort, like some of our uncles over there . . . I hope not."

He finds them amusing; I find them daunting. They are stern-faced and formal with one another, as befits the seriousness of the day, but not one of them seems visibly saddened by the demise of a brother. They lean inward as they meet, muttering a sentence or two, and sometimes a guarded smile passes between them, or a shake of the hand, or a cursory pat on the shoulder. But there's no warmth there, no fraternity.

I can't help noticing that my father, Fabrizio Stornello, the youngest at fifty-two, is standing slightly apart from the others. None of them is speaking to him. In fact, *nobody's* speaking to him—and nobody has, as far as I've been able to see, throughout the long day, apart from the occasional penitent or beggar, to whom he's handed a few *soldi*. And there he stands now—looking rather forlorn, a little bit adrift—not knowing quite what to do.

He has seemed fairly aimless recently. I don't know why. His business dealings haven't been going too well, I suspect, although I know little about such things. Belts have had to be tightened in the palazzo.

I know he's no longer on the Council of Ten and therefore not as much at the heart of things as he's been used to. He hasn't told me why. He hasn't said much at all to me in the month since it happened. Perhaps that's the reason for his moroseness. He used to be so full of rage and bluster aimed at the Council and what he considered to be their idiotic decisions, and we would bear the brunt of his incandescence. I haven't known him to be this crestfallen since my mother died five years ago. There's always been a distance between us—I know he doesn't much like me and never has—but now I feel a rush of sorrow for him. For a moment or two I feel like going over to him, perhaps just to stand with him, as a sign of solidarity. But I know if I were to do that he would only blink at me in bewilderment.

So once more I watch my uncles, his brothers. I see so little of them that I still struggle to put a name to a face.

I can identify Vincenzo because he's the oldest. He must be at least twenty years older than my father. He carried the coffin out of the church this morning, at the start of this interminable ceremony, along with my father and some of the knights of the Scuola di San Rocco. He's so very frail that he could manage only a few steps. I recognize some of my uncles by what they're wearing—Bishop Alfredo, obviously (there's talk of his becoming a cardinal soon), with his white and gold miter and his crook, and the two who are still members of the Council of Ten, in their official scarlet robes; one is Cristoforo, the other Tommaso, but I'm afraid I don't remember which is which.

Similarly I can never distinguish between my uncles Daniele and Ottaviano, because they are close to each other in age and look so alike, and in marked contrast to the other brothers they spend a lot of time in each other's company, forging various business deals, apparently. They're both immensely wealthy. They're said to have more than a hundred servants in each of their households. We have ten.

I see that my uncle Ubaldo has chosen not to be a part of this huddle of *cittadini influenti* but is walking among the other mourners, clasping a hand here or an elbow there. He's just a year or two older than my father, and I like him, mainly because he seems to like me, or at least to tolerate my existence. I attended lectures at the seminary with his sons, my cousins Liborio and Maurizio, and occasionally they invited me back to their palazzo. Not that my uncle Ubaldo is in Venice much these days. He's been spending more and more of his time at his villa on *terra firma*, especially since his wife died.

The most famous and instantly recognizable of the clan, Graziano Stornello, Captain-General of the Sea, isn't here, of course. He's in Cyprus with my uncle Lodovico. I know nothing of them, except by reputation. One is a war hero; the other the most successful merchant in our family, richer even than Daniele and Ottaviano. He has never married, has no offspring, and lives alone, apart from his servants, in a huge house close to the Rialto, which I've gawked at but have never seen the inside of.

It seems a bit strange that such a hermitlike individual with a preference for not stepping much beyond his own home, except to hunt, should suddenly have been dispatched to Cyprus, a hot and dusty and unwelcoming place, they say, and at least a thousand leagues away.

None of this would be of any interest to me at all, and I wouldn't have given it a second thought today, if I hadn't just heard the name of my ill-fated cousin Desdemona being called out over and over again.

She was a mousy thing when she was alive, I thought, really very plain—not like her sisters, who are pretty, especially Caterina, who's gorgeous. Also unlike her sisters, with their raven-colored hair, and therefore unlike most Venetian girls, she was blond, which set her apart, I suppose. I didn't see her very often, spoke to her two or three times at most and only by way of greeting, so perhaps she possessed hidden attributes. Something must have made her attractive to the man they call the Moor, whom she married shortly before the two of them left for Cyprus. He died with her, of course, of some pestilence, or so they're saying.

A lot of people are also saying that my uncle Brabantio died of grief.

The official line is that he'd been sick for months, but he passed away within a day of receiving the news of his daughter's death, which reached Venice just over a week ago.

One thing I do know (and maybe shouldn't) is that my uncle Brabantio didn't approve of Desdemona's marriage to the Moor. He fell ill soon after it took place. I know this because my father, who was on the Council then, told me of it—well, not me specifically; he bawled it out in a fury to anyone in the palazzo who was around to hear it. "Witchcraft!" he raged. "The blackamoor seduced her with spells and potions!"

All the things I know have come from his indiscreet explosions, which have now so abruptly stopped. I know Lodovico was sent out to replace the Moor as governor—or, as my father put it: "He's botched it. You can't put a man like that in charge of a country. It's their brains, you know, and all that heat and sun in Africa or wherever it is they come from. It shrinks their brains, the difference between a grape and a raisin . . . He couldn't squash the uprising there, and now they've sent out your incompetent uncle Lodovico to take his place, a man who's never been out of Venice in his life."

It hasn't been announced yet that Lodovico is the new governor, but it will be soon, I daresay. I presume my uncle Graziano is there to make sure he doesn't "botch it," as the Moor obviously did.

I've decided my uncles are a sinister band, holding secrets to their chests. I have the palpable feeling that there's much they are talking about that is *not to be known*, about Cyprus possibly, about Desdemona and the Moor—I'm becoming a cynic, *un vero scettico*.

But here's Doge Grimani at last. I've never seen him close before. He's the tiniest thing, or perhaps it's just that he seems to be coiled in on himself. He has to be helped down from his *portantina*, surrounded by important-looking personages who don't look too happy about being caught up in this whole business. The only one of them who seems cheerful—inappropriately so—is an expensively dressed boy. He can't be more than ten years old, but he's behaving as if he's the most significant person in the square, like a king receiving the acclamation of his subjects. "That's the Duke of Urbino's son," explains Benvenuto. "His father's very ill, probably dying, so they must have sent him along in his place."

"He looks like a conceited brat."

"So would you, if you were about to inherit Urbino."

Benvenuto's knowledge surprises me. I've always thought he cares for little but traveling and fighting and carousing with his fellow soldiers. "How did you know *that*?"

He shrugs. "I know what I learn on the battlefield, and the Duke of Urbino is a first-rate captain."

The coffin is lifted again and taken up the steps, in the wake of the Doge and his visitors, this time by six of my uncle Brabantio's stout servants. The grief on their faces is blatant. They are followed by my aunt Isabella, who I must say has seemed amazingly poised throughout the whole awful day, and her three remaining daughters, Rosalia and Severina and the exquisitely lovely Caterina, who's been weeping from the start of things but is now doing her best to stop her tears. Then the uncles enter the church, and now everyone else.

"If we hold back a bit," suggests Benvenuto slyly, "we may not be able to get in; we can just hang around out here. . . ."

He's right, because the Chiesa di San Rocco is a modestly sized building, compared to the Frari, which dominates the square like a beached galleon. But I berate my brother now. "Of course you have to go in—you're the eldest son, *il successivo*. You have to sit with Father."

My father breaks into a relieved smile as he sees his preferred son approach. If Benvenuto *is* killed in the wars, his world will collapse, as my uncle Brabantio's evidently did.

I *can* hold back, as I doubt anyone will notice my not being in the main body of the congregation, among the Stornelli. I slip around the edge of the crowd and lean my weary body against a sarcophagus.

I can just about see the coffin, which has been placed on a platform in front of the high altar, and the tops of the heads of the monks of the *Misericordia* and the Jesuits, whipping themselves and wailing out to Jesus. A choir of novices from the Monastery of Sant'Appolonia, who have the best young voices in Venice, starts to sing the *Kyrie*. My father has suggested more than once that I should become a novice myself. I suppose he thinks it the only honorable vocation for a bookish son with no physical abilities. But one of the many things I can't do is sing—or not like that.

High-pitched cadences and soaring threnodies always melt my soul. The more complex the harmonies, the more I am moved. Today is no exception. I feel the tears fill my eyes. I can only imagine what effect these angelic reverberations are having on those who have far greater reason to feel sorrowful than I do—in particular Desdemona's mother and sisters, up there in front of the coffin, creased with loss.

A shuffling of feet on the flagstones and muttered imprecations mean that the Eucharist is being given. I distinguish the tremulous voice of my uncle Alfredo, Bishop of somewhere, who's conducting the Communion—*Hic est enim calix sanguinis mei.* It's only the heads of the families and the first sons and the direct relatives of my uncle Brabantio who are to receive the bread and wine today; otherwise, it would take forever.

At last the business of Communion is over. I can make out a hairless, gnarled pate over the throng, but it's only when I hear the name of "Girolamo Stornello" that I realize the oration is to be delivered by no less esteemed a personage than my grandfather. I'd thought he was so very near death, at ninety-four, that he wouldn't be able to make it. I didn't see him in the square or during the procession.

I can't hear a word. Those I'm close to can't either. They're turning to one another and mouthing, "What? What? What's he saying?" I hoist myself onto the top of the tomb. Standing next to the old ninny is my uncle Vincenzo, of advanced years himself, murmuring into his ear, prompting him.

There's an impatient rustling in the congregation. I can see the Doge's horned hat turning this way and that. Others' chins are dropping to their chests. There are stifled yawns and the tapping of boots. Some of the youngsters are giggling quietly, earning admonitory looks and even the occasional slap from their elders.

I think the cantankerous old fool would be perfectly happy to babble on for all time, but suddenly I see *Il Principe Supremo* making his way, helped by a host of flunkies, toward the main door. He must have got bored, and who can blame him? He does have a republic to run, after all. At such an abrupt departure, even my senile grandfather knows he has to stop, and now he's guided away by another of my uncles, one of the Councillors. The choir starts to sing the *In Paradisum* as the coffin is yet again lifted. I realize soon enough that it's being borne toward me and the tomb on which I've been sitting. For a heart-stopping second or two I think I might be perched on Brabantino Stornello's sepulchre and I jump down quickly, but the procession passes on. I catch Caterina's glance. For a few seconds she's looking directly at me. She seems resolutely composed now, firm-lipped and high-chinned, but there is moisture in her big eyes. Why is there such beauty in sorrow?

"Let's get out of here," says Benvenuto, who's beside me again. "I'm off to Milan first thing."

"Don't you think we should at least wait until our uncle has been put under marble?"

"Why? Did you know him?"

I follow him outside.

Night has fallen and torches flare, and it's starting to snow. With the boys of Sant'Appolonia singing the *Lux Aeterna* within the church, quite lustily, all of a sudden there's an almost festive air to the occasion. Or maybe it's only relief that a long, cheerless day is coming to an end. It's bitingly cold and people need the comfort of their hearths, so nobody hangs around much.

I agree that there seems little point in staying. My legs ache, my buttocks hurt, and the snow's becoming heavy. I need food and a warm fire and a soft bed. So I nod and Benvenuto and I set off for our palazzo, which isn't far. He strides decisively, as he always does, and I hobble and skip after him, trying to keep up. I slide, as the ground beneath the settling snow is icy.

"It's all a bit strange, don't you think?" I say.

"What's strange?"

"People are saying our uncle died of grief. Father thinks so too; he says that our uncle never approved of the marriage to the Moor, and he fell ill just after they left for Cyprus."

"I can think of much better things to die of, like a sword straight to the heart, but grief?" Benvenuto puffs dismissively.

I blunder on. "Father also believes that Desdemona's husband, the Moor, messed things up over there—"

"Grief is a weak thing to die of."

"Have you noticed how sad Father seems, how quiet he's being?" I'm battering him with these questions because I see him so rarely.

"Can't say I have." To be fair, my warrior brother notices very little when he's in Venice. He hates being here. He's never happier than when out in the open country and in perpetual peril. He always appears to be so awkward on his visits home; it's as if he's too bulky and feral for the narrow streets and the packed *campi* and the boat-filled canals, trapped like a restless beast in a cage.

He looks very uncomfortable now. We've reached the street door of the palazzo. He puts a hand on my shoulder and looks at me with a sudden and surprising expression of disquiet. I haven't received such an admonitory gaze from him since I was a small boy, "Father often comes out with stuff he shouldn't."

"I know." I have to acknowledge what I suppose I've always been aware of—that my soldier brother is perhaps more astute than he outwardly seems.

He bangs on the door, and while Leonzino—our redoubtable but slumberous doorkeeper—shuffles toward it from within, Benvenuto mutters, "Be careful, little brother, be careful with that clever brain you've got."

The door opens and we enter, shaking the snow from our cloaks. I try to laugh it off. "You're telling *me* to be careful! You're the one we should worry about!"

"I'll be fine," he says. "I'm quite good at what I do."

And by all accounts he is. He's had letters of praise from the Holy Roman Emperor of Germany, no less, and one from the King of France. And he's still not yet twenty.

Welcome cooking smells fill our home. "I'm starving," I say. "Shall we go and see what Zinerva's got to eat?"

He shakes his big head. "It's straight to bed for me. I have to be up well before dawn."

"When do you think you might be back?"

He shrugs. "Not until the summer, or maybe later. It looks as if it's going to be a long campaign."

"Well, take care, brother," I say. "And good luck." We do that nervous and stiff fraternal dance around each other. He pats me on the head and then disappears to his chamber, boots banging up the stairs.

I go down to the kitchen. Zinerva, our plump cook, has made *un stufato di coniglio*, which is bubbling away in a great pot on the fire and smells wonderful as usual.

"Sad day?" she asks, washing her thick hands in the basin.

"Very sad," I reply. "And very long."

Balbina, our humpbacked, gap-toothed scullery girl, is sitting by the fireplace, shelling *fagioli di fava* into a bowl. "It's horrible about that Desdemona passing on like she did," she says. "What sickness did your cousin die of, do you know?"

"I heard it was some terrible plague that's killed off almost the whole island. Did you see the procession?"

"For a bit. I get pushed over a lot though, so I didn't stay for the whole thing."

"Did you hear them all cry out her name?"

"Yes. Everybody's talking about her now."

"She should be left to rest in peace, *piccina povera*," Zinerva declares. "It'll be proclaimed soon enough what she died of. Until then, let's not go believing tittle-tattle." Zinerva is dismissive of gossip of all kinds. She also knew Desdemona better than I did, or at any rate she was friendly with the girl's chambermaid, whose name I can't remember but who went with my cousin and her new husband to Cyprus.

I take a spoon and dip it into the rabbit stew, but I'm reprimanded. "Don't touch!" Zinerva cries. "You'll wait till your father's home and you can both sit down to a proper supper."

"But I'm so hungry!" I whine, childishly.

Balbina giggles and Zinerva, seduced as always by this tactic, relents. "All right, take a bowl."

"I'll take it up to my chamber if I may. I'm exhausted."

"Why are you limping like that?" Balbina asks as I falter toward the door.

"I fell over in the snow."

"*Ragazzo maldestro*," I hear Zinerva mutter as I ascend the stairs.

I sit at the table in my chamber, in front of the fire, gobbling *stufato* as Giovanni, my manservant, brings jugs of hot water to prepare a soothing bath. I stare out at the thick flakes of snow falling outside the casement and think of death.

What if I were to die, for some reason? Who would miss me?

But why am I pondering on my own death now? Apart from two childhood maladies—which I survived (although my younger brother and sister didn't)—I've never faced any sort of danger in my life and doubt I shall.

This, for what it's worth, is what my life has been so far, as one might scribble it in a diary:

Gentile Venier Stornello, b. in the sestiere di San Polo in Venice at the Palazzo Stornello Piccolo, July 23, AD 1507; father, Signor Fabrizio Stornello, merchant of Venice, sometime member of the Council of Ten; mother, Filomena (born Filomena Venier), d. August 9, 1517; two brothers, Benvenuto (b. 1503), soldier, and Ippolito (b. 1509, d. 1514); one sister, Flora (b. 1513, d. 1518).

Travels: Padua (eight times), Vicenza (once), Bologna (once), Ferrara (once). Outside Italy—none.

Educated mainly at the Patriarchal Seminary and at home by Friar Domenico Lovato (d. 1519), latterly, and at present at home by Baldassare Ghiberti, Doctor of Philosophy at Padua. Attending lectures and debates at Rialto School of Philosophy. Hoping to continue studies at Padua.

Rhetorical skills: two commendations from Patriarchal Seminary (distinguished and highly distinguished), three distinctions from Rialto School of Philosophy. Grammatical skills: four commendations from Patriarchal Seminary (three distinguished, one highly distinguished). Liberal arts and literary skills: two prizes in sonnet competition at St. Mark's, one prize for discourse on Virgil's *Eclogues* at St. Mark's. Musical skills: viol and recorder, acceptably proficient. Dancing skills: not good. Singing skills: dreadful. Sporting skills: none.

I'm destined for a lengthy and unthreatened existence that will consist mainly of books, which I love. My tutor, Baldassare Ghiberti, Doctor of Philosophy at Padua, who lives with us when he's not in Padua, tells me that I write reasonably well for a fifteen-year-old. I've penned a few sonnets and discourses and, as outlined above, won some awards. Perhaps I shall become a celebrated philosopher or, better still, a poet.

4. Two Graves in Cyprus

The Moor had left instruction that he should be buried "where he fell." He'd been fond of repeating that he thought himself a citizen of the world. He had no home, state or country to which he could claim to belong, and never revealed to anyone his place of birth, except to say that it was a fiery region and far away.

Those with the task of implementing his wish believed it had been made on the assumption that he would be laid to rest in or near a battle-field. But he had not died in battle. He had breathed his last in his bed-chamber, in an unexpected manner, in the citadel at Famagusta, a fortified town on the east coast of the island, which was where most of the Venetian forces were garrisoned.

His wife—surprisingly, perhaps, for one not yet sixteen years old—had left a last testament, in which she had written simply: *I wish to lie next to my beloved lord and husband in death as I have in life.*

There had been no lying in state, no dignified passage of mourners. The funeral had been immediate and cursory, conducted at speed by the Venetian Patriarch of Cyprus. The attendees had been the new gov-ernor, a small collection of hurriedly assembled local dignitaries, a few long-standing Venetian expatriates, and about ten senior members of the garrison. Some two hundred foot soldiers had been posted around the Cathedral of St. Nicolas in Famagusta to discourage any violence or insurgence.

Now, on a muggy afternoon some three weeks later, the freshly des-
ignated Governor, Lodovico Stornello, and his older brother Graziano,
Captain-General of the Sea, decided to pay their respects to the remains
of their late niece Desdemona—something they had not yet been able to
do, as they had been on the island for only a day and two nights and had
been preoccupied with other concerns.

All morning they had overseen the punishment of the jailers and
guards from the castle of Buffavento, or whatever the place had been
called, those who had somehow, through inattention or possibly collu-
sion, allowed their one and only prisoner to escape.

None of the men questioned had been cooperative or informative. It
had been almost impossible to communicate with them in any event, as
they had spoken a strange and guttural form of Greek, which bore no
resemblance to the tongue that the lords had reluctantly learned in
their youth. The handful of Venetians at the castle had vociferously
absolved themselves of all responsibility.

Lodovico Stornello had wanted all who had been at the castle to be
tortured and then publicly hanged. It would be a sign of the rigor with
which he proposed to rule. Graziano Stornello had persuaded him not
to be quite so impetuous. The slaughter of upward of fifty locals, he
advised, would not be the wisest first move for a new governor.

In the end, the Cypriots who had been closest to the villain's cell,
some ten in all, were hanged that morning in the main courtyard of the
citadel. The others had been flogged and then sent to suppurate in the
prisons of Famagusta and would be interrogated further in due course.
The four or five Venetians had been spared but deprived of their status
as soldiers. The heads of the hanged men were stuck on spikes on the
ramparts of the citadel, and their corpses had been thrown into the
street outside the gate tower.

It was around these naked, tangled bodies that the two Signors of
Venice had to step gingerly as they set out for the Cathedral of St. Nicolas, accompanied by twenty members of the garrison guard. The journey took longer than it might have in a less perilous town. The lords
were unable to walk more than a few paces at a time while their mind-
ers inspected every dark recess or doorway for potential assassins.

Graziano Stornello asked the man in command of these men, a grizzled Venetian: "How long have you been in Cyprus?"

"Two years, almost."

"A good while. You'll perhaps be returning home soon."

"I go where I'm paid to go, sir—and I've been to worse places."

"Yes, I've been to far less commodious places myself. I'd call this a pretty good posting. The wine's good—I've tasted it—there's no shortage of food, the weather's neither too hot nor too cold, and I understand that the island provides all sorts of other . . . pleasures."

"I'm not complaining."

"Perhaps some of the troops don't realize how lucky they are, Captain, having not known quite as much of the world as you and I have."

"I say to my lads, sir, they should try sleeping in a ditch where the rain's so cold it comes down on you like shards of glass, and you ain't eaten nothing for three days. Or to be out somewhere where you think you could cook to death like a roasted *porco* and it ain't rain in your face, it's sand."

"How many serve directly under your command?"

"Fifty all told, sir."

"And what's the mood, generally, among them?"

"They're good men, sir, and not one of them has been unruly." Like the excellent captain he undoubtedly was, he wasn't going to say anything bad about those he led. But the fact that he had vouched for them so keenly betrayed the fact that others had not been as well behaved.

"You lead them by example, I am certain of it," said Graziano Stornello. "Although I do understand there's been some disarray in the citadel—"

"Not from my lot, there hasn't," the man quickly interjected.

"Some bloodshed too, I understand—several men wounded and a fair number killed."

The soldier stiffened. The Signor laid a hand on his shoulder as they walked on. "Oh, come now, good fellow," he said softly, "do you think I'm here on holiday, to restore my old limbs under a bit of warm sunshine?"

"You arrived here with four ships and a thousand more men, sir . . . That don't seem to me like a Signor on holiday would do."

The lord smiled. "Why do you think there was such discontent?"

"I wouldn't know, sir."

"May there have been some provocation, some incitement?"

"In-*what*, sir?"

Graziano Stornello decided to be more direct. "How well were you acquainted with the man who I believe is referred to as the Mantuan?"

"The Mantuan?"

"I've no idea why he's called that; I can only conclude it's because he's from Mantua."

"If you mean Captain Iago, sir, who was personal captain to the governor, God rest his soul—I mean God rest the governor's soul, not Iago's, sir."

Iago.

In all his inquiries in the past couple of days, Graziano Stornello had not heard the name before. Even the Florentine had spoken of the criminal only as "the Mantuan."

What a curious name it was—not Italian, certainly. It had a Spanish ring to it. Iago . . .

"Yes, yes," he said. "Iago—how well did you know him?"

"I spoke with him now and then, but not much; he was closer to the governor than to us men, sir. He seemed a good type though; he wasn't standoffish, he'd come down to our quarters, to the wardroom or wherever, he was always ready to stand us a drink. Him and the men, they had a few sing-alongs; he had some tales to tell of the places he'd been to and the battles he'd fought in."

"So he was . . . *liked*?"

"From what I knew of him, I'd say he was the honorable sort . . . honest, I reckon—yes, *honest*, very *honest*—until he was clapped in irons and taken away, sir, for what reason I still don't know."

"You don't know why he was arrested?"

"No, sir."

This was an interesting disclosure. Graziano Stornello had presumed that it would be common knowledge that Iago of Mantua was a murderer. The Florentine had not told him that the slayings had been kept a secret. Indeed, the Florentine had so far told his brother and him very little—except that the villain was a traitor and a pestilence and that he had somehow infected the whole garrison, then killed the Moor and Desdemona in their bedchamber.

But now the captain leaned forward and looked over his shoulder to ensure he wasn't being overheard. "There's been talk, of course."

"There always is. . . ."

"Some are saying he was in the pay of the Turk, sir . . .

"I see."

"And there's others say he killed his wife."

"His wife?"

There was a nod. "Saw the woman dead on the floor and Captain Iago with a knife in his hand. . . ."

"You're telling me the Mantuan murdered his wife?"

The soldier once again glanced about the square. "I'm only saying what's been spoken of, sir," he said softly.

"And you believe it?"

"I know to believe nothing, sir, until it's been confirmed. I'm only saying it as you seemed to want to know. I don't trust gossip."

"Good man," Graziano Stornello muttered. "And the governor and the Lady Desdemona? How do people suppose they died?"

"There's no talk about that, sir." The captain regarded his questioner with astonishment. "They died of a sickness. That's what we were told."

"Yes, of course."

A sickness . . .

Graziano Stornello's opinion of the Florentine went up a notch.

"A sickness, yes," he murmured, as if he'd known that all along.

They'd reached the cathedral.

As a military man, Graziano Stornello did not readily confess to his liking for old architecture. It was a private enjoyment. Before entering, he had to look up. He was impressed. The building seemed to belong to another land. He was reminded of the soaring structures he'd seen in more northerly and far colder places—in France and the German Empire. He knew that men from those regions had been here—the Crusaders, predecessors of the Lusignan kings—and supposed they must have built it, either on their way to Jerusalem or on their return. It was not as grandly proportioned as those masterpieces, and it was made of warmer stone. But it was a striking replication.

It had the same tall towers topped by pyramid-shaped spires on either side of a huge circular stained-glass window with delicate tracery over the monumental main entrance, which was set in a pointed arch, as were the many other windows. Every one of the three substantial storeys of the cathedral was adorned with statues of the apostles, saints, and martyrs and certain Crusaders too, holding their swords at rest or aloft, and also a few kings. There were sculpted buttresses protruding from every corner, with the faces of ugly demonic creatures, as the northern churches had. It had been constructed, Graziano Stornello thought, with elegance and artistry, and there was a spiritual grace to it.

He considered the doughty men who must have built it—devout, courageous souls, doggedly creating, over decades and more, a place of beauty for their worship, in what was then an unchristian and inimical land. As far as he could see, it was easily the tallest and most noble structure in a sprawling, ramshackle, and sun-beaten town, the most dignified building he'd seen yet on this largely unprepossessing island. He decided to look upon it as a symbol of hope standing proud against the heresy and subversion that hemmed it in. Despite its Christian kings and recent Venetian occupation, the Ottoman threats continued and the people remained stubbornly hostile.

And now, somewhere out there, was this Iago of Mantua, perhaps an infidel himself.

"It might not be too safe, sir, to stay out here for long."

Graziano Stornello looked around the baking cathedral square. Some scrawny dogs sniffed for scraps. A few lethargic individuals dozed in doorways or under trees.

But the soldiers were looking edgy, and the Signor had already marked the captain out as a dependable sort, so he thought it best to follow his advice. And his younger brother, to whom one building was pretty much like another, was waiting irritably at the door.

The interior of the church was filled with shafts of spectral light. Graziano Stornello was pleased to see that at least two of the windows depicted the Lion of St. Mark. Below one of these, in an aisle to the right of the central nave, were the burial places of the deceased governor and his wife, toward which he and his brother were now guided. There was as yet no sign of any form of tomb—only two slabs in the ground, made of rough sandstone, with nothing carved on either. Which was the Moor's and which was their niece's, they could not tell.

Before these anonymous memorials sat the young Florentine. He seemed to wake from a reverie, straightening and blinking up at them.

A short, portly personage with a sallow complexion and a mat of greasy hair now rose from beside him and bowed sycophantically.

"Great Signors, good afternoon," said the Florentine, who, but for lack of a leg, would have stood too. "This is Pietro Bellini, a relative of the Bellinis, painters of Venice, with whom I'm sure you're familiar. He has made his home here on the island."

Graziano Stornello pondered briefly why a kinsman of so talented a family should have ended up in Cyprus. He must have been one of the less gifted Bellinis.

"Messer Bellini and I were just discussing the plans for the sepulchre," the Florentine continued. "He has sketches, if you'd care to inspect them."

The fat little artist hastily spread out a collection of parchments on the floor. "It will be an incomparable memorial, Illustrious Ones, to a great warrior and his wife, with a representation of the many celebrated battles he fought in, and there will be a fine depiction of her, perhaps gazing up at him in devotion."

Neither of the lords bothered even to glance at the plans. Instead, the new governor asked, "Who'll pay for this monument? Venice?" The price of things was never far from his mind.

"Venice won't have to fork out a ducat," the Florentine replied, through slightly gritted teeth. "The cost will come out of the late governor's inheritance."

"He made a bit, did he?" Lodovico Stornello inquired.

"He was a *condottiere*," Graziano Stornello explained. He was well aware of how much money a successful mercenary commander could make in a lifetime of warfare.

"An outstanding one too," declared the Florentine.

With a clatter of boots on stone, someone burst into the church. The soldiers surrounded the Signors protectively with rapidly unsheathed swords. The new arrival was sweating and disheveled and breathless. "I have a message," he cried, "from the Serene Republic for the Captain-General Graziano Stornello and the Governor Lodovico Stornello!" He was wearing a tunic adorned with the Lion of St. Mark, so the news was from the highest source.

"You can give it to me," said the captain of the guard, pushing him back toward the door.

"I admire your concern for our safety, Captain," said Graziano Stornello, "but I don't think he's travelled a thousand leagues to harm us."

The messenger was permitted to approach.

"How long has it taken you to get here?" asked Lodovico Stornello, remembering his own lengthy and storm-tossed voyage.

"Nine days, lord."

Graziano Stornello was impressed. "A swift vessel, then, friendlier seas than we encountered."

"It was a caravel, lord. We didn't stop anywhere; we docked half an hour ago."

"Well done. And?"

"I have a verbal communication, lord."

"Well, spit it out, then," said Lodovico Stornello.

The messenger coughed, as if readying himself for some great oration. "It is with extreme sorrow that his Excellency the Doge and the Great Council of the Serene Republic of Venice have to inform the Captain-General Graziano Stornello and the Governor of Cyprus Lodovico Stornello of the death, on the morning of the twenty-seventh of January of this year, of their brother—"

"Brabantio Stornello," Lodovico Stornello muttered, at exactly the same time as the man said the name and Graziano Stornello mouthed it too.

"*O Dio Mio Caro!*"

They turned. The Florentine had dropped his head into his hands and was mumbling, "Such a loss, his daughter and now him . . . two virtuous souls . . ."

"You knew our brother?" Lodovico asked.

"I knew him as a good, kindly, generous being, with a charitable heart." The Florentine looked up at the Signors, neither of whom seemed overly distressed. "You must be devastated, my lords."

His face was pale and tight with misery. Tears pricked his eyes.

Graziano Stornello felt a pang of compassion for the youngster. "Of course we are saddened. But our brother had been in poor health for some time, and I'm presuming that when he heard of his daughter's death—"

"Brabantio Stornello did not approve of the marriage of his daughter to the Moor, you know," Lodovico Stornello declared. "That's what made him ill in the first place."

Graziano Stornello shot his younger brother an admonitory look. There were those in the cathedral who should not be privy to such confidences or witnessing this whole disquieting spectacle. He chose to rid the place of all but himself, his brother, and the weeping Florentine. He would have liked to dismiss his brother as well, but the new governor was now technically his superior while they remained on the island. So the messenger was sent packing, along with the artist (with a not very convincing assurance that his plans would be considered in time) and the captain of the guard and his men.

Once the church was empty of all but the three of them, Graziano Stornello sat down next to the youth. "You've had quite a rough time of it, haven't you?" From the folds of his cloak, he produced a silk handkerchief. "Here, dry your eyes; it isn't becoming for a *nobiluomo* to blubber quite so blatantly."

The Florentine stretched the material between his fingers and turned it over. He touched the delicate colored patterns at its edges. "This is excellent stitching," he said.

Graziano Stornello did not recollect precisely how he had obtained the handkerchief—as a token of affection, perhaps, when he'd been a young soldier himself? He had had many female admirers once. But now it seemed a trifling thing and he couldn't understand why such an everyday object should hold such fascination.

"My apologies, Signors," the Florentine sniffed. "I am not commonly overcome by such emotion, but in answer to your question, Captain-General, yes, I have endured much and seen things that I would not wish upon even an enemy."

"Your removal from the governorship?" Lodovico Stornello gave a curl of the lip.

The Florentine managed a thin smile. "My lord, I've no regrets on that account. It was not a position I wished for. I was only following my commander's last written instructions. If anything, it afforded me some solace to address you the night before last: *I consign this government to you in the name of the most illustrious Signory of Venice.* They seemed sweet words to me, and I'm sure the island is now in far more capable hands."

"Well, you've certainly left it in a bit of a mess," his replacement snapped.

"I think, my lord, that the mess, as you call it, was not of my making, although I may not have handled it as well as I might."

"Brother." Graziano Stornello's tone was clipped. "I think it would be more productive perhaps if we permitted this unfortunate young fellow to tell us what has so troubled him, don't you?"

"Yes," the Florentine mumbled, "I should do that." He patted his face with the handkerchief a little more, wiped his nose with it, and then tried to hand the moist piece of cloth back to the Signor.

"No, please, keep it," said Graziano Stornello. "It is only a handkerchief, after all."

"What might be a trifle light as air to some can be of consequence to others," the young man said mysteriously.

Graziano Stornello touched the Florentine's forearm. "What things have you endured and seen?"

"I wasn't the first to come upon them."

"Come upon them? Someone *came upon them* before you did, is that what you're saying?"

"The chambermaid."

"The chambermaid?"

"She'd served my lady for many years. He killed her too."

"Was this woman by any chance his wife?"

The young man nodded.

Lodovico Stornello was perplexed. "How did you—"

His brother raised a hand to silence him.

The Florentine was looking up at the painted window. Light spilled through the great Lion of Venice and played upon his face. He seemed to be in a kind of trance. "He slit her throat. In front of me. He killed her because she found them in their bedchamber and then came running to me. It was the hour before dawn, I think; and I had been restless and could not sleep. I was pacing the Great Hall . . ."

"Pacing?" Lodovico Stornello scoffed. "With one leg?"

The Florentine did not divert his eyes from the window. "Perhaps hobbling more than pacing. My leg had been wounded, but I did not yet know it was infected. It had only just happened . . ."

"Were you in some brawl?" Lodovico Stornello sneered.

"I'm no brawler, my lord," the youth responded coolly, "but when you are attacked, you must defend yourself."

"Attacked? By whom?" Graziano Stornello sensed a new revelation.

But the Florentine only grunted. "Nobody of import," he said.

"A Cypriot? A rebel?" inquired Lodovico Stornello.

"No, a Venetian. A Malipiero . . . He wasn't of the garrison, so I only knew him vaguely."

The patricians glanced at each other. The Malipieri were not much liked by the Stornelli—in fact, the two clans had been enemies for decades.

"He was a lout and a braggart. He came running from the shadows, calling me all sorts of foul things. I don't know what I had done to offend him. He had a companion whom I could not make out in the gloom. I fought them both. The faceless one ran, but I managed to kill the Malipiero. Or I think I did. He crawled off like a miserable coward, and his body was brought to me later. His given name was Roderigo, I believe."

"And this happened shortly before . . ." the Captain-General began.

"The *murders*, yes." The sad young man stared at the unmarked slabs before him. "I could not sleep because I feared my commander might hear of the confrontation, and I had already fallen out of his favor."

"You had?"

"Again, I do not know why"—The Florentine straightened—"But what the governor thought of me is of no consequence."

"So you were in the Great Hall on your own . . ."

"I heard cries from their chamber. I heard Emilia scream."

"Emilia?"

"The chambermaid . . . 'Oh, my lady!' I heard a deep voice too—my commander's, I think. Then she screamed again, so very loudly that I thought the whole citadel might wake. She ran down toward me. They were both dead, she howled, murdered by . . . by him." The youth began to tremble. "And then *he* arrived . . ."

"Iago?"

"Who's Iago?" Lodovico Stornello interposed.

"He must have heard her wailing."

"From the bedchamber, I presume. He would have come from the bedchamber." Graziano Stornello was trying to form a picture of the events.

"No. He came from somewhere in the citadel, from below, I think, from the kitchens perhaps, bawling at her, calling her a villainous whore and other vile things, and she was shouting, 'Murderer, murderer,' and then he . . . he grabbed her from behind, and before I could stop him or call out, he had taken his dagger and . . . sliced her throat."

He retched at the memory. The handkerchief fluttered down between the graves.

Graziano Stornello asked, quietly: "If the Mantuan did not come from the bedchamber but from below, how did his wife know he had murdered them?"

"That I cannot tell you, Signor. He slaughtered her before she could say another word."

"But you believed her when she said he had killed them?"

"Utterly. Emilia was a loyal and sincere woman. She would not know how to lie." He did not lift his eyes from the graves. "I will try to recall word for word what she said . . . before the evil felon stopped her tongue."

"That would be helpful," Lodovico Stornello grunted.

"First of all she shouted that my commander, the governor, had murdered the lady Desdemona."

"So the Moor did it!" Lodovico Stornello exclaimed.

The Florentine shook his head in exasperation. "She then corrected herself and said it was her husband, Iago, who had done the deed, and he'd killed the governor also. She cried 'Villainy' many times. She called the governor a fool and a dolt for having trusted Iago as he had. She scolded me and everyone in the citadel for trusting Iago, for thinking him honest, because Iago was nothing but a liar and a vile assassin, she said, who had poisoned my commander—"

"Ha!" Lodovico Stornello barked. "So it was poison!"

"No, my lord, it was not—or not of the kind you may find in a potion or tincture."

"What sort was it, then?"

"Please, brother," Graziano Stornello said quietly, "let's hear the poor man out."

"Those were almost the last words she uttered, that her husband had poisoned the governor, had poisoned my lady Desdemona. Then he appeared, calling her those abominable things, and she cried out 'murderer' one last time, and that was when he . . ."

"That was when he killed her," Graziano Stornello whispered.

The Florentine took a deep breath. "Yes. It was quick, at least. I called out for the guards. I told them to take hold of him. It was hard for them to accept my instructions at first, because they thought of him as a comrade. They were shocked by the sight of the dead woman. I let them reach their own conclusions as to what had happened there. I did not tell them what she told *me*. I said only that Iago was a traitor to the state and should be taken at once to the dungeons. He did not protest. He simply spread out his arms and let the guards clap the irons around his wrists—and he smiled."

"He *smiled*?"

"A hard, spiteful smile. I'd never seen a smile from him like that before. I, too, had thought of him as a friend, and an honorable one. I'd always thought him honest. My commander too: He'd always called him honest. I questioned him—how could he, honest Iago, have performed the dread deeds he'd been accused of?"

"And how did he answer?"

"He said . . ." The Florentine tried to recall the Mantuan's precise response. "He said, 'Ask me nothing. What you know, you know.'"

"And he hasn't spoken a word since?"

The young man shook his head.

Graziano Stornello shivered. The sun had vanished, behind clouds perhaps, and no longer shone through the great windows. Lodovico Stornello appeared to be experiencing the chill as well. He was no longer striding up and down with his customary impatience.

"So, with the villain in chains, I went up to the bedchamber." The Florentine placed his arms across his chest and began to rock back and forth.

Graziano Stornello stretched out a hand again and patted his back.

"I saw . . ."

They waited as he endeavored to compose himself.

"I saw her first. I saw Desdemona, my lady . . . on the bed . . . her body, in her night shift, was twisted . . . as if she had fallen from a great height. Her arms and legs were white, and splayed, and crooked. Worse still, her head was covered. . . . I went to the bed. I wrenched the pillow from her face. It was whiter even than her limbs, and her mouth gaped open. Her eyes were open also, still staring in terror but unblinking. I put my own face close to hers to feel the slightest breath, but she'd gone. Do you know what I wanted to do then, lords?"

"Tell us."

"I wanted to . . . rearrange her. I tried to do so, but she was stiff, her body was stiff but still warm. Every part of her that I touched was rigid, though not yet cold."

"And the Governor, the Moor?"

"He was on the floor with a knife in his breast, a knife straight to the heart—his own. His favorite *pugnale,* a stiletto. He had bought it in Aleppo or someplace. It had a fine gold handle inlaid with lapis and amber and rubies and other stones. He was proud of it, fond of relating how many infidels had tasted its blade. He would use it only against barbarians and those who did not abide by Christian Law." With that, the young man lifted a closed fist and plunged it downward, in imitation of a dagger blow.

There was now only silence in the cold church. The Florentine's hunched shoulders relaxed a little as he continued to gaze at the graves.

Lodovico Stornello asked, "So the Mantuan, this Iago, he suffocated the girl and stabbed the Moor with the Moor's own knife?"

"No," the Florentine replied, almost inaudibly.

"Then who did kill them?"

"Oh, Iago killed them." He let his eyes meet those of the new Governor of Cyprus and said, with as much composure as he could muster, "I have already said to you, Signor, that he has his own way of killing."

"Yes, and I still don't comprehend it," Lodovico Stornello growled.

"Then I shall try to explain. He may not always strike with the *pugnale* himself. He may not drop the poison in a cup. He may not squeeze the life out of a young woman. He may not be present when the men of the garrison are busily stabbing and killing one another. But he is the killer nonetheless."

Lodovico Stornello looked more perplexed than ever. "Did he or didn't he murder the Moor and our niece?" he bellowed.

Graziano Stornello leapt to his feet. "Brother," he snapped, "do you wish everyone within a mile or more to know what occurred on that night?" He turned to the Florentine. "He is, as you told us, like a pestilence."

"Yes."

"An infestation that can invade and kill you before you even know you are sick."

The Florentine nodded.

"He is the very worst kind of villain. The sort who does not soil his own hands in the practice of his despicable endeavors."

The Florentine nodded again.

"Yes indeed," said Graziano Stornello, more to himself than to anyone else, "a particularly insidious form of poison, I think." He stood and gestured at the graves. "Which one of these is my niece's?"

The young man pointed to the slab on the right. Graziano Stornello crossed himself. "May God have mercy on her unhappy soul."

Lodovico Stornello also made a sign of the cross, in deferential imitation of his brother.

Crossing himself too, the Florentine said, "God will be merciful, for she was the most virtuous being I have known."

"Forgive me, Signor," said the Captain-General, using the respectful title for the first time. "But before we leave you—"

"We're going?" Lodovico Stornello asked.

"Yes, we are, brother. I think we should leave this excellent fellow to his obsequies." He addressed the Florentine again, in a low voice. "I believe you have let it be known, generally, that the late governor and my niece died of the plague?"

"Yes," said the Florentine, "of a malady they both caught on a visit to the town of Limmasol, on the south coast."

"Very good, very good. One would not wish to cause further turbulence. And what of Venice? What will Venice know?"

"The very same information was relayed to Venice."

Graziano Stornello's favorable opinion of the young soldier was growing steadily. "So, to be absolutely clear, Venice knows nothing as yet of the Mantuan or of his murderous ways?"

The Florentine nodded. "Though Cyprus knows him as a traitor—and it may well have got out that he killed his wife, as some saw her lying dead before him."

"No harm in that—she was only a servant. But for as long as possible, perhaps at least until we have caught the fiend, the fiction of them having died of a disease should be sustained, I think."

There was a commotion outside the building, and the captain of the guard burst in. "Excuse me, lords, but there's been a . . . a . . . what do you call it? A sighting."

"A sighting?" asked Lodovico Stornello. "A sighting of what?"

"Him, sir. The Mantuan. Captain Iago. No, beg your pardon, not Captain no more. He's in the mountains south of Kyrenia, where most of the bad ones hide."

5. *Two Inquisitors*

The Chief Inquisitor of the Serene Republic of Venice, whose name was Annibale Malipiero but who was known by many in Venice as "*Il Terribile*," by virtue of his profession and rank, was weary and discontented. In his rigorously self-critical view, the entire week's work had been substandard. He was looking forward to heading home and enjoying a good meal with his dear wife. Most of all, though, his thoughts were turning to the idea of a revitalizing sleep.

Tomorrow he would be leaving the city altogether and traveling to his second home on the Mainland, to open it up after the unduly lengthy and bitter winter. It was still chilly, for it was late February, but the flowers in the country would be doing their best to bud—the *campanule* and *iride* and *anemone* and the glorious yellow *ginestra* that would soon be in full bloom.

The Council of Ten had agreed to his request for a short break, and, despite his current dissatisfaction, he allowed the anticipation of time away from the noisome tribulations of the city and the often draining nature of his job to beat away the disquiet in his mind. He would be able to breathe clearer air, walk with his dogs, and hear birdsong and the soft lap of clean water at the dock of his villa. He did not suppose that Venice would collapse during his fleeting absence.

But before he could leave the Palazzo Ducale, he and his fellow *interrogante* Bonifacio Colonna would have to present their usual weekly report to the Council of Ten. He consoled himself with the fact that the session—though tiresome—would be a short one.

As the Councillors had not yet assembled, Bonifacio Colonna and he would have to wait in the *sala degli interroganti*, the room in which most of their work was done when they weren't in the *sala della tortura*.

There should have been three inquisitors, but the third, Roberto Fabbri, was sickly, and had been for a couple of weeks. Therefore, most of the tasks usually carried out by three *interroganti* had been performed over the past fortnight by only two. Little wonder that Annibale Malipiero, though healthy enough at fifty-five years of age, was feeling fatigued. The same could not be said of Bonifacio Colonna. There was no evidence of exhaustion in *his* demeanor.

The two inquisitors had nothing whatsoever in common aside from the job they shared. Even their appearances could not have been more markedly dissimilar. Annibale Malipiero, though solidly built, was tall and lean, with a narrow, bony face and a long white bushy beard, which he was fond of stroking studiously. A stranger might have judged him to be imposing but thoughtful and benign. There was no hint of meditation or benevolence, however, in his subordinate. Nor, by any stretch of the imagination, was Bonifacio Colonna thin. Despite being a few years younger than his colleague (he was fifty-two), he looked older and distinctly less physically energetic. His corpulence, in fact, was such that when he had to move, he had to *be* moved—lifted from wherever he was sitting to wherever he intended to sit next—except during one of his not infrequent rages, when he managed somehow to reposition himself without help. Atop his gigantic body sat a huge head, supported by what must have once been a neck but was now a mass of folded flesh. His face was a waxy bubble with a constant sheen of sweat; his eyes bulged with rheumy disdain; his bulbous lips dribbled continuously. He was quite the ugliest person Annibale Malipiero had ever known.

He examined the giant now, at the end of the long table at which they both sat. With no sign of lassitude, and indeed with some relish, the vast *interrogante* was inspecting an instrument of torture resembling a sandal made of iron bands, which had just been delivered to him from Germany. It was called, or so Bonifacio Colonna had informed him, "the boot." The unfortunate wearer of such a device could be secured within it by a chain at the ankle and a hoop that could be opened and closed around the lower leg.

"But this is the cleverest part." Bonifacio Colonna produced a thin cylinder with a small crank at one end.

Annibale Malipiero watched as he turned the handle; from the other end of the cylinder, a thin blade emerged. "And that is somehow attached to the boot?"

"Yes, here, do you see?" The other indicated a small hole in the top of one of the bands, above where the wearer's instep might be. He inserted the cylinder and turned the crank some more. The blade advanced downward, very slowly. He reversed the process and the blade slid back. Then the blade appeared again and advanced farther, then vanished, then advanced yet more, in small increments. "I've been told by the people who made this that the upper part of the foot between the ankle and the toes is far more sensitive to pain than is generally assumed."

"Who'd have thought it," said Annibale Malipiero.

"These chaps in Nuremberg know what they're talking about. And it is well within the prescriptions of the torture code, I believe, producing copious amounts of blood but inflicting little permanent damage."

However great his aversion to his fellow inquisitor, Annibale Malipiero had to respect the man's application. Bonifacio Colonna had no equal in Venice in the meting out of pain. *He* was, without question, the *terribile* one. He would no doubt be making much use of his recent delivery in the week or so that his colleague was going to be away. Perhaps he would even manage to extract a full confession from the boatman the two of them had been questioning for many days now, whose wife had accused him of raping two girls and fathering children by both of them.

Perhaps, perhaps . . .

But did Annibale Malipiero much care? He would soon be out of the city and silently wished Bonifacio Colonna the best in his assiduous endeavors.

"What are you so miserable about anyway?" his plump associate asked.

"I'm a little tired and feel we've not achieved as much as we should have in this past week or so."

"We got that miserable Turk to squeal, didn't we?"

"You did that, not I." Annibale Malipiero had not been present in the *sala della tortura* for the final interrogation of an infidel merchant who'd been accused of dubious business practices, but he'd heard the screams.

Bonifacio Colonna's globular eyes popped with pride.

There was a knock on the main door of the chamber, and a guard entered.

"There's someone to see you. With a missive, he says."

"Well, let him in."

"I told him I could bring it to you myself, but he's insistent."

These guards, thought Annibale Malipiero—so flushed with unmerited self-importance. "So let him in," he repeated.

"We have to be careful, Signor, of who we allow to—"

"Yes, yes . . . Let him *in*."

The messenger was a graying, thickset creature, weather-beaten, unkempt, and close to exhaustion, but the winged lion stitched upon his tunic testified to the authority of his mission. He held a sealed scroll in his callused hands. "Which one of you nobles is Annibale Malipiero?" His eyes fell on the iron boot and the blade with which Bonifacio Colonna was still fiddling, but he didn't flinch.

"I am. You have something for me?"

"Yes, lord, and only for you."

Annibale Malipiero beckoned the man over. He thought he could detect a salty tang. "You have traveled far?"

"Yes, sir. I cannot say from where, but you will know soon enough when you read this." He handed over the scroll.

"You look as if you've run halfway across the world!" Bonifacio Colonna's gross body wobbled with mirth.

"I'm strong enough, sir, but I have run from the Arsenal."

"The Arsenal, eh," Bonifacio Colonna mumbled. "Where the warships dock." He raised a knowing eyebrow in his colleague's direction.

"Are you a sailor?" Annibale Malipiero inquired.

"No, sir, a soldier. A land fighter, sir. I don't much like the sea."

"A pity. I was going to send you back with a reply."

He'd seen the name on the seal of the scroll; it could only be from Cyprus.

"I go wherever Venice sends me, my lord," the soldier announced.

Annibale Malipiero dismissed him with a brisk wave of the hand, broke the seal, and unfurled the scroll.

Bonifacio Colonna leaned forward as best he could, which wasn't very far, and endeavored to discern from his colleague's expression if the document might contain anything of alarming significance. But while the *Capo degli Interroganti* scanned the paper with increasingly intense concentration, he gave nothing away.

Honored Signor,

I write to you in spite of the long differences that have kept the Stornelli and the Malipieri from a mutually convivial association between our families, the cause of which I myself have never been able to comprehend. But I am led to understand that during your tenure as an investigator you have proved an excellent and patient judge of character and that you have had singular success in extracting truth from those in your charge, not solely by the more obvious methods sometimes summarily and often ineffectively applied by lesser and more impetuous questioners but by the application of exhaustive inquiry based on the examination and under-standing of a person's temperament and disposition. It is for this reason that I write to you.

You alone must know of what I am about to tell you. For reasons of security and because of the delicacy of the situation that I shall impart to you, it is imperative that not even His Excellency our illustrious prince, or any member of the Council, or your fellow inquisitors should be apprised of the contents of this message, and I request that you destroy it after you have fully absorbed its substance.

My brother, now installed as Governor of Cyprus, and I arrived on the island only three days ago. Our journey was far lengthier than we had anticipated, owing to inclement seas and the need to take shelter from them during the voyage. No doubt Venice has learned by now what we discovered upon our disembarkation—namely, that the Governor my brother was sent to replace is dead, as is his young wife, my niece Desdemona. The interim governor, a Florentine who has since been deprived of his position, sent an announcement to the Doge and the Council that their deaths were the result of a sickness that they had both incurred on their travels around the island.

I have ascertained since—and here, Signor, I reiterate my demand that you treat what I have to tell you with absolute confidence—that the late governor and his wife were in truth both murdered, by a single inhuman and venomous individual.

This person—by report, because I have not yet met him—is no ordinary criminal. He is a barbarous being with no respect for life or for anyone's happiness. He has been responsible for many other deaths on the island—some fifty in all, or perhaps more—not, as I understand, by his own hand but by methods whereby he incites others to fulfill his heinous intentions, which I have no doubt are to encourage disaffection and chaos. I have not yet been able to establish if he is in the service of the Ottoman, but it is a possibility that must not be discounted, and I intend to investigate it with rigor, with the help of my brother and the full force of Venetian justice. He also killed his own wife, slicing her throat in full view of the Florentine to whom I have referred above. She was chambermaid to my late niece.

I should clarify that although I say he "murdered" the governor and the lady Desdemona, he did not kill either of them directly. But that he was responsible for their deaths, I am certain. I believe that by means of some poisonous form of suggestion, some insidious implication, he caused the governor to smother his wife with a pillow. When the governor realized the error of his action, possibly by being told of it by the chambermaid, he took his own life by stabbing himself in the heart. This is a picture I have formed for myself and that can be established as truth only when the man is properly interrogated.

The Florentine himself has described the creature as a poison, or as a pestilence or infection that can creep unnoticed into the blood and kill a man before he knows he is sick.

He was summarily arrested and incarcerated in what was claimed to be a secure prison at the very top of a precipitous mountain. From this place he has managed to escape nonetheless, by some as yet unfathomable means.

I intend to hunt the inhuman brute down and return with him to Venice. He has, I am led to believe, said not a word since his apprehension. Torture failed to open his lips, but I suspect that in Cyprus they are perhaps not as up to date and efficient in the questioning of criminals as they are in Venice. I believe that a judicious examination of motive and nature, for which you, Signor, are renowned, will produce a more satisfactory and enlightening outcome.

This Iago, for that is his name, though most know him as "the Mantuan," was for many years in the service, as a soldier, of the deceased governor of this island, whom you will know as the Moor. He was a good soldier and the governor thought him a loyal one. They fought together in many battles, including those of Novara and Marignano. They have been to Naples, to Sicily, to Rome, and to several other Italian states. They have both traveled to France, the island of Britain, and deep into the lands of the infidel.

I have learned that Iago's villainous nature and acts came as a surprise to everyone when he was arrested. He was until that moment thought to be jovial, generous, companionable, and decent. The word that has been used most often to describe him is "honest."

Again I ask you to keep these matters entirely to yourself, at least until I have brought Iago to Venice. You of all people will know that if word gets out of this creature's whereabouts and of the heinous extent of his crimes, there will be the usual calls for his immediate torture and execution, and I trust you will concur by now that he is, despite being incontrovertibly evil, worth deeper and more prolonged study before he meets his inevitable fate.

Although I doubt it has any relevance to the matter of Iago, you may also wish to know, if you do not already, that a relative of yours named Roderigo Malipiero, I believe, was killed out here by the Florentine—though not out of malice but as a consequence of his having been subjected to an assault by the said person.

I should be grateful of a brief confirmation of your having absorbed *and understood all that I have written, and I shall keep you informed of any progress here. Our intermediary can be the man who brought this dispatch to you. He is entirely dependable. He has served the Republic unwaveringly for thirty-five years. He would be thankful for any pecuniary reward you are in a position to offer him.*

I trust I have not burdened you unduly. But I am sure you will agree that a monster like this Iago of Mantua does not come into the world very often, mercifully enough. I look forward to returning with him to Venice in time and placing him in your capable hands. I also relish the prospect of meeting you myself. I hope that we might, despite the sometime differences between our families, become friends. I have the honor of being a grateful ally in our mutual endeavors from now on. With respect and anticipated amity, I am your servant,

Graziano Stornello, Captain-General of the Sea

"Interesting news?" Bonifacio Colonna had been eyeing his co-inquisitor with unswerving curiosity throughout the twenty minutes or so that it had taken Annibale Malipiero to read the letter.

"Not that interesting," said Annibale Malipiero, affecting a yawn. "Just a communication from an old friend." He rose from his place at the table and walked to the great chimneypiece at the far end of the room. The fire therein crackled and spat and sent his tall shadow across the heavily curtained chamber. He threw the papers into the flames and watched them redden and curl.

"He had a goodly amount of news to impart, clearly," the other observed.

"Yes, a fair bit, we haven't seen each other for a time."

Bonifacio Colonna continued to look mistrustful, but then he always did.

Annibale Malipiero turned his back on the fire and warmed himself. He was feeling rather gratified and no longer disaffected. He'd been flattered, after all, by a fulsome paean to his abilities by no less a personage than Graziano Stornello, Captain-General of the Sea. Annibale Malipiero was not by nature a proud man, but it was nice to hear such things.

He thought as he'd read the message, that he might have to cancel his holiday. But even if this Mantuan were to be arrested again soon, or already had been, it would take time to bring him to Venice. The Chief Inquisitor doubted that a week on the Brenta Canal would hold things up unduly. He was fired by fascination nonetheless. This villain was clearly much more challenging than the daily round of petty thieves, forgers, fraudsters, foolish critics of the state, suspicious foreigners, rapists, ruffians, and general scum that swilled around *La Serenissima*. With some enthusiasm, he anticipated meeting the fellow, if and when he finally arrived in the city.

Once he'd returned to the table, he scribbled:

Esteemed Graziano Stornello,
I am in receipt of your missive and have understood the information contained therein. I am grateful for the task assigned to me and shall not disappoint you or the Serene Republic in my inquiries. This remains, I understand, a matter that is to be known, for as long as you require it to be so, by yourself and myself and nobody else. Venice is so far aware only of the deaths of the governor and his wife, your niece, and that they died of a sickness. The populace's appetite for rumor has inevitably meant that there is talk of other causes for their sad demise, some of them quite preposterous, but to my knowledge nobody is speaking of the circumstances you describe in your dispatch. Please accept my profound condolences for the passing of your niece. It may be of some comfort to you that the people of Venice appear to have taken her name to their hearts. I look forward to continued correspondence between us. I remain your respectful servant,
Annibale Malipiero, Chief Inquisitor of Venice

He called for the messenger, rolled up the paper, dripped wax upon it, impressed his signet ring into the wax, and handed over the scroll. He then took out a purse from the folds of his cloak, and gave the man five hundred *soldi*. It was a substantial sum, and the burly old soldier looked appropriately amazed. "You may have to travel across the water a few times in the next few months, my good man," said Annibale Malipiero. "Perhaps you'll become accustomed to it."

"Not as extensive a letter back as the one you received, I notice," said Bonifacio Colonna, once the messenger had gone.

"What can I possibly tell my old friend that would be of any interest to him?" *Il Terribile* smiled. "I spend all of my days, and too many of my nights, in this musty room—with *you.*"

6. A Fateful Encounter

I'm hurrying across the Campo Sant'Angelo, in the black garb that we Stornello mourners must continue to wear for another few days at least. This is not a safe place for a Stornello to be, especially as it'll soon be dark. Carnival is almost over, which is the worst time, when you think about it. There's despondency and violence in the air. I should have chosen the more circuitous route home, but Venice is still bitterly cold, even though it's early March. As yet there's been no sign of spring. This morning I read more of *The Decameron* with my tutor, Baldassare Ghiberti. It was one of Boccaccio's less impious stories, which my tutor prefers. He'd wanted us to continue with our studies of Herodotus, but I said that four consecutive mornings of Herodotus were quite enough to tax the brain of even the most studious and dedicated student, as I trusted I'd proved to be, and that I needed a respite from writings in Greek about wars and yet more wars, and that even Boccaccio, although Italian, wrote in a language far removed from our current way of writing and speaking, so I might have something to learn from him. My tutor relented, on the condition that he picked the tale.

So we read the narrative of Lisabetta and the pot of basil—the fifth tale of the fourth day. It moved me, although a basil pot is a bizarre sort of receptacle in which to bury the entire head of a man, never mind that the man is one's former lover. I thought of the pots that our cook,

Zinerva, grows her basil in, and none is large enough to contain a head. I mentioned this to my tutor, who scolded me for unnecessary frivolity and for being overliteral, and talked of *licenza poetica*. I suppose this means that a poet can make up all kinds of things without worrying too much about the truth.

At my tutor's insistence—probably as a punishment for my playfulness—I went this afternoon to a lecture at the Seminary of San Marco by the eminent philosopher from Bologna, Pietro Pomponazzi. He's extremely famous, so the audience was sizable. Much of it, I'm afraid, went over my head, although I understood that he believes only some of the soul can be guaranteed immortality. His views, according to my tutor, have caused a deal of controversy—but I've read something similar in Aristotle.

I didn't manage to catch which bits of the soul will remain immortal when we die, although I got the impression that death will deprive us of most of it, and whichever parts remain with us on our journey to heaven—or to hell, or to wherever in between—will be so insignificant as to be hardly worth hanging on to. I can see why Dottore Pomponazzi's observations are hotly debated and even despised. Most of us, I'm sure, would like to think that our souls will leave this world reasonably intact.

So I'm thinking of severed heads and what happens to you when you're dead as I scurry toward the welcoming—but in the circumstances very distant—entrance to a *calle* on the far side of the Campo Sant'Angelo.

I'm sincerely wishing I could be wearing some silk, some finery, some *color*, so that in my obvious black I would not be so marked out.

"Hey! A Stornello! Get him!"

My heart sinks to my legs, a great weight.

In seconds I'm pounced on by a baying pack of about fifteen brutes, thrown to the ground, and kicked around a bit. Recent heavy rains have made the streets and squares of Venice slushy, so I'm quickly caked in all sorts of filth. From their yellow-green and scarlet hose, I know at once that they're all from the Malipiero family. I couldn't be in a worse situation. A Malipiero boot is raised within inches of my upturned face. I'm about to have my nose broken into a thousand pieces when a voice, the same that cried out before, husky and derisive, yells, "Bring the rat to me now!"

I'm dragged like a broken *burattino*, knees scuffing the wet but still painfully stony ground, to be dumped unceremoniously at the feet of the person who issued the command.

My eyes travel upward, taking in the gold buckles on his shoes, the parti-colored hose, the somewhat shockingly short and open-fronted doublet with a braided low-necked shirt beneath it, the maroon velvet cloak thrown over his left shoulder. He's not much older than I am but definitely taller and well shaped, with broad shoulders and slim hips. His hair, under a crimson brimless hat with a peacock feather, is a tumble of chestnut locks, reaching almost down to his waist. It frames a face that you could call a painter's dream—with a strong chin, a fine straight nose, and piercing hazel eyes. All in all he's almost ridiculously good-looking. He scowls down at me.

I know who he is. Most of Venice knows who he is. He's the despair of his family on account of his three main proclivities, which are women (above all else), and drink, and violence. He's Jacopo Malipiero. I've never met him to speak to but I've seen him around—at functions and ceremonies or on the streets, through which he swaggers, always followed by his fawning cohorts. I've overheard whispers, both censorious and admiring, of his carousing and general misbehavior. He does have an *atmosfera* about him—*una presunzione*. I think he likes being looked at and up to, as I'm doing now.

But my gaze does not stay long on this Apollo, or not as long as he might wish it to, because my eyes are quickly diverted to the person standing beside him with an arm tucked firmly into his. She's quite the most beautiful creature I've ever seen.

As with Petrarch with his Laura, I fall first and foremost in love with her eyes.

> *On a day when the sun's bright glow*
> *Had been quenched in sorrow for its creator,*
> *I was captured, and defenseless,*
> *Bound as I was, lady, by your beautiful eyes.*

Huge dark orbs they are, with thick long lashes, staring down at me with what I take to be disdain. Her examination doesn't last long. I'm dismissed as a dull boy, I think.

As I'm hauled up by Jacopo's acolytes I see her more clearly. She's wearing a plain green kirtle over a white linen *camicia* cut low enough to reveal far too much for the lovelorn swain that I've so instantly become. I can see *the tops of her breasts.* They are the color of burnished copper, as are her long neck (adorned with a pearl necklace, her only ostentation) and her face—the loveliest face imaginable, with a small pointed nose and the fullest, sweetest lips. She's hatless, so that her russet-colored hair falls loosely about that stunning visage. She has a look of the country about her—there's no Venetian pallor there, and certainly no paint. She is no *puttana* or *cortigiana.* She emits a pastoral vitality—*un brio rustico.* She's not of Jacopo's class, or mine—and I don't care a jot.

I don't stare at her for long. Anyone who stares too long, I suspect, would pay a savage price. Besides, she's looking at *him,* not at me.

"Which particularly scummy part of the Stornello cesspit have you crawled from today, louse?" he asks.

"I am Gentile, son of Fabrizio Stornello," I reply.

"I don't think I've heard of him," he snorts. A short debate ensues among the assembled adherents about whether any of them have heard of Fabrizio Stornello, and the conclusion is that none of them has. There's a lot of laughter and slapping of thighs. He continues: "And what is it that makes you think that you, a Stornello, and from a *very* humble fragment of that family, can invade my territory in this rash fashion?"

I respond that I've not been aware until now that in this free city of ours there are places into which a person of noble birth isn't allowed to wander without permission.

He punches me in the stomach so severely that I'm winded beyond belief. For a time I can't breathe, let alone speak.

He fires questions at me, curt and direct and brooking no pause or vacillation.

"You are in mourning for the death of your uncle?"

"Yes." I splutter.

"And also for your cousin?"

"I didn't know her well . . . or scarcely at all."

"Does that mean you don't mourn her?"

"Yes, I mourn her. She died too young."

"Of some disease, they're saying, in Cyprus, she and her black husband. Do you believe that?"

"Well, that's what was announced."

"But do you *believe* it, worm?"

"I believe what I have been told."

"Oh, really," he growls, his face an inch or two from mine. "You are so worthless and negligible a Stornello, are you, that you're unaware of what everybody else in your family *knows*?" I can smell wine on his breath.

Out of the corner of an eye I see she's looking at me again. In a frenzied effort to raise myself a notch in her estimation, I do my best to stand a little taller, to look tougher than I'm feeling, and I say, as steadily as I can, "My family won't take kindly to your denigrating me thus. And I can assure you that no Stornello believes . . . such . . . such idle theories . . . and if there was any truth to such chitchat I would know it."

I'm making this all up, but ever since I watched my cold uncles conferring in hushed voices on the day of my uncle Brabantio's funeral, and despite the official proclamation sent about Venice that my cousin and her husband caught the plague, I've felt that there is something *we've not been told*.

For a moment I feel rather pleased with my staunch rebuttal. Then I'm punched to the ground again and kicked about the head and in the gut and the groin. Throughout the ordeal, I see her angelic luminous face somewhere above. In my extreme pain I grasp at the suggestion of a crumpled brow and the smallest indication in her eyes that she's not partial to what's being done to me.

Now he's above me, breathing on me, a hand to my throat, as his loutish admirers pin the rest of me to the muddied ground. He leans into my face and he hisses, "So you're saying they weren't *murdered*, is that it?"

"Oh, no," I pant. "By the Turks, you mean? No, that didn't happen." I have to appear to be *on top of things*, even though, at this moment, he's literally on top of *me*.

"Not by the Turks, you ignorant bug. By an *Italian*!"

Now this I've certainly *not* heard—of course I want to ask, "Italian? What Italian? Who?" But I've just told him I know all there is to know. Instead I say, "Oh, *that* old story . . . that was dismissed *weeks* ago."

He blinks and jerks his face away. "By whom?" he demands warily.

"The family. None of us believes that anymore."

Now he's heaving me up, shouting to his yobs to stand off, and, with an arm locked around my neck, he marches me to the fountain in the center of the square. I think he may be intending to throw me into the freezing water, but he forces me instead to sit on the fountain's rim and drops down beside me. Whatever conversation we're about to have, he wants it to be private.

With my neck still caught in the crook of his arm, he wrenches me closer. "Why should your damned family know any more than I do about what happened in Cyprus? It's a thousand leagues across the sea."

"Well, I do have two uncles there," I remind him. "And one of them is the new Governor."

He doesn't much like being wrong-footed, I think, but he nods almost imperceptibly and lets out a small grunt. He loosens his grip a little. "So they don't believe it was the Mantuan, then?"

The Mantuan . . . It means nothing to me. Mantuan what? Mantuan who?

Now he's crushing my neck again, so hard I can scarcely draw breath. "Tell me, you scum. Tell me what the upright and knowledge-able Stornelli have been saying about the Mantuan."

"Ah, yes, the Mantuan—there's really no substance to that particular theory, none whatsoever."

I don't dare look at him directly, in case he catches the duplicity in my eyes. Besides, I'm gazing at her again now. She's still standing where he left her, playing with a tress of her lovely hair, and perhaps looking rather reproachful that he's paying more attention to me than he is to her.

"You said that already," he growls. "But what's the theory that's being dismissed?"

"More than one theory, actually . . ." I try not to flounder too much and elect to throw as many ideas into the ring as possible. "As I said, it's all been denied by my family, but there was talk of him—the Mantuan, I mean—having killed them, some say with poison, or that he ran them both through with his sword, or that he strangled her and stabbed him. There've been many rumors."

He's let go of my neck entirely now, so I feel a bit emboldened. I'm even beginning to enjoy these extraordinary fictions of mine. "There's one story that he shot them both, with arrows, from a distance, as they were hunting. Oh, and another that he suffocated them in their bed-chamber while they were asleep." I might be getting a little too imaginative, I think. "If any of this is true—and it's all been denied, as I said—he sounds like a nasty sort of brute."

"I'll say he's nasty," he mutters. "Are they denying that he killed all those other people too?"

"All . . . those . . . *other* people," I find myself repeating, before I can stop it. Who is this bloodthirsty monster he's talking about? "It was a slaughterhouse over there, I've been told."

His gaze is drilling into me, trying to find some shred of deceit. "But that's all nonsense too, is it?"

"Well, I don't know about the, the *others*, but he definitely didn't kill the governor or my cousin," I reply, with just the smallest gulp.

Then he says, "He killed *my* cousin."

"*Your* cousin? Well now . . ."

"Not that your lot would know about that, or care."

This allows me to confess to some ignorance at last. The murder of a Malipiero would not interest my family much. "You're right, I wasn't aware of that. I'm sorry—"

"No, you're not," he snaps. "Why should you be?"

He's shaking slightly. He starts to kick at the ground. "I've heard nothing from him for *weeks*, not since Christmas." His cheeks flush and his mouth tightens.

I sense that beneath the anger he is also quite sad. "Were you close?"

"Roderigo was my best friend. We had a few adventures together, I can tell you." He stabs his heel into the ground and clenches a fist. "That bastard Iago, I *know* he killed him."

Iago—

It's not a name I've heard, even from our kitchen girl Balbina, who's the main source of gossip in our house. It sounds more Spanish than Italian. Iago . . .

But Jacopo Malipiero has had enough of such confidences. The girl is now looking *very* impatient, I would say. He smiles at her. He may be a sadistic lout, but I can see how such a smile might send a flutter through the heart. It's simply extraordinary, absolutely dazzling. If that was petulance on her part it melts away in an instant. She dips slightly, in a half curtsy, and puts a finger to her mouth. She even seems to shudder a little. Then she smiles back.

And as for *her smile*—I shall have to write a whole sonnet in praise of it. If I get out of this square alive.

Perhaps he's regretting what he's told me or that he's let his usual brash confidence slip in my presence, because now he gets up and, no longer smiling, he stretches and flexes and punches the air.

"Stand up," he says.

I do so, having no immediate alternative. I could try to run, but I wouldn't get far. He floors me with one immaculately aimed fist to the chin. The back of my skull hits the hard edge of the fountain.

I'm away from this world for a while. I don't know for how long. When I come around, his face is over mine again. He's got his hands to my throat and he's straddling my chest. Around him and beyond him somewhere, his bullies are circling, grinning, sneering. "Leave this bug to me!" he shouts abruptly, with such force that they instantly back off.

He spits on me. "I think I know rather more than you do, cockroach, and maybe more than your uncle the governor, or that captain-general, or any of your uncles. Unless you've been lying to me all along and know it already. *Have* you been lying to me, insect?"

"No!" I choke.

"Yes, you have. A sailor returning from that dismal place told me this. I had to hurt him very badly to see if *he* was lying. The black man and your pathetic little cousin didn't die of a disease. They were murdered, in their bedchamber, by the Mantuan, Iago—not by a Turk, or by anybody else, but by the Mantuan, Iago. He killed my cousin, and other people besides, lots of people—soldiers, proud Venetian soldiers. He even killed his own wife, who was your cousin's chambermaid. That's the bastard he is. Did you know that?"

"No!" I can only admit. If what he said about the chambermaid is true, then Zinerva, our cook, might know about it; they were friends of a sort, when Desdemona was still in Venice. But I'm not going to tell Jacopo Malipiero *that*. He might try to beat the facts out of her too, although I daresay, she'd put up a pretty good fight.

He slaps me across the face, once, twice, three times, four. "I don't think you know anything, worm. I think you're just an insignificant, ignorant Stornello, I might have to stamp you out."

"Please," I squeak, "Please . . . please . . . I can find out for you, I can ask my father, my uncles!"

With his hands around my throat, he lifts my head and slams it back onto the ground. "What? What can you find out?"

"Everything—anything you want to know. I can ask about Iago, if it's true . . . to . . . to . . . confirm it, that he . . . that he killed your cousin!"

"So you want to be my little Stornello spy," he snaps. "Is that it?"

"Yes!"

"Then you shall be," he says. "And I will come looking for you, slug, if you don't come to *me* with what you learn." He punches me on the nose, then he thumps me on the mouth for good measure.

He gets up, leaving me crumpled and in exceptional pain. I see him hazily above me, turning his head to look down at me, those enviable locks of his swaying as he does so. "I'd advise you," he says, "not to go blabbing about what I've told you—about Iago, or my cousin, or anything. It can be our secret."

"Then how am I supposed to find anything out?" I burble through a mouthful of blood.

"That," he says, "you'll have to work out for yourself. You may be ignorant, but I can tell you're no fool." He moves out of my vision and I hear him call out, "Franceschina! Have you missed me, my love? I'm all yours now!"

I hear a scuttling of feet. I close my eyes and wait for the blows.

Franceschina . . . I may die, but I know her name.

"Leave him be!" The squelch of expensive shoes on muddy cobbles stops. Then a snarl: "For the present."

7. A Place in the Hills

Graziano Stornello, the Florentine, and a score of soldiers had been up in the northern mountains of Cyprus again. There had been another so-called "sighting," the fifteenth in the month or so that the lords had been on the island, and still fairly close to the castle from which the villain had escaped. This time he'd been said to be hiding in an abandoned shepherd's hut on the impossibly steep side of a concealed valley.

The Florentine, despite his disability and a great deal of awkward negotiation up and down narrow paths and across streams by the men bearing his chair, had proved to be a first-rate guide to the vicinity, to the obscure tracks and gaps between the peaks. They had approached the hut from above and beneath, with stealth, but its only inhabitant, a wild-looking ancient with a beard down to his knees, had run off into the hills.

Graziano Stornello believed that many of these "sightings" had been deliberately concocted in the hope of financial gain or out of mischief. His brother, the Governor of Cyprus, was adamant that the insubordinate liars who'd been responsible for these wasted forays should be hanged.

As their cheerless labors had come to an end only two hours before sunset, and the trek back to Famagusta would take at least three more, the Florentine had tentatively suggested to the Venetian Signor that he might like to rest awhile and enjoy some refreshment, perhaps even a meal, at the villa he had bought for himself in these hills and in which he intended to live out the rest of his days. "It's no distance from here, lord, and I can offer you a passable wine, a few modest but appetizing morsels of local food, and a view to rival any in Italy."

To the Florentine's obvious delight, Graziano Stornello had accepted the offer. His legs ached and he was sorely desirous of something to eat and drink. He was also becoming fond of the young man's company and conversation. He could be gallingly pedantic and sophistic at times, but the veteran liked his fervor and his challenging mind. He had once possessed such discursive zeal himself.

They'd talked a goodly amount in the preceding weeks—usually as they'd set out for or were returning from yet another ineffective expedition into the countryside in search of their worryingly elusive prey. The eager young lieutenant had hung on the seasoned soldier's every word as he was regaled with descriptions of great battles, the names of which could resonate with import in the mind of even the most casual student of recent military history—names like Novara and Ravenna and Brescia and Marignano. But he was full of questions too—about this advance or that retreat, or about the precise position of phalanxes and vanguards and rearguards, the placing of cavalry and infantry and archers and crossbowmen on the field. He was clearly a tactician, a *strategist*; his interest was in *arrangements*—talking of the ranks of men who had to endure the mayhem of warfare as if they were merely pieces on a chessboard. He had evidently not experienced many battles for himself.

They had talked about the Moor too. He had also fought at Marignano. It was there that his skills as a *condottiere* had first come to the attention of Venice. Graziano Stornello had gleaned much that he had not known before about the Moor's temperament in general and more significantly about how he had behaved as a man and not just as a soldier.

The young man from Florence had been in the Moor's service for only a year but spoke of him as if he'd known him for far longer—as one might of an admired mentor or favorite older relative. He would brook no criticism of him, even though, as he revealed during one of their conversations, the Moor had taken against him most vehemently shortly before his death and had even stripped him of his lieutenancy.

"Why did he do that, Michele?" Graziano Stornello had asked. He'd only just started to address the youngster by his given name, as a sign of growing affection and trust.

The Florentine had shrugged. "At the time I could not fathom it. I became the very center of his fury. When I asked him if I had offended him in some way, he only shouted more, demanding I leave his sight and that he wished never to see me again. Your niece, the good lady Desdemona, pleaded on my behalf, I know she did, but her pleas made him yet more vehement in his loathing of me."

"Do you fathom the reason now?"

"I believe I do, lord. I should have been suspicious at the time. My commander at once gave the position he'd so summarily taken from me to the man we are now hunting in these hills."

"And that did not make you mistrustful of the villain?"

"No, Signor. As I've said before, he was at that time known only as a trustworthy and honest man."

"Your commander must have retained some liking and respect for you, however," Graziano Stornello had observed, "or he wouldn't have left instructions that you should become governor in the event of his death."

"That," the youth had said sadly, "was an oversight, I imagine. He was so generally distracted, I think, that he very probably forgot that he'd ever composed such an edict."

The Florentine had frequently spoken of the Moor being "distracted"— and it would seem he had been so almost from the moment he had landed in Cyprus. Although the Florentine could avow to the deep love that the Moor and Desdemona had held for each other, the Moor's preoccupations had given no indication of happiness, only fretfulness and fractiousness and rage. Some darkness of tribulation had descended upon him. He would weep openly, and cry out nonsense, and thunder about the citadel like a fuming lion. On occasion he would lock himself away, granting access only to the Mantuan.

The garrison, seeing that the Governor was no longer the confident master of their destinies, took advantage, as soldiers will, of the license they thought this change in his conduct would give them, and so the disorder had begun—the drinking, the fighting, and all variety of licentiousness. Squabbles had broken out, often provoked by lust and jealousy over the loose women who were regularly brought into the barracks, and men had died. The Florentine and other decent officers, alarmed by the turmoil, had tried their best to take control, but to no avail. He had no doubt now that Iago had incited the soldiers to be even more unruly than they might otherwise have been.

The two men spoke of Iago now as they made their way toward the Florentine's villa, in a late-afternoon light so calmingly mellow that it almost rid the patrician of his irritation at the disappointments of the day. They were both on horseback. The young man could ride well, despite the absence of a leg.

"I was wondering if I might have met him," the Captain-General began.

"You may have. He was usually at my commander's side when they were in Venice."

"I met the Moor on only a few occasions. Tell me, Michele, how would I *know* the villain? And what will I see when we finally catch him?"

"If you're expecting, lord, to see someone who is visibly the devil on earth, whose countenance reveals his malevolence, through some disfigurement, say, or perhaps an obvious expression of foul intent, then you will be sorely disappointed. He's a most ordinary-looking man. He's not handsome, nor is he ugly. He's thickset and . . . short."

"Short?"

"He might come up to your shoulder, Signor. But he's robust, with a bulletlike head, which he shaves, I suspect. He had a rough upbringing in the countryside, he once told me, but other than that I know nothing of his antecedence, or why he calls himself a Mantuan. He's no city-dweller."

"So you think he could wander around this land without drawing too much attention to himself?"

"He's paler than the average Cypriot, although by now the climate may have darkened him."

The villa that the Florentine had chosen had once been a farmhouse, he said. It was a compact two-storey building, which looked very old and still a little dilapidated, but its ochre wash made it pretty in the evening sun. Bright flowers clambered up its walls. Graziano Stornello didn't see it as the home of a soldier. He thought it rather feminine. As they arrived at the house, a woman emerged. Graziano Stornello dismounted and the Florentine was lifted from his horse.

"Permit me to introduce my bride-to-be, lord," the youth beamed. "Her name is Bianca, and she is from these parts."

Bianca curtsied and bowed her head, smiling in a mildly flirtatious manner. She wasn't pretty, which surprised the Captain-General, because her intended was undoubtedly handsome. She was also notably older than the man she was going to marry—perhaps in her late twenties. She had the dark skin of a local and an abundance of loose black hair. She would have looked like a peasant if it had not been for her clothes: a deep-red square-necked gown with a gray *camicia* beneath it, set slightly too low for the old man's taste. She had also painted her face somewhat excessively and was sporting rather too much cheap-looking jewelry. Graziano Stornello allowed himself the thought that she might once have been a prostitute, or may still be one—there was a louche air about her that reminded him of the whores of Venice.

"I call her my Aphrodite." Still wreathed in smiles, the Florentine took her hand. "You know that Cyprus is known as the land of Aphrodite?"

"No, I did not know that."

"She emerged, the Goddess of Love, from the sea just south of Paphos, so perhaps Cyprus should also be called the Land of Love." He squeezed the hand that held his and murmured something in Modern Greek, which he was learning. His loved one disappeared back into the house. "I think we shall eat outside tonight," he said. "It's warm enough, and it's what all the Cypriots do, for the rest of the year now, until the cold comes back in November. Let me show you the view, Signor, before it gets dark."

The terraced garden sloped down from the villa and was almost overwhelmingly replete with vividly colored and scented flowers and shrubs, vines, acacia trees and lemon trees and orange trees, for spring had truly arrived here. As the two men made their way through this abundance of vegetation, the Florentine, who may have picked up on his guest's questioning look when introduced to Bianca, said, "This country may have a libertine reputation, lord, but not all Cypriots are wanton sybarites. Most indeed are good and Christian people."

"If a trifle insubordinate," mused the Captain-General.

"I believe the defiant ones are in a minority. Most simply want to get on with their lives and earn their bread. But even those who wish to thrust off the yoke of Venice do it only for love."

"Love?"

"Yes, the love of their land, the love they hold for their island, for the island of love."

"Are you siding with the rebels now, Michele?" Graziano Stornello asked, with a raised brow.

"My loyalty to Venice, while I serve her, is paramount. But as your own experience as a great soldier must tell you, it helps to know what those you are fighting are fighting for themselves."

"That's true indeed."

"And these people *do* fight for God and their country, have fought for hundreds of years against their oppressors—the Byzantines, the Crusaders, the Lusignans, and now the Venetians. Who knows, they may one day have to endure and struggle against the oppression of the Turks."

"Not if I have anything to do with it," the redoubtable old soldier grunted.

"I am certain you will keep the Turks away from these shores for many years, lord. But if, for the sake of argument, they do manage to overrun this country, then I shall assuredly fight for Cyprus, for the island of Aphrodite. Just look at it, just look at how beautiful she is. Sit, Signor, please."

They had reached a small pavilionlike structure at the farthest and lowest part of the garden—an agreeable octagonal arrangement of wooden posts and slats and a conical roof, with a bench around its inner edge, upon which Graziano Stornello now sat. The Florentine declared that such delightful buildings were common in Cyprus and in the countries to the south and the east, and with his fondness for the derivation of words, he explained that it was called a "gazebo," which he thought came from the vernacular Latin for "I shall gaze." So the weary patrician gazed—over a sweeping coastline stretching into the far distance, with a wide white beach below him and sharp hills above it and beyond, darkening now as the sun descended quickly, casting a deep red glow over the whole impressive spectacle. It was as fine a view as the Florentine had promised.

In the center of the peculiar little hut was a circular table on which certain delicacies had been laid, as well as goblets and a flagon of wine. Graziano Stornello was excessively hungry and set about the morsels with relish. He tasted things that reminded him of his travels to still-hotter climes, and he pronounced them all delicious—pastes made from olives and from aubergines and roe, into which they dipped the crusty unleavened bread, and all manner of beans in rich garlicky sauce, and small cheese pies and leaves wrapped around rice mixed with meat, and cubes of tender herbed lamb on skewers, and many types of small fish, which had been fried to crispness and could be eaten whole.

"All prepared by Bianca," said the Florentine proudly.

"She's an excellent cook," Graziano Stornello mumbled through a full mouth.

The young man merely picked at the food as he, too, stared at the view, which was being enveloped by blackness now. He seemed to be in a wistful frame of mind. "I introduced them, you know—I introduced your niece to my commander. I knew her before he did."

Whenever the Florentine mentioned Desdemona, Graziano Stornello had already noted, it was in a melancholy tone. "Last summer I spent many contented days in her company and that of her delightful sisters, and her mother, and her father Brabantio of course, your late brother—may his soul rest at peace in heaven, and that of his daughter Desdemona too. I was new to Venice then, a lost soul in a strange place. I think your brother took pity on me. He and his wife and daughters were most welcoming. Yes, it was a happy time." For a while he was lost in his own recollections.

"And how did you introduce her to the Moor?"

"A benevolent man himself, he knew of your brother's charitable ways and wished to discuss with him the notion of a foundation for indigent former soldiers." His voice became still softer, still more contemplative, as he spoke of his late employer and of the girl he had married. "So on a spring day last year, I brought him to your brother's palazzo, and from the moment he set eyes on Desdemona he was entranced by her, I could tell, by her . . . vivacity, her strength of spirit, her cleverness. She was exceptionally intelligent for someone so young—but you, Signor, know that, of course."

"I did not know her well, I'm sorry to say."

The Florentine betrayed some surprise. "You did not know your *niece*?"

Graziano Stornello shrugged apologetically. "We are a large family, Michele. I have a score of nieces, maybe more—I lose count. But do go on with your story."

The youthful soldier smiled to himself. "My commander would often say that we had *both* courted Desdemona, that we went a-wooing together." Again he fell silent, and the smile faded. But then he appeared to pull himself up somewhat. "Although that was not true. I was simply a messenger between them, and I composed many a doting letter at his instruction, as he could not write as well as he could speak. But when he did speak, then her eyes shone with wonder at the tales he had to tell, and I could see that she was spellbound by him, and so I watched her fall in love with him, and he with her."

Graziano Stornello could not help but think that the youngster may have been more than a little in love with the girl himself.

"Yes, they were happy times," the Florentine repeated, almost in a whisper. He stood up from the bench and, with a taper, took a flame from an already burning candle and lit a number of lanterns that hung from the ceiling. The Captain-General could hear the whir of crickets in the garden behind them and the distant pull of the surf on the beach far below. Such quietude, he thought, merited talk of happier times.

The young man referred once more to the darkness that had descended on the loving couple and to the change in his commander's behavior. "Such a strange transformation," he said, as he returned to his seat. "I still cannot fully grasp how the finest, the noblest, the most able of men, as my master unquestionably was, can be thrown from their best intentions and endeavors . . ."

"As the course of a war or a battle might?"

"Perhaps, lord, but it was no force of nature or whim of fate that altered him. It was the wicked determination of a single individual."

"Oh, please, dear boy," the seasoned soldier interjected, "let us talk no more of Iago, not tonight at least."

A second course was brought out, copious measures of it, by the Florentine's *innamorata* and a couple of servants. There were meats of many kinds—boar, and kid, and pigeon—and stews of pork and rabbit, and crumbled-lamb pies topped with layered vegetables in oil, and mullet cooked in lemon, as well as salads of lettuce, cucumber, tomato, and olives topped with salty cheese. More wine was placed on the table too.

Graziano Stornello stared in wonder at the feast. "Some of this should go to the men waiting on the road for me."

"I already do that," said Bianca, in broken Italian. "They in kitchen, they eat now."

"You will be marrying a most considerate woman, Michele. I congratulate you," Graziano Stornello declared.

"Sit with us, Aphrodite," said the Florentine, patting the bench beside him. "Do you mind if my wife-to-be joins us, Signor?"

"Nothing would give me greater pleasure," Graziano Stornello replied. He had already drunk a little too much, he thought, and sensed that his speech was becoming faintly slurred. They talked of many things after that, but no further mention was made of the Moor, or Desdemona, or Iago. Memories of sorrow and savagery did not suit the tranquillity of the night.

At one point, much later—by which time pastries of wheat covered with honey and nuts had been delivered along with yet another jug of sweet Cyprus wine—the Florentine reiterated his affection for the Cypriot people and expressed his hopes for their future. He raised his goblet in a toast to their eventual liberation from all foreign oppression, and Bianca raised hers too. Graziano Stornello did not lift his own goblet but opined—without spite, for he retained a fondness for the youth—that he thought there were certain places in the world that were made to be conquered, through some weakness in their very nature. "I do not, of course, mean to criticize your future bride, Michele, for she does seem a sturdy and most capable person."

"She is, lord," the Florentine responded, "and without a rebellious bone in her body, and yet she still loves her land." For her benefit, he translated what he'd said.

Bianca smiled too, quite demurely, and murmured, "I am . . . good woman."

"I'm certain you are," said the captain-general, lifting his goblet in her direction. He drained it and made a move to get up. "But it's late, and I must return to Famagusta."

"The garrison at Kyrenia is closer, sir, only half an hour away. I could accompany you there—unless you'd prefer to spend the night here? There's an extra chamber with a moderately restful bed."

"I wouldn't wish to impose," said Graziano Stornello, although he considered it an appealing option. As he'd tried to stand, his legs had felt less sturdy than they should have. And to wake in the morning with a view like the one he'd seen before night had fallen would be refreshing.

"Yes . . . you *stay* . . . in Villa Michele," Bianca trilled, clapping her hands. "I bring more wine. We sing. I dance."

So the old soldier stayed.

8. Home Comforts

"Gesu Cristo e Santa Maria Madre di Dio!" little Balbina lisps as I hobble into the kitchen through the street door. I am covered in the mud and shit of the city and in extreme pain.

She tugs me to a chair by the fire and sits me down. Without ceremony, she unties my shirt and stares in horror at my battered torso. "Dio mio, he's black all over!" she squeals.

I can see only through my left eye. I have to move my head to the right and left in order to scan the room, and moving any part of me at the moment is excruciating.

The kitchen is busy, because my father is just back from a business trip to Verona. His returns to the palazzo after a time away invariably provoke a fluster of apprehensive activity among the servants, and Zinerva knows that he will want to be fed well. I can smell a herbaceous soup of some kind bubbling in the great pot over the fire; it's probably her inestimable zuppa di fagioli, which my father loves. One of the domestici, Hostolana, is peeling and chopping vegetables; the other, Geanna, her sister, is scaling sardines. Zinerva herself is slicing cuttlefish, to put, I hope, into her delicious risotto nero, because, despite being pounded half to death, I'm hungry. The only person who's doing nothing useful, as usual, is Paganello, our recently acquired serving boy, who is crouched in a corner, half asleep.

Oh, and Baldassare Ghiberti, Doctor of Philosophy at the University of Padua, is sitting at the table, close to Zinerva, grabbing at scraps. He's often down here when a good supper is being prepared, drawn from his garret at the top of the house by the scent of Zinerva's cooking. She rebukes me and slaps me away whenever I try to snatch at something or dip a finger into a bowl, just as he is doing. "You eat well enough!" she cries. Baldassare eats well enough too, but she indulges him. As a consequence, he is exceedingly plump.

Balbina is prodding and poking and pulling at various bits of me. I yelp when she jabs at anything particularly sensitive. I must look a fright, because everybody else in the kitchen is gaping at me, apart from Zinerva, who's tight-lipped with disapproval. "Nothing's broken, anyway," Balbina concludes.

"Are you sure of that? I think my nose has been smashed."

She gives it a tweak. I whimper.

"No, just bruised," she pronounces. She goes to the cubicle where she sleeps and pulls out a selection of small bottles and pots. She has a myriad of vividly colored lotions and ointments in there. There are those in our *quartiere* who think she's a witch. The fact that she's tiny and bent and misshapen, poor girl, only adds to their suspicion. She busily applies her concoctions to my bruises. Some are soothing, others sting like the devil.

Baldassare, nibbling on a chicken leg, is the first to have the decency to ask what happened. "Have you been in the wars, *coniglietto*?" He's called me his little rabbit since he began teaching me four years ago and still does even though I loom over him these days, despite being short for my age.

"I ran into a Malipiero. Quite a few of them, actually."

"How often do I tell you not to go to those places?" Zinerva snaps reproachfully.

"What places?" I protest. "I was only walking through the Campo Sant'Angelo." Balbina begins to wipe the caked blood from my injuries with a warm wet cloth. She does worry for me, the ugly thing.

I know that Zinerva worries for me too, but she's in a very stern mood today. I'll have to win back her good opinion soon, because I need to know more about my cousin Desdemona's chambermaid, or Jacopo Malipiero will ensure that the next time I meet him, Balbina won't be able to declare with such confidence that there's nothing broken.

"You should still be cautious, *giovanotto*," Zinerva grunts, somewhat mollified. "And what your father will say when he sees you looking like a beaten dog dragged from the gutter don't bear thinking about."

I'm dreading this too. He will expect me to eat with him, though we never speak much and sometimes it's as if I barely exist for him.

Balbina is doing her best to clean me up. And her mysterious potions are easing the pain slightly. I'm even managing to see a bit through my right eye.

Something about her touch—and, malformed though she is, she cares for me more than any other girl I know—makes me think now of the unequaled being that is Franceschina, my Laura, my Amaryllis, the unknowable beauty who has stolen my heart.

My chest heaves, and Balbina feels it. "That's a big sigh," she whispers.

"I'm in love, Balbina," I groan, loudly enough for everyone to hear.

"Ooooh, in love," the maids Hostolana and Geanna titter.

"With a Malipiero?" my tutor asks.

"That wouldn't be clever," Zinerva sniffs.

"No, with a girl who was there."

There's a flutter of excitement from the maids. "Who is it who is it who is it?" they cry in unison.

"Is she pretty?" Balbina asks. I sense her stiffen and back off.

"Not as pretty as you, Balbina," I say disingenuously.

"Oh, you charming *nobiluomo*!" she squeaks, administering a jab in the ribs, which makes me shudder and let out a little whistle of pain.

"What's her name what's her name?!" the maids plead.

"Franceschina," I reveal. "I don't know her family name."

"Is she in love with *you*?" Balbina asks, quite warily.

"No, Balbina, she belongs to another."

"A Malipiero, I'd guess," Zinerva says.

"Yes, to a Jacopo of that ilk."

"Oh, oh, oh, Jacopo Malipiero!" Geanna and Hostolana do a dance around the kitchen, slapping their hands together and blowing make-believe kisses and spreading out their skirts and bobbing up and down.

Little twisted Balbina knows who he is too. "He's a handsome boy," she says softly, as she gives my brow a final mop. "But handsomeness isn't always the way to a girl's heart."

Zinerva, who probably hasn't heard of Jacopo Malipiero but for whom the name Malipiero alone inspires caution, shouts at the maids to stop their foolery and get back to their work. She's finished with her fish by now and comes to the fire to check on her soup. She takes a closer look at me. "You'll live," she announces. "But if you want my advice—"

"I always welcome your advice, Zinerva." I smile as best I can with my swollen mouth.

"Keep away from Malipiero boys, however fine-looking, and their girls too, however pretty. Your father won't be pleased with you consorting with that family."

" 'Consorting' isn't the word I'd choose."

"How are you going to explain that black eye and that fat lip?"

"I'll say I tripped and fell onto some stones."

Dottore Baldassare Ghiberti, who is now cutting into a large wheel of fontina cheese, decides, as I thought he might, to expostulate on the subject of beauty. *"Nimium ne crede colori,"* he begins solemnly, "as Virgil so sensibly wrote—"

"Do translate, pray," Balbina interjects, mocking him with the formality of her words and a crooked curtsy.

"It means you should never trust the beautiful," I tell her.

"Well, that's what I said—sort of—wasn't it?" Balbina exclaims. "Except I said it in Italian and it comes from me, not *Virgil*, or whatever you called him."

"Petrarch was Italian and was there before you, Balbina," says Baldassare. *"He* said, 'Rarely do great beauty and great virtue dwell together.'"

"Wasn't he the clever one," Balbina trills.

"Youth craves only what is dazzling; age knows better," Baldassare intones, continuing the Petrarch theme.

"You mean old cranks like you," Balbina sniggers. The girls shriek with high-pitched laughter. Baldassare looks indignant.

I throw some Ovid back at him: *"Auxilium non leve vultus habet!"* I translate for Balbina. "A pleasurable countenance is no disadvantage."

"Theocritus would consider that to be—"

"Is this some philosophy school—if that's what they're called—or is it a kitchen, where there's a supper to be got ready?" cries Zinerva, who's now back at the big table, hollowing out *melanzane*.

We're silenced. I was going to remark to my learned mentor, and probably will, that if any of the several poets and thinkers who mistrust instant loveliness had seen Franceschina, all their philosophizing would have vanished in a moment, because they would have been startled into a dumb acceptance at the very first sight of her, as I was.

At this point Paganello, who has—surprisingly—been listening, rises from the corner and mumbles, "What I say is, if you've got it, flaunt it, and if she's half pretty, go for it." He lopes out of the kitchen to make himself presentable for the duty of waiting on my father. He gives Hostolana and Geanna a sly wink as he goes, and they giggle again.

"Ragazzo arrogante," Zinerva mutters.

"There now." Balbina steps back. "You could *almost* pass for a handsome enough *nobiluomo* who's just had an ordinary day."

"Apart from the puffy mouth and the black eye and the torn jerkin and shirt and ripped hose and the slime and piss of the Campo Sant'Angelo all over you," Zinerva proclaims.

I have some cleaning up to do, clearly. First of all I have to rise from the chair that Balbina plopped me into, which proves painful. Walking is even more so. How I made it from the campo to home, I don't know. All the same, I somehow get to the kitchen door and upstairs to my chamber.

Giovanni, my manservant, gasps at my appearance.

I tell him to pour me a hot *bagno* and lay out some new clothes.

I feel marginally revived as I sit opposite my father in the *sala da pranzo*. The candles gutter, the fire fizzles and snaps, the curtains stir as a high wind roars down the *calle* outside. It's all rather murky, and I'm thankful for the gloom. My fresh clothes cover the bumps and bruises on most of my body. Only my face, if examined closely, reveals the scars of my encounter with Jacopo Malipiero. But as ever, my father barely looks at me anyway.

At least he's hungry. He's demolishing what Zinerva has prepared—the bean soup, the *melanzane* stuffed with her *risotto nero*, the fried sardines, the lark pies, all of it. I can't eat as readily, despite my own hunger, because I'm still hardly capable of opening my inflamed mouth. He's thirsty too. He glugs the wine down, slams the cup on the table, and demands more from Paganello, who obediently pours—with a wily smirk in my direction. I really don't like this new boy. "We'll call for you when we have need of you," I growl at him, nodding in the direction of the door.

I try to start a dialogue. My father's an unwilling conversationalist at the best of times. "I trust your visit to Verona was productive—"

"It wasn't."

So that's one reason for his being so glum. I know very little about his dealings, but I'm alert enough to what's going on in Venice to know that there are more and more threats from the Ottoman. My father's primary commerce is silks from the East, just as his father's was, and back for generations; our fortune, such as it is, is dependent on those routes remaining free and secure.

I know he has been trying to save money. Our gondola, for example, is a leaky old vessel. Constantino the boatman is always griping about it. He calls it *un relitto e un imbarazzo per la famiglia,* which should have been sold for scrap years ago. My father says that so long as it still floats and gets him to where he wants to be taken, we will keep it. "Until it sinks with him in it," Constantino grumbles. And while Zinerva will always do her best to provide us with the comforts of her mouthwatering cooking, she's had to scrimp on her provisions lately, bargaining harder at the market than she's used to, or getting Balbina, who can drive a tough deal, to do it, or not being quite so fussy as to quality, because she's been told to watch the *soldi.*

"Have you had news from Benvenuto, Father?" The mention of my brother normally cheers him up. I do need to *get him to talk* . . .

He lifts his eyes to mine at last, but only with a glare. I hastily cover my bruised mouth with one hand and my purple eye with the other.

"News from Benvenuto? *What?* What are you talking about? How am I meant to have had news from Benvenuto?

He's right to be bemused. It's a preposterous question. Benvenuto rarely writes.

And I've hit a raw spot. He misses Benvenuto and is worried about him. Now he's shouting: "Where's that boy? Boy! More wine, boy!"

In a split second, Paganello is back and replenishing his cup.

I persist. "I was thinking, at Uncle Brabantio's funeral, of how very upsetting it must be to lose a child—a daughter or a son—especially as Benvenuto left us on the very same day."

"Why are we discussing such a thing?" he exclaims very loudly. He's shifting uneasily, and now he tries to bat the topic away with a flick of the wrist. In doing so, he knocks over his goblet and the wine spills over the table. Paganello gasps and picks it up. When he tries to fill it again, he sees that the jug he's holding in his other hand is empty. He looks around the room for further supplies of wine, but there are none. "Run and fetch some more, lad!" my father snaps. The lout scuttles off.

With Paganello gone—but for only a couple of minutes, probably—I have to get to the point. "To lose someone close, a daughter, as my uncle Brabantio did, or a son, as you might—"

"What's that boy's name?"

"Paganello, Father." I take a breath. "But as I was saying—"

"Where did we get him from?"

"From Uncle Cristoforo's household, Father, soon after you fired the last one because he was asking for more money. But I was wondering—"

"Well, *he* has no shortage of staff, now, does he, your uncle Cristoforo? How many would you say he has? Fifty? More than that?"

"Around that number."

"At a meal like this he'd have ten or fifteen standing about, just to attend to the two of us. Whereas I have to make do with—"

"Father!" I yelp, quite forcefully and rather bravely, I think.

He turns to me blearily. "What?"

"There can be nothing more dreadful, Father, can there, than to learn of the violent death of a son or a daughter?"

He stares at me again. There's no suspicion in his look, only puzzlement. I don't bother to cover the injuries to my face. At least he's listening, or starting to. "As I said, at Uncle Brabantio's funeral, I thought how sad it would be if we had to learn of Benvenuto's death, in battle perhaps, because of course it's being said that my cousin Desdemona died violently too."

Now I have his full attention.

"*What?* Violently? Who's saying this?"

"Maybe it's only rumor."

"I should say it is. Damnable gossip! It was *announced* she died of a sickness!" But he repeats: "Died violently?"

"Yes, Father, and her husband too."

"Her husband died violently?"

"Yes."

"You mean the blackamoor?"

"Yes. They were both murdered."

"Murdered?"

"So it's being said."

"That they were *murdered*?"

"By a man from . . . from Mantua, Father . . . a man called Iago."

I've never seen him quite so flummoxed, even when he's been as drunk as he is now. It's obvious he knows nothing whatsoever. I suddenly wonder if Jacopo Malipiero might have made the whole thing up, possibly to frighten me. Perhaps there's no Mantuan, no Iago, no murders.

But I go on: "There's also talk that he—the Mantuan, Iago, I mean—killed a Malipiero by the name of Roderigo."

He screws up his face. "A Malipiero? Why are we talking about a Malipiero now?"

I give up. I dip my head and say contritely, "I'm only relaying what I've heard around the city, Father."

He thumps the table. The crockery, the goblets, the tureens, and the serving dishes shake and clatter. For a short time he sounds quite like his old self. "Damn what you've heard on the streets! Damn the people and their wild guesses as to what might be and what might not be! It was announced!" He repeats it. "It was announced!" He repeats again: *"It was announced!"*

Somewhere toward the end of this tirade, Paganello reappears with another jug of wine.

He approaches my father with some nervousness. As he gets closer, my father grabs the jug and pours himself another cupful. He glugs it down and wipes his mouth with the back of his hand. Again he looks at me, his eyes narrowing. It's quite a malevolent look. "You *believe* what you hear around the city, do you? All this *prattle?*"

Paganello's obviously thinking: *Prattle? What prattle?*

"No, Father."

"You know more than I, do you? I'm not . . . up to speed on things, is that it?"

"Father, I—"

"You think I'm . . . *out of touch.*" His tone is no longer aggressive but morosely self-pitying. "I was on the Council of Ten, you know."

"Yes, Father."

He looks up at the boy. "Did you know that?" he asks him. "Did you know I was on the *Council of Ten?*"

Paganello can only gape and shake his head. He's looking a bit frightened. He's new; he hasn't experienced one of my father's palazzo-shaking moods before.

"At the . . . hub . . . I was," my thoroughly inebriated father now mumbles, staring down at the table. "At the very *hub.*"

I've the feeling that if he's not taken to his bed soon, he'll start shouting around the palazzo, berating the Council, berating the Doge, berating everyone in power, as he used to.

I get up and walk gingerly around to his side of the table. "Come, Father." I hold out my hands.

"What?" he splutters. "Haven't finished supper yet."

"Yes, you have, Father. Look: You've cleared the table of everything Zinerva's provided."

"Good old Zinerva," he slurs. "What would we do without her?"

"Indeed, Father. Come now."

He tries to stand but can't. He plunks back down into his seat. I have to lift him from one side, wincing but trying not to show it, and gesture to Paganello to do the same on the other. The two of us guide him out of the room and I call to his personal servants. In my present state I definitely can't manage to get farther than the door.

As we reach it, my father grunts, "A Malipiero murdered, eh? In Cyprus. Well, one less Malipiero can't be a bad thing, can it?" Manfredo and Sansone, thundering down from the top of the palazzo, have arrived. As they take hold of him, the old man eyes me again. "What happened to you?" he asks. "Been in a fight?"

"No, Father. I fell."

He looks me up and down blearily. "No, you'll never be a fighter, will you—head buried in books all the time." He sounds disappointed.

And my sorry old father is lugged off to his bed.

I'm ready for mine too. I sit in my chamber awhile, trying to read. I know I shan't be able to sleep. The wind outside is even stronger now, whistling and squealing along the canal and swirling like an enraged specter around the building. I have to think of what I can tell Jacopo Malipiero when he comes knocking, as I'm sure he will if I don't return to the Campo Sant'Angelo with *something* to tell him.

If anybody's still awake at this hour, it'll be Zinerva, and she'll be alone, as she so seldom is—down in the kitchen, pounding and shaping the dough for the bread she makes every night. The delicious smell of Zinerva's excellent bread wafting through the palazzo is what gets everybody up in the morning.

My father demands a supply of it wherever he is traveling. Benvenuto's letters, when they do arrive, always contain a plea for Zinerva's bread to be sent to him, and Baldassare won't venture anywhere beyond the city without at least a couple of her exceptional loaves.

Zinerva despises all the bakers in Venice. She won't even contemplate buying the other things they provide—*torte* and *paste* and *pasticcii* and *dolci*—because she makes them too, and they're also mouthwatering.

I haven't been down to the kitchen to taste Zinerva's dough for some time now. But I think I must do so tonight.

She isn't quite alone. Little Balbina is in her cubicle by the great fire, but the girl's dead to the world. Zinerva has her broad back to me and is bent over the table, thumping away. "Can't sleep?" she asks, without even turning.

"It's the wind," I say.

I approach the table and reach gingerly for the mound of dough. "No!" she snaps. "Not till I've mixed it proper. Pass me the oil."

I hand her the flagon. She pours a glob into the paste.

"What's the secret of first-rate bread making, Zinerva?"

"Nothing much," she says. "Just the right time to let it rise, the right heat and the right time in the oven is all."

"I think it's more than that, Zinerva. I think it's what you put into it."

"Well, that's whatever I fancy or whatever's around. Fetch me some *origano* and some *timo* too."

It's too early in the year for the fresh herbs she likes to grow on the *loggetta* at the top of the palazzo, so I collect dried sprigs from where they hang in neat bundles.

Her hands are chubby but deft. She strips a few stalks of their pungent leaves and scatters them into the blend. Now she puts a forefinger into the pasty mass and savors the results of her labors. She seems satisfied. She spreads her palms and motions for me to have a taste, but as I reach out with a finger too, she cries, "No, no, no, I won't have you touching my bread. What with where you've been today, who knows what you could have picked up! Get yourself a spoon!"

So I do. I can taste the oregano and the thyme, the yeast and the salt, and there's something sweet too. She's told me that she often adds honey. She's been known to add other things—other herbs, or sliced olives or chopped nuts, or spices like *cannella* or *moscata*—but tonight she is making what she calls her *pane rudimentale*, which is fine by me.

"Exquisite," I say.

"Exquisite, is it?" she huffs. "You with your fancy words." She smiles, revealing her paucity of teeth.

She's shaped five fat loaves already, and now the sixth lies beside them, ready to rise. In five hours or so she will wake again to put them in the oven. She goes to the basin to wash the delectable mess from her hands. She looks tired.

"Are you feeling better after your fight?" she asks.

"A little, thank you," I say. "But I wouldn't describe it as a fight; I didn't stand a chance. I was attacked by at least fifteen of the brutes."

"That'll teach you not to go ambling into places you shouldn't." She wags a finger as she returns to scour the table with a moistened hand brush. "And don't go back there or you'll end up dead, and then where will you be?"

"In a coffin, I suppose, and that would be the second Stornello funeral in just over a month." Then I add, "Or the third in two months."

"The third?" she asks, rubbing feverishly.

"Yes, my cousin Desdemona, you know, in Cyprus?"

"Ay, yes!" she exclaims softly. "Your poor cousin—"

"You knew her better than I did," I interject quickly.

"Not well," she says. "She was a lady and I'm a cook."

"But you knew her chambermaid, didn't you? What was her name?"

For a second she stops her scrubbing and I notice her big body stiffen. "Emilia," she says quietly.

"Have you been to the palazzo since the funeral?" I keep my tone as casual as I can.

She cocks a bushy eyebrow in my direction. "What palazzo?"

"My late uncle's."

"Why should I want to do that?"

"You used to before. To call on Emilia."

"*Call on?*" she snorts. "We servants don't go *calling on* each other!"

"Well, to visit her, then."

"How d'you know I visited her?" She's beginning to sound wary.

"You used to tease me about my . . . feelings . . . for Caterina—my *debolezza*, as you called it. And you would come back from there and say, 'Caterina was looking very lovely today.'"

She grins slightly at the recollection. I did once express to her and to everyone else in the kitchen at the time that I thought Caterina was beautiful. It was all I said, a passing remark about someone I'd had barely two words with, and I was mocked for it for weeks.

"And do you still?" she asks.

"Do I still what?"

She sways her hips a little and says in a faintly coquettish voice, which doesn't suit her, "Have *feelings* for Caterina?"

I don't respond.

"Ah, no," she sighs. "Your heart is elsewhere now, isn't it? It's with the girlfriend of a Malipiero who nearly broke your bones." She returns to the basin, washes her hands again, yawns generously, and then moves to the large blanket-covered chair on which she sleeps, next to the oven. She doesn't have a bed. She has no need of one, she says. *"Ragazzo imbecille e infatuato,"* she murmurs as she settles herself. Her eyelids are starting to droop. She doesn't want my company any longer.

"I was only wondering, I suppose," I persist, "what the mood was like at the palazzo since my cousin's death."

"What do you *expect* the mood to be, *giovanotto stupido*?" she says drowsily.

"Has Emilia returned to Venice?"

Her answer isn't helpful. "I don't know."

"But I thought you were friends."

"Not so close that I know every move she makes," she says irritably.

"So she hasn't . . . written to you then, from Cyprus?"

She becomes alert enough to give me a withering stare. "Written? You think we go writing to each other? She can't write, nor can I."

Of course I know this. I feel very foolish, a *ragazzo stupido* indeed.

I also now know, from the way she talks of Emilia in the present tense, that she isn't yet aware that the woman is dead—if in fact she is.

Her chin has now dropped onto her voluminous chest. I risk a final, direct, and what will seem to her entirely inexplicable question. "Is she . . . married?"

A lid opens and a single eye surveys me with blatant suspicion. "Yes, she's married. Why?"

"I . . . I'm . . . glad of it," I flounder under her brief glare. "That she has a husband to . . . to support her in her . . . her . . . sorrow at her mistress's death."

But Zinerva's head has fallen forward again and she's asleep. There's nothing for me to do now but sleep myself, or try to.

For the time being I'll forget the demands and threats of Jacopo Malipiero and my utter failure to discover anything, or have anything confirmed, that might stop me from being thrashed, kicked, broken, and probably killed. As I lie in my comfortable bed, with the wind still sweeping up and around the palazzo (named the Palazzo Stornello Piccolo, to distinguish it from the other, far grander palazzi that my uncles and their families inhabit), I consider the consolations of the place I call home.

Right now, I decide, I wouldn't wish to be anywhere else. I feel *protected* here, by our very trifling collection of servants—crooked little Balbina; the two tittering maids, Hostolana and Geanna; stout Zinerva, with her stern concern for my welfare; my stupid but loyal manservant, Giovanni; my father's two personal servants, burly men both, Manfredo and Sansone; Constantino, the complaining boatman; Leonzino, our powerfully built but slumberous doorman; and maybe even the new boy, Paganello (yes, perhaps I should give him the benefit of the doubt)—and by Baldassare, my tutor, of course, plump and perpetually troubled and always unaccountably worried for me in some way. The concern of those who were in the kitchen as I hobbled in earlier this evening was palpable and reassuring.

I suspect that if my brother Benvenuto had been here and not away at the wars, he, too, would have been enraged on my behalf, if only out of loyalty to the family name. He might even have gone looking for Jacopo Malipiero to avenge me. Jacopo Malipiero would not try to bully *him*. The only person who shows me any coldness in this house is my father. But he also cares for me, I'm sure, in his crabby fashion. He berates me for my bookishness, but he pays for Baldassare to live with us and for my education.

And these are the comforts of our unassuming *casa*. The loyalty and protection of those closest to you, I think, is what makes for true succor—a shield against the fears of the night and the perils of the world outside.

9. The Chase

Iago had once again been "spotted"—though this time there was reason to be relatively expectant at last. The fifty or so apparent sightings of him in the past two months, all of them in the northern mountains, had yielded nothing. The perpetrators of such false leads had been tortured, decapitated, hanged. It had been quite a toll.

One of these, an old blacksmith from a village much farther to the south, had cried before dying, "But he's in Palekhori! I know it! I've seen him! He's in a cave on Mount Olympus! He's been hiding there for weeks! I can take you to him!" He didn't get the chance.

Governor Lodovico Stornello had instantly demanded that the village called Palekhori, a well-hidden place that sat under the shadow of the tallest peak in Cyprus, be burned to the ground and that all the villagers be arrested and tortured. Graziano Stornello had as usual advised a more guarded response. He'd suggested that the villagers should not be aware that they were under suspicion, because if they did know of it, Iago would know of it too and might flee. So a scout had been sent out to see what he could see. This spy had been a steadfast Cypriot endorsed for his dependability by the Florentine, and he had, he reported, indeed espied Iago washing himself under a waterfall one morning.

The journey south and then west from Famagusta had taken a long day. A lone horseman could have done it in three hours at most. But

Graziano Stornello had with him more than a hundred soldiers—crossbowmen, archers, and handgunners, as well as the ordinary militiamen. He wasn't going to let Iago escape this time.

He'd also brought with him a dozen or so loyal Cypriots who knew the area well and who had been recommended to him by the Florentine. The young soldier accompanied him too. When Lodovico Stornello predictably asked why his brother should be so keen to take the "whelp" with him wherever he went, Graziano Stornello had explained sharply, "Because he knows the island, and what is more, in contrast to any other Italian here, he is *liked*."

As the two men rode together at the head of the great column of troops, with the Florentine's chair lumbering after them on a carriage, they talked—or the Florentine did. Graziano Stornello mainly listened. The youngster was especially exercised on this occasion as to what motivated soldiers to fight. The veteran's view was that most men fought for money or booty and little else. The Florentine looked crestfallen but voiced the opinion that if only a Christian army could be spurred by faith, to fight for God, as the Ottoman undoubtedly did, then the infidel might be more easily overcome.

"It's been many years since anyone on our side fought for God, dear boy," Graziano Stornello sighed.

"Then Venice—why not for Venice, why not for the love of your state or your country?"

"Look behind you, Michele. How many of these do you think are Venetian? One in ten? Most are mercenaries, from all over Italy and beyond, paid per engagement. Soldiering is a profession now, young fellow, not a vocation."

High black mountains soared around them. The warmth had left the air. Dark clouds were building overhead.

To their right was a narrow track which, one of the Cypriots informed them, was the "road" to Palekhori. Instructions were quickly sent back to the troops to stop marching. A gruff command was also relayed to them to stop chattering too, on pain of a good whipping. On the main road from Famagusta to Limmasol, the coastal town to the south of Mount Olympus, a force of more than one hundred heavily armed Venetian troops would not provoke undue attention. Men were marching up and down it all the time. But if such a very conspicuous multitude were to turn off that road and venture into the mountains and arrive within even a mile or two of where Iago hid, Graziano Stornello was certain that the alarm would be raised, and the villain would vanish like a thief on a black night.

The Captain-General gave the order to set up an encampment, there on the main road. Night was falling swiftly, so any apprehension of Iago would have to wait until morning. He told the captains of the army to get the troops to start moving up the path before dawn on the following day. He himself hoped to be able to see something of the layout of the area in which Iago was hiding and perhaps calculate how many men might be protecting him, so as to be able to work out how best to surprise and capture him when light returned.

He, the Florentine, fifteen or so selected soldiers, and the small band of loyal Cypriots did not reach Palekhori for a good hour, partly because the Florentine, of course, had to negotiate the path with a crutch under one shoulder and one of his dogged personal bearers under the other.

The soldiers and the Cypriots were told to make their own camp a little way short of the village, and Graziano Stornello and the Florentine and his man, and one Cypriot whom the Florentine had said he particularly trusted moved on through the darkness. Night crashed in on them. Absolute silence reigned too, aside from the howling of a dog. They lit a couple of torches, but that did not help much.

Graziano Stornello felt a jolt of frustration. He could see nothing. And in the inky night with rain starting to fall, it felt bitter enough to freeze the bones. He was also hungry. "There must be an inn of some kind, even in an ungodly abyss like this." He would not, if he could possibly help it, be spending the rest of the night in the open, even under the protection of a canopy.

"With respect, my lord," declared the Florentine, "there's a greater concentration of churches and monasteries in these mountains than in any other part of Cyprus, so to describe it as ungodly is surely inappropriate."

The patrician rewarded him with a grunt.

The young man continued: "I'm sure there will be a hostelry here. Hundreds of pilgrims visit Mount Olympus. There's a shrine there to Aphrodite—"

"Ah, yes, your beloved Aphrodite."

The Florentine consulted the Cypriot. This squat but reliable-looking individual said a word or two in reply and ran off into the gloom. "There is a place he knows of, a small *locanda*. I'll not be joining you there, if you'll forgive me. I shall encamp with our chosen men just outside the village. I would not want to be recognized."

"Who's likely to do so here?"

"Signor, I may have been governor for less than a month, but I tried in that time to get to know as much of the country as I could, so I've been to these mountains before, indeed to this village. My lack of a leg also sets me apart. Iago would know who I was and would suspect my purpose instantly."

"You think that he could be here in the village and not up in his cave?"

"He may have come down from the mountain for warmth and refreshment. It can't be too comfortable for him up there."

"He might be sitting in an inn, in this very place, without a care, even though he's the most hunted man in Cyprus?"

"He's fearless," the Florentine said. "And he doesn't care too much for being alone. So, yes, I believe he might."

The night felt colder still to Graziano Stornello. The rain was getting heavier.

The Cypriot reappeared and whispered into the ear of the Florentine, who then translated. "Panos has spoken to the innkeeper. He told him that he is in the service of an Italian gentleman with a fascination for churches and monasteries who is making a tour of the vicinity and needs a place to sleep."

"That was clever of him."

"It was what I instructed him to say."

"Thank you," said Graziano Stornello.

"I think it might be sensible, lord, if Panos were to remain with you in the inn. He speaks some Italian. He's a strong chap as you can see, even though he's on the small side."

"Like Iago," said the Captain-General.

"Yes, and, like Iago, he's a fierce fighter. Panos will defend you to the death."

"Let's hope such a sacrifice won't be necessary." Graziano Stornello was keen to get out of the rain, which was becoming torrential. "I'll be down at the camp by first light."

He had chosen the most unassuming clothes in his possession, all of which were now soaked through. Nevertheless he provoked a degree of attention upon entering the *locanda*, as any stranger would, having to stoop under the lintel of the low door as he did so. But the dozen or so individuals in the cramped space glanced up only briefly before returning to their cards or backgammon and their inaudible conversations.

At least it was warm and dry. A fire roared. The innkeeper seemed trusting and hospitable, grateful perhaps for the arrival of an outsider with some money to spend on such an uncongenial night. He showed him to a table set a bit apart from his regular patrons. He produced wine, which was rough, and bread and cheese and olives and other dishes, which Graziano Stornello set about with gusto.

From the relative darkness of his corner, he tried to scan the faces in the room. The light from the fire and a few lanterns flickered and shifted, so sometimes they were in shadow and sometimes distinct. He supposed they were all men from the village—perhaps they constituted its entire male population. They looked craggy and mahogany-brown and weather-toughened. The Captain-General tried to discern if any of them fit the description the Florentine had once given him—of a short, ordinary-looking man with a bulletlike shaven head—but the only one who did so in any way was the Cypriot, Panos, who sat at a respectful distance, fidgeting nervously.

When he'd finished his meal, he glanced up. He was met by stares so unremittingly hostile that it almost made him flinch. He wondered for a moment if he'd been recognized—although how this might be he could not fathom.

Panos appeared to be even more anxious, for they were watching him too.

Graziano Stornello instinctively put a finger to the hilt of his short sword, a *cinquedea*, buried within the folds of his cloak. He soon enough acknowledged to himself that even with this weapon to hand, and the smaller *pugnale* that he also carried, he would stand not a chance of survival against such an assemblage of ruffians. He'd put up a fight, but in the end he'd lose.

So the lord of Venice did his best to appear to be what he was pretending to be—a passing Italian tourist with a liking for churches, caught out by the inclemency of the weather. He smiled at the unprepossessing group, lifted his cup of wine to them in salutation, and summoned the innkeeper.

After a little translation through Panos and the dispensing of coins from Graziano Stornello's purse, the innkeeper explained to the company that the generous traveler from Italy was of a mind to buy them all a drink, and as much as they liked. That quelled the tension momentarily. Some were even gracious enough to raise a cup in his direction. Soon they were back to their games and their murmuring.

He was devilishly tired and ached for whatever apology for a bed the innkeeper might have for him. He knew he couldn't move, however, until the others had left the inn. They might still elect to pounce upon him in the night. He began to regret his munificence. His eyes drooped and his head dropped forward onto his chest.

He was shaken awake by the innkeeper, who gesticulated in the direction of a passage at the back of the room and said something in Greek. Graziano Stornello looked about for Panos to translate, but he wasn't there. Neither was anyone else. He quickly checked that his sword and dagger were still under his cloak. They were. And so was his purse.

"Where is Panos?"

"Panos?" said the innkeeper. "Ah, Panos . . ."

The Cypriot came running in through the door to the alley. "Forgive . . . Signor . . . You sleep . . . I go for *passeggiata*."

It seemed faintly strange that the fellow should have chosen to take a *stroll* in such inclement conditions; he was now wet through.

"Giorgos show you bed," said Panos. "I stay down. I sleep here."

The innkeeper led the patrician into the passage and gestured toward a rickety ladder leading up to a hatch.

There wasn't a bedchamber as such. The bed, which was no more than a thin mattress, a pile of frayed coverlets, and a bolster, lay in the center of the gabled attic, surrounded by chests and old boxes and all manner of clutter. The noise of the rain was deafening, and a copious amount of it was finding its way through several holes in the roof.

He did not undress, as it was so damned cold and he was still contemplating the likelihood of his being attacked; he decided to keep his sword and dagger close to hand and unsheathed. Frequently, he had to get up and move the mattress to avoid it being too heavily dripped on, as the storm outside became steadily more severe.

Exhausted though he was, sleep was impossible, and he was now endeavoring to recollect if he might ever have seen Iago in Venice. He had pondered this often since the Florentine first described the beast. He was rarely out of the Moor's company, the young man had said. And yet no image came.

He must have slept eventually, because, not long before dawn, he was woken by a virulent whiteness forcing itself through the gaps in the timber above him, and by an almost simultaneous and extraordinarily loud crack of thunder and the clatter of hail on the roof. He snapped upright and heard himself cry out. After the light had vanished, he could see only blackness. But when his sight returned, surely only seconds later, he thought he could discern the silhouette of a man standing a few feet from him.

There was another blast of shimmering luminescence and another bone-shaking crash, and he saw, or thought he saw, the creature's face—an ordinary enough face, unshaven, the skin blackened and weathered, the nose crooked, perhaps broken. The hair was cropped almost to baldness, the head small and solid and round as a cannonball. The mouth was tight and the eyes forbidding. Light glinted on the blade of the knife raised in his right hand.

At last, Graziano Stornello thought, *I know that face.*

He has come for me.

He's known all along that I'd end up here.

The darkness returned and the figure hurled himself toward the Captain-General with a howl of rage. Graziano Stornello pointed his unsheathed *cinquedea* upward and his assailant landed upon it, and then upon him, with a gurgle of pain. The patrician extricated himself from beneath his now jolting, screaming aggressor, pulling the sword out of the man's stomach as he did so.

A third flare revealed the attacker to be Panos, the supposedly loyal Cypriot, now whimpering at the Venetian warrior's feet, doubled over in agony, holding his bloodied, gaping wound, and staring up at him with frightened eyes.

"Who made you do this?" Graziano Stornello demanded. "Who told you to kill me?"

Perhaps the quivering impostor did not have enough Italian to understand what he was being asked. He blubbered and trembled and gave only a thin wail. Graziano Stornello aimed the tip of the *cinquedea* at the recreant's perfidious heart and pushed downward.

He clambered hastily down the ladder and out of the inn, into the beginnings of dawn. The storm had passed as quickly as it had arrived. Hailstones the size of billiard balls covered the ground, quickly dissolving. Sword still in hand, he glanced to right and left and behind him as he hurried toward the main track out of the village. He set a few dogs barking and didn't doubt that he was being watched.

Once on the path, he stopped and surveyed the valley around him. It was densely forested with cypress and pine and oak. Inaccessible-looking peaks reared up on all sides. Iago had chosen a good place to hide.

He would send the band of soldiers closest to the village to encircle the cave. They were Venetians to a man, handpicked for their bravery and skill in hand-to-hand combat.

The main body of his army, the foot soldiers and gunners and cross-bowmen and archers, would already be making its way up from the Limmasol road. They would take their positions at the base of Mount Olympus to prevent the possibility of escape.

The Florentine's encampment lay to the right of the track, hidden within a grove of cedars. There were five tents in all, four for the soldiers and one, slightly larger and more ornate, for the Florentine.

An open fire still smoldered, but the place was completely still. Not even the birds had woken in this leafy grove. Had the men set off already? They would not have done that, surely, without him to command them. Perhaps they were still asleep. He would berate them sorely if they were.

The first tent he reached was empty—but a troubling spectacle nonetheless. There was evidence of some kind of struggle—mattresses askew and gashes in the canopy.

He lifted the flap of the second. "*O Dio Mio e Gesu Cristo* . . ." He crossed himself. Three Venetians lay there, limbs splayed and twisted. All had had their throats slit, with diabolical efficiency. A fourth had sustained wounds to the stomach and the chest, but he was still alive, if only just.

"Who did this?" Graziano Stornello whispered into the failing man's ear. "What happened?"

"Don't . . . know . . . sir," the soldier breathed. "Came from . . . nowhere . . . A gang of them . . . knives out . . . tried to fight them off, sir . . . did my best . . ."

"Cypriots? All Cypriots? Was there one of them who might have been *Italian*?"

The soldier's head fell forward onto his breast.

"Hold on, man, the rest of the troops are headed here, hold on."

In the third and fourth tents he saw much the same—slaughtered Venetians, most of them sliced across the throat. From a hasty count of the slain, he calculated that some of the soldiers, at least, must have managed to escape and were probably now stumbling toward the forces who he very much hoped were coming up the track.

He steeled himself as he approached the Florentine's tent at last. Perhaps the young man had also fled this carnage.

The retainer the Florentine had chosen to bring with him to the village, who had so loyally carried him everywhere, was slumped just inside the entrance. He'd obviously been dispatched before he could even look up to see his attacker and before he could defend his master. The fresh-faced soldier from Florence, the sometimes infuriatingly voluble young-ster whom Graziano Stornello had grown to like for his thoughtfulness and rare optimism, sat in a chair with his head lolling backward, an open, blood-caked mouth, and a cruel gash across his neck.

His shirt had been ripped open and a message had been carved in Greek across his chest. Another message, also in Greek, had been daubed in blood across the tent wall behind him.

The Captain-General of the Sea dropped to his knees and, though he was no stranger to all manner of cruelty that man can inflict on man, wept a little. As he did so, he thought he heard the Florentine's joyous words ringing in his ears. "What better place to fall in love than on the island of love?" he'd declared. And as his wife-to-be danced and sang he'd cried, "Let's drink to love and Cyprus and Aphrodite!" And Gra-ziano Stornello had joined him in the toast.

He could hear the tramp of boots and the clank of arms and armor heading in his direction. The man responsible for the events of this ter-rible morning would have fled his mountain aerie by now. But the Captain-General would order them to burn the village to the ground and hang everyone in it, as his brother Lodovico had suggested.

A lieutenant who could speak and read Greek scrutinized, at Gra-ziano Stornello's command, what had been written into the Florentine's chest and on the fabric behind him. "That's the Greek word for free-dom, sir—"

"And there, on the wall, what does that say?"

"Well, that's more words, sir. And they got a crazy way of putting words in the wrong order, so it's difficult—"

"Do your best."

"I wouldn't put my life on it, lord, but what it says, I reckon, is DO NOT DARE COME NEAR ME NOW."

10. *The Effects of Love*

Dante put it like this:

> My normal strengths were hampered from the moment I saw that apparition, for they were wholly devoted to that graceful being, so that soon I was so weak and incapacitated that my friends became concerned for my appearance. I said that it was Love who had caused my state, for the signs of Love could not be hidden from my demeanor, and when they asked: "Who is it that Love has chosen to make you so unhappy?" I looked at them and smiled and stayed silent.

But I've spoken to nobody about *my* love.

I could talk to Baldassare, he is my *confidente* in most things. But I suspect he'll only give me his stern look and tell me stuff I know already from the poets and philosophers we read together. He'll say it is not LOVE but an obsession of the eye, because all I've done is *see* her. You may as well fall in love with a painting. Love isn't LOVE if it is governed by beauty alone, for beauty fades, and true LOVE never weakens.

What does Baldassare, my fat little tutor, know about LOVE, except from books? How can a man who lives solely in his mind know about the truth of LOVE?

I've stopped eating. My throat contracts. Even those rich aromas that float up from the kitchen entice me no longer. I don't think I've tried to dip a spoon or a finger into any of Zinerva's pots for more than a month. She used to scold me for doing such a thing, and now she's offended. "What's the matter, *giovanotto*, not hungry?"

I'm sick. It's early May, and the days are warming up but the nights are still cold—except in my chamber, where it seems as hot as a muggy August. I throw the covers off my bed and pitch about like a boat on the *bacino* when the wind's up. I call to Giovanni to douse the fire. I shiver and burn at the same time. I rarely wash or change my clothes. Giovanni doesn't lay out a new shirt and new hose every morning, as he used to. He's given up on me altogether. I must reek like a canal rat. I probably look like one too. My hair is stringy and matted. I've started to grow a wispy excuse for a beard.

Some know, or suspect, that it is LOVE that has done this to me. Balbina stares at me and says I look like *un scheletro* and that I should be in a casket. She offers potions to restore me. I refuse them. She whispers, "I have a cure for LOVE too, in my cabinet." I think she has a remedy for *everything*. "I'm not sure I want to be cured, Balbina," I say. The maids Hostolana and Geanna give me sidelong glances and they even flirt with me a little, much as they do with Benvenuto on his rare visits home, batting their eyes and pouting. They've never done that before. Oh, the unfairness of it! You fall in LOVE and suddenly girls become interested in you, but not the one you ache for.

I write her sonnets. They're not good, but she won't ever read them anyway.

I show some of them to Baldassare, who nods and scratches his chin, making comparisons, usually not favorable, with the great poets. If he talks about the *subject* of the poems at all, and he hardly ever does, he'll mention Beatrice or Laura or Corinna or Amaryllis or one of the other fictitious sweethearts of literature. I want to grab him by his chubby shoulders and shake him and cry, "Don't you understand that the girl I'm writing about is *real*—gloriously, perfectly, vitally *real*?"

I lurk daily at the edges of the Campo Sant'Angelo. I talk to her, blathering beneath my breath like *un pazzo*. They should put me away. Mainly I just tell her how staggering she looks, but sometimes I express concern, if she seems a little paler than usual, or I can be censorious if I think she's overdressed, with just too much finery or paint. "No, no, it does not suit you, you look too much like *un cortigiana*, my lady!"

She's never there without *him*, of course. Why would she be? But he's regularly there without *her*, strutting about, jostling with his eager cohorts, roaring in and out of the drinking den he frequents—the Albergo Tre Stelle, which of course I've never ventured into but which they say is full of thieves and whores.

He hasn't spotted me, thank God, skulking in dark passageways or peering around the corner of a *calle* like a scared rodent. I've found a ditch into which I can vanish if there's the slightest chance of being noticed. I emerge from it moist and stinking. I've become what he's called me—*un verme scrofoloso*.

I haven't seen either of them for a few days now. Maybe he's gone to the country. He has a villa there, of course. Apparently it's almost as ostentatious as his huge palazzo on the Grand Canal, one of the biggest in Venice, which I've stared up at occasionally with a mixture of awe and revulsion. It's entirely his. His father died last year, and now, terrifyingly, he's technically the *capo* of his branch of the family, at seventeen years of age.

Perhaps he's in the country with *her*, just the two of them—it's an awful, stinging thought. But he'll be back. The pull of violence will bring him back.

The last time I watched Jacopo from my shadowy vantage point, I saw him and about thirty Malipieri clash with another gang, the Dandoli. The leader of this pack, Fabietto Dandolo, is an ugly thug to whom Jacopo Malipiero has taken a particular dislike. Blood was spilled and bones broken, but I don't think anybody died. I watched only Jacopo anyway, in the very center of things. When the *poliziotti* finally intervened, he seemed virtually untouched, tossing his locks back over his shoulders, grinning in triumph—even though he didn't technically win anything.

I'm surprised he hasn't come looking for me, as he threatened to. If I had something to tell him, I might approach him. I'd sway into the square with head held high and a self-important grin. "I have news for you, Jacopo Malipiero . . ."

I haven't much thought of the Mantuan, or my cousin Desdemona, or what may have happened in Cyprus, for an *age*, it seems to me. This is the effect of LOVE. You've no interest in anything or anybody else. You don't eat, you fall ill, you smell, you stand in the wind and the rain or sit in the sludge and shit, and you don't care. You wait for hours, soaked to the skin and shivering, and you don't care. When you see her finally, the sight of her astounds you. It's as if you've never seen her before. Her beauty is like a punch to the stomach—like one of Jacopo Malipiero's punches—winding you, making you fight for breath. She's the sun and she blinds you to everything but her radiance.

11. *Zinerva's Bread*

I might have guessed that if anyone was going to make a determined effort to drag me up and out of this insanity of LOVE, it would be no-nonsense Zinerva.

There's a commotion outside my door as she shouts at Giovanni to "shift his good-for-nothing bones." I hear a protesting grunt as he rises reluctantly from the pallet in the passageway on which he sleeps. Then she's in my chamber, with a yawning Giovanni in her wake. I'm not asleep, of course, but lying sprawled on my back on my coverless bed. She claps her chubby hands. "Up!" she cries. "Up, up, *up!*"

She pulls open the casement shutters. A feeble light—it's barely dawn—seeps into the room. She sniffs as she surveys it. I feel ashamed. She rarely comes up here, indeed hardly ever leaves the kitchen. And my bedchamber is a complete and squalid mess.

"It stinks like *un cesso* in here, *una sala da merda!*" Zinerva exclaims. She picks up the piss pot by my bed. "When was this last emptied?" she asks my quivering manservant. She thrusts it at him, spilling some of the noxious liquid. "Empty it now!" she demands. "And bring a basin of water from the *cisterna!*"

She turns her attention to my filthy, sweat-stiffened bedding. "Up!" she barks again, and I'm barely standing before she's pulling the sheets and the coverlets and bolsters off the mattress and dumping them in the passage. She looks me up and down. "You sleep in those?" She eyes the clothes that I haven't removed for days.

"I don't sleep," I reply.

"Rubbish," she says. "Everyone sleeps, even when they think they can't. Off!"

"What?"

"Off, take everything off!"

"But, Zinerva—"

"You think you're too old now, do you, to let me see you *nudo*, and not yet sixteen? When did you last wear fresh linen? Off!"

I begin to undress while she delves into my chest to find something unsoiled. She mutters, "It's no surprise you're sick, with no new linen on you and dirty as a beggar and no food in you and the air in this room as sour as it is. I'm taking you downstairs, *ragazzo bello*, and I'm going to feed you up!"

With a clean shirt in her hands, she starts to peruse my bony body, tutting to herself as she does so. Giovanni reappears with the basin, and before I can protect myself she throws its contents over me. If I looked like a rat before, I look like a properly drowned one now. I howl because the water is icy cold. "There," she declares, "that will do for the moment, but you need a proper *bagno*." She walks to the tub in the corner of the room. "And how long has this not been emptied?"

Giovanni shrugs.

"So empty it," she snaps. "And then fill it up again with good hot water from the kitchen."

She snatches a towel and proceeds to rub down my shivering skin. She hasn't done such a thing since I was a mewling child—and I feel like one again now. She dries my hair, too, digging into my scalp with her fingers. She hands me the shirt and clean hose that she's also taken from the chest. I put them on. She clasps my wrist. "Now, *bambino cretino*, you're coming with me."

I resist only a little. As we pass Giovanni in the passage, she issues yet more instructions: "When you've done that, light a fire, get the maids to put new linen on the bed, take that bundle of filthy bedding down to be washed—or maybe we should burn it. I want this room spotless!"

"You shouldn't be so harsh on him," I say, as we descend. "It's not his fault."

"Yes, it is," she replies. "He should have taken you in hand. We all should have taken you in hand."

The aroma of her bread is starting to fill the house, as it does every morning. I haven't tasted it in weeks. I haven't tasted anything.

Apart from Balbina, who's still asleep in her cubicle, the kitchen is empty. Zinerva pushes me down onto the bench at the main table and takes four freshly baked *panini* from the oven. "Eat," she says.

They smell wonderful, but my throat still tightens. "I can't," I gasp.

"Try," she says. She puts cheese in front of me too, and a big jug of milk, and *pancetta* fried to a crisp, and oranges cut open. Oranges are expensive. She shouldn't be doing this.

I tear weakly at one of the *panini* and tentatively put a piece into my mouth. It does taste excellent—sweet and sharp at the same time; I detect olives and almonds and honey. "It's good," I mumble.

"Of course it's good," she snorts. She plops herself down on the bench opposite me. "Now," she demands, "as we're alone, apart from the little mite over there who's lost to the world, tell me what's making you mope about like this, not eating and saying you're sick and looking like a near-dead *topo* in a trap." Because her hands can never be idle, she begins to pluck at the feathers of a half-cleaned goose lying on the table.

"I'm in love, Zinerva."

She snorts. "Yes, with a girl who belongs to a Malipiero. What was the name of that *briccone* again, the one who thrashed you?"

"Jacopo."

"Jacopo, yes. The girls—and others too—have told me about him. Don't go near him, *bello*, he's *un bruto pericoloso*."

"I know."

"And you say you're in love with his *fidanzata*?"

"Yes. Although I wouldn't call her that. He has other women."

"I've heard that too," she says. "I didn't believe you were in love then, and I don't believe it now. You *giovani* are all the same; you get one look of a pretty face and you call it love."

"I've seen her more than once," I say. "I've seen her . . . six times."

"Where?"

"Where I first set eyes on her, in the Campo Sant'Angelo."

She slaps a palm to her forehead. "*Ragazzo pazzo*, don't *go* there, I've told you before!" Balbina stirs in her hole. "You want to end up being dragged from a canal?"

"I'm careful, Zinerva. I don't let myself be seen."

"Eat!" she commands again. She pushes the honey pot toward me. "Put some of this on it. Here, break it open and fill it with this." She points to the crunchy strips of *pancetta*. "Have an orange. Oranges are good for the brain; they clear it out, get rid of all the nonsense." Balbina yawns. "Oh, good morning, little miss," Zinerva snaps. "And isn't it time you were on your way to market?"

Balbina groans, then sees me. "Oh, you're eating!" she cries. Her body lurches from her bedding. "And you're *clean*!"

"Won't be properly clean until he's had a good *bagno* and all the foolishness scrubbed out of him," Zinerva says.

"You still look like *un cadavere*, though," Balbina giggles. "You need fattening."

"What do you think I'm trying to do," says Zinerva.

Balbina dances about until she's behind my back. "A lover must look his best for his maiden," she whispers cheekily into my ear. I can feel myself flush.

"Off with you now!" Zinerva barks. "Get yourself to the market, girl, or the butcher will have sold the best meat!" Balbina pouts and hobbles toward the street door, slipping a *borsetta* made of fustian over her neck. It's almost as big as she is. "And make sure you beat that thieving *macellaio* down!"

The girl limps out into the cold *calle*. It's still barely light outside.

"I have to send her off early; it takes her longer to get there than most. She's a good haggler, mind, and always brings back good meat and good fish at a good price. It may be they just feel sorry for her. That *mascalzone* of a butcher has a soft spot for her, I know that. And he knows he'll have me to contend with if he sells her short or tries to palm off some rotten old carcass that he's been keeping in the back of his shop for days. Eat!"

I'm on my fourth *panino* now.

"You want more?"

I nod. I've realized I'm starving.

"Take some cheese too; that'll build you up."

She walks to the oven, plucks out four more little rolls, and places them in front of me. Then she slides the big flat *pala* under the larger loaves. They smell extraordinary. Soon that sweet odor will be waking the rest of the household.

She comes back to her bench, thinks about plucking the goose some more, but then pushes it away and leans toward me, hands clasped, her burly forearms on the table. "*Bello*, if you want to fall in love, go for a respectable girl—not some *puttana* on the arm of a Malipiero who could kill you."

"She's not a whore!" I protest.

"You haven't even spoken to her but think she's pure as the snow on the Dolomiti because she's pretty. *Madonna mia*, what are we going to do with you? Forget her, *figliolo bravo*; there are other good-looking girls in Venice."

"Not for me."

She reaches over and gives me a quick slap across the top of my head. It's not very hard, but it takes me by surprise. "Wake up, *idiota*! This will come to no good! Remember how we care for you! We don't want you murdered!" Then she says, "What about Caterina? She's pretty."

"Caterina who?" Names other than the divine one seem to have slipped from my mind.

"You know which Caterina, *sciocco*!" she cries. "Weren't you in love with *her* once?"

I shake my head. "I was never in love with her. I just said once how good-looking I thought she was, and you teased me about it for weeks."

She returns her attention to the goose. "She's clever, is Caterina," she says in a low voice. "She's not some dumb street girl. She likes books, same as you. She could do with the company of *un intellettuale*—someone with more than just feathers in his head, like those *bambinoni* dancing 'round her. She needs some comforting, poor dear, after what she's been through."

"So you've been back there, then."

"Back where?"

"To my uncle Brabantio's house."

"A couple of times."

"To see my cousin's chambermaid, I suppose—what's her name?" I say as blithely as I can.

The cleaning of the goose stops abruptly. Zinerva lays her beefy palms upon the table. She seems to choke a little. Her lower lip starts to quiver.

"Her name was Emilia," she reminds me softly.

"*Was?*"

"Yes, *was.*" She grabs the goose—which is pretty much stripped by now—and takes it to the *lavandino* to wash it. "That's all I'm saying and that's all you need to know." She scrubs feverishly at the bird's bald brown flesh.

"You mean she's dead?"

"Yes, she's dead."

"But you must be . . . devastated," I gasp.

"I don't have the time to be sad," she announces, although her slightly crumpled face says otherwise.

"What did she die of?"

"Same thing as her mistress," she replies curtly, without actually mentioning the plague. She slaps the goose back onto the tabletop, and lugs out its innards. Then, forgetting for a moment her determination not to elaborate, she says, "She was as strong as *un bue* though, was Emilia Borghetto. Never had a sickness in her life. There was a pestilence in Assisi, where she came from; she was the only one in her whole street who didn't die of it."

"So you think it *wasn't* the plague that killed her?"

"I don't think nothing!" she snaps. "And there's an end to it!" To underscore the point, she takes a *mannaia* and chops off the goose's head and neck with one deft blow. "Have you finished?" she asks, surveying the remains of the food she placed in front of me. There's a little cheese left, and a few olives, but no oranges and certainly no *panini*.

"Yes, thank you," I say meekly.

"Feeling better?"

"Much better, thank you."

"Good," she says. "Now make yourself useful and fetch me *origano, timo, salvia,* four lemons, two limes . . ."

I collect the dried herbs speedily from the *credenza* and take the lemons and limes from the jars in which she preserves them in vinegar over the winter.

"And what about her . . . husband?" I can't stop now.

"Husband? What husband?" She squeezes a lemon hard into a bowl, then another.

"You told me she had a husband."

"Did I? Why would I tell you a thing like that?" She repeats the process with the other lemons and the limes.

"You mean she *didn't*?"

"Yes, she had a *husband*." She shreds the herb stalks of their leaves.

"And where is he, then? Is he back in Venice?"

"Who knows where he is?" she mutters, with a shrug of her hefty shoulders. "Nobody knows where he is. There's no news of *him* dying of the plague."

I can hear something approaching loathing in her tone.

"Bring me the oil," she commands.

She pours a great slug into the bowl. I can hear stirring and shuffling upstairs. The palazzo is waking up.

"You don't sound as if you liked him much." There's a dryness in my throat.

She starts to rub the mixture she's made into the skin of the goose. "Didn't know him too well, but what I say is never trust a Spaniard. Shifty lot, they are."

I think I may have to sit down. "He was . . . Spanish, then?"

She's lost briefly in her own musings. "But she loved him, she said, and that's why she followed him to that stinking land, just like your poor cousin followed her husband, and look what's happened to them now." She looks up at me. "There's the power of love, *giovanotto*," she sighs. "It's not just falling for a pretty face." She wags a finger. I can see that her eyes are watery.

"You said he was Spanish?"

"Well, he said he came from Mantua, but his name sounds Spanish to me. And they're all *assassini*, aren't they, the Spanish?" It's thrown away so casually, this assumption. Is she simply giving vent to the usual prejudice, or does she know something deeper?

Now I *do* have to sit down. Dare I ask the name? There's a clattering of enthusiastic feet on the stairs. So I do.

"Iago," she says. "Does that seem Spanish to you or not?"

"It does seem quite Spanish. Is he still in Cyprus, then, this . . . this Iago?"

The kitchen is suddenly full of people. Our entire little household, it seems, is crowding around Zinerva's oven. She uses her *pala* as a weapon, batting away the hungry mouths. "Off, off! Let them cool."

I need to get to the Campo Sant'Angelo. It's still early though, so perhaps I'll have that bath. I'll put on some fresh clothes too—my finest doublet, I think. As Balbina said, a lover has to look his best for his loved one.

12. *Drinking with the Enemy*

I'm feeling quite the dashing youth, *un pavone orgoglioso,* as Zinerva might call me. I perch, as nonchalantly as I can manage, on the rim of the fountain in the center of the Campo Sant'Angelo. I've scrubbed up, I've washed my hair, Giovanni has shaved the wispy stubble from my chin, and I'm dressed in the best clothes I possess—which admittedly aren't as striking as those worn by some of the Malipieri or by the wealthier youth of my own clan, but if Franceschina sees me now, she won't be able to deny that I've made an effort. I'm wearing a gray shirt and black hose, but at least my doublet has some color in it—it's green and gold. I've taken care to pull the shirt through the slashes in the arms, so that I look properly fashionable. My shoes have been buffed to a shine.

The sun has just appeared over the roof of the convent of Santo Stefano. Today is going to be a cloudless one. I'm starting to feel quite hot, even though it's still cold for the time of year. I've been here for more than an hour, and the only signs of life have been a couple of priests leaving the convent deep in conversation, three or four beggars, a hawker with a cart full of old clothing, a bird-seller laden with cages, and a hurrying handful of others. Nobody wants to stop for long in the Campo Sant'Angelo, even when there aren't a bunch of intimidating Malipieri lolling about.

I hear a sneering voice behind me. "Well, well, look who it is."

It isn't his voice. I can't forget *his* voice. This one's high-pitched. I turn and there, standing on his own, a fist to his hip, is a boy who's barely in his teens. I dimly remember his thickset little face and his scowl. "What are you doing here?" he demands of me.

Because he's so very short and, as far as I can tell, alone, I respond with a tone of similar condescension. "And you are . . . ?"

"Nicolo Malipiero," he announces boastfully. Jacopo has three siblings and Nicolo is one.

"I have some news for your brother."

"He's not here," says Nicolo.

"I can see that."

"Tell me what it is and I can pass it on to him."

"It's for his ears alone."

"He's at home."

"All right, then, I'll call on him there." I make to get up from the rim of the fountain, but I'm not very assured about it.

"I . . . wouldn't do that if I were you . . ."

"Why not?" I sit down again.

"He's . . . busy . . ." the whelp sniggers.

"Busy at what?" I can't picture Jacopo Malipiero being busy at anything but drinking and fighting and womanizing.

"Never you mind what he's busy at. Give me the message and I'll pass it on." He's striding up and down now, self-importantly, on his stocky little legs. "He won't see you anyway. Give it to me, louse."

"Don't call me a louse," I say. "I'm bigger than you." I stand up again to leave him in no doubt of it.

He balks, but only a bit, and lifts himself onto his toes. "I can get my other brothers and cousins to come and kick it out of you." He really does have an unpleasantly puglike face. He doesn't share his brother's good looks.

"Buy me a drink," he snaps.

"What?"

"Buy me a drink and I won't get my other brothers and cousins to beat you up, and I won't tell Jacopo you tried to thrash me, so he won't kill you."

It might not be completely fruitless to spend a bit more time with this minuscule delinquent. I could learn something more about France-schina.

"I don't have any money on me," I say.

"Doesn't matter. The Tre Stelle takes credit. I'll vouch for you."

The Albergo is below pavement level, appropriate to its infernal reputation. No light enters it, except when the door is opened, so even on a bright May morning like this one, lanterns and candles battle to penetrate the gloom. If anything reprehensible is going on, I can't make it out (there are rooms upstairs for that sort of thing, apparently), and the people that I can see are quietly drunk, or comatose, or both. There are women here who have the trappings of the cheap *zoccole* you see on the streets, daubed with paint to hide their wilting skin. One of them has her sagging breasts open to view over her unlaced bodice. I shudder as I think of Franceschina in such company.

A few call out to Nicolo as he enters. "Nicoletto!" they cry, or "Nicolino!" as if addressing a child, and he isn't much more than that. He beams smugly and waves. Has he already been with such *meduse*, I wonder? He shouts to the *locandiera*, a skeletal crone who I presume is a procuress too, to bring us a jug of wine. "No credit for strangers," she announces when Nicolo tells her I'll be paying for it later. He chuckles. "You can trust him; he's honest; he's a *Stornello*!"

He's revealed this rather too loudly for my liking.

He slides onto a bench against a wall behind a small table. I'm not sure his feet can even touch the floor. I've no choice but to sit opposite him, with my back to the room.

"So we're known for our honesty, are we?" I'm surprised that my integrity can be guaranteed so easily.

"Well, you're all priests and councillors and magistrates and procurators, aren't you?"

"There's an archbishop, yes, and there *was* a procurator, and of course one of my uncles is captain-general of the sea," I say immodestly.

"*We* have an *interrogante* in our family," he declares haughtily.

"Really? I didn't know that." And I didn't.

"He tortures people," the horrible little hooligan takes great delight in informing me. "*Il Terribile*, he's called."

"Good for him," I say.

"He's the chief inquisitor, the top dog." He smirks. "You don't want to get on the wrong side of *him*."

"No, that wouldn't be wise."

"All I have to do is put a note about you in the *Bocca di Leone* and he'd haul you in, put you on the *strappado*." He glowers and takes a slug of wine.

I have a cup before me too, but I don't touch it. "Do you think your brother's likely to turn up at any time soon?" I try to sound nonchalant. I turn and survey the room, taking the opportunity to check for threats.

"Like I said, he's busy." There's that snigger again.

"What's so funny about his being busy?"

He grins more horribly still and then makes that gesture that even I, in my relative ignorance of things salacious, recognize—the forefinger of one hand being pushed in and out of the encircled forefinger and thumb of the other.

"Oh, that kind of busy," I say. "Well I'm sure he wouldn't wish to be disturbed doing *that*."

"Too right." Nicolo smirks. "Burst in on him doing that and he'd kill you for sure."

"Is she . . . pretty?" Part of me dreads hearing the answer.

"Of course she's pretty."

The boy looks over my shoulder. I freeze, expecting a crack to the head or a knife at my throat from whoever is standing behind me.

But a manifestly feminine hand begins to stroke my hair. "Who's this *nobiluomo bellissimo,* then?" a hoarse voice purrs.

She slinks to my left. From what I can make out of her face beneath the paint, she's not as hideous as some that I've scurried past in the streets. She's relatively young, possibly not yet thirty. She's not wearing a *camicia* under her tightly laced bodice, so I can see a generous portion of her white-powdered breasts. She exudes lubricious odors—I can detect musk and ambergris, and too much of both. She leans in to whisper in my ear. "Have you been with a woman yet, *tesoro*?" I can smell stale wine on her breath.

I don't answer.

"He's rich!" Nicolo cackles.

"Rich, is he?" the whore mews. "Shift over, *amore*," she instructs the boy, and slips onto the bench beside him, without taking her eyes off mine.

"I'm not rich, actually," I say. "I'm nowhere near as rich as you or your brothers, Nicolo Malipiero. I don't have a vast palazzo to call my own."

"I'm not rich neither," Nicolo Malipiero complains sulkily. "Jacopo keeps all of it to himself."

"Ah, *bambino indigente*," the woman murmurs soothingly, letting a scarlet-nailed finger run up and down his pudgy arm.

"I suppose he has other things to spend his money on," I suggest.

"He spent some on *me* once," the *puttana* muses sadly. "Ah, Jacopo Malipiero, *il riccone generoso*. Every girl in the Albergo Tre Stelle had trinkets from him once."

I can make out a few regretful mutterings of agreement elsewhere in the room, from those she has flatteringly referred to as "girls."

"He's not so generous now, then?" Maybe he's throwing it all away on Franceschina.

"Doesn't come in here these days so often as he did," the slattern moans. "Now we have to make do with the other *giovanotti* for company, like Nicolino here." She ruffles the boy's hair. He squirms with embarrassment.

Others chime in on the subject.

"He's not been here for weeks," one mutters.

"He comes to the square, but he don't come in here," another grumbles.

"Hasn't been to the campo for over a week," a third echoes.

"Don't even see him out and about anywhere."

The slut sitting opposite me concludes, "That's love for you, I reckon."

"Jacopo Malipiero is in *love*?" I exclaim, hoping not to reveal excessive interest.

"Yes," Nicolo Malipiero spits, "with a *servant* . . . from the *country!*"

"I was a country girl once," a *puttana* chuckles from a corner.

"Weren't we all, darling?" another shrieks. "And servants too!"

"Ah," sighs the wench sitting opposite me, "if only we'd all been blessed with skin like copper and tits like pomegranates."

"And eyes like they'd eat you alive," comes a wistful near-whisper from behind me.

The whore across the table pinches Nicolo Malipiero's cheek. "Ah, but you think her pretty too, don't you, *piccolo amante*? Never mind she's from the country and a servant."

Nicolo wriggles again, trying to break away, but a grin of admission crosses his lips.

The scrawny harridan with the breasts hanging over her bodice says to the boy, "Are you jealous, little one, that your big brother is fucking pretty Franceschina? Are you?"

I have to stand up. My head reels. I feel a gurgling in my throat and a need to retch.

As I make for the door I'm being clung to by two of them at least, hands all over me. "Are you going, *ometto bello*? We have only just met."

"I have no money."

"I'll give you credit."

In the relatively unsoiled air of the campo, I am momentarily blinded by the noon sun.

I need another *bagno*. Earlier this morning I stank of the slime and defecations that swill around this squalid city. Now I reek of something far worse.

Zinerva is right. I must forget her, and him, and the Campo Sant'Angelo. I must move on. I'll go back to my books. I'll become a model student. I may even talk to my confessor, Fra Ignazio Trissino, about seeking a position as a novice. I need to be cloistered away, safely out of reach of the world and its sordid, futile temptations.

13. A Letter from Cyprus

From Graziano Stornello, Captain-General of the Sea of the Empire of Venice, to Annibale Malipiero, Chief Inquisitor

Eminent Signor,
This is my fifth dispatch to you in the ten weeks that I have been in Cyprus, and it will perhaps be my last.

With the resources I have at my disposal, I am no longer confident of capturing the villain who has been the subject of our correspondence. Since my last communication, sent two weeks ago, he has vanished off the face of the earth, or from Cyprus at least.

The defiance of the population grows. His name is often on the lips of those we torture and hang. I have a suspicion that the name "Iago," so vociferously repeated by the insurgents here, must have reached Venice by now.

The troops allocated to my charge for the purpose of finding and apprehending the criminal are becoming disenchanted and fearful. Their misgivings are understandable. I have already described to you the two occasions when we were close to catching our prey—the first in the central mountains of this island, when twenty soldiers and the Florentine were massacred in the dead of night, and the second when another thirty of my soldiers were ambushed and slain in a bloodbath of extreme ferocity as they were marching toward the town of Pafos, where the Mantuan was reportedly hiding in a church. In neither case was there an opportunity for proper engagement. Such occurrences are not conducive to the maintenance of good morale.

I will confess to you, Signor, and to you alone, that I have become discouraged. I was, as I am sure you were, looking forward to meeting and questioning the despicable individual responsible for such carnage. I suspect it is not to be. I shall soon return to Venice. I wish to make a direct appeal to His Eminence the Doge and to the Council for more soldiery to quell the uprising here, as my written requests so far have been to no avail. I must also dedicate my full attention now to the task initially assigned to me, namely the defeat of the Ottoman.

When I set sail, I shall do so in secrecy. I fear that my lack of success condemns me to no more than an anonymous reentry into La Serenissima. I am not the victor that I had hoped to be in this venture.

I trust that despite our shared disappointment we can remain friends, as I feel we still have much to discuss—and perhaps we might be the architects of an accord between our families.

I remain, in anticipation of our meeting, your dedicated and admiring associate in future undertakings,

Graziano Stornello, Captain-General of the Sea

Annibale Malipiero stared at the single scroll of parchment on which the sad letter had been composed, in a hastier scrawl than the previous ones and in an altogether more personal tone.

He was seated in a small side chamber off the *sala degli interroganti.* The letter had been delivered to him, as usual, by the reliable old soldier to whom their passage of information had been entrusted. Its arrival had interrupted the not entirely successful questioning of a minor fraudster; Bonifacio Colonna had started to shout a lot, an increasingly commonplace practice that rarely produced quick results. So it was with some relief that Annibale Malipiero had escaped into this little room to read the scroll. He could still hear the corpulent inquisitor yelling next door.

Through his ever-alert network of informants on the streets, Annibale Malipiero had learned that word of the villain had indeed traveled to Venice—albeit thus far in muffled undertones, veiled references to "the Mantuan," and, on occasion, even by name. Some whispered that he had killed the hapless Desdemona. *She* was certainly on people's lips and had been ever since that alarming outpouring on the day of her father's funeral. Death had elevated her to celebrity. Makeshift shrines had been cobbled together outside the palazzo in which she'd been born and brought up as well as beside her father's tomb in the Chiesa di San Rocco.

There was no talk yet of Iago as a fomenter of rebellion, though reports of the continuing and mounting troubles on the island had reached the Signory alongside the governor's and the Captain-General's appeal for more troops. The request had provoked a fiery session in the chamber. The Stornelli had naturally sided with their brothers, but most of the Council felt that quite enough money had been spent on that godforsaken place already.

"We don't send an army to every unruly outpost of the empire!" a Malipiero had declared.

"They're not as close to the Ottoman as Cyprus is!" a Stornello had retorted, and others in that family had shouted, "Remember Rhodes!"

"Rhodes was lost through bad leadership!" a second Malipiero had exclaimed, and proposed that a motion be passed indicting both Lodovico and Graziano Stornello for failure of command.

"Their incompetence has increased the infidel threat, not lessened it!" yet another Malipiero bawled, and yells of "Arrest them! Hang them!" echoed around the chamber. Blows were exchanged, and the ducal guard had been summoned to subdue the worst offenders in the brawl. Annibale Malipiero himself had remained silent throughout. Iago hadn't been mentioned once.

The only time the chief inquisitor had heard the Mantuan's true name from the lips of anyone but his spies was after he had found, on one of his daily emptyings of the messages left in the *Bocca di Leone*— that slit in a wall not far from the chamber of the Council of Ten, into which the citizens of Venice were encouraged to drop their gripes and accusations—a scrawl that, despite its illiteracy, had made him curious: *I KNOWS WERE IAGO IZ.* The writer had been bright enough to leave his name and his whereabouts, which were more intriguing still, as he was a servant in one of the less noteworthy Stornello households. He'd been summoned accordingly.

It had turned out that the boy, for he was no more than that, had overheard a young scion of that branch of the family conversing with his father. "He said to him they was murdered, sir, Desdemona, sir, and the black man, by Iago, from Mantua, sir."

"I see."

"He was also saying Iago killed a Malipiero, sir, name of Roderigo, and you're a Malipiero, ain't you, sir?"

This was, of course, what Annibale Malipiero had already learned from the Captain-General of the Sea. He had made subsequent, though halfhearted, inquiries within his own family about the death of a Malipiero in a far-off land, but none seemed to have heard of any Roderigo Malipiero, so he hadn't pursued the matter further.

"But you claim to know the whereabouts of this Iago, whoever he may be? Do you?"

"He's still in Cyprus, sir. That's what the cook said."

"The cook?"

"She says Iago killed his wife . . . she knew his wife . . . she spends a lot of time there, sir, at the palazzo where Desdemona's mother and her sisters live."

"Is that it?" the *interrogante* asked of the somewhat surly lad, in whom he nonetheless discerned a keenness to divulge, and betray, which was always useful.

"And your name is?"

"Paganello, sir. Does I get paid now?"

"Certainly not," said *Il Terribile*, adopting a glassy glare. "But as you're obviously a brat with no sense of loyalty, I might have need of you in the future, and *then* you might. And, incidentally, if you talk to anyone else of what you know or say that you have visited me, you will very probably end up at the bottom of a canal. Is that clear?"

"Good luck to you, Signor, and your endeavors," Annibale Malipiero now muttered to Graziano Stornello, as if his words might carry across the sea, and he tore up the Captain-General's scroll and threw the fragments onto the fire.

He'd spent almost three years now in the company of the very worst of humanity—schemers and desperadoes, racketeers and blackmailers, hustlers and pimps, rapists and child molesters, traitors and foreign agents, petty thieves and hardened housebreakers, and of course murderers aplenty. But he'd been looking forward to meeting Iago of Mantua.

Of the lowlife he'd interviewed, the killers had always interested him most. Unlike his associates, he liked to go beyond the business of confession, to delve deeper into their dispositions, to understand what drove them. He'd been selective, of course. Those who killed out of anger, or merely for gain, were of no interest to him. Neither were the vermin who had known nothing other than killing. But in a few instances he had encountered men who weren't poor, jealous, enraged, or stupid and yet had committed murder. Some motive beyond circumstance, some *patologia*, had driven them to it.

Iago of Mantua would have been his finest subject yet, his last great case—for in just two months his tenure as chief inquisitor would be over.

The shouting next door had stopped. He rose wearily and reentered the *sala degli interroganti*. The fraudster had disappeared, and so had Bonifacio Colonna. Roberto Fabbri was alone in the room.

"Success?"

Roberto Fabbri was a shriveled, sickly man, as thin as the other inquisitor was fat. Also unlike Bonifacio Colonna, he rarely spoke, and now was no exception. He shook his skeletal head.

"So where have they gone, to the *sala della tortura*?"

Roberto Fabbri nodded.

There was a kerfuffle beyond the main entrance to the chamber.

"Cosimo!" Annibale Malipiero exclaimed with a smile, as he opened the door.

Cosimo Dandolo was a patrician of some distinction in Venice—a prominent *Avogadoro*, a member of the *Collegio*, and a successful merchant—but the sentinels had shown scant regard for his status. They held him firmly by both arms, and his hair and clothes were in some disarray.

"He was trying to enter without an appointment—"

"Let go of him! He is known to me! Leave him be!"

Annibale Malpiero was not a very sociable man, but he would

sometimes dine with Cosimo Dandolo, and considered him a friend. However now and then their encounters had been more brusque than cordial, because Cosimo Dandolo had a particularly intemperate son— not that the chief inquisitor held him in any less esteem on that account, for he had disorderly young relatives of his own . . .

On this occasion Cosimo Dandolo seemed puce with fury, and not just at the way he'd been manhandled.

"Is it about Fabietto?" the *interrogante* tentatively asked. "What's he been up to this time?"

"I need to talk to you," Cosimo Dandolo fumed, "about *your* murderous nephew."

Annibale's Malipiero's spirits, already lowered by the news from Cyprus, sank yet further.

14. A Difficult Nephew

The sleek and commodious gondola provided for Annibale Malipiero during his tenure as inquisitor made its stately progress from the Palazzo Ducale toward the northernmost reaches of the Grand Canal. In two months he would have to return the vessel. He wouldn't miss much about the job, but he'd be sad to lose the boat.

The *interrogante*'s mission on this occasion had nothing to do with his professional duties, or not exclusively. It was more of a family chore.

"How much longer?" he called from his curtained cabin. Ercole, a reassuringly muscular Goliath who doubled as his personal *gondoliere* and bodyguard, said, "It's the traffic, lord; I'm going as quickly as I can."

As the days got warmer—although summer still seemed unwilling to make itself felt—the waterways were increasingly crammed with skiffs, ferries, *barconi*, *barcaccie*, and merchant ships trying to offload onto the wharves of the palazzi or the market quays, all of them bustling and squabbling noisily for space.

"We'll go back by the lagoon route."

"It's choppy out there, lord."

"Good," said Annibale Malipiero. "The choppier the better." He was on a venture where water at its worst—and he himself did not much like water—might prove useful.

The Palazzo Malipiero Grandioso was indeed by far the largest of the Malipiero homes in the city, dominating the northern end of the

Grand Canal and dwarfing every other structure in its shadow. Five storeys high and with a canal frontage measuring at least eighty yards, it had been built a decade or so previously, *alla Romana* (or so Annibale Malipiero thought he'd heard it called, not that he had the least interest in architecture). It boasted an extraordinary number of windows, some thirty on each level, and ten or so massive Doric columns on the water-front alone (with more on each façade).

The inquisitor thought it one of the most ostentatiously self-satisfied edifices in the whole of Venice. As the owner of a smallish establishment on the Giudecca—a decidedly unfashionable location, which he'd chosen for its distance from the bustle of the city—and a modestly functional villa on the mainland that amply satisfied his desire for seclusion, he simply could not comprehend why anyone should choose to live in such a hulking pile. It was more a statement than a home—a haughty announcement of inordinate wealth.

The owner—whom Annibale Malipiero had come to see—was as vainglorious as this monstrosity, and a violent libertine. More infuriating still, he was just seventeen years of age. He had inherited the palazzo from his father, Stefano Malipiero, a man of great riches and vulgar taste, who had died six months earlier. The delinquent had inherited his father's profligacy too—choosing to fritter away the millions of ducats that were suddenly his in as rapid and arbitrary a manner as possible. His mother had expired many years previously, so now he was master of all he surveyed.

Here then, thought Annibale Malipiero as he pounded the knocker on the solid canal door, was a youthful example of the kind of miscreant he had been thinking about only yesterday, with a propensity for savagery without apparent reason. Of good birth, education, reasonable intelligence, vigorous health, good looks, and more money than he could possibly need, he was still possessed of a predilection for acts of shocking cruelty.

After several minutes of hammering, as the inquisitor considered sending Ercole to ram upon less sturdy entrances on the *calli* that surrounded the palazzo, the door creaked open.

Standing before the *interrogante* was an extraordinarily pretty girl—

dressed in the simple *camicia* and fustian kirtle of a servant. She had a rural look to her and quite surprised him by her diffidence. She lowered her eyes to the ground and curtsied. Most of his nephew's maids were former *puttane*, or still were *puttane*, with the coiffed conceit that such women flaunted, just as his male servants were cocky and boorish, like their master. He felt a rush of concern for the wench, wondering briefly how she might have ended up in so libidinous a household.

"Where is Jacopo Malipiero?" he demanded.

"He's sleeping, sir," the girl replied, with a degree of puzzlement as to what else her master could be doing a few minutes before noon.

"Go and wake him, will you?" said the Signor, but then he had a better idea. "On second thought, I'll wake him myself." An unanticipated entry was often a productive prelude to an interrogation.

He moved quickly past the demure maid into the vast ground-floor *sottoportego*. In most of the great palazzi, there would be a commotion of mercantile goings-on at this time of the morning, with boats being loaded and unloaded on the quayside, crates and barrels being carried in and out, deals being struck and payments being made, and other activities too—laundry girls washing clothes, food being collected from the larders and taken to the kitchens above, wine and oil being decanted, and water heated in tubs. Here there was nothing but a moist silence.

"Where *d'you* think you're going?" a voice croaked. The house's *portiere* had been half asleep beside the door and too lazy, or inebriated, to open it himself.

"I am here to talk to my nephew." Annibale Malipiero ascended the stairs to the *piano nobile*.

"He's not . . . receiving," the man called after him.

"Oh, he'll receive me," said the inquisitor, "I'm sure of it."

Unforgiving sunlight filled the *sala grande*. Its marble floor did not gleam; its paintings and tapestries were coated with dust; its costly silverware and glass failed to glitter.

"You!" Annibale Malipiero poked at a comatose figure sprawled on a nearby couch, apparently the only occupant of the huge space. Not more than twelve years old, the boy was too expensively clothed to be a servant. He was probably a relative, or one of Jacopo Malipiero's groveling devotees. He was quicker to react than the *portiere* had been—up in an instant, a hand gripping the dagger that hung from his hips. Undeterred, the Signor demanded, "Take me to where Jacopo Malipiero is sleeping."

"And you are . . . ?" the pup growled, fractionally unsheathing the blade.

"I don't know why you should know that, but I'll indulge you. I'm Annibale Malipiero."

The brat flinched. Relative or not, he'd know the name. *Il Terribile* had entered the building.

The inquisitor was led up a wide staircase to the second floor, which was more fully inhabited than the first. There were servants here, male and female, but none was notably occupied. Other young men were slouched on daybeds or cushions on the floor, and there were other women too, in disheveled and unlaced bodices and gowns. A musty odor hung in the air.

Annibale Malipiero felt as if he had stepped into the aftermath of a *baccanale*. He probably had. He knew well enough of his nephew's *feste* and of their notoriety. The youth of Venice—or the disreputable portion of it—would clamor and fight for admittance. He'd occasionally had to drag the odd participant in for questioning after some wine-fueled scuffle had gone too far.

He was pointed in the direction of a passageway leading off the main chamber. Carefully skirting a pool of what he presumed was vomit, he walked to the door at its far end.

Before entering the chamber, he drew breath. He'd had a son once, a boy named Carlo, not much younger than the nephew he was about to burst in on. He'd been clever, upright, and assiduous in his studies and had been destined for the University at Padua, but had died of a still-mysterious sickness. Annibale Malipiero often thought of his late son prior to apprehending some vile young degenerate in the course of his duties. It strengthened him and gave him hope, for it provided a welcome reminder that not every youngster of noble blood was susceptible to the diseases that appeared to be infecting the offspring of the city's eminent families, *gli giovanotti aristocratici*. It also made him angry.

There was a large key on the inside of the door. He turned it, then secreted it in his doublet.

Annibale Malipiero had expected to come across at least one whore toying with the thick tousle of curled chestnut-colored hair spread across his nephew's bolster, but, uncharacteristically, Jacopo Malipiero appeared to be alone in his enormous bed. It was almost insufferably hot in the room, so the youth had cast aside a plethora of embroidered throws of velvet and silk and sheepskins and calfskins and lay, snoring slightly, beneath a satin sheet.

The Signor looked for somewhere to sit, but there were no chairs or couches as such, just piles of overstuffed cushions of various fabrics and colors and a couple of mattresses draped with intricately woven damasks. There were two or three clothes chests and an elaborate dressing table covered in combs and brushes and bottles and jars, backed by an oval mirror. There were other mirrors in the room too—rather more, Annibale Malipiero thought, than any man might reasonably need. Gilt sconces still sputtered lazily, and an ornate candelabrum hung from the ceiling, casting a sultry ochre glow.

He strode to the weighty brocaded curtains that hid the windows and, with some effort, hauled them open. Daylight flooded in and once again revealed that everything was dusty, grubby, unpolished, unwashed, and frayed. The youth stirred and gave a drowsy complaint. After a few more minutes he mumbled, "Damn you, what time is it?"

"Gone noon, I'd say."

One eye blinked open, and then the next.

Annibale Malipiero smiled.

"Uncle . . . ?" Jacopo Malipiero groaned. "Oh, God, what have I done now?"

The *interrogante* moved toward the bed. "I was thinking of sending out the *Signori di Notte* to make an official arrest and to subject you to the attention of my less tolerant colleagues. But as you are, most regrettably, my late brother's son, I thought that the matter should be kept within the family. For the moment, at least."

"You wouldn't torture *me*," the unconscionable youth snorted.

Annibale Malipiero leaned forward. "You think," he hissed, "that because you're a blood relative and the head of a household in my family that I, chief inquisitor of the state, with bounden duties to perform in her service, will not scrupulously investigate, with torture if required, accusations that have been leveled against you?"

"What accusations?" Jacopo Malipiero still appeared unthreatened. He'd already been accused of so much in his short life.

Annibale Malipiero itemized them for the lout's benefit. "How about debauchery, whoremongering, gambling, drunkenness, bullying, the encouragement of dissipation and violence—"

"You can't torture me for those," the lad murmured.

"And *murder.*" Annibale Malipiero let the word hang awhile and then pulled the sheet up and away from the recumbent hooligan. As he'd suspected, the boy was naked.

Jacopo Malipiero was off the bed in an instant, making for the door. "You've locked it."

"Get dressed." The *interrogante* withdrew the key from his doublet. "We're going to take a little trip."

The thug banged on the door. "Beppino! Danilo! Nicodemo! I'm locked in! Bring the other key!"

"They can't help you now, boy," his uncle said.

"My servants dress me."

"Let's see if you are capable of so onerous a task. You won't need much where we're going—just a shirt and hose." The patrician picked up two items of clothing from the array that was scattered about the room and threw them at his nephew.

Boots pounded down the corridor. Annibale Malipiero quickly went to the door and inserted the key to stop it being unlocked from outside.

Trapped now, the boy reverted to his customary sneering arrogance. "Why should you trust a Dandolo anyway? The Dandoli are scum, vermin. Of course they're going to accuse *me*, they *hate* me—they hate *all* the Malipieri, you included probably."

"I said nothing of any Dandolo." The Signor gave the churl a crack around the head. It provoked a howl of pain. For a man of fifty-five, Annibale Malipiero could pack a formidable blow, though he rarely resorted to brute force. He was proud of his physical aptitude. He believed in Juvenal's dictum about a sound mind in a sound body. "Get dressed. *Now!*"

"Are you all right, master?" a servant called from the passageway.

"He's fine," the *interrogante* called back. "And unless you all want to go where he's going, I'd recommend you move away from the door."

Jacopo Malipiero pulled on a shirt and hose. Despite his parlous circumstance, he was unable to resist checking his appearance in the dressing-table mirror and neatening his disheveled hair.

"That'll do." The inquisitor unlocked the door.

"What? No shoes?"

"Nobody wears shoes in the dungeons of the Palazzo Ducale."

There were about twenty young reprobates outside the chamber, including one or two quivering, openmouthed girls. Even the burlier servants looked afraid. The inquisitor thought it odd indeed that these children—for that was how they appeared to him—should hold such sway over certain areas of the city and be capable of the savagery for which they were notorious.

"This is the *real* Jacopo Malipiero," he announced, gripping his nephew by the neck. "Like most bullies, he's a coward at heart. Remember what he looks like, because you'll never see him again."

The degenerate did his best to affect an expression of haughty indifference as he was marched along the corridor and down to the *sala grande*, but finally he whispered, "What do you mean they'll never see me again?"

Annibale Malipiero said nothing.

The pretty maid still stood in the *sottoportego*. The boy writhed slightly under her bewildered gaze. The *interrogante* instructed Ercole to take him to the gondola, then, without ceremony, he grasped the girl's wrist. "Leave this place," he breathed.

She could only stare back at him with lustrous, faintly glistening eyes.

"You sure you want the lagoon route, lord?" Ercole asked as they set off.

The *interrogante* closed the cabin curtain and turned to his problematic nephew as the vessel heaved out into the busy waterway.

"I'm going to give you a simple choice," he said briskly. "You can either make your confession here and now, or we can wait till we get to the *sala della tortura*, and that means I'll be placing you in the care of my fellow inquisitors. Which would you prefer?"

"I haven't murdered . . . anybody . . ." Jacopo Malipiero gasped.

"Let me ask you this, then." His uncle endeavored to remain patient. "Where were you just before midnight on Tuesday?"

Jacopo managed a befuddled shake of the head.

Annibale Malipiero slapped himself on the thigh. "Were you drunk, is that it?"

"Probably."

The Signor stretched out his arms and drummed his fingers on the woodwork of the gondola. "Let me jog your memory," he said crisply. "You were in the Campo San Sebastiano—not your usual stomping ground—and, yes, you were *roaring* drunk. What were you doing there?"

"I . . . don't . . . know."

"It's more Dandolo territory, isn't it, the Campo San Sebastiano?"

"Dandolo territory?"

Annibale Malipiero let out a sigh. He'd hoped to get this exchange over with long before they reached the Palazzo Ducale. The gondola began to rock as Ercole steered it out into the lagoon. "What is it that you have against the Dandoli? You called them scum. Are they *all* scum? Or do you have a reason to hate Fabietto Dandolo in particular?"

"Who?"

The boat was pitching and rolling now, and the patrician had to hold fast onto the gunwale. The boy clutched the edges of his own bench too.

"Are you acquainted with water torture?"

The braggart's eyes widened. "Has it . . . got something to do with . . . water?"

"It has. Filling a person up with it, little by little. Those who've endured it say it's the most frightening experience they've ever had; they say it's as if they are going to explode from the inside. Not all of them survive, of course. There's been the odd regrettable mistake—a little too much water, that kind of thing."

The youth started to pant rapidly.

Annibale Malipiero called, "Ercole! Take us out into the *bacino*!"

"It's mighty rough out there, Signor . . ."

"Do it!"

The gondola swayed more heavily.

"We usually do it in the comfort—for us, at least—of the *sala della tortura*. But why not in real water, good salty water?"

The woodwork shuddered and creaked as the boat hit the swell head on. "But I haven't *done* anything!" Jacopo Malipiero wailed.

"Ercole, drop anchor!"

The chain scraped and the boat steadied a little.

The Signor leaned into his nephew, close to the face that all the girls in Venice were in love with, apparently. He couldn't see it himself. The boy's lips were pursed like those of a baby about to bawl. Snot was starting to drip from his nose. "In the *sala della tortura*," the *interrogante* said, "we use a barrel and a rope. But here we have Ercole and the sea—"

"All right, all right," Jacopo Malipiero cried. "I may have thrashed him a bit."

"Thrashed him? Is *that* what you call it?"

"And, anyway, he's been insulting me, so if I went a bit far . . . and it wasn't just me, you know. *Everyone* hates Fabietto Dandolo."

"Ercole!" Annibale Malipiero bellowed over the crash of the waves. "He's all yours!"

The swell was so ferocious now that the gondola was undergoing a form of water torture itself. Jacopo Malipiero dropped to his knees and echoed the vessel's agonized protests.

The inquisitor surveyed his nephew awhile, letting him suffer a little longer. Then he instructed his helmsman to take them to the *riva*. The boat was threatening to break apart, and if it did so, they'd all drown.

The anchor chain ground its way back up again, and the craft bucked and headed north.

"How did he insult you?" Annibale Malipiero asked as they slid into calmer waters. He doubted the answer would interest him much, but it would pass the time before they docked.

"He said he was glad my cousin had been killed."

"Cousin? A cousin killed? What cousin?"

"Roderigo—"

"I don't think I know a nephew called Roderigo."

"You wouldn't. He was my best friend."

"And when did this happen?"

"Months ago. In Cyprus."

So here was the *interrogante*'s nephew confirming what he'd been cursorily informed of by Graziano Stornello first and what had been corroborated by the serving boy he'd interviewed—and the boy had said that Iago was the killer.

Annibale Malipiero had to ask: "Who killed him?"

"The Mantuan."

"Mantuan? What Mantuan?"

The waters beneath the gondola were more quiescent as they slid across the edge of the city, along the northern shore of the Giudecca Canal.

"*You* know." Jacopo Malipiero smirked.

"What do I know?"

"The one they call Iago. Everybody's talking about him."

The *interrogante* stroked his beard, affecting to try to recollect the name that had been obsessing him for weeks. "No, doesn't ring any bells."

"Oh, come on," his nephew mewled. "You're an inquisitor—you're the *chief* inquisitor."

"I am indeed," said the chief inquisitor. "And, as such, I never trust gossip."

"It's not gossip. It's true. He killed that woman in Cyprus, and her husband, the black man, and he killed my cousin too!"

"Oh, *that* Mantuan . . ." Annibale Malipiero picked at a loose thread in his cloak. "There's no truth in that, none whatsoever. And, believe me, I'd know if there was. No, no, no, he doesn't even *exist*. He's a *fabrication*."

The boat creaked into the Rio di Palazzo. The investigator knew it by its utter stillness and its stench. All the small canals of Venice were sewers, but this one stank worse than most. It ran between the Prigioni Ducale and the Palazzo Ducale and therefore received an abundance of excrement from both buildings. The patrician had sometimes pondered upon the irony of the shit of a Doge and the shit of the lowest form of felon meeting somewhere in the middle of this putrescent waterway.

The vessel clunked against the *imbarcadero* of the *prigioni*. Annibale Malipiero swept open the curtain and took his nephew's hand. Ercole was already at the massive door of the plain black edifice that contrasted so markedly with the intricate ornamentation of the palazzo opposite. The bridge that connected the two buildings, across which prisoners were marched to their interrogations and executions, was directly above them. No sunlight ever entered this particular reach.

Jacopo Malipiero retched a little at the pervasive odor and peered up at the sullen, windowless structure. "What's going to happen to me here?" he whimpered.

"You'll be interrogated," declared the inquisitor. "Unless of course you're willing to sign a confession at once—which would perhaps be the wisest course. I'm going to leave you in the capable hands of my colleagues."

"If I did kill him . . . I didn't mean to," the wastrel wailed. "Can't you . . . vouch . . . for me?"

"That would be most unprofessional."

The reprobate grasped his uncle by both arms. "Please . . . Please don't let them torture me. . . . Please don't let me be hanged." Tears coursed down his smooth cheeks, snot from his classical nose.

Annibale Malipiero extricated himself from his nephew's grip and plucked thoughtfully at his beard. He asked, as a confessor might, "Are you truly repentant for what you've done?"

"Yes, yes, *yes!*"

The *interrogante* stared into the wretch's eyes. "Listen to me," he whispered. "And listen carefully."

"Yes, Uncle."

"Fabietto Dandolo isn't dead, though he might as well be. He has a broken rib, a broken nose, a broken skull, and three or four stab wounds; one punctured his lung and another was very close to his heart. But for the moment you're not a murderer. I'm tempted to arrest you for serious assault, but, to be frank, I can't be bothered. I'd prefer never to see you again, but regrettably I doubt that'll be the case."

"You're . . . not taking me in there, then?"

"Not for the time being."

The immediate relief that swept over the churl—a sudden reversion to type, a scowling smile, a lifting and straightening of the shoulders, a flick of those full locks—only revolted Annibale Malipiero further.

He turned to the huge tarred prison door, and Jacopo Malipiero asked, "Can Ercole take me back in the gondola?"

The chief inquisitor stopped in his tracks. The boy's temerity was astounding. "Certainly not." And with that, he and Ercole swept into the Prigioni Ducale and the door clanked shut behind them.

He'd done what he'd intended to do—which was to frighten his appalling nephew out of his wits. It *might* persuade the lout to think twice before throwing his weight about quite as much as he had.

Halfway up the stairs to the corridor that led to the *sala degli interroganti,* the *interrogante* came to a halt. For a few seconds he felt the imposing stone walls spin around him and the contents of his stomach rose to the back of his throat. Fortunately, he was alone. As he produced a handkerchief—a delicate one, embroidered by his loving wife—to wipe his mouth, he put his nausea down to the rough ride on the *bacino.* He'd been almost as fearful of drowning as his nephew had, though of course he hadn't shown it. Or perhaps it was the exceptionally foul odor that he so loathed as he entered the Rio di Palazzo, though he should have got used to it by now. Or maybe it was merely a reaction to his having had to sit for a time in the company of so disgusting a relative.

Mercifully, the *sala degli interroganti* itself was empty of other inquisitors (they must have been upstairs torturing someone), but a man stood by the long table.

"Forgive me, lord, but they permitted me to wait for you here." It was the storm-beaten old soldier who'd brought the despairing missive from Cyprus that morning. He clutched another scroll now.

"Shouldn't you be halfway to Cyprus?"

"No need, lord. I have a new communication for you."

The disgusting relative, meanwhile, still stood on the flimsy, creaking dock of the Prigioni Ducale. The only way off it was by boat. But few boats passed through the Rio di Palazzo. And on those that did, the boatmen refused to acknowledge Jacopo Malipiero's increasingly frantic waves and calls. With his soaked shirt and hose and matted hair and bare feet, perhaps they thought him a recently released felon.

He felt humiliated, wretched, slightly embarrassed, and not a little enraged. His pride had taken a real mauling. He needed to restore it somehow. There were usually two ways of doing that—to make love to a hapless, adoring girl or to beat somebody up. Or, better still, both.

15. A Second Battering

The loud pounding on the *porta da canale* doesn't betoken a friendly visit, and it has interrupted my siesta. I rise from my bed and look tentatively out of the canal window. From here I have to crane to see who's doing the hammering, but I don't dare lean out farther, because what I do see is not reassuring. There are three or four of them down there, puffed up as usual, bridling and punching the air, spoiling for something vicious.

Faces are appearing in the windows of the houses and palazzi on the other side of the canal and from the *loggette* on the rooftops, incensed at having been disturbed at this time of day.

This, to say the least, is a disconcerting intrusion on an otherwise tranquil period in my life—almost three weeks, in fact, of near-monastic existence. I haven't actually entered a monastery—though now I'm thinking it might be better for me if I had—but I've stayed at home most of the time, keenly devoting my mind and my heart to books.

I've tried to avoid studying love too much, for obvious reasons. If I've read any poetry, it's been Theocritus, who writes about love between boys, so I don't feel too affected. Mostly, though, I've stuck to hard facts, to the cold historians—to Herodotus, Tacitus, Thucydides, Livy. I dislike history, and military history most of all. But I've tried to study ancient wars. My tutor is delighted with my diligence. He thinks it will be good for my Greek and my Latin, as the more you abhor a subject in an old tongue, he says, the more you struggle—and therefore learn—to master it. He's also pleased with my interest in Theocritus, because Theocritus is his favorite poet.

I'm becoming interested in astronomy too. I'm trying to understand Ptolemy, which is difficult. But his theories sometimes take me up to the *loggetta* at night, where my mother often used to sit, so that I can contemplate the movements of the moon and the stars on their journey around the world, or the sun when it comes up. Perhaps this is my way of getting as far from the world, and reality, as I can.

Reality is thumping on the door now. "Open up!" someone's bellowing. It isn't *his* voice. "Open up or we'll bloody kick our way in!"

Who's around to protect me? My father isn't—he's in Ferrara, I think. Where's our sturdy *portinaio* Leonzino, our lion, our personal Cerberus, when he's most needed? He's visiting his sick mother in Treviso. My father's servants Manfredo and Sansone, who are almost as pugnacious, are presumably wherever my father is. Giovanni, my own servant, will be cowering somewhere. Paganello won't bother to defend me, if he's in (he spends most of his days away from the palazzo, I don't know where, but he's probably up to no good). Baldassare will already have locked himself in his garret. So that leaves the women. Zinerva will be grumbling at having been woken up, as this is the only point in the day when she gets a decent sleep. She might send the brutes packing, if she bothers to descend from the kitchen. The housemaids will be clutching each other in terror. And little Balbina—she, perhaps, is hobbling toward the door at this moment.

I'd better try to beat her to it. It's me they've come to see.

"Well, hello, and what's your name, pretty one?" There's a cry and a crash. Balbina's been sent flying.

I face them in the *sottoportego*. Two have entered; the others are still pacing on the dock outside.

Balbina is doubled up on the floor. The sight of her there makes me angry. "You didn't need to do that; what harm has she done you?"

"Who are you to tell us what to do and what not to do, louse?" a brute growls, imitating the creature he serves.

I help Balbina up. She doesn't seem to be badly injured, although it's always difficult to tell with her. "Go now," I say.

She limps off up the stairs. But before she leaves the room entirely, she turns to the one who hit her and declares, "You are a most discourteous *giovanotto*, Signor . . ." I want to run to her and plant a kiss on her crinkled brow. I may do so later, if I live.

The youth laughs. "I like a girl with spirit! *Porca miseria*, she's an ugly thing though, isn't she?"

"I don't know who you are," I say, trying to maintain a brave front, "but I'd guess you're here on some mission from Jacopo Malipiero. Doesn't he have the courtesy or courage to confront me himself?"

The lout swings toward me and thrusts his bestial face into mine. "We're here to take you to him," he growls.

As I'm carried out, I hear a distressed howl from Zinerva, presumably as she sees Balbina. I'm dumped with a crash into Jacopo Malipiero's gondola. Like him, it's a brazen thing—long and luxuriant and polished to a gleam.

There are six of them, if you include the *gondoliere*, who looks as nasty as his passengers. I have a reprobate on either side of me, two facing me, and in the prow sits Jacopo's little brother Nicolo, who turns to me with a sneer. "You didn't deliver your news, did you?"

"Well, he wasn't there, was he; you said he was busy—"

"That was ages ago," the little thug snarls.

"Where am I being taken? To the Campo Sant'Angelo?"

"No. We're going home."

I know the Palazzo Malipiero Grandioso, of course. All of Venice does—it's not easy to ignore. It's a monstrous cube at the northern end of the Grand Canal. It makes our own humble house look like *una baracca di un povero*. But I've never entered it—as I am not a member of the *giovanotti splendente*, the *bel mondo giovanile*, who hungrily fall over one another to be invited to one of Jacopo Malipiero's infamous *feste*. Besides, I'm a Stornello, and no Stornello would ever get an invitation to an occasion hosted by a Malipiero.

Although it seems I have received one now.

I'm surprised that I haven't yet been kicked or punched or stamped on. They must have been instructed to keep me relatively intact. They don't seem pleased about it.

What was it that I had to tell him in the campo all those weeks ago? Confirmation of a sort that Iago killed his wife and a suggestion that my cousin didn't die of the plague but was murdered by him. Such news seems distinctly paltry now.

What's the worst he can do to me? A boot to the face again, the breaking of a few bones, some ingenious form of torture I haven't yet contemplated, or a knife to the throat? Has he ever *killed* anyone? I don't know, but if he hasn't, it can only be a matter of time.

I could of course make something up. I regard myself as something of a poet, after all, and a poet could be said to be a fabricator . . . I'm going to have to fabricate something pretty convincing.

I'm heaved out of the gondola and across the palazzo's private *imbarcadero* (much larger than ours), through the big thick door into the *sottoportego* (twenty times larger than ours), up some stairs into the *sala grande* (fifty times larger than ours), and out into the building's central courtyard (we don't, needless to say, have a courtyard).

He's standing in the very center of this vast plant-and-statue-bedecked space.

And so, *Madonna mia*, is she. They're alone together.

I haven't seen her for what seems like an age, so it's almost as if I'm experiencing this smack to the heart for the first time. Her untied hair is over her face. She looks a bit disheveled, *un po' spogliata*. She's wearing her simple servant clothes, which make her in my view more glorious, not less. One sleeve of her *camicia* has slipped off a soft brown shoulder. He seems somewhat undressed too—all he's wearing is a shirt and hose, and he's barefoot. His hair is slightly matted and he looks wet. What is it, sweat?

As I'm hauled closer, she turns to me and appears to be a little put out. Her already dark skin flushes darker. There's a sheen about it—a hint of moistness. It's very hot in this courtyard. I think they've been canoodling.

He plants a kiss on her cheek and murmurs, "Off you go now, *cara mia*."

She looks at me for a moment before leaving. I sense some concern there—for what I'm about to endure, I suppose.

I don't risk following her with my own gaze. I hear the scrape of sandals on pebbles.

Jacopo Malipiero kicks me in the groin. Even though he's not wearing boots or shoes, the pain is extreme. I yowl and stumble backward. His vile henchmen, bunched behind me, push me toward him again. He punches me in the stomach, then adroitly spins me around and gives me a chop across the back of my neck. I'm on all fours on the sharp gravel. He drops to his haunches and wrenches up my head by the hair.

"You had some news but you didn't bring it to me. Why not?"

"I was told you were busy."

"Busy? Busy at what?"

"I told him you've been back for *weeks*," I hear Nicolo whine.

"It had better be good, whatever it is, to justify the wait." Jacopo Malipiero thwacks me across the skull. He clicks his fingers. "Nicolo, give me your *pugnale*." Now I have the tip of a very sharp stilettolike blade resting on my right cheek. "Because if it isn't, I shall have to cut your nose off."

"Oh, it is, it is," I gasp. "He did it—he killed his wife, and the Moor, and my cousin—"

"Of course he did, everybody knows that." He slides the knife under my nose so that its point is now in one of my nostrils. "I don't care about your pathetic cousin; I only want to know if he killed mine."

"Yes, yes, he did!" I cry out.

"How do you know?"

"I was . . . I heard it . . ."

"Who from?"

"From . . . well . . . our cook,"

"A *cook*?" he barks.

With a quick outward slice, he tears open the bottom of my nose. As I know from my first battering, a nose wound can produce a lot of blood, and such is the case now. It's spurting everywhere. I have to raise a hand to stanch the gush.

"Stop blubbering, it was just a nick. Now I'm going to chop it off and then I'm going to kill you."

It may be just a nick, but it hurts like hell. "Please," I gurgle, because my mouth is full of blood, "please don't kill me. It wasn't only the cook—I heard it from others too."

He seems momentarily confused. "What?"

"Oh . . . my family . . ." I go on lying wildly.

He's on his feet again. His handsome face has taken on a kind of demented frenzy. This is probably what murderers look like right before they strike. What on this great earth can I tell him now?

He turns to his acolytes, arms swinging. "What's the bug saying? I can't understand him. Nicolo or someone, give him a handkerchief. He's burbling. *I need to know what he's saying.*"

An obliging thug scurries toward me with a cloth. It's a prettily embroidered thing, rather too feminine to be in the possession of such a hooligan. I spit blood onto it and put it to my nostril.

"Get up," he snaps. I struggle to obey; I feel distinctly giddy. "Hold him; he's going to topple." I'm supported from beneath each elbow by his troops.

"If it wasn't just the cook, who was it?"

So he heard *that* part all right.

"Family," I splutter.

"What?"

"My . . . my father . . . my . . . uncles."

"How are they saying he was killed?

Oh, God, I should have known he'd ask me how his cousin was murdered. He's bound to want the gory details. Or he's probably heard them all already, from that sailor he beat up, and whatever I say won't match what he's heard.

"*And how come you haven't been to tell this before?*"

"I was waiting . . . to have it all . . . confirmed."

"Confirmed? Who by?" He starts to prowl around me, tapping the blade of the *pugnale* on his palm.

"I was waiting to have it confirmed by . . . by . . ." And then, from somewhere in my desperate brain, I blurt out, "*My uncle Graziano.*"

I grab the name because it has some weight. Everybody in Venice knows who Graziano Stornello is. Unfortunately for the story I'm starting to invent, he's in Cyprus.

This is the sorry truth that Jacopo Malipiero picks on now. "He's in Cyprus," he growls.

Now the knife is at my gullet, or just above it, under my chin. "I think I will have to kill you," he says. "I can't kill you here, though, not in my own home. We'll have to take you out into a side alley somewhere, so your rotting corpse won't be found for days, maybe weeks."

"Oh, but he's not!" I suddenly exclaim.

"Not? Not what?"

"He's not in Cyprus. My uncle Graziano. He's here in Venice. He's come back. That's what I was waiting for, for him to return, because I knew he was going to, and now he has."

At least my mouth isn't full of blood anymore. And by pressing on my nose, I've managed to stop the flow there too.

My capacity for fiction in a crisis is—I must admit—incredible. Under sentence of further torture and imminent death you will invent anything and can even be quite inspired.

He's not convinced. But he's dropped the blade from my throat. "No, he isn't," he says. "If your famous bloody uncle came back, there'd be ceremony, the whole fleet out to greet him."

Damn it, he's right. To give what I say next some kind of authenticity, I lower my voice and mutter confidentially, "Well, he didn't want anybody to know he'd come home. It's very . . . secret."

"Why? What is?"

"I think," I whisper, "it should be something that is known only to you . . . and maybe not *anyone else*?" I flick a glance in the direction of his followers and the two louts still holding me.

"This isn't some trick of yours, is it, bug?" he growls. "Because even if I send them away, I still have a knife and I'm still minded to kill you. I may not need a knife." And he puts the hand that isn't holding the knife around my neck, which makes his adoring horde whoop.

"Get out of here!" he bellows to his apes.

They scuttle reluctantly into the palazzo.

"So . . . ?"

"It's because of the Turks."

"What have the bloody Turks got to do with it?"

"My uncle doesn't want the Turks knowing he's back in Venice. It's all got to be very secretive, very hush-hush . . ."

"I don't give a rat's ass about the Turks!" he yells. He grabs me by the collar of my doublet and lifts me off the ground. The knife he's still got in his right hand is again dangerously close to my cheek, to my right eye, in fact. "I will kill you here, right here and now in my *cortile*. Why not? What the hell, I can always say you were trying to rob me, a Stornello pauper trying to steal from a rich Malipiero. Or we can just dump your corpse into the canal."

"Please don't do that." God, he's strong. I hate how weak I am.

He bawls into my face, *"Where's Iago, louse?"*

The answer is simple enough. Iago is in Cyprus, if he's anywhere. What I come up with next is going to have be pretty dramatic. My very life depends on it.

"I . . . I was coming to that," I pant. "He's here too."

"What?"

"Iago. He's here too."

He pushes me away so that I land on my behind, with one leg buckled under it. That hurts too. "Don't lie to me, maggot!" he roars.

The cry brings his brood of drooling bullies back into the courtyard. They don't want to miss a thing.

He stands over me, raises the dagger, then puts it close to my pounding heart.

I squeal, "I'm not lying. That's why it has to be a secret. He's been brought back to Venice . . . by my uncle. That's what I was going to tell you!"

"Get the hell out of here!" he shouts to the animals.

He drops to his haunches again, one arm resting on each knee, tossing the knife from one hand to the other, catching it expertly by the hilt each time. He cocks his head, examining my expression for any sign of guile. Luckily for me, all I can display at this moment is blind dread.

"How do you know he's been brought back?"

"I know it from my uncle."

"He told you himself, did he? The first thing your famous uncle does when he comes back to Venice is to tell you—and only you—something that nobody else in Venice is allowed to know, is that it?"

He's being sharper than I'd expected—as keen as the blade he's toying with.

"I . . . heard him talking about it to my father."

"Where? When?"

"Two nights ago . . . in my father's study. I listened at the door."

"You little sneak."

He fires a cannonade of questions at me, hard and fast, as I imagine an *interrogante* might, barely giving me time to think, trying to make me slip.

"Why should it be a secret that Iago is in Venice?"

"Because . . . because of the Turks. He's a Turkish spy . . . and they don't want the Turks to know they've got him."

"Bloody Turks again." He spits in my face. "And why have they brought him back to Venice? Why didn't they just hang him in Cyprus?"

"Because they need to . . . interrogate him . . ."

He's inspecting the blade of the dagger, turning it around, letting it glint, and looking at the blood—*my* blood—on the tip.

"Why couldn't they interrogate him over there?"

I'm not sure how long I can keep this up. "Because . . . they're not very good at it in Cyprus?"

"That's possible," he mutters. "Venice does have the best inquisitors. When did they arrest him?"

"Oh, soon after the murders."

"But they were months ago!"

Oh, God, he's right again. His fingers tighten around the handle of the *pugnale*. He tips his decorous head to one side, looks me up and down, as if considering where on my body to insert it. "If he's been in Cyprus for months, why have they brought him back only now?"

Good question. Perversely, though, I'm starting to enjoy my capacity for invention. I'm so steeped in untruth by now that I may as well make a meal of it. "Well . . . he escaped for a time."

"Escaped? To where?"

"To somewhere in Cyprus . . . into the mountains. He was helped to escape by the rebels." In a sentence, I've encapsulated all that I know about Cyprus—that it has mountains and rebels. "But they caught him again, and now they're interrogating him here."

"Where are they keeping him?"

"Where do they usually keep the worst villains and enemies of the republic?"

Jacopo Malipiero suddenly plunges the dagger into the ground, so hard that the blade almost snaps. He stands and glares down at me intently. "I have an uncle too, you know, *nearly* as well known as yours. Although you won't know him, because you're so damned virtuous, aren't you? Like all your damned family."

"Who?" I ask.

"The chief inquisitor. *Il Terribile.*"

This is the uncle that Nicolo mentioned in the Albergo Tre Stelle.

"So if you're lying," he says, "I'll know about it, won't I?"

"Yes, you will," I groan.

Jacopo Malipiero looks up at the open sky. He sniffs the air, like a predator checking for prey. "I *thought* there was a new stench in Venice these past few days."

He walks away. "Bring me my *cinquedea*!" he barks. "The one with the ivory handle—oh, and my misericorde too!"

He pushes his way through his gang, who are crowded and bobbing and whispering to one another in the doorway. "Throw the louse into the canal; let him swim his way home."

Two of them come toward me. The others follow him like a set of eager hounds.

I could try to grab the dagger he's left in the ground, but when did I ever know how to use a dagger?

I'm dragged back into the palazzo, across the *sala grande*, down the stairs, and across the *sottoportego*.

There, if but for a split second, I see her again, with some other servants, all girls of around her age, washing bedding in a great *tinozza*. She scrubs away at a sheet on a washboard, pounding at it with her delicate copper-toned hands. As I'm lugged past her, she glances up and down again, too quickly for me to tell if there's any sympathy there. And I'm pushed into the Grand Canal.

I've never been fond of water at the best of times—which, for a boy who lives in Venice, is unfortunate. I've watched ragged urchins grasping their noses and buckling their knees as they've leapt hooting into canals around the city, on muggy days like today, so I have the sense to close my mouth and hold my nose. I discover that Archimedes's principle of buoyancy—once described to me by Baldassare, something to do with making yourself lighter than the mass of water you're in—actually works. *Mirabile dictu*: I float. But I still can't swim.

Then an angel comes to my rescue.

She doesn't hold out a hand for mine to grasp and pull me up and into heaven, but she's leaning down over the edge of the dock, saying something I don't hear at first. "There." She's pointing. "Hold on to that, then pull around to the next one."

It's the first time I've heard her speak. Her voice is a bit deeper than I'd expected—a country burr, I suppose you'd call it. It seems quite lovely to me—darkly different and enticing.

I'm so rapt for a moment that I forget what it is she's telling me to do. But I finally look in the direction she's indicating, grab a stave, haul myself to the next one, then the next, and finally I reach the bank. There are steps up from the water onto the narrow *calle* on this side of the palazzo.

I must look appalling. Her gaze confirms it. She wrinkles her little pointed nose. "Thank you," I say.

"Do not tell Jacopo, Signor," Franceschina says. For a second I'm surprised by her formal address, but then I remember that she's a servant and that I—however drenched and bruised—am a *nobiluomo*. She glances back over her shoulder to see if she's being watched.

"Here, take this." She pulls a handkerchief from a pocket in her kirtle. "For your nose."

It's a simple white linen square. The embroidered one I was using to stanch the blood earlier is still in Jacopo Malipiero's courtyard. I have to stretch, and every part of me hurts, but somehow I manage to take it. Our hands don't touch.

Then she's gone, and I hear the overcarved canal door of the Palazzo Malipiero Grandioso slam shut.

As I enter our kitchen, it's time for Balbina to squeal once more. "*Madre di Dio e il Figlio Santo*, where have you been this time!" She screws up her face at the stench of the sewage.

The maids recoil and put fingers to their nostrils. "Pooooooo!"

Paganello the serving boy grimaces.

Balbina applies some form of sticky stinging paste to my nose, then binds it with strips of brown gauze. I have the appearance of that misshapen fool—the revolting character they call Pulcinella in those scandalous shows that the Neapolitan acting troupes sometimes bring to Venice whose beak is the mark of a cuckold.

"But what about you, Balbina, aren't you hurt?"

"I'm used to being pushed about," she says, cleaning the caked blood from my face and checking the rest of me for breakage.

"*Ragazzo cretino*," Zinerva cries. "*Mamma mia*, what shall we do with you? You are *un incurabile*, *un zimbello demenziale*; nothing I say to you goes in! Now you are letting them into our house, the *bruti*, the *assassini*, the scum, *la feccia della terra*—the Malipieri *animali*! What will your father say when he learns of it?"

"Perhaps he doesn't need to know . . . ?"

"He will know of it, *bambino stupido*—all the *quartiere* knows of it. They all heard them shouting out there, and some saw them coming in too! *Dio Santo*, the disgrace!"

"*He* didn't let them in," Balbina says, trying to defend me. "I did."

"Yes, and look what they did to you, the dogs! Setting upon a helpless cripple! If I'd got there quicker, they'd have felt the end of my *trinciante*, I can tell you!" She flourishes the great carving knife she's holding.

I feel a need to pour my heart out to someone though. I clamber painfully up to the very top of the palazzo and knock on the door to Baldassare's chamber.

He opens it only slightly. He, too, looks disapproving as he peers at me through the crack, but I also think he seems quite pleased to see that I'm alive. He eyes my bandaged nose. "Oh, *coniglietto*, what have you done now?"

"What have *I* done?" I exclaim. "Are you going to say it's all my fault too?"

"You smell dreadful," he says.

"That's because I almost drowned in the Grand Canal. Does my smelling so bad mean you're not going to let me in?"

"All right, but please don't sit anywhere."

There's nowhere to sit anyway, apart from the chair at his table. Every other item of furniture, including his narrow bed, is buried under books and manuscripts and scrolls and parchments and scraps of paper. They're all over the floor, too, and more stacked volumes cover the walls. We don't have lessons in this tiny room, with its one small casement overlooking the canal. This is his hermit's cave, his retreat from the inconveniences of humanity. I've suggested he should move to a bigger room, as his collection of literature gets ever larger—but he says that he's content here, and that if he were to move, he wouldn't know where to find anything.

And even though this is where he sleeps and reads and thinks, he does have the run of the palazzo. He's welcome here. He's liked. My father finds him amusing, if incomprehensible. The rest of the household enjoys teasing him—for his studiousness and absentmindedness, for having his "head in the clouds" all the time, and for knowing nothing of the real world though it's not fair to accuse him of that. Being small and fat and distracted, he's easy prey for the bullies out there. He doesn't go out much as a result. But he has to travel to and from Padua, where he teaches, and he's been robbed twice on his journeys. He was once thrown into the lagoon on the coast outside Malcontenta and would have drowned but for a passing fisherman.

I tell him now that I, too, have been rescued from a watery grave, by my own Amaryllis, my Laura, my Beatrice.

"And, like a Nereid, she caught your hand and sang sweet songs as she pulled you up from the canal?" he asks sardonically. "Did she take you to her silvery cave and feed you fruits and wine?"

"No, but she gave me this. . . ."

I produce the handkerchief, soaked in blood. I notice for the first time that there is a small "F" stitched in purple in one corner.

"Ah, a love token," he says. "Or perhaps she simply could not bear to look at your sanguineous nose. Perhaps she's just squeamish."

"She *pitied* me, Baldassare."

"And was it her boyfriend who did that to you?" He waves a finger in the direction of my nose.

I nod. Then I tell him everything—or everything that I can remember. He's my only true *confidente,* after all.

I find a place to sit and it takes a while for me to come out with it all, because there's quite a lot of explaining to do. There are great gaps in the knowledge of my knowledgeable instructor. The present day is as foreign to him as the ancient world is to most.

When I've finished, he paces about his room, stepping carefully over the piles of books and papers, and strokes his pudgy chin. "It's not a good thing to lie, Gentile. As Socrates advised—"

"I know what Socrates said about lying: It infects the soul. But what if you're about to be killed?"

"Lies come back to haunt the liar," he muses, most unhelpfully.

"But what should I *do*?" I plead.

I don't expect *il Dottore* Baldassare Ghiberti, esteemed philosopher from the University of Padua, to come up with some all-embracing, instantly useful, Socratic solution. And he doesn't. All he can offer is: "I'd bolt and lock the doors for the time being, *coniglietto.* That's what I always do when I hear trouble coming."

16. *Imprisonment*

Massive crash. Shaken from fretful sleep, and my chamber full of people. Half a dozen or so. Don't see faces because hooded, like monks. But they're not monks. Thick black cloaks; velvety, quite glossy in the flames of their torches.

Assume at first, naturally, it's Jacopo and his gang. How did they get in? I've told Leonzino to admit no one, *no one*. Even bolted my own door. I see now it's on the floor and its hinges dangle on the broken jamb, and Giovanni's cowering form is framed in the doorway.

"Up." A muffled voice. "Get dressed."

"Who are you, what do you want?"

"Shut up. Get dressed."

Grab a shirt and hose and put them on. On the bed, partially concealed under a bolster, is Franceschina's handkerchief, still bloody. I was kissing it as I fell asleep. Snatch it, hopefully not observed, and slip it under my shirt, against my chest—*un ciondolo come portafortuna*. May it bring me luck.

Leonzino shrugs apologetically at the open canal door. Nobody refuses entry to the *Signori di Notte*.

On our little dock, I look up to see only one small window with a light burning in it—Baldassare's. My father's casements are dark.

Head pushed down and thrown into the cabin of the gondola—larger even than Jacopo's, but it cuts through the water with the same slick speed, or even faster. Hardly any traffic at this time of night. The very dead of night . . .

We head south. No sound but the efficient swish of the keel. Three black-cowled figures in the cabin with me, heads bowed.

Recognize the familiar rocking—more palpable in the darkness—as the boat slides out of the calm of the Grand Canal into the rougher waters of the *bacino*, then we swing left and all is still again—horribly silent, and there's a nauseating odor.

It's too dark to make out much of the inky bulk of the building before me, but I glimpse its oily stones by the light of a brazier as I'm tugged across a few wet planks to a thick tarred door almost level with the water.

Heart pounds and seems to jump into my gullet, and sour sickness rushes up from my stomach.

Held by both arms, I'm dragged down a steep, dank flight of stairs, with the water of the *rio* following us in a torrent. And more stairs, seemingly down and down . . .

I shouldn't be here. Noblemen don't get taken here. They have cells at least at ground level, with windows, or so I've heard. This is where the scum are put, *la feccia della terra* as Zinerva calls them, the murderers, rapists, violent madmen. This is the place of perpetual night, the *pozzi*, the city's very own Inferno.

"You can't do this to me, I am *un nobiluomo!*" I scream. "I am Gentile Stornello, son of Fabrizio Stornello, nephew of Graziano Stornello, Captain-General of the Sea!"

I'm cracked around the head.

Thrust into complete blackness.

Can only hear, and feel, and smell . . . mutterings and curses and grunts and groans and hoarse rasps and sometimes a high wail of hopeless dejection . . . shoves and pokes and sometimes a smack to the pate or a thump to the stomach . . . overwhelming stink, worse than the filthiest corners of the city . . . fetid unyielding air, scouring the back of my throat . . . uneven ground, no floor as such, only sludge, and water, sometimes reaching my knees.

So many bodies. I bump into one. "Hey, keep off!" I fall face forward into a puddle of God knows what . . . almost solid, tastes foul . . . I gag . . . a slippery hairy thing runs over my hand . . . I weep . . .

> *Lasciate ogne speranza, voi ch'intrate . . .*
> *Moans, protestations, and loud cries*
> *Echoed through the starless place,*
> *And from the very start I wept.*

"Hello." A sinister voice in my ear. "Who's this then?"

"It's a Stornello," another snarls, equally close.

"A Stornello, eh? Must be rich, then," says the first.

Hands and fingers trace my face, my neck, my whole body. Not an inch of me is left unexplored. I'm sniffed at, like a bitch by a dog. "*Smells* rich." Horrendous, reeking breath. I'm pawed. A whisper. "Feels *good* too."

And then: "Welcome to hell, pretty one."

17. *Interrogation*

"You are Gentile Stornello?" I'm being addressed by a tiny withered man with a bald head that looks like a skull. He has a reedy, whining voice.

He's seated behind a long table covered with a red cloth. On the table are three sputtering candelabra and a brass handbell, to be rung, I would guess, if things should ever get out of hand in this room. There are papers on the table too, neatly stacked, and an inkwell and some quills.

Beside this corpse sits the fattest person I've ever seen. He's monstrously obese, his bulbous, rubicund face framed by greasy, stringy hair and globular, protuberant eyes, a pug nose, and a thick, dribbling mouth.

Both men are dressed in scarlet robes and *berretti*—the official garb of the *Interroganti della Republica Serenissima*.

I wonder if one of these might be Jacopo Malipiero's uncle—the *chief* inquisitor—but the Malipieri are a generally good-looking tribe, and neither of these could be called that.

I see no instruments of torture here—not that I'd recognize one. Aside from the table and the chairs on which the *interroganti* sit, there's no other furniture in the paneled and thickly curtained chamber. The only light comes from the candles. There's a huge fireplace against one wall, but as the night is so warm, it's empty.

I didn't have to spend long in the *pozzi*. A man crashed into the dungeon, swinging a lantern up and down and from side to side as he tramped about the repellent space. The wretches into whose company I'd been thrown scuttled away to the nearest dark corner. I suppose I'm going to be sent back down there when this is over. Unless I'm to be taken somewhere else.

My nose wound doesn't seem to be bleeding too much, but I must look a desperate sight. The thin one is still waiting for an answer.

"Yes, I'm Gentile Stornello."

"You are sixteen years of age?"

"Not yet."

"Do you know why you have been brought to us, Gentile Stornello?"

"No."

"Can you guess?"

"No."

"You won't even hazard a guess?"

"Because I have done something wrong?"

"Have you?"

"I don't know."

"So you don't deny that you *may* have done something wrong."

"We all do things that are . . . wrong . . . sometimes."

"What is that you think you might have done wrong that has brought you to us?"

"Perhaps *you* could tell *me*."

I'm sensing some impatience from the fat one. He's not said anything yet, but he's grunted a bit, like a pig, and his rheumy eyes are bulging so much I think they might burst from their sockets.

"Would you say you were an upright sort of character?" the skeletal one asks.

"I endeavor to be."

"You say your prayers, you go to Confession . . ."

"Yes."

"When did you last go to Confession?"

"Three weeks ago."

"That is a sign of an upright person, is it, someone who has not been to Confession for three whole weeks?"

"There's no point in going to confession, Signor, if you feel you have nothing to confess."

"So you are wholly without sin?"

"None of us is *wholly* without sin, Signor . . ."

The corpulent one drums his chubby fingers on the table.

"You are a godly person, are you?"

"I believe in God, sir, if that's what you mean."

"I only wish to know if you respect the laws of God."

"I do, yes."

"And the laws of the state? Do you respect them too?"

"I obey them, Signor, I don't think I've ever broken a law in my life."

"That's for us to decide, I think." He turns briefly to his colleague, who harrumphs in agreement. Then he asks, "But do you *respect* the law? Many *obey* the law, because they fear the consequences if they don't. You're not one of those, are you, Gentile Stornello? Someone who obeys the law only because you might be punished if you break it?"

I'm sure that this shrunken *interrogante*, who looks old enough to be my father's father, has a thoroughly sharp brain in his small, wrinkled head. The fat one, I think, is fairly stupid, but he worries me because, although he still hasn't said anything, he looks like a very large firecracker waiting for a spark.

"I obey the law because I believe that it is fair and just," I say.

"So you respect your government, do you?"

"Very much."

He seems surprised. "Really? I thought all you clever young chaps quite liked to kick against the government."

"I don't. I admire it."

"What do you admire most about it?"

"It models itself on ancient Athens," I declare. "And, as such, every-one has a say in how it is run."

"Not quite everyone, Gentile Stornello," he corrects me.

"By everyone, I mean the *ottimati*, those with the status and the . . . the intelligence to participate."

The rotund one is looking bored now. I go on, hoping to impress with my erudition. "However, as Pericles said in his famous oration, recorded for posterity by Thucydides, good government favors the many and not just the few—"

"What happened to your nose?" the disgusting one thunders, making me jump.

I cover the injury with a hand.

"Don't do that, boy!" he blasts. "Come here, show it to me!" Five sausagelike fingers beckon me forward. I'm still standing, as there are no seats on my side of the table. I lean toward him. His fleshy eyelids close slightly as he peers at my nose. "That's a cut, that's a knife wound. Have you been in a fight?"

"No, Signor."

"Bit of a brawler, are you?"

"No, Signor."

"No, you don't look much like one," he sniffs. He then asks, "Would you say that a person's character can be judged by the company he keeps?"

It's a strange sort of question, coming out of nowhere, but I understand that we have now reached the interrogation proper. I say, "I think a person may spend his time in the company of people perhaps less honorable than himself, although that does not inevitably mean—"

A mammoth hand crashes down on the tabletop. Sweat bursts from his brow. Phlegm flies everywhere. "Don't come over all equivocal with *us*, boy! Your intellectualism won't help you in here! You will from now on answer all questions directly! We're not here to waste any more time on debate or academic claptrap; we want answers, yes or no!"

His spectral associate slides silently from my vision. I protest, "Some questions, Signor, cannot be answered so simply."

"Yes, they can!" the mountainous one roars. "Mine can! I ask you a question, you answer yes or no; seems simple enough to me."

I hear the other's voice again: "It would be best for you, Gentile Stornello, for all of us, if you answered as simply as you can."

I follow the voice with my eyes. He is standing with his back to me in front of a painting, the only one in the chamber, as far as I can tell in the candlelight. It's a Madonna and Child—finely depicted. She gazes beatifically out at the room. What things must she have seen, I wonder.

"Then, yes," I mutter, defeated. "A person might be judged by the company he keeps."

"Good," says the hog. "Now, do you consort with whores?"

"Whores, Signor?"

"You know what whores are, don't you, boy?"

"I know what whores are, Signor." As he wants either a yes or a no, I say, "No, I do not," and realize that it's my first lie, or a sort of one.

"You've never spent any time with whores?"

"No, I have not," which makes it a *real* lie.

"So you've never lain with a woman of low repute?"

This at least I can answer honestly. The relief of being able to do so makes me quite eloquent. "I can state most truthfully, Signor," I declare, "that I have not lain with any low women, or even any *high* ones, for I have not as yet lain with any woman at all."

He jerks back, insofar as he can considering his titanic girth. I also hear what sounds like a small wheeze of surprise from elsewhere in the room. Perhaps these old men think that all the boys of Venice—or the *giovanotti nobile,* at any rate—are busily copulating all the time. Well, a lot of them are. But I'm not one of them.

"Do you drink?"

"If you mean do I consume alcohol, I sometimes take a little wine, but not much, as it does not agree with me."

The beast grunts in obvious disappointment.

"Do you know any Turks?" the thin one whines, from somewhere behind me.

"Turks, Signor? Yes, I know some Turks." Once more I can be honest.

There's a rustle of interest. "What Turks are you acquainted with?"

"Only those my father trades with, when they come to the palazzo. He's a merchant in spices and silks from the Levant and beyond, as you may know."

"Do you talk with them?" the emaciated one asks.

"No, Signor, they are businessmen. I know nothing of business."

The huge one looks even more disenchanted. He lets his stout shoulders drop and exhales damp air from his porcine jaws.

"Do you know Fabietto Dandolo?" They do this, I suppose—shoot new questions at you that have no discernible connection with those before—but it's definitely the strangest so far. Why are they asking me about Fabietto Dandolo? I know *of* him. I've never spoken to him. I've seen him. He's an enemy of Jacopo's—I saw them fighting. I saw that big ruckus in the Campo Sant'Angelo.

I can still be truthful. "No, Signor, I do not know Fabietto Dandolo."

I hear a hiss of admonition from beside the painting of the Madonna. The great oaf shrugs, insofar as he can, and lowers his eyes. The thin one asks (as if he's read my mind, and maybe he has), "How well acquainted are you with Jacopo Malipiero?"

I must tread carefully. When they asked if I should be judged by the "company" I kept, they meant Jacopo, obviously. Do they think I'm in some way an *associate* of his—a fellow hooligan? They can't. I'm a Stornello, he's a Malipiero.

"I have . . . met him." I try not to sound too guarded.

"How many times?"

"Twice."

"Only *twice*?"

"Yes. I have seen him on other occasions but met him only twice."

"So you would not call yourself a friend?"

"No, Signor. Our families are not friendly."

"Were they lengthy encounters?"

"They were . . . lengthy, yes."

Now the gargantuan one butts in. "Why would you have lengthy conversations with an enemy of your family?"

I turn to him. "They wouldn't have been lengthy if I'd had my way, Signor." I'm still standing my ground, I think.

"They were against your will?" the lean one inquires.

"Yes."

"You were *forced* to have these talks, were you?" This is from the hulk.

"Yes, Signor."

"Bullied, even?"

"Would you describe Jacopo Malipiero as a bully?" the high-pitched voice asks.

I'd better not be too truthful, much as I'd like to be. I still haven't absolutely decided that neither of these men is Jacopo Malipiero's uncle. "He likes to have his way, Signors."

"Did he do that to you?" A stubby finger jabs at my injured nose.

I nod.

"Did you provoke him?"

"No, Signor."

"He cut your nose for the hell of it?"

I nod.

He looks unconvinced.

"Where and when did you first meet Jacopo Malipiero?" the scrawny one asks.

"In the Campo Sant'Angelo, some time ago now."

"Be specific, if you please."

"In March, Signor. Soon after my uncle Brabantio's funeral."

Foolishly perhaps, I'd hoped for some sympathy here. But I get none.

"Why were you in the Campo Sant'Angelo?"

"I was on my way home from a lecture."

"Yet you knew, did you not," the fleshless *interrogante* says, moving back toward the table, "that the Campo Sant'Angelo would not be a safe place to pass through? As you are a Stornello and the Campo Sant'Angelo is known to be Malipiero territory and your families are not friendly . . ."

"I don't usually let family feuds affect me, Signor, or I didn't until that day."

"You've since learned differently?"

"Yes, Signor, I know now not to go there unless I want to be pounced on."

"You were pounced on?"

I nod. The vast one lets out a soupy chortle. The thin one slides silently into the chair he occupied at the start of the interrogation.

"When did you last encounter Jacopo Malipiero?"

"Yesterday, Signor."

"That's when he sliced your nose, was it?" There's another poke in its direction, so close it almost touches.

I wince. "Yes."

"Where was this, in the Campo Sant'Angelo again?"

"No, at his palazzo."

"And why were you at his palazzo?"

"I was taken there."

"Taken? You did not go willingly?"

"Far from it."

"And what happened there?"

I tell them. I describe, in meticulous detail, every punch, every kick, every slice. I try not to put too much hatred in my voice. And finally I tell them how I was thrown into the Grand Canal.

The monster wobbles with mirth. I stare back at him with a rage I can no longer conceal.

There's a silence as they examine me, the fat one with a baleful glare, the thin one tipping his skull sideways and grilling me with his pin-sharp eyes.

"What troubles me," the wraith eventually says very quietly, "is why he should have taken against you so. It can't be only because you are a Stornello, can it? It seems, if I may say so, very personal."

I'm exhausted—too shattered to go into the ins and outs and whys and wherefores of my relationship with Jacopo Malipiero. And I'm still in a great deal of pain. They probably know all there is to know anyway. "Are you sure you are telling us the truth, Gentile Stornello? Because I'd advise you to be careful. Lying to an *interrogante* is punishable in its own right."

"I'm not lying."

"We can find that out very quickly." He means torture, obviously.

"Yes, we can," his heavy associate grunts.

"Let me furnish you then, Gentile Stornello," says the other, "with what we already know and with what we have heard."

"Who from?" I have to ask.

"*Silence!*" the obese one bawls. "*We* ask the questions! *You* listen, and you answer!"

"You have visited the Campo Sant'Angelo often," the wizened inquisitor states, "not just on that first occasion but many times since."

"Yes, but that was—"

"Silence!"

"You did on a particular morning—although you have denied it—spend some time consorting with loose women there."

The floor seems to shift beneath me. I thought that my visits to the campo were clandestine, unobserved by anyone.

"It seems to us, Gentile Stornello, that your outings to the Campo Sant'Angelo have been more frequent than you are ready to admit and that, if I may say so, you haven't been there reluctantly."

"I can explain—"

"Silence!"

"Indeed, we have learned that even your first visit was entirely of your own volition, that you sought the place out—"

"That's not true—"

"Silence!"

"We understand that you were drunk, that you went roaring into the square, that you even endeavored to abuse a girl there."

"But that's ridiculous!" I cry.

"Damn you, boy, be silent!"

"I advise you," I'm told with steely quietude, "to heed the counsel of my colleague."

I can't do anything anyway but be dumbly amazed as the accusations are leveled at me, absurdity piled upon groundless absurdity. "You've become obsessed with this girl, who's a servant of Jacopo Malipiero. You're envious of Jacopo Malipiero, as she's his and not yours. You've pursued her; you've waited for her, skulking in corners. Sometimes you've leapt from these places and tried to have your way with her—"

"What?"

"Silence!"

"Finally, Gentile Stornello, when your passion became uncontrollable, insatiable, you went, only yesterday, to the Palazzo Malipiero Grandioso, you demanded entry, you were drunk again, you leapt on the girl and had congress with her, in a violent fury of lust and jealousy, in the courtyard of the palazzo. When Jacopo Malipiero saw you there, he—with good reason—attacked you, cut your nose, and threw you into the canal."

"Who . . . who . . . who . . ." I stammer, "who told you this? Did Jacopo Malipiero tell you this?"

Of course he did. It's as sonorously clear to me now as the great Maleficio bell in the Campanile, tolling out gloom and imminent public execution. After I was dumped into the canal yesterday, he came here, to his uncle (*is* one of these his uncle?), to check on what I told him, and when he learned that I'd been lying, he decided to cast me into the mire still further by accusing me of pouncing on and ravishing my solicitous girl, my rescuer.

"Did Jacopo Malipiero tell you this?" I scream again.

Two hands are raised. One, more of a bloated fist, sways out toward me in a great arc but doesn't reach me before crashing down on the table. The other, a bony claw, is simply lifted to silence me. "These in themselves—enforced molestation, rape—are truly heinous crimes that must be met with the full force of the laws of Venice. However, there is one more crime, one more allegation, that I have not yet mentioned."

"One more crime?"

"Yes, for which the punishment is execution."

"What crime is that?" I gulp.

"Murder."

I gape. I try to swallow. Nothing comes from my mouth but a gurgle. The chamber is spinning; the candles flash at me.

"You claim that you do not know Fabietto Dandolo or any of his brothers."

What's this? Fabietto Dandolo has been murdered? And *I'm* thought to be his murderer? Oh, God . . . oh, my God . . . Jacopo Malipiero has told them I'm a murderer!

"So you have lied to us on this matter also."

"You're quite the fabricator, aren't you, boy?" the capacious one growls.

"I . . . I've never killed anyone . . . never . . . or harmed anyone . . . ever . . ."

"No more interruptions if you please, Gentile Stornello," says the wraith. "Two nights ago you went to the Campo San Sebastiano, which you well know is Dandolo territory, to look for him."

I have the sensation of falling now—as if the pit is opening beneath me. I'm sick with confusion and fear. If it wasn't so very terrifying, it would be laughable. Horror and hilarity are strange but constant bed-fellows.

"I've no idea, Gentile Stornello," the ghostly one continues, "why you should feel such rancor toward Fabietto Dandolo. Perhaps an insult in the past or a love spat over some girl? It seems you get quite heated in female company."

"Whatever the motive, he passed away this afternoon, of injuries inflicted by *you*." The slavering beast stares at me, narrowing his waxy eyelids, insofar as he can.

"What?"

"Perhaps you did not know he was dead?" the other suggests. "He didn't die immediately. You may not have been aware of that."

"He's dead now," the monster affirms.

"You do seem surprised, so it's very possible you *didn't* know—"

I cling to some semblance of rational argument. "I'm surprised at the lunacy of these allegations."

Neither says anything more for a time. They both examine me. The silence is interrupted only by the heavy breathing of the porcine inquis-itor. His brows are lifted, with anticipation, I think.

Are they expecting some response, some vindication? Do they allow that?

I feel as if I'm an actor in some theatrical *scena* authored by Jacopo Malipiero. Or perhaps I'm the *marionetta* and he's my puppeteer. And I thought *I* was the weaver of fantastical tales.

"Do I now have the opportunity to speak in my defense?" I ask as coolly as I can, trying to work out where I might begin.

"No," the thin one says with unsettling finality. "We've already heard your side of the story."

"Plenty of opportunity we've given you," the fat one agrees. "Shall we get straight to the confession?" His look darkens. "Unless you still feel inclined to protest, in which case we can take you *upstairs*." He starts to sort through some papers and the thin one reaches for a quill.

"I have been locked away at home for weeks," I blurt. "A hermit very nearly, devoting myself to my studies—my servants can vouch for me, my tutor, ask them! Ask my father!"

"Hardly the most impartial of advocates," says the thin one. "Your immediate family, your household . . ."

"Your *tutor*," the pig snuffles with disdain.

"It's Jacopo Malipiero who has invented this!" I cry.

The papers stop being shuffled; the quill drops to the table.

"Ah, yes, Jacopo Malipiero," the specter rasps. "Was he to be your next victim?"

"No!"

Now he's reaching for a particular document. "What exactly was this tale you told him?" He reaches for a particular document. "Yes, I have it here. Some . . . nonsense about a murderer coming from Cyprus . . . Someone whom he claims killed his cousin. You told him he was here, in Venice."

"Iago, yes. I can explain . . ."

They look at each other. There's no recognition of the name in their expressions. They must have heard of it. They're *interroganti*.

The thin one gets up and walks over to the Madonna again. "Jacopo Malipiero came here; he called this man's name. Was that your intention? To have him arrested for causing an affray outside the Prigioni Ducale?"

"My intention was to keep him from murdering *me*!"

I feel cowed and defeated. Where's the point in saying anything more?

"As has already been noted," the spectral inquisitor pronounces, "you seem to be an accomplished fabricator."

"A liar through and through," his colleague snorts.

"A fine capacity for falsehood. How can we believe anything you say?"

"I . . . didn't . . ." I'm so tired I can barely speak.

"Right!" A gelatinous palm thwacks the table. "Let's take you upstairs! See what the torturers can do."

But something emboldens me, steels me for what's to come. It won't take much, I think, to make me crack. But I've found a strangely noble streak in myself that I didn't think I had—I'm going to stick to the truth, unless of course it *really* hurts.

18. *The Madonna's Eyes*

W ere one to approach within a couple of feet of the painting of the Madonna and Child in the *sala degli interroganti* in the Palazzo Ducale (which nobody but an *interrogante* is permitted to do), one would notice a certain abnormality, despite the excellence of the work. Her eyes, which artists habitually struggle to render both placid and striking, appear to be entirely blank. Closer examination would reveal that where they should be, there are two black holes.

Annibale Malipiero had spent a good hour in the small chamber next to the *sala*, his face pressed to the wall, peering through them. He had been forced to stand for the entire time in order to do this, and because the Madonna's eyes were not level, had had to adjust the angle of his head to match hers. It was not a comfortable stance. Annibale Malipiero had a troublesome lower back, which, despite his robust constitution, was worsening with age. And now his neck was also extremely stiff.

The all-seeing Madonna was a recent addition to the *sala degli interroganti*. It had been Roberto Fabbri's idea and Annibale Malipiero had thought it a good one. To watch someone without their knowledge had its uses—especially if you were a keen observer of facial expression and the truths that could sometimes be observed in the unsuspecting demeanor of the accused. This, however, had been the first time the chief inquisitor had spent quite so long witnessing an interrogation.

"It would be more convenient if the painting were lower on the wall, so that one could at least sit down."

"I fear that might look . . . odd, Signor," Roberto Fabbri whined. "We wouldn't wish to draw undue attention."

"Then perhaps we need a stool, one of those tall ones?"

"Yes, that's a thought."

"And her eyes, do you see, they're askew, as her head is inclined toward the Christ Child. Perhaps we could tip the painting itself, like this?"

"Also a little odd, I think," Roberto Fabbri opined.

"Then maybe we should commission another"—Annibale Malipiero's tone was clipped—"with horizontal eyes."

They were both standing before the painting. The immensely corpulent Bonifacio Colonna was still at the table.

The interrogation was over; the Stornello boy had been sent away— but not to the *sala della tortura*. The chief inquisitor had told the guards to take the lad elsewhere.

The sight of the youngster had shocked him, with his cut nose and the putrid slime of the *pozzi* upon his clothes. He was little more than a child, and a fragile one, with an almost feminine face.

Nevertheless, he had proved resilient and bright. For the most part he had controlled his anger. He'd shown fear often enough but had stayed resolute in the conviction of his own fundamental honesty. Annibale Malipiero was impressed.

He'd had no choice, however, but to bring the understandably bewildered youth into custody. He'd been accused of murder, after all.

Fabietto Dandolo had died the previous afternoon of the wounds inflicted on him two days earlier, and the perpetrator of these injuries— with an irony that was not lost on *Il Terribile*—had made his way to the Prigioni Ducale of his own volition.

Once Jacopo Malipiero had been informed that he was now under arrest for murder, he had done everything possible to pin the killing on the unfortunate Stornello along with a host of other charges.

Whilst the object of these accusations was clearly neither a murderer nor a rapist, the sooner his appalling nephew was hanged the better, as far as Annibale Malipiero was concerned. But the allegations of Jacopo Malipiero, now safely incarcerated himself, had provided much else of interest. He'd been caught, even drunker than usual, howling the name of Iago through the prison windows that opened onto the *riva,* vowing all manner of vengeance on the villain. And when brought before his astonished uncle, had declared that he knew Iago was in Venice, because he had been told so by a boy called Gentile Stornello. Furthermore, this boy had apparently relayed certain other details regarding Iago in Cyprus that were disturbingly close to the truth.

Gentile Stornello now interested him greatly, and not just because of his uncanny grasp of clandestine matters. Rarely had he witnessed such an amalgam of astuteness and decency in one so young, with the exception perhaps of his own late son. To be both smart and good was a rare thing indeed. In a Venetian youth it was remarkable.

"Well, Signors"—Annibale Malipiero turned to his colleagues—"I thought that a most successful session."

"Successful? What was successful about it?" Bonifacio Colonna grunted. "He didn't confess to anything."

"Because he has nothing to confess."

"A waste of an hour, then," Bonifacio Colonna moaned.

"The establishment of blamelessness can sometimes achieve as much as the confirmation of guilt," the chief inquisitor said cheerfully.

"So your nephew accused him to divert the blame from himself."

"Obviously." He turned to the thinner of his associates. "Incidentally, Signor Fabbri, I thought your interrogation most excellently done. Bringing up those fabrications of his just before the end. A fine capacity for falsehood . . . Very good."

"Why . . . thank you." Roberto Fabbri wasn't used to being congratulated for his efforts but still could not raise a smile. He was looking even more deathly than usual, if such a thing were possible. He was also swaying a little.

"And rape?" Bonifacio Colonna asked glumly, clutching at straws. "Is he innocent of that too?"

"Does he look like a rapist to you?"

"He did consort with whores." Bonifacio Colonna's eyes glistened.

"Only once, according to my extremely unreliable nephew, and I doubt he got up to much."

"He was seen hanging about the square, drooling over that girl!"

"By the servant I have encouraged to keep an eye on things. But drool is all he did."

The chief inquisitor watched Roberto Fabbri fade further. "Might I suggest we sign off Gentile Stornello and call it a night—assuming we all agree he's guiltless?"

"Why not?" The emaciated Signor picked up a sheet of paper and dipped a quill into the inkwell.

But Bonifacio Colonna persisted: "What about Jacopo? Where've you put him? Let's bring him down." His appetite for torture was insatiable.

"Much as I appreciate your assiduity, you will get your hands on my nauseating nephew soon enough," Annibale Malipiero said. "But at present I fancy that Signor Fabbri is ready to snatch some sleep."

Roberto Fabbri blinked and caught hold of the edge of the table to stop himself from toppling. He signed the document in a spidery scrawl. Bonifacio Colonna grabbed a quill of his own and added a vigorous scribble. Annibale Malipiero signed last, under the printed words DICHI-ARAZIONE DELLA INNOCENZA. Above this he wrote the boy's name, to leave nothing in doubt.

"And the release form too?"

Annibale Malipiero stayed the thin inquisitor's hand. "Perhaps not just yet. I think I'd like to talk to him again, on a personal level—"

Bonifacio Colonna gave him a rheumy glare of suspicion, which he ignored. He summoned the guards to guide Roberto Fabbri to his gondola.

"I was thinking of asking the Council to replace him," he said to his fellow inquisitor, once their ailing colleague was gone. "But tonight, I have to say, he was rather good."

"And I wasn't?" Bonifacio Colonna boomed.

"You, Signor Colonna, were your usual imposing self."

The two men left the *sala degli interroganti*, and the Madonna on the wall surveyed the empty chamber through her blank, nonjudgmental eyes.

Dawn had come and gone. A strident morning light forced its way through the windows of the covered bridge that led from the place of inquisition. It was so very bright that Annibale Malipiero had to close and open his eyelids. It was a dark world he worked in.

He had an appointment to keep, and he suspected he might be a little late. Instead of following his lumbering associate across the bridge, he turned left from the chamber and strode down a corridor, and then another, and another. These passageways became ever wider, the woodwork more intricately carved, the walls more tapestry-covered.

He reached a pair of particularly ornate doors, beyond which lay a room three or four times larger than the *sala degli interroganti*. Tall, clear windows filled it with a soft luminescence. There was a great deal of gilt—the pilasters were gilt, the lintels and cornices were gilt. There was a vast sculpted fireplace depicting some mythological scene he did not recognize (his knowledge of mythology was limited). Similarly dramatic scenes adorned every wall and the ceiling above him. In the course of his weekly visits to the Council of Ten, he had long since decided that the colors that now surrounded him were turbulent to the point of excess.

It was empty of people this early in the morning, apart from the guard who admitted him and who now led him to another door in one of the painted walls.

Standing in this plain little side chamber, lit only by a single square casement, were four men. Annibale Malipiero had never been in the company of four Stornelli before—or not at such proximity. Two were known to him, at least by their frosty demeanor, because they were both on the Council of Ten. The third he did not think he had previously met; he was younger than the councillors and seemed somewhat nervous and bemused, as if he had just woken to discover himself somewhere he did not wish to be.

The fourth Stornello smiled. Though his dress did not indicate his standing or profession, he had an authoritative bearing and the visage of a man more weatherworn than his companions, with their customary Venetian pallor.

Annibale Malipiero had not met this Stornello either, but he felt he knew him well. "Welcome back to Venice, Captain-General," he said.

19. A Figure in the Darkness

What circle of the Inferno am I in now? A higher one, though not by much. I'm still below the level of the *bacino*, I think, and this is as dank and stench-filled a place as I was thrown into before. But there's a long thin grate at the very top of one of the walls. The light that seeps through it is intensely white. Venice must be waking to a sunny morning.

I can hear the boatmen calling to one another on the *molo*, and the fishermen bringing in their catch, and the tradesmen setting up their stalls, and the seagulls. The scuffling shadows of passing feet cross the grate, and sometimes I see the snouts of dogs that do more than just sniff but use the opening as their *gabinetto* too.

At least I'm on my own.

There's no color in this world. I didn't think I'd miss color as much as I do. I'd give anything, I think, to be able to see the scarlet and gold and purple of the clothes of the *ottimati* going about their business, or the plainer gray and white of the ordinary people, or the ochre of the churches and palazzi caught in the sun, or the aquamarine of the lagoon on a good day, or even the sludgy greenish-brown of the canals, or my blue bedchamber walls, or the yellows and reds of a snapping fire—or the deep copper of Franceschina's skin.

There are only sounds and smells down here—the miserable echoes of the most desolate of humanity, in other dungeons now, and the appalling malodors that are a world away from the scent of spices near the Rialto, the fruits and flowers on the market stalls, and the sweet fragrance of Zinerva's bread.

I hear a noise that is not a groan or a whine or a lamentation or a plea. It's a grunt, followed by a cough.

Behind me, quite close.

It would seem I'm *not* alone.

20. *A Breakthrough*

Annibale Malipiero, state inquisitor, Graziano Stornello, Captain-General of the Sea, Cristoforo and Tommaso Stornello, Councillors, and Fabrizio Stornello, citizen and merchant of Venice, were seated around a table in the little room to the side of the *Sala del Consiglio dei Dieci.*

"He is securely incarcerated, away from all others?" Graziano Stornello was eager to get on with things.

"Absolutely," Annibale Malipiero replied reassuringly. "I've put him in a cell that's been forgotten about for years."

"His guards are reliable?"

"To a man. And they have no idea who he is."

"And Gentile?" Fabrizio Stornello blinked. "Where have you put Gentile?"

"He's safe enough," said Annibale Malipiero crisply.

Graziano Stornello leaned his elbows on the table and crossed his fingers. In a low voice, he began, "It is Signor Malipiero's wish, and I respect that wish, that nobody, nobody but those in this room, should yet know of Iago's—"

But he wasn't permitted to finish. Sounds of a disturbance in the main chamber prompted Annibale Malipiero to rise from the table.

Three or four guards were attempting to halt the progress of another, whom the inquisitor knew to be from the *prigioni.*

"He spoke, sir!"

"Let him pass," Annibale Malipiero snapped. "He's one of mine." Closing the door behind them, he said, "You can talk now. You should not have done so before—"

"I think we heard it: He spoke," the Captain-General whispered. "For the first time in over four months, he *spoke*."

"Spoke?" Fabrizio Stornello spluttered. "What are we talking about? I've been brought here from my bed, I've slept barely an hour, having just got back from Ferrara, and my son's been arrested—I haven't the vaguest idea why. I'd like to know *what the hell is going on!*"

"Your exceptionally clever son, Signor, is going to be of great service to the Serene Republic," the *capo degli interroganti* responded with as much composure as he could muster. "I think you should be very proud of him."

Part

II

21. A Shocking Companion

When I heard that cough, I froze.

I turned gingerly and could just make out a shape—a crouched, contorted creature: man or beast?

A callused finger found my face.

"Please . . . no . . . don't hurt me!"

"Cease blubbering."

The bent figure swung around and scuttled back to its corner.

The sun, in its ascent over the *bacino*, in time allowed me to make out more. He'd stretched out on the ground. Maybe he'd gone to sleep. I couldn't see his face, because he had a muscular arm thrown over it, but he had a cropped, bulletlike head. He was tough-looking, though short for his bulk. His clothes, a fustian shirt and frayed hose, were filthy. So was he. He had what seemed to be caked blood on that arm, and more on his bare lower legs.

Without knowing who he was or what terrible things he might have done, I felt pity for him. He was in a far worse state than I.

"Stop looking at me," he grumbled. Then, more loudly: *"Stop looking at me."*

I stared down at the soggy ground.

"What are *you* doing here?" There was scorn in his voice.

I was too scared to speak.

"Why—are—you—here?" He enunciated each word, as if to a child.

"I don't know," I squeaked.

"You must be here for a reason," he said wearily. "What is it that you've done?"

"I've been accused of murder."

"You don't look like the killing kind."

"I'm not."

His view of me must have been better than mine of him. He was surveying me with some scrutiny from under that arm.

Then he chuckled. "I know that voice. You're the boy who was protesting earlier, as they brought you in. You're a Stornello."

I saw no harm in admitting to it. "Yes, I'm a Stornello."

I don't know which was the more terrifying—the sudden wolfish howl, which seemed to be as full of pain as it was of rage, or the realization that I was being attacked. He was on me in an instant, pinning me to the floor, not by my flailing arms or legs but by my throat.

On at least three occasions in the past day and night I've considered the possibility of death. Now I was certain of it.

"Up!"

"Off!"

"*Bruto! Lascia lo! Basta, assassino!*"

I felt him hauled off me; rough hands caught me beneath my arms and dragged me out of there.

"That was close," cackled one of the guards who'd thrown me into the beast's presence to begin with. His foul breath seared my face.

I turned to check that the door behind me was securely shut and that my assailant was safely on the other side of it. It was and he was.

I trust that's the way it'll stay.

22. *A Stupid Man*

It had been immediately apparent to Annibale Malipiero that the boy's father was a fool.

Everything about Fabrizio Stornello—his demeanor (flat-faced, low-browed, narrow-eyed), his conduct (capricious, befuddled), his words (noisy and somehow off the point)—confirmed this initial opinion.

It would have been better for everyone concerned if Fabrizio Stornello had not been at the meeting, but his son had been imprisoned and now would not be released, very possibly, for a considerable time. So he'd been dragged from his bed for things to be spelled out to him, as best they might.

"Iago? Who the hell is Iago?" he'd asked. His brothers had raised their eyes to the ceiling, almost in unison, at this display of ignorance. Just about all of Venice knew by now who Iago was.

Apparently the buffoon had once served on the Council of Ten although he'd been dismissed. "And why was that?" the *interrogante* had asked of Graziano Stornello, in a moment of private conference.

"I should have thought that was obvious," the Captain-General had whispered back.

Fabrizio Stornello didn't appear to like his youngest son much, calling him overly bookish and "too bloody clever for his own good." But there'd also been a lot of bluster about "family honor" and "stains on my reputation" and so forth. Indeed, there was so much hot-blooded indignation that the *interrogante* had become concerned that any secrets the imbecile may have managed to absorb were in danger of not staying secret for long.

So he had offered Gentile Stornello's father a lift home in his official gondola.

"This is swish," Fabrizio Stornello observed, as he surveyed the craft. "You should see mine. It's about half the size and falling to bits."

Once aboard, Annibale Malipiero didn't mince words. "You will understand, I trust, that none of what you have learned today must be divulged to anyone—*anyone*. As far as you are concerned, the felon we have spoken of remains on the loose in Cyprus, and your brother Graziano is still looking for him there. The consequences of your disclosing anything to the contrary will be calamitous, not only for you but also for your son. Should it be discovered that you have been talking to others, the act will constitute a crime against the state, and it will be my duty, as chief inquisitor, to investigate it."

"And what am I supposed to say has happened to Gentile?"

"You tell the truth. He's been arrested on suspicion of the murder of Fabietto Dandolo."

"Damn it, look at him, he couldn't hurt a fly—hasn't the muscle for it."

When they reached the Palazzo Stornello Piccolo (appropriately named, the inquisitor thought), a motley bunch of servants came tumbling onto the unsteady *imbarcadero*. A handful of retainers, three maids (one of whom was severely crippled), and a large, flour-covered woman all asked of their master, with apprehensive faces and in trembling tones, what had happened to "poor Gentile, kind Gentile, *il ragazzo sfortunato*."

The boy Paganello, who'd first alerted the inquisitor to the existence of this modest household and since reported little of use, was grinning at him presumptuously. There was another person whom he recognized too but hadn't expected to see there—a short and portly figure with a troubled demeanor and a satchel of books around his neck.

"Dottore Baldassare Ghiberti of the University of Padua!" the inquisitor exclaimed. "What are you doing here?" He explained to Fabrizio

Stornello, who could not have seemed less interested, "This excellent and clever fellow once taught my son!"

Baldassare Ghiberti was setting off for Padua.

"Allow me to offer you the use of my gondola to get you to the mainland," Annibale Malipiero proposed. "But before you go, I recommend you assemble some reading matter for your pupil. He'll welcome it, I'm sure." Then he turned to the quaking servants: "He'll need some food and clean clothes too—a substantial quantity of both."

23. A Prison Visitor

Having been dragged away from the dreadful creature, and in the nick of time, I'm in yet another cell, higher up than the last one, and now I'm definitely its only occupant. It has a window—yes, a window! It's not big and it's barred, but through it I can snatch a view of the *molo*, and the *bacino* beyond it, and of the people going about their ordinary lives out there—the tradesmen and boatmen and beggars and casual passersby.

They also have a view of *me*. I'm not looking good. I'm wearing a soaked, torn shirt and hose and filthy breeches, my hair is clogged with whatever noxious deposits I picked up in the dungeons below, and my nose and cheeks and chin are crusted with blood.

These cells are reserved for prisoners of breeding. When I was out there myself, I'd sometimes peer in as my own audience does now. I'd wonder about the misdemeanors of the felons within, just as they are doing, very vocally.

"What is it you done, then?"

"Fraud, was it?" someone else grunts. "Larcenous bastard! They're all thieving crooks, the *nobiluomini*."

"Did you murder someone?"

"He couldn't murder nobody; look at him, he's a boy."

"Rape, was it, then? Did you rape someone? Who did you rape?"

Someone else decides that I don't look much like a rapist either, so I must be the recipient of the lascivious attentions of others. "He's a bum-boy, I reckon."

The unanimous conclusion is that I must have perpetrated some atrocious crime against the state, that my offense, in short, is treason. I'm judged and found guilty, and my punishment is decided upon: I should be flogged and stretched, I should be hung from a hook by my ass, I should have my eyes torn from their sockets and my tongue ripped from my gullet, I should have my bowels slashed open and be made to eat my own innards, and my head should be displayed, as turn-coats are, on the traitor's plinth outside the Basilica di San Marco, just around the corner from here.

Aside from the (dubious, I'm now thinking) advantage of a window and a stone floor on which I can manage to stand without falling over (although much of it is covered by fetid water), I have what I suppose I must call a bed—a narrow pallet with a flea-ridden coverlet and one minuscule bolster—and a rickety table and a chair. I have a bucket too, which I imagine is to serve as my *gabinetto*, but maybe I'm meant to wash in it as well.

I've tried to sleep, as I'm so damned tired, but with little success, because of the cannonade of condemnation from the pavement.

A short while ago my jailer arrived with a bag of food. Wafting over the stench of his own breath came the unmistakable aroma of Zinerva's cooking: four loaves, morsels of goose and pig and rabbit, a dozen or so *salsicce piccanti*, half a wheel of cheese, and pickled fruit—pears and peaches and oranges—in jars.

When I asked who'd delivered them, the toothless oaf replied, "Not strictly permitted to say, but she was a bent little bug." When I wanted to know if Balbina had demanded to see me, as I'm sure she would have, he announced, "No visitors *permitted*, on account of no communication with the prisoner being *permitted*."

"And what about that lot?" I protested, pointing at the window. "They've been communicating with me all morning!"

There are also clothes—a new doublet and breeches, four clean shirts and hose, and two pairs of shoes. Zinerva and Balbina evidently think I'm going to be here for some time. Baldassare must think so too. He's sent me books, in a great satchel. He wants me to continue with my education. He'll be lucky.

I suppose if Zinerva, Balbina, and Baldassare know of my where-abouts, then so must my father. I trust he's protesting somewhere on my behalf, for the sake of family honor if nothing else.

The rasp of bolts being drawn back heralds the arrival of someone who, if the obsequiousness of the jailer is anything to go by (he's practi-cally on his knees), must be very important indeed.

He cuts an authoritative figure—tall and lean and upright. He twirls and tugs at a long white beard with the fingers of his right hand. He surveys me with a pair of acute, surprisingly blue eyes. It's not a hostile look though; there's the suggestion of a smile on his lips.

"Leave us." He waves the jailer away and sniffs the putrid air. "Signor Gentile Stornello, please accept my sincere contrition, and that of the republic, for the . . . inconveniences you've had to endure."

He glances around the little room with mild distaste. He seems unfa-miliar with such places. "This isn't much," he says, "but I hope you'll concur that it's better than where you were taken last night. Yet another example, I'm afraid, of the *Signori di Notte* taking matters into their own hands. They've been berated for it, I can promise you. Ah! I see you've been furnished with something to eat, at least, and some reading matter; good." He approaches the table on which I've already tried to sort the books. "Poetry," he sighs. "I believe you're a diligent scholar, but I see no purpose in fictitious musings myself. Where was it you were hoping to continue your education?"

Hoping to. That sounds ominous. "Padua."

"Padua. Yes, yes." He nods. "I had a son bound for there myself. . . ." He's momentarily distracted. "And what was it you were intending to read?"

It's that disturbing use of the conditional again. "Poetry," I answer contritely. "But you will notice that my tutor has also supplied me with Herodotus, Thucydides, Tacitus—"

"There's much to be gleaned from history," he interjects. "The study of what has occurred is generally more productive, I find, than that of what has been invented." He glances sharply in my direction.

"My tutor would agree with you."

"Your tutor, whoever he may be, sounds like a sagacious fellow."

He stands imperiously before the small barred aperture and raises himself to his full height. The gawkers cringe in retreat, mumbling to themselves. "How people like to feed upon misfortune," he mutters. "Do they talk to you?"

"It's more shouting than talking."

"What do they shout?"

"That I should be tortured and ripped to bits and hanged."

"But they don't know what it is that you've done," he says softly.

"They are not alone in that." His genial loftiness is making me angry. "I haven't done anything that justifies my being dragged from my bed in the middle of the night and thrown into a stinking black hole full of revolting men, then being hauled up for an interrogation during which my protestations of innocence clearly fell on deaf ears, and then being thrown back into another dark cell with another criminal, who looked as if he might be about to kill me."

He tilts his head to one side and examines me yet again, then bats my complaints away. "Yes, yes, as I've already explained, that was a blunder."

"The interrogation was a *blunder*?"

"Perhaps not the interrogation," he says calmly.

"But why? I haven't done anything!"

"Your band of spectators cares very little about that," he retorts. "They have no desire to let the truth get in the way of a good execution."

"I prefer to stay away from executions," I say.

"We are alike, then, in that respect at least." He claps his hands. "Do you feel like a walk?"

"A walk?"

"I'd like to carry on with this conversation of ours," he says. "And you look as if you could do with some air. So, indeed, could I. I hate being cooped up, don't you?"

I know who he is. Who else could he be? There are only three state inquisitors, after all. He's Jacopo's uncle—the *Capo, Il Terribile.*

24. A Walk to the Arsenal

There's an *impazienza* about him. He strides ahead of me, head turning from right to left, as if to check that he hasn't been seen. I don't know why he should be so anxious. But then, I suppose that the chief inquisitor must have more than a few enemies out here.

He let me change into fresh clothes. He even had the courtesy to stand before the window of my cell with his arms raised, so that his cloak could act as a screen. "There," he said, when I'd put on a clean hose, breeches, and doublet and slipped into a pair of shoes polished to a gleam by Giovanni. "You look quite the young aristocrat again."

"I could do with a wash."

"No time for that." Instead, he dabbed a handkerchief reluctantly in a nearby puddle and endeavored to mop away the evidence of his nephew's assault.

He turned to my jailer as he permitted me to pass through the door. "This cell is a disgrace! Are they all like this? These are for the *nobiluomini* and should be furnished accordingly. Clean it out at once; mop up the floor; put down a carpet. I want a proper basin and *comoda* and that accursed window covered with a curtain!"

He guided me, with a hand on my shoulder or pressed against my back, through a labyrinth of dim passageways. "I sometimes still get lost here myself," he murmured. "And I've been working in this awful place for almost three years."

"It must be difficult to escape from."

"Impossible! Even those of us who aren't prisoners can't always find their way out!"

An unremarkable door led directly onto the *riva*. I was knocked backward by an abundance of light and noise and activity.

But we're heading east, not west toward the buzz of the Piazza di San Marco; this isn't just a stroll.

"You said earlier that you were thrown into a cell, after your interrogation, with a man who tried to kill you?"

"Yes."

"Were there others in the cell?"

"Only him."

"Oh, dear." He clicks his teeth. "And when you say he tried to kill you. How did he do that, precisely?"

"He put his hands around my throat."

"Oh, dear, oh, dear." He shakes his head. "How very unfortunate. You must have been terrified."

"I was."

"I shall have to look into this further. In a cell of his own, you say?"

"Yes."

"Only those of noble blood, such as yourself, have cells of their own."

"Maybe . . . maybe he's been put in a cell of his own because he's in the habit of trying to kill anyone who gets too close to him."

"Perhaps, perhaps," he muses. "But he wasn't shackled, was he? He can't have been, if he tried to strangle you." He plucks at a strand of his beard. "I don't suppose he told you who he was, did he?"

I shake my head.

"Oh, well," he sighs. "There'll be a record of it somewhere."

He grasps my arm, guides me to the water's edge, then spins me around. "Do you know that palazzo?"

Everyone knows it. Doges have been born there. It's the grandest house on this section of the *riva* and one of the finest in Venice. It has many arched windows on each of its three storeys and a balcony under almost every one of them. There's an abundance of delicately carved tracery, always a sign of great riches. It stands out not only because it's bigger than any of the others but because it's very *pink*.

"It's the Palazzo Dandolo," I say.

"Yes, but which member of the Dandolo family owns it?" He sounds impatient.

"I'm afraid I—"

"Cosimo Dandolo," he informs me. "A good friend of mine. He's more than a little upset at the moment, and I can't really blame him. His son died yesterday, from wounds sustained in a fight."

He's scrutinizing me, as if he thinks he might discover the key to the violent tendencies of Venetian youth in my physiognomy. "Where does it come from?" he asks. "This savagery?"

"I've never been savage to anyone, ever," I say.

"There's always a reason for any cruel act."

"And I definitely didn't kill Fabietto Dandolo."

"Come along," he snaps. He clamps an unyielding hand around my arm and we continue our journey, still heading east. I stumble a bit as he strides on, not releasing his hold. The crowds are beginning to thin.

"Take the person you had the misfortune of spending some time with earlier this morning. There's a reason, I'm sure, for the cruel things he's done."

"What *has* he done?" I ask.

He slows down a little. "As I told you, I've no idea. But he's no angel, that's certain."

"He asked me what my crime was," I blurt.

"And did you enlighten him?"

"I told him I'd been *falsely* accused of murder."

"So you spoke together?" He lets go of me. "Did he have a devilish sort of voice, would you say?"

"I'm not sure what a devilish sort of voice is."

"Low, gruff, sneering—that sort of voice?"

"Actually he was coughing a lot. I think he's ill."

He halts again and blinks at me in surprise. "Are you feeling sorry for this beast, Gentile Stornello?"

I shuffle awkwardly under his gaze. "Not after he attacked me, no."

"But before he pounced?"

"A little maybe. He looked . . . a bit . . . pathetic. He'd been beaten, I think, tortured. He had blood on him."

"There's no harm, I daresay, in having compassion for someone you don't know and of whose crimes you're unaware."

"He was kind enough to say I didn't look much like a murderer."

"And you don't, Gentile Stornello." His smile is momentarily reassuring. "Although I'm not sure one can tell whether or not a man is a murderer simply by the way he looks."

We must have crossed four or five bridges. The houses are getting smaller. To our right, the *bacino* has opened up into the great lagoon, an endless expanse of calm, sparkling water.

Because our surroundings are quieter now and less crowded, I hear the tramp of feet some way behind us, almost echoing our own. When I pluck up the courage to look around, I catch sight of two squat figures in black with hats pulled over their eyes, shrinking back into the medley of passersby. But I could be imagining it.

"Did you talk about anything else?" He still hasn't let go of me, and his tone of indifference doesn't match his persistent interest in what was said in that gloomy cell.

"He knew my name."

"Your name . . . And why should he know your name?"

"He'd heard me shouting it out in the *pozzi*."

"I see, I see."

"He recognized my voice."

"I see."

"And that was it, really. Then he attacked me."

"Because of your name?"

"I don't know," I say. "Perhaps my name meant—"

"Well, that's as may be," he announces, with a dismissive flap of the hand. "Why are we talking about this miscreant anyway? What's he to us? Another degenerate who'll get his just deserts." Then he asks, "Have you ever visited the Arsenal?"

We're not far from it. I can tell by the noise and the way the stones are starting to judder slightly beneath our feet—the uproar of an immense industry. It's been louder and more incessant than usual recently. In the small hours, you can hear it all over Venice. It's because of the Turkish threat, they're saying—more ships needed to fight the Ottoman.

"You've not been *inside* it, I'll venture. Let me proffer you a guided tour. Courtesy of the state."

He lets me follow him freely now, without hanging on to my arm. He knows I won't escape. Just before we turn north off the *riva*, we pass a modest dwelling, dwarfed by grander ones on either side. "Do you know who used to live here?" I call after him.

He stops and turns. He looks blank.

"Francesco Petrarcha, Italy's pride, a god among men."

I stumble on in his wake.

"He came here to get away from a plague in Padua, and Venice gave him that house."

"You're something of a sonnet-monger yourself, aren't you, Gentile Stornello?"

A *sonnet-monger*! As if poets were merely purveyors of fodder or chattel! I feel the blood rush to my cheeks. Has he read my poetry? God, I hope not.

Now I'm sure we're being followed. We cut through a narrow *calle*, just the two of us for the moment, and I'm convinced I can hear a scraping on the cobbles behind us.

We're among people again, a rush of them, as we cross the bridge that spans the Canale dell'Arsenale. We push our way toward the towering gatehouse, through a throng of indigent hopefuls, clambering over one another for the possibility of employment.

"Word's got out." He turns to check that I haven't vanished into the multitude. "Whenever there's talk of a full-on war in the offing, this is where the people run to. It demonstrates a rather admirable loyalty to the republic in the face of the enemy, don't you think?"

"Or maybe they just need a job."

He gives me a stern look.

"And *is* there?" I ask.

"Is there what?"

"A full-on war in the offing?"

"I wouldn't know," he says. "I'm not a warrior."

At last we succeed in reaching the massive doors, which are stead-fastly closed. Great marble pillars stand on each side, and a vast Lion of St. Mark glowers down at us from above.

"You have a warrior uncle," he shouts to me over the clamor of the crowd and the thumping stridor emanating from within. "The Captain-General of the Sea, no less. Why don't you ask him what's in the offing?"

"He's in Cyprus," I yell. "And even if he wasn't, he wouldn't tell *me* anything. I hardly know him."

Set into the doors, which are opened only for ceremonial occasions, there's a smaller means of ingress, with a grille and a flap. After a muf-fled conversation through the bars, it is unbolted.

The rumpus of our great navy being built and mended and supplied is now overwhelming, and so is the smell. It sears the back of my nostrils. "Tar," he bellows. "Boiling tar!" There's a stench of sweat too in the crush-ing heat.

Over the heads of an army of artisans, I can make out masts of dif-ferent heights, a bucking and swaying array against the sky. He propels me up a flight of wooden steps to a gallery that runs around the entire perimeter of the colossal dock. There must be more than a hundred ves-sels within it, sleek ones and bulbous ones, little ones and enormous ones, squat ones and tall ones, and all shapes and sizes in between. Some are falling to pieces and in need of repair, some almost wholly dismantled or only partly built, but many are brand-new.

Over these vessels, men clamber and scuttle like insects, hammer-ing and sawing and painting and polishing. It's an awe-inspiring sight, and even if I could be heard above the din I'd be speechless.

"The very center of our power, Gentile! The beating heart of our great empire!"

If I've made him out correctly, it's the first time he's addressed me solely by my first name.

He leads me on and up another set of steps into a small pavilion screened from the thunderous uproar by relatively solid walls and a line of windows, with glass so thick that you have to squint through them to see what's going on out there. It's still noisy, but at least we can hear each other speak.

"This is where the city's most illustrious guests are brought, and it's where the Doge sits when he visits," he informs me.

"I feel honored," I reply, even though for the life of me I don't know why he's brought me here.

In the middle of the room there's a globe of the world on a pedestal. At its rear, facing the windows, there's a throne on a dais, with smaller chairs on either side of it. Benches line the other walls, which are hung with rich tapestries, depicting various victories at sea (Venetian victories, I presume), and there are books and maps on tables.

"In all honesty, I'm not too interested in ships," my guide confesses, inspecting one of the tapestries. "One boat looks much like another to me. I try to avoid the sea and everything about it. In fact, I'm fairly nervous of water in general. And I live on the Giudecca, which means I have to face my trepidation daily."

"I don't like water much either," I say.

"I know you don't."

Does he know everything about me? He knows I write sonnets; he knows I hate water. What other details of my trivial life are in his possession?

"Still," he goes on, "we can all do our bit, even us landlubbers. At least, I like to think that I do mine." Then he asks, "Do you do yours?"

It's the oddest question so far. I'm not too sure what doing "my bit" might entail—but I've always been loyal to Venice in my fashion, so I reply, "Of course. If you mean am I ready to serve the republic, of course."

"Your brother's doing his bit isn't he?" He gives me a wry smile. "He's at the wars in the west, I think."

So he knows about Benvenuto too. "Yes, he's fighting for the Emperor of Germany."

"Who is currently our ally in the fight against the French, is he not?"

"I think so."

"I agree; it can sometimes be quite difficult to know who's a friend and who's an enemy. Only a year ago we were fighting with the French *against* the Germans. Now it's the other way around. All very confusing."

"I don't interest myself in wars much, except where it concerns Benvenuto, where he might be and what might happen to him."

He's gazing down at the globe. "Do you know what this is?" He beckons me to approach it.

"It's a globe," I reply. I've seen one of these rare objects in Padua. That one wasn't enclosed in its own stand though, and this is much larger and made of gilded copper. It can be turned within its casing. He does this now.

"Do you know who invented these things?"

I shake my head.

"The infidel." He chuckles. "And talking of the infidel, look here . . ."

I lean forward. I know that he's focusing upon the great swath of Ottoman territory, ominously dun-colored in contrast to the bright blue of the sea or the yellow boot that is Italy, which looks vulnerably small by comparison. Someone has tried to make Venice look far bigger than it is by painting an amalgam of buildings and towers (all the other cities of Italy are tiny flecks), with the words VENETIA SERENISSIMA above it. There's no question that this is a Venetian globe.

"Read what it says here," he instructs me, finger hovering.

The words are written in a bold but carefully scripted hand. HIC SUNT DRACONES.

I look up at him. "Here be dragons?"

"And, believe me, there *are*," he murmurs. "Millions of them." He crosses his arms over his chest and raises a hand to twist a tendril of his generous beard. "The trouble is, they're also here." He stabs at VENETIA SERENISSIMA. Again he inspects me. "You know some of them—Turks, I mean."

I quickly defend myself. "I've never spoken to any of them. My father has commerce with them, that's all. It's just business; he never invites them in."

"They're not an especially sociable bunch anyway, are they? Huddling together, never leaving their *quartiere* unless they absolutely have to—in order to trade with your father, for example."

"He's not the only one who has dealings with the Turks; hundreds do! My father says if we didn't trade with them, Venice would collapse!"

"That's as may be." He twirls his beard once more. "The problem of doing business with people with whom we're also at war is not mine to solve. My job is to safeguard the republic from those minded to overthrow it from within." He moves toward the Doge's great red and gold throne. With a flourish of his cloak, he steps onto the dais and sits. That's not quite permitted, I think, even for a chief inquisitor. "My concern," he exclaims, "is the possible subversion from within of *La Serenissima* by the Ottoman!"

Then suddenly he becomes cordial, soft-spoken again. "I'm only asking you to *know your enemy*, Gentile Stornello. Do you know what your Turk is capable of?"

"I've heard stories."

"He's not known for being merciful."

"So I gather."

"They hate us, did you know that? To the depths of their souls. To them, we are the infidel. It's a holy war they're fighting. They'll stop at nothing to achieve their purpose, which is, quite simply, the eradication of all Christians from the face of the globe." He waves a finger at the sphere in the middle of the room.

The sounds of the Arsenal seem to grow louder, much louder. The clangs and crashes and scrapes are more relentless, more insistent. I think of my sea-captain uncle Graziano fighting off the predatory Turks and of the taciturn strangers that I see sorting through silks and spices and haggling with my father in the *sottoportego* of our palazzo. Some have acknowledged my presence with a formal, stiff-backed bow and sometimes even a smile. Can it really be that all they want to do is kill me?

"The Turks themselves interest me less than those they collude with to help them in their cause, those who feel disadvantaged, dispossessed, mistreated—the underbelly of our fair city." His voice is full of revulsion. "You, of course, have met quite a few of that sort recently," and he adds, with a tone of contrition that I don't quite believe, "for which again I must apologize."

"I wouldn't call it meeting them. I couldn't see them. It was pitch black."

"Yes, yes . . ." He appears to ponder, no longer looking at me. "Who's to say how many of the lowlife of Venice might be secretly working for the Turks? That frightening fellow in the cell—you saw *him,* didn't you? He could be a Turkish agent; who's to know?"

Then, from his lofty position: "You admire Venice, don't you, Gentile Stornello, her laws, her system of government?"

"Yes I do." The thought now strikes me: He was there last night, hidden away somewhere, listening to every word. Of course he was. He's the *capo.*

But now he asks something that I wasn't asked. "Would you be ready to die for Venice?"

That rather frightens me. "I'm not sure."

"I respect your honesty, Gentile Stornello," he mutters. "It's not too common an attribute among the young nobility." He eases himself even deeper into the throne. "If it's any comfort," he says, "I'm not entirely certain I'd be prepared to die for Venice either, although I like to think I serve her well enough in my way."

"You *do your bit,*" I venture cheekily.

He chuckles. "Exactly, just as I hope you will do yours."

I've the feeling that our talk, and my visit to the Arsenal, is over. The impression is confirmed when he claps his hands and within moments two men have entered the pavilion, dressed in the black velvet doublets and short black cloaks of the *Sentinelle di Prigioni,* the ones who've been following us all this while. They seem as nonplussed as I am by the temerity of where he's chosen to sit, but they grab hold of me nonetheless.

"*Non troppo brutale,*" he instructs them.

They relax their grip a little.

"So I'm not being released?" I inquire wretchedly.

"I'm afraid not," he says.

He calls after me as I'm led away. "*Buona ventura,* Gentile Stornello!" And also: "*Sta risoluto!*"

I'm part of some plan of his, I suppose, which probably has something to do with the Turks. Beyond that, I can't think what might be in store for me. I don't dare to.

25. *In the Dark*

Well, I certainly didn't expect *that*.

Sono nel profondo.

Men being pulled to pieces on the gallows prior to their hanging beg for death. I've heard them, much as I haven't wanted to. They cry out to God for it. *La liberazione della morte.*

I must have screamed for it too, although I don't think I can be dead, because there's still so much pain.

So I have been there, to the room that everyone talks of but only the unfortunate few get to visit. I saw the famous *strappado*—though I wasn't stretched on it. No, I was dunked in water upside down, repeatedly, each time almost to the point of certain drowning. And then there was the whipping . . . I won't go into details, because I'm trying to close my mind to it. I feel a surge of nausea and fight for breath. *What did they want from me?* There was no sign of the *capo*, just the two of them, the huge one and the skinny one. They asked no questions at all. I think they only wished to hear me howl.

But what place am I in now? Perhaps I'm in death's antechamber. It's definitely Stygian in here.

As my heartbeat slows, I can make out the echoing plink of water on stone—then the rasps, snores, snuffles, and occasional sobs of others in this blackness.

Unbelievable pain makes you crave, if not death, then sleep. And at last it comes.

I'm in water, but I feel no fear. I'm not struggling for air. Around and above and below me are smiling girls, who are more like fish than girls—girl-fish, with flickering silvery skin. They point downward and beckon me to follow yet deeper. She sits in a cave, with myriad jewels for walls, at the very bottom of the sea. Her nymphs attend to her, braiding her caramel-colored hair. She's still incontestably beautiful. She's Galatea, daughter of Nereus and granddaughter of Poseidon, and I'm her Acis, son of Pan, brought to her like a trophy. I'm offered honey-soaked cakes by her handmaidens.

But Polyphemus the Cyclops, her husband, is enraged that she's in love with me and not him. He reaches into the cave. His hand is almost as big as I am. He roars. I screech and start to swallow water. The sea has become an angry place once more. I'm lifted into the air. His ghastly one-eyed face grins at me, revoltingly close. Soon it becomes the face of another—a huge, dribbling, lardaceous countenance, that of the immensely fat inquisitor; next to him, the skull of his skeletal associate seems to grin. "He's a wriggler, this one," says the giant. Then, as Polyphemus was wont to do, he starts to eat me.

"Stop that wailing!" he bellows, covering me with phlegm and spitting mouthfuls of my flesh into the boiling waters below.

"Give me peace! Stop that noise!"

It's not Polyphemus or the gross inquisitor.

It's *him*, his voice like scuffed gravel. Of course, they've put me back in with him, in the cell I was thrown into before. Is that what they intend, then, to let him finish me off?

I'm awake, on my back, soaked in sweat, and the pain still sears. A fragile gray light creeps through the thin grate set high in the wall. There are some early morning stirrings up there on the *molo*.

"Who's the girl?"

It's the oddest question.

"You—Gentile Stornello: Who's the girl?"

"That's a *Stornello*," I hear from whoever else is in this place.

"Oh, we have a *nobiluomo* among us, don't you know. Aren't we honored?"

"Are you deaf? Have they broken your ears too?"

"No."

"Then who is she?"

I suppose he deserves the courtesy of a reply, as the question has caused such discomfort. And maybe I should reply anyway, because if I don't he'll probably be at my throat again.

"I . . . don't know . . . who you're talking about." I discover that speaking after torture can be nearly as painful as the torture itself. My gullet burns; my chest feels as if it's being prized open.

There's something like a chuckle, succeeded by a lacerating wheeze. "You're a fickle lover, Gentile Stornello, that you should recollect her name only in your dreams."

He's eloquent. It belies a dialect that is definitely not Venetian and to which there's a rural, uneducated drawl.

I can now see something of the others. There are five of them, huddling together in some attempt at comradeship, legs thrust before them and backs against the pitted wall. They're as far from him as it's possible to be.

I dare to glance at him from behind slightly parted fingers. He's coiled, with his face hidden. There are flashes of metal around his wrists and his ankles. He's been shackled and chained to the wall. So that's why he hasn't attacked me.

Guards burst in and one of the criminals is dragged out. Then another, and then the third, and the fourth, and the fifth, over time. None of them returns.

He hasn't moved. Not a muscle.

"Why have they not taken you?" he asks eventually.

"I expect they've got their hands full." I could ask why nobody has taken him.

He rolls, with some effort, onto his back and turns to face the wall, pushing his legs up into his chest. I watch the shadows cross the grate, hear the clop of feet. The dogs are starting to sniff again and to cock their legs at the bars.

I think of Jacopo Malipiero. Where is he now? Crowing at my fate in the Albergo Tre Stelle probably, with his whooping followers and his drooling whores. "Here's to the Stornello louse, and to a good hanging!"

The *capo degli interroganti*, sitting Jove-like on the Doge's throne, wished me *buona ventura* as I was led from his presence—which, when I think about it, was a bit rich coming from him, as he is in command of whatever fortune awaits me, good or otherwise.

I need good fortune now, because—*Madre di Dio*—they've come for me again.

25. A House on the Giudecca

The arrest of Iago of Mantua had been so very simple that the Captain-General was forced to wonder why he hadn't thought of the idea before. The villain had been entrapped, as are many men, by the allure of a woman. The Siren in question, the former prostitute Bianca, had come up with the notion, soon after the slaughter of her husband-to-be, the Florentine.

Iago knew her from the time when she had consorted with the soldiers at the citadel at Famagusta. Cyprus was a place of whispers, so it had been relatively easy for her to get messages to him, never written down but conveyed through a series of insinuations, which became more brazen by the day, about how his notoriety, his reputation for mercilessness, had made him more appealing to her, not less. She craved his mastery; she wished to support his cause. If they could but meet, she would demonstrate to him her limitless devotion.

In the chapel of a small monastery on the western coast of the island, Bianca had clothed herself as a penitent, contrite for her many sins, but she had been careful not to cover herself too excessively. Iago had brought men with him, of course, but only five or six, and they'd been easily dispatched as the woman had distracted the criminal by falling at his feet, calling him her potent lord.

It had still taken some fifteen of the stoutest Venetian troops to over-power him, but when finally overcome he'd appeared deflated, like the sails of a ship suddenly becalmed. His months in the mountains had made him ill.

Graziano Stornello had resolved that there would be no triumphant return to Famagusta. Rather, the felon had been manacled in the bowels of a waiting caravel with the Captain-General and a few guards as his ever watchful company.

As far as Cyprus (and Venice) knew, Iago of Mantua had vanished from the face of the earth, and so had Graziano Stornello. If Iago was to seem as if he had somehow evaporated, then he must melt away as well, or questions would be asked. Not even his brother the governor had knowledge of where either of them might have disappeared.

To ensure his continued anonymity, the old soldier had accepted the hospitality of the man with whom he'd established a copious correspondence while in Cyprus and to whom he had delivered his prisoner. Annibale Malipiero, Chief Inquisitor of the Republic, lived on the Giudecca, close enough to the city for relatively quick access and information but far enough to retain a certain unfashionable obscurity from prying eyes.

The Captain-General sat in Signor Malipiero's house now, awaiting the return of his host from a day's work. It was decidedly a *house*. It could in no sense be described as anything grander. It wasn't even fronted by a canal but nestled in a narrow and sparsely lit street of similarly sized two-storey buildings. The place was extremely well cared for but monastic. The furniture was limited and functional; there was little ornament, few pictures.

After two days and a night in this unassuming domicile, the renowned naval commander was starting to feel confined. His only company, apart from servants, had been the *interrogante*'s wife—a demure, modestly dressed, and timorous woman. She'd barely dared to exchange a single word with him.

He'd seen almost nothing of the inquisitor himself. The two men had snatched only brief confidences outside the chamber of the Council of Ten, and Annibale Malipiero's visit last night had simply been to ensure that the Captain-General was comfortable.

But here he was now, as he'd promised he would be, stamping the rain from his boots, with the servants bobbing about him to remove his hat and cloak.

He appeared prodigiously tired, and the dinner that followed—which had been prepared by Annibale Malipiero's wife—was not, in Graziano Stornello's opinion, by any stretch of the imagination good. It consisted of a watery soup, an unidentifiable fowl accompanied by overboiled vegetables, and a fruit-topped pastry that more closely resembled a suppurating wound than an inviting delicacy. The wine was only marginally more palatable than the fare.

The men confined themselves to small talk while the lady of the house was still present.

"Grimani's just died," Annibale Malipiero announced through a mouthful of gristle.

"The Doge? Who will replace him?"

"The favorite is Gritti."

"I know Andrea Gritti! We've fought together."

"Venice has need of a soldier to lead her."

Once his wife had left (after being graciously congratulated by the captain-general on her culinary skills), Annibale Malipiero said warily, "I hope you're not minded to tell your old friend of our secret prisoner."

Graziano Stornello shook his head impatiently. He was keen to get to the nub of things. Annibale Malipiero had brought notes, which he now consulted.

"Anything of interest been said?"

"Not as yet. I never suggested it would be a quick process. The felon revealed some curiosity about a girl that your nephew is in love with. Aside from that there was . . . oh, yes, I have it here . . ." The *interrogante* squinted at something he'd scribbled. "He has a surprisingly felicitous turn of phrase, does Iago. Here's what he said after the boy was brought back from torture—"

The soldier raised a hand. "You're *torturing* my nephew?"

Annibale Malipiero looked up. "I thought I told you we might have to do that. To allay Iago's suspicions, do you see? He has to be treated like a fellow criminal. And it seems that the creature is feeling some pity for him." Presuming he'd allayed Graziano Stornello's anxieties, he went back to the notes. "This is what Iago said: 'What they know, they know. Words slide over them like ghosts. Say not a word to them more. Silence is the wisest course.'"

The other looked pensive. "He said much the same after his first arrest in Cyprus, or so I was told. 'What you know, you know, and I shan't say another word,' or something along those lines." He lugged a large fustian shoulder bag onto the table and began to rummage through it.

As he did so, Annibale Malipiero went on: "I put some other male-factors in with the two of them for a time. I thought it might make him less wary, I also wished to see if he might speak to them too."

"And did he?"

"Not a word."

Now the soldier extracted from the bag a small bundle of papers, folded many times over and held together by a faded yellow ribbon, which he untied. They tumbled onto the table, opening a little as they did so, like clams. The chief inquisitor's eyes widened.

"Letters to Iago," said the captain-general. "Found in a pocket of his doublet when we took him."

"Letters from whom?"

"That we don't know. They're not signed, or not by name. We also found this . . ."

Graziano Stornello produced a lock of fine blond hair, also tied with a ribbon of yellow.

"Letters of affection, then?" The *interrogante* fell hungrily upon the collection, spreading them out across the table and starting to unfold them, one by one. There must have been more than twenty of the things. "So the creature was loved."

"More lusted after, I'd say."

"Yes, yes . . . possibly. You've perused all these?"

"Naturally. Some are rather"—the warrior cleared his throat—"frank."

"Yes, I can see that. But a cultured hand, I think."

"Certainly. And there's a lot of French."

"A courtly affectation, I think."

"And she was"—a second cough—"married."

"I haven't reached that particular revelation as yet."

"She mostly writes as if she were not."

Annibale Malipiero suddenly dropped one of the letters as if he'd been burned by it and hurriedly diverted his attention to the lock of hair. The strands were indeed fine and still shone, or seemed as if they did, in the glow cast from the fire in the austere room.

"You'll have noticed . . ." The captain-general coughed again. "That it's blond."

The inquisitor glanced up. "Yes?"

"Not . . . common."

"Not in Italy, but in Cyprus perhaps?"

"Even less so in Cyprus." The distinguished Stornello Signor took a deep breath, leaned forward, and stared fixedly at his host.

Annibale Malipiero waited.

"My niece, Desdemona, God rest her soul, was famous for it."

"Famous? For what?"

"Her blond hair. It was . . . it was her only distinguishing feature."

26. A Face at the Window

I'd never thought a mattress would be such a welcome thing—even a thin scratchy one that provides nourishment and comfort for an army of bugs.

The man in the cell below, after I'd been hauled back into his presence yet again, advised me that I must remain silent under torture. "They want to break you," he said. "They are not concerned with what you have to say." I've been able to do little more than howl anyway, as I don't know what it is that they want. They don't say a thing, the fat one and the thin one, as they put me in the hands of a brute in a mask (they introduced him as *il tormentatore principale*), or as they let the guards who lug me back and forth beat me up along the way.

But now I'm back in my cell, the one on the level with the *riva*, my bulky jailer has become quite solicitous. He's produced relatively fresh water, so that I can wash my wounds, and a few strips of old clothing as bandages. I'm in dire need of Balbina's soothing ointments. I asked him if she had visited again, and when he shook his head I said, "If she does, maybe you could instruct her to return with her medicines?"

"Not sure medicines is permitted," he sniffed.

He's made the cell marginally more hospitable. He's laid down a couple of frayed carpets, brought in three more chairs, one of which has cushions, a *comoda* of a sort (an unstable stool above a bucket), and a basin on a stand behind a threadbare folding screen. He's even hung a tattered woolen blanket over the window. I also have a larger and more reliable table, upon which he's arranged my books between two lit candles. Franceschina's simple linen handkerchief—the one she gave me to hold to my cut nose after I'd been thrown into the Grand Canal—lay beside them.

It was newly laundered and pressed and neatly folded. I picked it up and put my nose to it. It smelled of roses and of lavender. "Did you wash this too?" I asked my jailer.

He shook his head.

"Who did?"

"Not *permitted* to disclose."

Now the cloth, with its woven purple "F," has blood on it again, from a gash beneath my right eye.

Some hours ago the clang of the Marangona bell of the campanile marked the conclusion of another day. It's quiet out there on the *molo*—only the lapping of the hulls of boats put to rest until morning, or the yap of a dog, or the occasional scuff of hasty footfalls. But now there's a sound beyond the makeshift curtain—a kind of scraping. There's a slight movement of the material too.

"Signor?"

It's just a whisper, breathy, hurried, anxious, *feminine* . . .

"Signor Stornello? If you are not Signor Stornello, I apologize for having disturbed you—"

I'm up from the bed in a second. I pat down my matted hair, feel my face for palpable disfigurements, pull my filthy torn shirt closer to my bones.

The blanket is heavy and nailed to the wall. It can't be pulled back, so I have to scramble under it. She skips back, her hands to her mouth, her eyes enormous. Yes, I'm a horrendous spectacle.

She's in the usual plain kirtle over a white *camicia*. She has a thin woolen shawl over her shoulders. It's a warm night though, and by the light of a single sconce jutting from the outside wall she *glows* . . . she *glistens*. Her hair is untied.

She lowers her terrified stare and turns away. She's seen a monster, something from her worst nightmares. She begins to move off.

"Please don't go!"

She doesn't. She approaches me gingerly, her delicate hands clasped in front of her, and raises her shimmering eyes.

"You are badly hurt." I think I detect *some* sympathy. "Is it . . . the . . . torturers who have done this?" I nod. She steps back and gazes up at the grim façade of the building. "This must be a cruel place, Signor . . ."

"It is. Come closer."

There are still people out there: stragglers, a boatman or two tying up and unloading. Some are noticing her. Well, you would, wouldn't you—the loveliest girl in the world, standing alone on the *molo* in the middle of the night?

"Please," I whisper again. "How did you find out I was here?"

"It is known, Signor."

"Is it known why I'm here?"

She nods.

"What's being said? Tell me."

She can't bring herself to reply.

"Tell me!" I snap, so vehemently that I make her recoil. "Please," I say more softly. "I have to know."

"Murder," she eventually murmurs, her full lips curling at the word.

"Who's saying I'm a murderer? Jacopo? Is that what he's saying?"

"No!" she squeals.

The night-walkers slow their swift steps; the men at their boats glance up. She flushes. Her limbs tighten. Those incredible eyes of hers flash. She's angry. Oh, God, she's angry—with *me*. I didn't know she could display such blazing rage. Again she's turning from me.

"Franceschina, no! I beg you, don't leave!"

She halts, her back to me, her sweet shoulders rising and falling. Then she swings around and returns. She's still livid.

"Was it Signor Jacopo you killed? He is nowhere to be found."

Before I can answer, there are coarse shouts to her left. She turns in their direction, scared. Now there's the approaching bang of hard boot heels on the stones of the *molo* and a cry: "Hey! You! *Puttana!* No soliciting outside the Prigioni Ducale! *Zoccola sordida!*"

She's vanished. I hear the slap of her sandals scurrying eastward.

I scrabble out from under the blanket.

I sit on the floor of my cell, my back against the wall, my knees against my aching chest, and I weep.

Her handkerchief lies a few feet from me, close to the bottom of the bed where I dropped it, crumpled again and wet and admonishing.

27. Letters to a Murderer

A nnibale Malipiero picked up a six-branched candelabrum from a dresser and set it upon the table, beside the rows of creased letters, and read what had been written, in a clear but childish hand, to Iago of Mantua.

Esteemed (may I say admired) Sir—
Your lack of contact since we last had the pleasure (may I say delight) of each other's close companionship betokens only, I hope, that you have been too busy to think much of your little kitten—and not that you have assumed a coldness toward her, for a reason I cannot deduce. If the latter, what offense might she have caused? Her memory of the last "réunion agréable" is that the gratification in it was as much yours as it was hers. I trust, then, that my trepidation is groundless and that you have indeed been "très occupé" with grave, though I pray not dangerous, military matters—and that a small though loving kitten, however eager and obliging, is but a negligible trifle when set against the weighty concerns of her brave and strong master. As a token of the kitten's continued devotion, she sends her master a cutting of her softest fur, recently chopped, with the wish that it will remind him of her unquestioning deference and her inalterable adoration and also serve as a memory of the pleasures exchanged between owner and pet, who offers you this greeting: "Je suis absolument de vous, mon seigneur magnifique—votre chaton petit et fidèle."

The beneficiary of these endearments was tardy in his response, if he replied at all.

Your kitten, sir, is fretful, for you have not provided her with any indication of your continued regard. She is comfortless, bereft. Her tiny frame trembles. "Elle a mal; elle languit; elle souffre." You should see her abed, sir, as she thrashes and gasps, cold and hot by turns, remembering and imagining and pining for your touch . . . "votre splendeur virile."

As the silence presumably persisted, the letter writer hypothesized as to its various possible causes:

If it is your fear, sir, that your kitten may have been tempted to stray in her affections, forgoing her devotion to you and diverting it to the solicitations of others who demonstrate their own fondness, then she begs, with a sweet purr of remonstration, that you dismiss such apprehension as baseless. You remain her "maître seul et superbe."

Or this (put more bluntly in a subsequent letter):

Is there another whom you now hold more closely to your manly heart than your kitten? If it should be so, sir, then she hates her rival and would remind you a kitten has claws.

To which was added a rebuke (that at the same time flattered):

Was she misguided, then, in your own assertions of ardor, unreservedly avowed many times, on the occasions you could meet alone and away from the eyes of others—the memories of which still warm her? Can you be as capricious in your contentions of fidelity as most men are reputed to be? She cannot believe this of you. Sir, she worries.

Concern was expressed that the receiver of her attentions might have now and again felt overwhelmed by her own accomplishments, when undoubtedly she was the subjugator and he the subdued. Appropriate to his profession, she used a military analogy. She also, on this occasion, dropped her pretense of speaking on behalf of his kitten and addressed him straightforwardly, as herself.

I was your besieger and you were the castle besieged. I climbed your strong walls, "vos bâtiments, vos tourelles," your mighty bastions, and you were vanquished by my wiles. Was I mistaken to be the victor in our skirmishes? "Avez-vous été distrait quelquefois, mon seigneur puissant, par mon pouvoir?" I noticed no discomposure at the time but gladness only.

Then she wrote of her suspicion that a disparity in status might be troubling him (again quite directly put):

Are you cold to me now, as you were not once, because you consider our circumstance of birth to be so at variance? Are we to be separated for eternity because I am of noble blood and you are not? These are but the irrelevant annoyances of custom, dearest omnipotent lord. In our allegiance you are the paramount one and I am the underling. You are the general, I am the humble soldier. You are the governor, I am the subject. All that you are is godly to me—your origins make you more hypnotic, not less. "Vous êtes un campagnard, et je vous adore; vous êtes rugueux, et je vous adore; vous êtes brutal, de temps en temps, et je vous adore."

Buried amid these increasingly frantic paeans, there was a sole mention of the woman's husband (unidentified and patently despised), as if he were a minor inconvenience barely worth thinking about. Indeed, she seemed to derive great pleasure from the need to keep her adulterous carnality a secret. Circumspection and betrayal intoxicated her.

Do you suppose that you have an adversary for your kitten's adoration? He is but a dullard, sir, who owns her in name alone. Her vows of obedience to him were forced upon her. She detests him. He sickens her. Did you not believe her assurances when you were alone together, seeking dark corners to be away from him and those who surround him? It behooves her to show him respect and some devotion before the eyes of others, as all entrapped kittens must, but beneath her enactments of loyalty there lies only revulsion, and she sheds hidden tears of solitude and longing—"pour vous et seulement pour vous, mon vrai seigneur."

More succinctly, she wrote:

Can we no longer enjoy the covert places that so elated us once? Then let us defy propriety! "Courage, mon maître, mon commandant brave! Venez!" Come to me! "Libérez moi!" Rescue me from this prison of loneliness and misery!

The later letters displayed even further desperation, and the last of all was sullen, accusing, but still somehow hopeful. Had the object of her obsession responded to a single one?

You are cruel in your muteness. Weeks of unresponsiveness can signify only that you have rid me from your mind. I was your trifle, your bauble, readily forgotten. If my perseverance in articulating my undying desire for you has been displeasing to you, an irritating distraction, then silence me forever by killing me, for I want nothing but death in my desolation. Come to me and kill me, as you do others, my sturdy warrior. But I shall crawl away like the obedient kitten I am. I shall write no more. "Bonne chance" in your future endeavors, seigneur. I shall still fear for you and whatever dangers you encounter. More than that, as I said to you when we last touched, when we last kissed, I shall always hold you to my heart, if not in actuality, then in spirit. I shall always love you.

Annibale Malipiero carefully folded this final communication along its creases and then did the same with all the others, tapping them into a pile and retying them with the frayed yellow ribbon. He blew out the six candles on the candelabrum and sat awhile in the darkness.

He searched in his heart for some compassion for the misguided child-woman, articulate and highborn certainly but still desperately naïve, who had been so fervent in her veneration for a common soldier.

Although she could not have been aware that he was a brutal murderer (*her* murderer eventually?), he could feel no pity at all—only abhorrence at the mania of her craving.

There was a small canal at the back of Annibale Malipiero's home on the Giudecca, at the very end of the sizable and well-tended garden of which he was rightly proud. Despite his aversion to all things watery, he sometimes chose to swim in this unassuming conduit, as he occasionally did at his other home, his villa on the Brenta. The fear of it braced him; it cleared his mind and cleansed his soul.

Even though it was the very dead of night, he walked to the end of the garden, stripped himself naked, and jumped in.

28. Hope Abandoned . . .

asciate ogne speranza . . .

Dante's three simple words have taken on an import I realize I'd never truly understood.

The Stornello clan is not renowned for a quick response to anything—even in its business dealings—but I've stupidly assumed that some attempt might have been made beyond these grim walls to protest on my behalf. It must be two weeks at least since I was taken. Hours, days, weeks, months, mean nothing to me now.

There have been no more deliveries of food, no fresh clothes, no new books from my tutor. After my request to the jailer, I did receive a small bag of unguents and salve-soaked bandages from Balbina, and they've soothed the demolition of my body to a degree—but they, too, are running dry.

I've not been taken up to the *sala della tortura* again. The guards are now my sole tormentors. They've taken to hitting me with clubs. I suppose I should count myself fortunate. At least I'm not being flayed, or half drowned, or burned, or pierced with spikes, or having bits torn off me with pincers.

I'm visited by nobody. My jailer squats like some morose anthropoid outside my cell door, barely raising a glance as I'm heaved in and out. He used to be quite voluble. Now when I try to speak to him he grunts. My *comoda* regularly overflows and stinks. Fat flies buzz about it in the rising heat of early summer and buzz about me too.

The improvised curtain over my window has been replaced by three or four wide planks of wood, tightly set against one another so that barely a chink of light can get through them during the day. They seem to embody my utter separateness from the world.

I've discovered that when you're set apart from all participation in the down-to-earth recurrences of other people's lives, which you so take for granted when among them, you will turn to anyone, no matter who, for the simple fulfillment of connection with another being.

My only communication of any kind, therefore, is with the chained, perpetually prone figure in that even darker cell somewhere below mine and into whose company I've been thrust over and over again. It's usually just the two of us down there. Sometimes a whimpering wretch or two will be thrown in with us and then whisked off again, screeching for mercy, but mostly we're alone now.

When he deigns to address me, I find I'm grateful.

Curiously, he doesn't appear to object to my presence, or not much. He can even sound, in his way, quite genial about it. "So you are with us again," he might say, not too antagonistically, or, "Once more we have the pleasure . . ." He almost always uses the plural pronoun, even when it's just him in the place, as if he were some grandee and I his pliant subject.

Sometimes he affords me comfort of a kind.

He'll ask what they've done to me, and I'll oblige him with a catalog of injuries. He'll offer restorative advice: "Hold your head forward, not back—do you want to choke yourself on your own blood?"

"They've cracked my nose."

"Can you breathe through it?"

After a sanguineous deluge through my nostrils, I found I could.

"It's whole," he diagnosed. "It will heal itself—as the body does, until death comes, when there's no remedy."

He quite often wants to know if I've "squealed." I tell him that I have not because I have nothing to squeal about.

"Does a beast set for slaughter ponder the reason for the knife at his gizzard?" he once asked, and another time he said, "Even saints under torment may confess to sins they've not committed." And then: "But you've stayed dumb, as I said you must. If you had not, you would not be here. You would be down in the *pozzi*, awaiting the rope."

When he talks, it's never much above a gruff whisper, and out of some kind of deference, or perhaps straightforward fear, I respond in like fashion. It's possible he simply cannot speak any louder, in case he sets off another fit of coughing, or perhaps he's worried that we might be overheard. He's revealed no secrets as yet, or none that I've been able to identify, but I reply with a similar air of confidentiality.

Our interlocutions regularly falter. Frequently there's just a morose, sunless hush—hour upon hour of it. He hardly ever sits up. I still haven't seen his face. If there's the slightest chance I might, when the dungeon door is heaved open as another hapless victim is kicked in or pulled out, or I am, he hides it quickly, with a weather-roughened hand. Mostly he's lying on his back, with an arm across his eyes, or on his front, with a bent elbow still concealing his visage, or on his side, usually turned away from me and intertwined with himself, almost clutching himself, rather like a baby.

More often than not he's asleep. I can tell he's sleeping, because when he's awake there are snuffles and rumbles of disaffection (of soreness in his bones or more general irritation, or both, I can't tell) and a fair amount of coughing. Recently there's been less of that though—or not so many of those lengthy, gorge-scraping, seemingly unstoppable choruses of his. Perhaps he's getting better. He said the body can heal itself, except when death comes.

He said to me once that he longed for sleep, but only, I think, because I was boring him. I'd been blathering on about something or other, probably my guiltlessness. "Stop your prattling," he groaned. "I'm away now, and heaven help you if you wake me."

"Sweet dreams," I said.

"Pah! Dreams are deceivers."

Nevertheless, he does find peace in sleep, I believe. I watch his squat but brawny torso rise and fall. He says he is wary of dreams. I wonder if he has any.

I try not to sleep down there myself, endeavoring to save my slumbers for my own cell, where at least there's a bed—not much of one, but a bed all the same. And I'm still nervous of him. I imagine that if I do fall asleep, he may somehow loosen his fetters and grasp my throat again.

But sometimes—unavoidably and too often for my liking—my head falls forward (because I do my best never, and in defiance of all temptation, to lie down) upon my sapped and insubstantial chest.

"How many times," he once asked, as I emerged from one of these fitful lapses, "have I had to suffer her name, this darling you call for? Who is this beauty?"

He then enunciated—with some elegance, I thought—her name. "Franceschina." He seemed to roll it around in his mouth, savoring it. "Franceschina . . . Franceschina." Even in his rough, hoarse brogue, it had a sweet lilt, like a melancholy song.

"She's just a girl," I lied.

Once—and only once—I had the nerve to ask him why he was in prison. I have after all told him why I'm here—for murder, I think, and I've even given him the name of the person I'm alleged to have murdered. I thought it only fair, I said courageously, that he should furnish me with similar information.

He didn't, or not in any specific way. All he said was, "I'm quite the notorious felon, lad."

I've decided it's probably wise not to inquire further.

He, on the other hand, has learned pretty much everything there is to know about me.

I've told him of my monklike existence in the weeks before I was arrested, aside from the time I was dragged into Jacopo Malipiero's vicious presence, and how after I'd had my nose cut and was thrown into the canal I scurried home and locked myself away again. I've also told him of my certainty that it was Jacopo Malipiero who killed Fabietto Dandolo. The loathing in my voice provoked a spark of interest.

"Describe this lout," he demanded.

"Conceited, a bully, rich, and ridiculously good-looking."

"Favored to make women false," he said, or something on those lines. And later: "I'll warrant you'd like *him* dead."

"That I would."

"And you'd like to do the deed yourself."

"Willingly. He's strong though."

I heard him whisper, "If I was free of these shackles, I'd teach you how to stand your ground, boy, against an army of Jacopo Malipieros."

I've no craving whatsoever to have him unfettered, but the thought of some masterly, merciless vengeance against Jacopo Malipiero is a sweet one. I've imagined the two of us, my dark companion and me, with him at our mercy, dependent on our lenity, and we would give him none.

So I have confided in this shadowy being in the immeasurable time that I have spent in his dungeon. Yesterday I told him of the fable I concocted to save myself from death at Jacopo's hands, which I had initially thought might be the reason for my being brought here. I went into some detail, as he didn't seem inclined to stop my blathering. When I asked him if he knew, or had heard of, a villain called Iago of Mantua— presuming that there was a good chance he would have, being a villain himself—he did not deny or affirm it. He only pronounced, "You've a mettlesome imagination there, Gentile Stornello."

He's tired of me now. He's never given any indication of enjoying my company; it's always been mere tolerance. But he's not said a word, or indeed shown signs of much life, for the best part of two days and a night, although I've been with him all that time aside from a couple of hours of respite on my own bed, after a particularly savage crack on the back of my head by one of the most bloodthirsty of the guards.

I find that I'm longing for further conversation, however intermittent or diffident, or at the very least some acknowledgment of my presence. But there is none now.

29. A Fat Cook

Thee was to be no ostentation about Annibale Malipiero's second visit to the Palazzo Stornello Piccolo—no lordly gondola arriving at the shaky *imbarcadero,* no pounding on the main *porta d'ingresso* on the landward side of the unassuming dwelling. He had little desire to encounter the boy's numskull of a father again if he could best avoid it. A professional arrival would guarantee all sorts of fuss.

Instead, he knocked on a small door down a sunless side alley shortly after dawn, on a mid-June day. He heard voices within—one high pitched and another that, though feminine, sounded deep and almost manly. "I don't know who that could be at such an hour."

"Should we answer it?"

"Best not. Pass me the *prezzemolo.*"

The aromas of some variety of gastronomic preparation wafted through the door's deteriorating planks, and they were, in the *interrogante's* opinion, delectable.

His wife was not the best of cooks, he knew that. He tolerated her culinary attempts—and had for many years—because he loved her. He had even praised her at times, particularly on the infrequent occasions when others had eaten at his house. But even so dispassionate an individual as Annibale Malipiero had to admit that the smells issuing from the kitchen of the Palazzo Stornello Piccolo were exceptional. He could not precisely make out what they were, but there was a multiplicity of them, and some reminded him of the scents in the garden of his villa on the Brenta.

He knocked again, with greater purpose.

"Who's there?" the near-masculine voice inquired crossly.

Not wishing to advertise his identity to anyone within earshot apart from those in the kitchen, he leaned into the door and hissed, "Annibale Malipiero, Chief *Interrogante* of the Republic. Open up at once."

His command was obeyed by a severely bent scullery maid with a paucity of teeth. He faintly remembered having seen her among the modest assemblage of servants on his first visit. The cook he recalled instantly—a weightily built woman, half as broad as she was tall, with a demeanor of perennial suspicion. She was at the big table in the center of the kitchen, with her sleeves rolled up to her spheroid shoulders, with a pair of astonishingly muscular arms pummeling and bruising the shorn carcass of a small lamb, unsparingly rubbing herbs and oil into the pink skin with her generous fingers. He at last recognized a particular bouquet—that of mint. But there were more fragrances drifting over from elsewhere in the steamy room, and he went immediately to the two large iron pots bubbling over a hot fire and dipped his head, the better to catch their extraordinary richness. "This smells good," he said. "What is it?"

"*Stufato di coniglio,*" he was reluctantly informed.

"May I taste it?"

"Not without a spoon, you won't."

"May I have a spoon?"

"If you can find one."

The crooked midget quickly obliged him. The taste was so instantaneously, so unarguably delicious that Annibale Malipiero, who had believed himself fairly indifferent to flavor until that moment, immediately wanted more. But when he tried to dip the spoon into the pot again, he was speedily and tersely rebuked. "You want more, you'll have to get yourself invited to supper," announced the cook.

The malformed maid was more fawning. "Have you come to tell us about Signor Gentile, lord?" she lisped. He was amazed she could speak at all.

"I'm afraid not."

"But is he . . . well?"

"Yes, he's well," the inquisitor lied.

"Will he soon go for trial?"

"As I said, I'm not here to talk about Gentile Stornello."

"But he's not a bad man, lord. You can see that just by looking at him."

"As I said—"

"What *are* you here for, then?" demanded the ample cook. She lifted the lamb by its hind legs, swung it almost over her head, and slapped it down on the table again, belly upward.

"I'm here to talk to you." Uninvited, Annibale Malipiero pulled back a chair and sat down.

She cocked a thick eyebrow. "What's there to talk to me about?"

"What are you going to do with that?" the *interrogante* inquired, nodding at the lamb. "Roast it?"

"Haven't made up my mind yet."

"I'm sorry, I don't know your name . . ."

"No reason you should. Zinerva Brigante."

"And where are you from, Zinerva Brigante?"

"Arezzo."

"Have you worked here long?"

"Since I was younger than this poor waif."

He asked nothing more for a while. He didn't feel he could. The maid was scuttling around, half hobbling, half hopping—busy at something, though he could not see what. She was never far from him, tipping her ugly face, squinting at him with her unparallel eyes. So he sat and watched Zinerva Brigante work. Bubbles of sweat pricked her wide forehead; rivulets of it coursed down her brawny arms. He was perspiring most uncomfortably himself.

She began to chop at the lamb with the edges of her glistening hands, dexterously but thunderously along the length of its stomach. Turning it over again, she did the same along its back.

"What are you doing that for?" Annibale Malipiero had to ask.

"Tenderizing it. We don't want it chewy."

He thought of the unidentifiable meat that his wife prepared. "No, one would not wish it . . . chewy."

The cook may have noted his discomfort at the continued proximity of the bobbing girl, because she then snapped, "Off with you to market now, Balbina!" The asymmetric thing, with a pout of remonstrance, put a bag that was very nearly the same size as she was around her neck and limped outside.

The *interrogante* heard suggestions above him of an awakening palazzo—a scuffle of feet, doors creaking, morning coughs. "I believe you knew Emilia Borghetto, who worked in the household of the late Brabantio Stornello."

She stopped battering the carcass and went to the sink to wash her hands. She remained silent.

"Did you or didn't you?" He turned in her direction to see her take a brush and scrub determinedly at her palms and her fingers, leaning downward to inspect them as she did so.

"Come now, Zinerva Brigante, you must realize it's not wise to hold things back from a state inquisitor."

"What are you going to do, arrest me?"

"You knew her, though not well, from occasional visits to the palazzo of Brabantio Stornello. You've been there since her death too—to commiserate with the rest of the *casa,* I presume."

She stopped scrubbing. "If you know all that already, why bother to ask me?"

"Do you know *how* she died?"

She took a cloth of linen and vigorously dried her hands, still checking for dirt. "Of the plague, wasn't it, like they all did?"

"You believe that?"

"I believe what I'm told to believe."

"Like the good *cittadina* that you are." He rose from the table.

"It does no good to go listening to gossip," she said, looking up at him impassively.

His own gaze did not flinch and was equally unrevealing—until he hinted, by a glimmer of the eyes, that he did know something she didn't. As a consequence, after a good couple of minutes, she conceded, "I reckon *you* know how she died, and more besides."

"Oh, I do. . . ." But he wasn't going to tell her more.

To most of Venice, Iago of Mantua still remained a creature of myth, monstrous but indistinct—and, crucially, not in Venice.

How long it could stay thus, Annibale Malipiero wasn't sure, despite the villain's having been hidden away in a long unused cell that only the *interrogante* and a few of his most constant guards knew about. Even Bonifacio Colonna and Roberto Fabbri were still unaware of the dungeon's existence, or of who was held there.

But the Prigioni Ducale, famously secure though it was, was a leaky old hulk when it came to talk. And the Palazzo Ducale itself, only a narrow canal and a short bridge's span away, was, perhaps inevitably, just about the most gossip-strewn building in Venice.

The great edifice was also, of course, a place of labyrinthine jealousies, populated by those jostling for advancement—every one of whom, if it was to his benefit, might be ready to betray another. Annibale Malipiero was on slippery ground, and he knew it. He was, after all, secretly harboring a traitor—an act of treachery itself.

The exercise of putting the boy together with the villain in the unfrequented cell, alone together for as many days and nights as he could risk without rousing the Mantuan's suspicions, had so far proved disappointing. Yes, Iago had continued to speak, but tersely and in annoyingly low tones. Annibale Malipiero had sat listening for hour upon uncomfortable hour, with his ear to the cell door and often unable to make anything out at all.

The youth had been considerably more loquacious, and louder too, revealing much of his own short and largely uninteresting life. The guards had continued the pretense of torture, again to stay the villain's suspicions, sometimes with undue enthusiasm.

Annibale Malipiero knew well enough that agony and fear were enemies of reason but had been somewhat surprised that Gentile

Stornello had not yet managed the slightest inkling that he was face-to-face with the protagonist of his own extraordinary imagination. Perhaps the boy was not quite as clever as he'd first supposed.

In the meantime, the inquisitor had decided to find out what he might from a woman who'd been acquainted with Iago's savagely murdered wife. He was not interested in Emilia Borghetto or her sad fate, however. It was her mistress he'd come to talk about.

"Did you ever meet or speak to the lady Desdemona?"

The smell of freshly baked bread now filled the kitchen. Zinerva Brigante picked up a heavy wooden paddle from beside the *credenza*. She held it in one hand and tapped it on the palm of the other. For a moment or two it seemed as if she might be about to strike him with it. Her look now was not just uncooperative but actually quite aggressive.

"Why do you want to know about her?" she asked icily.

"I understand she could be quite a . . . What's the word? A minx? *Una civetta?*"

The allegation—a complete invention on his part—produced the anticipated outrage. Now he really did think she might hit him with the *pala* she was still holding. "Just because she went with a black man don't mean she was bad, like Signor Brabantio thought. With all that talk of spells, of *incantesimi—incantata*, he was saying she was . . . Just because she had a mouth on her . . ."

The conversation was getting interesting at last, and more speedily than Annibale Malipiero had dared hope. Something—some affection for the girl, some need to come to her defense?—had made the cook garrulous.

He sat once more at the great table. The lamb's gleaming corpse, sprawled on its belly, legs outstretched, seemed to gaze on him with its dead black eyes.

The oven was set into the kitchen's great chimneypiece. Zinerva opened its rusting iron door, releasing further heat and still more of the heady aroma of perfectly baked dough. "Just because she had a mouth on her," she repeated, "and could talk and talk—she talked beautiful she did, and in French too; the way she spoke could tempt the birds down from the trees, Emilia said—that don't make her a . . . what you called her . . . and what her father called her too, except worse."

"Yes indeed. Remind me: What was it her father used to call her?"

"The very worst thing you can call a girl, and only fifteen too. Untouched as snow she was. No wonder she cried."

"She . . . cried? When was that?"

"Only the once when I was there, in their kitchen, with Emilia. She came down from shouting at her father. Like I said, she could talk, but she could shout too—yowling like a cat she was. '*Non sono una puttana*,' she was shrieking."

"A cat?"

"*Si, come una gattina. Povera ragazza piccina*, she was no *puttana*, I tell you."

Now Zinerva Brigante dug into the fiery abyss with her *pala* and produced loaf after smoky loaf, crusty and cracked on top and malleable below, sliding each onto the table before him. Some were small, little more than a couple of mouthfuls each, some impressively grand; one or two were nearly as big as the lamb they settled next to. He drew their perfume deep into his lungs—the perfume not only of freshly baked dough but of herbs, too, and oil, and honey.

She felt for the readiness of each loaf with heat-resistant fingers. A smile of reminiscence played on her lips. "They used to call her that—*la gattina della famiglia*—because of the way she could yowl, but I suppose you know that too, like you know everything."

"Of course."

She placed her fists on the table and stared down at him. "But there's something maybe you don't know—even you, *L'Inquisitore Principale della Repubblica*." She looked behind her to check that there was no one else in the room. "It was Emilia's husband called her *la gattina* first. It wasn't the only bad thing he put into folks' heads neither. I never trusted that Spaniard from the first time I set eyes on him. Oh, he had a *fascino* about him; he could charm, could Iago. He charmed Emilia, didn't he? And even the lady Desdemona trusted him; it was like they were best friends." Her eyes flashed. "Why haven't you caught him yet, *il demonio*?"

He shrugged and pouted. "We're trying." He was quite proud of the pretense.

Now it sounded as if a whole army of boots, and other footwear besides, was clattering down from above. "She was rather good at French, I gather?" he asked hastily.

"Spoke it like a native, or so Emilia said. *Come una dama istruita; molto elegante*. She wrote in it too, poems and the like."

"Poems?"

Her expansive shoulders lifted and fell. "Far as I know. Can't read, can I?"

The household froze as one at the sight of no lesser a personage than the *Capo degli Interroganti della Serenissima* sitting calmly at the great kitchen table. "Good morning." He scanned the faces of the small assembly. To his relief, the Signor of the house didn't appear to be among them.

Annibale Malipiero rose and made to leave. But before he did so, he pointed at one of the rolls, a gleaming herb-infused *panino*, and asked, as humbly as he could, of Zinerva Brigante, "May I take one of these?"

"Be my guest," the cook replied gruffly.

Once outside, he broke the roll in two and put one of the halves into his mouth. It was so very delicious, at once both sweet and tangy, that it almost made him breathless.

He was still savoring the matchless taste when the aging kitchen door creaked open behind him to reveal Baldassare Ghiberti, who now followed him, sweating and apprehensive. "Please, Signor Malipiero," he gasped, "do you have news of Gentile?"

"He's well enough," Annibale Malipiero said.

"But . . . but . . . we have heard nothing . . . and we are not permitted to visit him any longer or to send him provisions. . . . I have books for him."

The patrician stopped walking. He looked the tutor up and down. The fat fellow was almost blubbering. A wave of something like compassion passed through Annibale Malipiero then. The man seemed so very fretful for the boy's welfare, so very . . . what was the best word to describe it? So very *loving* toward him.

He decided that it would do no harm to give some small measure of reassurance. Provided the man could guarantee his prudence, of course. "Can you give me your word that what I say next will remain confidential?"

"Of course."

"On no account must you speak of it to anyone."

"Yes, yes, you have my word."

The *interrogante* paused a moment before leaning forward and whispering, "Gentile Stornello is performing a service to the state, for which the republic will be grateful in due time."

The tutor's eyes seemed to pop.

"More than that, I cannot say." Then, in order to set a seal upon the man's silence, he added, "The state may have need of *your* services at some point in the future too, Dottore Ghiberti." He left the academic nodding wordlessly and utterly overcome.

Munching on the remaining half of the exceptional *panino* and reaching at last the piercing sunlight of the nearest campo (it was by now fiendishly hot), he decided not to return immediately to his place of work. He was very much in Stornello territory. The church of the Frari was just a short stroll away, beside it was the humbler Chiesa di San Rocco, where Brabantio Stornello was buried—and not too distant from that was the late Signor's own palazzo.

It was on the landward *porta grande* of this imposing building that he now knocked. He stepped back to look up at it. Though as outwardly modest as its late owner, it was still at least five times bigger than the house he'd come from.

The door was opened not by a servant but by Desdemona's eldest sibling. What was her name? Caterina? She was a striking girl, tall and confident, and her expression was not welcoming.

"I believe your sister wrote poetry," said Annibale Malipiero, as amiably as he could muster. "I should like to take a look at some of it, if I may."

"Malipieri are not welcome here."

Thickly impenetrable timber was slammed in his face.

30. The Truth

I f this were a play, the audience would now bawl at me, the beaked fool, *"Imbecile! Infantile! Ma che pazzo!"* What's the likelihood, after all, in the great scheme of things, of fabricating something so preposterous and then discovering you are at the center of the story you've created?

No wonder I'm in prison.

He's not speaking to me anymore—not a word. He's sullen and dangerous, as he was before. But during the past few days he he's been startlingly talkative.

"We have a new door, did you notice? The carpenter's been in. A pretty good job he's made of it too. Take a look."

I didn't notice the new door when I was thrown through it, because for the first time I saw his face. It was around noon, so the sun was slanting down from the grate. He made no effort to hide behind a folded arm. His hands lay, palms downward, on his lap.

I'd presumed there'd be a scar or two, or a mouth deformed into a permanent snarl, with bared, broken teeth perhaps—something more in keeping with the ghastly malefactor I've always supposed him to be.

What I saw was, if not exactly commonplace, then hardly threatening. It's weather-worn certainly; his skin looks charred and is reddish-brown. There's none of the pallor you'd expect of someone who's spent a long time in darkness. He's managed to chop at his beard somehow—so that it bristles almost comically from his cheeks and jaw and chin. His whiskers are wiry, deep black with a few flecks of gray. He has absolutely no hair on the top of his head. He's either bald or has succeeded in shaving it, and it shines like burnished copper. That is perhaps the most notable thing about him—his naked head, which, if one were to remove all its other features, would resemble a cannonball.

He is, I suppose, what one might call handsome and was probably good-looking when he was younger (he is, I think, in his forties). Everything is in proportion—the nose strong and angular, the mouth full but not too much so, the chin slightly jutting with a small dimple at its tip, the cheeks (inevitably) sunken. If there's anything that should have made me instantly wary, it's his eyes, which are wide, grayish-green, and intense.

He had been given fresh clothes—another surprise. They were frayed and full of holes, but his shirt and hose were dirt-free. He remained barefoot. There was no caked blood on him anymore. He'd been "scrubbed up." That was how he put it himself. "Look at me," he chuckled. "I have been scrubbed up—like a chicken ready for cooking!" I'm still tattered and pallid and filthy and battered. By contrast, he seemed to glow with rugged health.

He pointed. "There," he said. "We've been given furniture too!" There had been none before. Now there's a table of sorts, and chairs with rush seats, and a flimsy bench against one of the walls. On the bench are a bowl and a jug, and there's a bucket on the floor. At last we have somewhere to go about our ablutions and evacuations (or he does, as I tend to try to save mine until I'm in my own cell).

"We could play cards," he said. "See, they've left a pack. Do you play cards?"

"No, I don't."

"Then I shall teach you. *Trappola*, that's what they all play here in Venice. I should warn you, though, that however good you get, I'll outsmart you every time."

Later he announced, "I'd venture we're ripe for a hanging, wouldn't you?"

"What do you mean by that?" I asked, with a hint of a tremor.

"One or the other of us, or both. They don't throw all this at you unless there's a change afoot."

Then he did something that froze my bones. He stood up. After stretching his limbs, he stepped away from the wall. He'd been freed. The chains and shackles still dangled, but he now had the freedom of his dungeon. He was master of it, king of his realm; he could go wherever he wished within its confines.

He's shorter than I thought he'd be. His body nevertheless exudes a powerful muscularity—squat but indomitable. I think if one were to see him in the street, one might well avoid him. His arms are too long, hanging to just below his knees, but that may be because his legs are bent a little too much outward. His hands are too big for the rest of him. As he moved around the cell, he rolled rather than walked. I'd call the look simian. It didn't put me at ease.

He went to the new door to give it closer scrutiny. "Not as solid as before," he pronounced. "If we were of a mind to escape, we could kick it open in a trice." He put his ear to it, listening for activity outside. I don't know if he heard any.

He seemed singularly spry as he loped about. And then, amazingly, he started to sing—nothing melodic—under his labored breath (he's still not entirely healthy). It was in some guttural language I couldn't recognize—not French, which I do (although I'm not much good at it), or Spanish (which I know to sound a bit like Italian). German perhaps?

"What's that tongue?" I asked.

"English," he said. "I learned some of it when I was there. It's a cold hell, where men speak little, for fear of a gale rushing down their gullets and silencing them for good."

"And the song?"

"A ditty of love unrequited." His tone was deprecatory. "Written, they say, by the King of England himself."

"They have a king who writes songs?"

Then he sang another, in the same vernacular as far as I could tell, but it had more of a thrust to it. He enjoyed it more than the previous one, evidently. To me it sounded even less tuneful.

"And that . . . ?"

"A drinking refrain only, fitting to the homeland that spawned it, as the English are potent in potting, because it's so damnably cold."

"Potting?"

"Drinking, boy."

"I preferred the first song."

"That you would," he said. "As you are a lad in love."

He teased me about Franceschina. "More dreams, Gentile Stornello, have you had more dreams?"

"She doesn't love me," I sighed.

He'd been shambling—almost prancing, or dancing—around the cell, his arms out at a level with his shoulders. Now he stopped. "How can you know that?"

"She's given me no sign of it."

"You require signs? They've been trained."

"Trained? Who?"

"Those daughters of the *nobility*." He virtually spat the word. "It's their education—to learn to shrink, to be bashful, to hide their hearts. You must know it's so, Gentile Stornello, as you are of the same pedigree—born in a velvety bed as you were."

"She has a noble soul, I'm sure of it," I said. "But she isn't of noble blood. She's a servant."

He discharged a sharp cackle—a sound I'd never heard from him until then. "Well, now," he said, "our aristocratic pup has an inclination, has he, for bitches of no breeding?"

I didn't much care for this new suggestive tone. "No!" I cried. "She's just unbelievably pretty."

"Have you tupped her?"

"Tupped"? It wasn't a word I was cognizant of, but it didn't take much to work out what it meant.

He wished to leave me in no doubt. "Had your way, made the beast, the one with two backs, coupled, yoked, had her sit upon your saddle . . ."

"No, of course I haven't."

"Why not? She's but a servant. I thought all you rich young braggarts would think it a necessity—no, more than that, a right—to mount any pretty servant girl you have sight of."

"There may be some who are that way disposed," I replied. "But I am not one of them. Nor am I rich."

"Not rich? You might not be as rich as some, lad, but as sure as hell is said to burn you're richer than most in this world."

Unavoidably, I thought of Jacopo Malipiero then and muttered resentfully, "I'm not as rich as Jacopo Malipiero, nowhere near."

He snatched at the observation. "Oh, yes," he sniggered, "your rival for the heart of Franceschina . . . Franceschina . . . Franceschina . . ." (Oh, God, there he went again, plucking at her name, like a lutenist.)

"He's no rival. He has her. I don't."

He went with the verb. "Has her, does he? *Has* her." He glanced up at the grate. "What time of day would you say it was?"

"Early afternoon, I'd guess."

"Siesta time," he mused. "Perchance he's *having* her now."

"He's disappeared, apparently," I said, to console myself.

"There are women who've a liking for brutes," he observed. "Or mayhap she just likes his money—the jewels he buys her, to pretty her up."

"She's not that sort!"

"And what sort is that?"

"The acquisitive sort, the garish sort. She's demure . . . and without vanity."

He clicked his teeth, peered down at me, cannonball head tilted. "My, my, Gentile Stornello, she must have captured you headily, for you to champion her so."

And then he delivered his conviction that love doesn't exist anywhere in the world. He said it was "a permission of the will." At another time he put it more pithily: "It's merely a lust of the blood."

His way with words can sometimes be astonishing. "We are but beasts in nature," he once said, "and like beasts we must have our concupiscence. We must sniff and we must rut. But as beasts have no reason or conscience, they go at it shamelessly. We would do so too, if reason did not stay us, and it is shame alone that gives our own carnality the name of love."

I don't dare dispute his opinions, but I don't agree with him. What else can I call the yawning void in my heart whenever I think of never seeing Franceschina again? What's that if it isn't love? Or the thud in my chest and my gullet when he tortures me with his talk of "tupping," if it isn't love? I wonder if he speaks thus because he's never known love himself.

Later still he announced, "Myself, I go the other way round . . ." I'd been dozing, so I didn't quite catch his drift. He elaborated: "I'm poor, you are not. You have a taste for the poor, I have a taste for those who are not."

"A *taste*?"

"A highborn mare is what I delight in!" he bragged. He performed that little mime I've seen the Neapolitan actors do in their lewd shows— knees bent, fists at waist level, hips thrusting back and forth. "You should hear how they neigh, Gentile Stornello!"

"And have you had many of these fine mares?"

"Many more than you, boy."

"That wouldn't be hard." I'd already told him I was *intatto*, an admission that provoked some hilarity. His assessment of me as a lightweight, a sissy, a "lily-livered whey-face," led him at one point to do something extraordinary and, to begin with, very frightening.

He destroyed a chair, tearing it apart as if it were no more substantial than paper. He took one of the legs and threw me another. I didn't catch it, of course, so had to scrabble about for it. He barked at me to stand up. I did so. Grinning, he tossed the chair leg he was holding from hand to hand. Then he made a few swipes at me, swishing it close to my face, and once thwacking me hard against my upper arm. Compared to the pain of the past weeks it was nothing, but I still howled.

"You think that by squealing you'll get help? It's me and you, boy, no one else. There's nobody to aid you now, Gentile Stornello."

He cracked me about the head. I reeled. This time the wail was genuine. Still no one came.

"Fight," he growled into my face, then leapt back. His fingers pointed inward at his chest. "Strike me!"

I tried—and missed. He didn't even have to step out of the way.

"Again."

I managed a blow, or more of a brush, to his upper left arm, for which I earned a wallop just below my rib cage.

Winded, I crumpled, but he grabbed me by the hair and hauled me straight.

"Fight," he snarled.

"How?" I pleaded.

"Like this."

In an instant I found myself once more on the floor, his arm so tight around my neck that I feared I was about to breathe my last.

"Please don't kill me," I wheezed.

I felt his breath against my ear. "Do you think you'd be alive now if I wanted you dead?"

He was up again, looking down at me as if he might still be considering it.

Then he laughed, swinging away. He began to saunter about the cell, relishing his thorough command of it. "What do you think I am," he asked. "A wayward murderer? Is my sport killing? Is that what you think?"

"I don't know what to think or what you are."

"May I not just be an ordinary fellow?"

"You wouldn't be here if you were."

"But you are here, Gentile Stornello, and if you will pardon the remark, Signor . . ."—and with this he gave a scraping bow, pretending to doff a cap and flap it about his legs—"for I know how easy it is to affront *un nobiluomo*, you are, in my most humble analysis, a very ordinary young man."

"Yes," I said. "Unexceptional indeed."

Since then, over the past two or three days, there have been more lessons in combat: parries and thrusts and arm holds and neck holds and carefully directed kicks and punches and tumblings and overturnings and mock duels with chair legs. If I'm still no good, I'm better than I was.

I thought his effortless victories might grow tedious to him. But he persisted. Then I drew blood. The chair legs we'd been using had splintered during our jousting, with sharp edges and projections, and it was one such that caught him unexpectedly against his right biceps.

He stared for a moment at the wound, then up at me. It was not a pleasant look. "A hit," he grunted. "A palpable hit."

It seemed as if he was about to clout me in return, and indeed he brandished his own weapon, lunging at me with it—but not with any great force, and I skipped readily aside.

"Who was in your head then, as you clipped me so?" he asked.

"In my head?"

"Was it your girl's pretty stripling?"

He'd often brought up Jacopo in the course of our duels, to incense me, I suppose, into a greater enthusiasm for the fight. He'd call him my "fine-looking contender" or my "bonny ill-wisher" or my "fetching adversary." Jacopo, he'd say, was a "bed-presser" or a "carpet knight"—"and who lies spent on that precious carpet now, my boy," he once asked, "with her limbs spread and all a-tangle?"

He's quite the conjurer of pictures you'd rather not have in your mind. I've told him about the ridiculous magnitude of Jacopo's palazzo, been openly indignant at its size compared to my own. Naturally he's run with this too: "And where in his many-roomed mansion has he resolved to tread her today? How many bedrooms does he have? Or it may be in one of his *stanze di bagno*, or in the kitchens, or up on the *loggetta* under an open sky, or on the marbled floor of the *piano nobile*, in full view of that callow army you've talked of. Where is he *ramming* her now, boy?" He flourished the chair leg he was clasping, calling it as he did so "the very thing that pleases her." And as we were, at that time, on the subject of size, he said, "A woman may declare she has no bother for comparison, but when a boy has a pike to be proud of, she'll bow as she must."

When I lashed at him so hard that I made him bleed, my fury was aimed at *him* too. He'd become my second tormentor.

I'd admitted to him that, yes, it was Jacopo who was "in my head" as I'd swung at him, and after a few more swipes and counterthrusts, he had my neck in an armlock once more, his every sinew tautened. "I'll kill the blackguard for you, Gentile Stornello. Or, still better, I'll weaken him so that you may have the final dispatch. How would you wish to see him slaughtered?"

"Slowly," I panted.

"So that he wails for mercy?"

"Yes."

"As vengeance for the pain you've suffered, not solely at his hands but in here too?"

"Yes."

He released me, and of course I crumpled. I landed on my front, so he tapped at me with his foot, pushing it beneath my belly and raising it, turning me over as if I were no more than a piece of meat on a spit. Then he glanced up at the white light pouring through the grate. "The revenge you crave will be yours, and I'll gladly help you," he muttered, "if we could but escape from this hell."

Again his eyes turned to the door, which he'd already pronounced could be easily smashed open if we had a mind to do it. I also looked at the somewhat makeshift set of planks that separated us from the rest of humanity and realized that all our scraps over the previous days and nights had been engineered by him for one purpose only. No whimpering sissy could aid his escape. He was still not in full health; he couldn't do it single-handedly.

"I don't think we'd get far," I whispered miserably.

"They are accoutred to the teeth on the other side of that door." He, too, kept his voice low. "What an armory we'd have if we could overwhelm them. We must look to our anger, Gentile Stornello. Soldiers fighting for a cause they believe in have an arsenal more masterful than any number of swords and daggers and pikes and axes and clubs—more so even than the pistol or the mighty cannon."

He seemed to revel for a while in this talk of men versus munitions—as if fondly remembering conflicts he himself had been engaged in. And it was at that point that I asked, "Were you once a soldier, then?"

His response may have been mere bluster, but I don't think so. His body appeared to swell, with self-esteem, as he clenched his fists and bulked up his chest. His conceit had made him momentarily candid—and incautious. For the first time in the weeks I'd spent with him, he spoke of who he was, or what he'd been.

"I was at Marignano," he said.

I confessed I hadn't heard of the place.

"Why should it matter where it is?" he huffed. "It's a fragment of land and a village. Nothing much grew there, though now it might, fertilized by the blood of twenty thousand men."

"That's a lot."

"The bloodiest conflict of them all. Anyone who knows of war will know of Marignano."

"There you have me," I said. "For I know nothing of war."

"I can credit that." He gave me another contemptuous look.

I thought of Benvenuto. Marignano will mean something to *him*. If I ever get out of this hole (and if he himself is still alive), I shall have to ask him about it—and about the other battles in which my cell mate now claimed to have participated: Ravenna, Chioggia, Agnadello, Novara, Cerignola.

"Was it for a cause that you fought?" I asked.

He laughed. "I fought for pay, lad, and for booty, as most men do. I fought to put money in my purse. There was no cause to wrestle for. Those battles were over land merely, and so they still are." His tone was briefly wistful, then reproachful, acrimonious. He spoke of thousands having died "so that this lord or that, or such a king or such an emperor, or a duke here or a marquis there, might get richer."

"Have you fought for many states and rulers, then?"

He leaned against the wall from which the chains still dangled and slid down it, head lowered. Suddenly he looked quite frail again. "I've traveled from army to army, hired to the highest bidder, and many have been more gracious than your fine republic, boy. They have *remembered* my loyalty." He listed them: "Ferrara, Firenze, Milan, Pope Leo . . . Mantua . . ."

The last—unless hindsight has given it a resonance it did not possess at the time—he appeared to dwell on, with a melancholic sigh.

Then he shifted on his buttocks and slapped a thigh. "But now we have a cause for which to fight, do we not, Gentile Stornello?"

"We do?"

He nodded. "And we may have to die for it."

I gulped a little. "What cause is that?"

He thumped the other thigh. "Injustice," he said. "Oppression. We must fight them, lad; we must fight for liberty."

"Must we?" I said unenthusiastically.

He wasn't amused. "I've seen men die for their liberty!" He glowered. "I've watched them fight and be killed, with smiles on their faces, strengthened only by what they believe in. I've seen them victorious too—weaponless men, conquering with their bare hands."

"Where was that?"

"It doesn't matter a fig where it was, boy. Their courage can be a lesson to us."

He pulled himself up again and cracked a hand across my skull. It really did hurt a lot. "You have been grossly arraigned, have you not? You've complained of it often enough."

"Yes, I have," I groaned.

"As have I," he said. "As have I."

It was darkening in the cell now, and I could hardly see him in the shadows. From time to time he struck out like a pugilist against an invisible opponent, as he muttered about unfairness, unpardonable wrongs, and Venice's lack of gratitude.

He spoke of walls of privilege that must be dismantled, of the oppressors and the oppressed. He railed against the disparities between rich and poor, as if they were not simply the way things are. He exclaimed that he himself had nearly died for lack of food. He, too, had worked for little gain—in unyielding fields that might as well have been deserts—and had been beaten for his labors.

I'm aware that some men talk thus in hidden cabals, but it was the first time I had ever heard such perfidious notions so directly and eloquently expressed.

Coward that I am, I did not wish anyone out there to think that I myself might concur with these heretical opinions. "But Venice is not like that. Venice is a democracy!"

"Pah!" he spluttered, and pronounced my city a place run by self-serving oligarchs who only feign some obeisance to equivalence among men. "And what of the others your precious *Serenissima* plays the tyrant over? Those lands across the sea she calls hers? Does democracy—or even a pretense of it—rule there?"

It was not just Venice, he said, that was out of balance, but the world.

And so the world must be turned upside down. Perhaps not in his life-time, or mine, or for many lifetimes to come, but it would happen. And it would be bloody.

In the silence that followed, I realized that I was, for the first time, alone with this person in the middle of the night. Normally I'd have been hauled away to my own cell by now and thrown back in again with the coming of day.

An hour or so passed. There were no shuffles or coughs from outside the cell. But he wasn't asleep. I can tell when he is by the deep regularity of his breathing. So I put the question to him that I'd risked once before but to which I'd only received a vague answer: "What is it that *you're* alleged to have done?"

He didn't respond immediately. Perhaps he was running them all through his head. "Name a crime and I'll be sure to have performed it." Tentatively, I did so. Perfidy? Of course. Theft? Naturally. Fraud? *Ma senz'altro.* Violence? Many times and in many forms. Rape? That also, and again often, and a host other perversions besides. Murder? Oh, a hundred or more. Then he announced, quite loudly and clearly not for my ears alone, "Can such a villain exist? Can *any* man be so very bad?"

Then he slept. I didn't. Shortly before a silky illumination began to steal through the grate, and as I heard the noises of the *molo* awakening, I reached my final deduction. Here was a being loathed by Venice. Here was a soldier who had traveled the world and hated it. Here was one who'd admitted, I think, to a liking for women of higher breeding. Here was a killer who was still willing to kill. And here was a man who spoke of Mantua with longing.

He stirred and seemed momentarily surprised that I should still be with him. After a moment's silence, during which I never let my gaze move from his, he asked, "How is it that you're always here? How is it that it's just you and me? Why should that be?"

I'd been asking myself the same question. I had wondered, in the blackness, why I'd been placed in a cell with Iago of Mantua. Was it my punishment for having had the impudence to stumble upon the truth? Or was I here for a purpose?

"You know I once talked of inventing a story to save my life?"

He nodded.

"About the man who is said to have murdered my cousin Desdemona?"

He blinked. For a moment or two he looked away.

"I thought it a silly fabrication, but . . ."

He waited.

"Are you he?" I asked.

More time has slid past since that final inquiry, but he's said not a single word further. He's folded in upon himself and covered his face once more.

He doesn't even stir when the rickety door rattles open and four guards burst in. They pull me up. I'm an obliging, unresisting puppet in their hands. I'm marched out.

I feel quite cheerful—quite *released*. I don't know why.

My optimism is short-lived. Standing before me, filling almost the entire antechamber of the cell, with a great grin on his lardaceous face, is the immensely fat inquisitor, whom I've not encountered for a while.

31. An Angry Inquisitor

"Stupid, *stupid* boy! You've ruined everything!"

The *Capo dei Interroganti della Repubblica Serenissima* is livid.

But I'm pretty livid too.

"How, exactly?"

"You've told him that you know who he is! Moreover, and perhaps even worse you have also revealed it to one of my . . . my colleagues."

"I think your fat friend knew anyway. I think he'd been listening. He didn't seem too surprised when I told him, after I'd been beaten to a pulp again, I might add—"

"Be silent!" He's plopped himself onto my bed. It twitches beneath his weight. He yanks at his beard. "*Allora,*" he says finally, "these are your instructions. You must try to loosen his tongue again. I shall give you two days and two nights. I want to know where he was born and in what circumstances. I am presuming in Mantua, but we can't be certain. I need precise locations. I would like to know about his childhood. I've no curiosity about his exploits as a soldier, or not here in Italy—I presume they were bloody and random, like most military adventures. Ask him about them if you think it may get him to talk again, but I know where he's been. I don't want another list. I do need details, however, of his activities in the East, with the Ottoman, and you must find out if he has any associations with the Turks in this city. You will have to be subtle in your questioning there, Gentile. It won't be information he'll readily divulge."

He's become more avuncular, less furious, so I decide to be helpful. "He did say he'd seen men fight and die for their beliefs. Did he mean the Turks, do you think?"

"Certainly. But more recently the contumacious Cypriots. Many have fought and died there, calling out his name."

"He spoke of the world being overturned."

"Probe him on the matter. But if he proves to be stubborn, move on. I need to know about his"—he coughs slightly—"relationship with your cousin."

"Relationship? I'm stunned. He killed her, didn't he?"

"Yes, and her husband, and her maid. Although not in any way you might think."

"And what way was that?"

"There are things it's still better for you not to know."

"*And why must that be?*" I cry. The fury that's been building within me has reached the bursting point. My sense of disentitlement, the maddening ignorance of the past weeks, the feeling of being useless and of being used, of being no more than a plaything and a conduit, a hapless, unknowing intermediary, there for his sole convenience, to say nothing of the brutality, the beaten head and limbs, the scarred and stretched body, the terror, and the sheer bloody loneliness. "Why?" I sputter again, as he listens—tranquilly, to my fulminations. "Why are there things I still mustn't know? And why didn't you tell me who he was in the first place? It might have saved a lot of time and . . . and a lot of pain."

He maintains his habitually level gaze. "It's the way of an inquisitor, I'm afraid," he says. "Nothing must be known until strictly necessary." He clasps his fingers across his lap and leans toward me. "It's not my habit to make a clean breast of things. In the pursuit of truth, I consider it best for those in my charge to draw their own conclusions. And believe me, Gentile, I can sometimes be as uncertain of that truth as anyone."

I'm not sure I'm any wiser. I sense nonetheless that it's taken him some effort to be so open with me, if that's what he's being. He straightens. "Anything you can find out about his murderous techniques will be both interesting and useful, but I'm more concerned with what lies *behind* his crimes and now you must be too. Can you do that?"

"I . . . can . . . try."

"Splendid!" He raises himself from the bed and moves to the cell door.

"Promise you won't have me tortured again!"

He drops his head but doesn't turn. "Find out what I need and I . . . promise."

I still don't trust him.

"And what if nothing comes of this? What if he stays silent? What then?"

He sighs. "Then I shall almost certainly have to indict you for the murder of Fabietto Dandolo."

"But you know it was your nephew!"

Still, he doesn't turn. "Of course it was my nephew," he says quietly. "But we've had to release him, I'm sorry to say. And the Dandoli are understandably eager for us to provide them with a culprit."

With that he leaves me.

32. *Balbina's Ministrations*

"Here's the ugliest goblin in Venice come to see you," the jailer sneers. *"Ma che nana ripugnante!"*

Balbina doesn't even glance at him; her already twisted lip curls even more as she mutters, "You're no oil painting yourself."

She digs into her capacious *borsa* and lays her ointments and pastes, her lotions and salves, her bandages and makeshift splints, and small spoons and tiny knives neatly on the table. She takes out a candle and waves it at the jailer. "Light this!" she demands, so peremptorily that he can only oblige.

She looks at me and crosses herself several times. *"O Madonna mia e tutti i santi nell' cielo! Buon Dio! Nostro Salvatore!"*

She pulls off my ripped, blood-caked shirt. *"Giovanotto povero . . ."* She touches my injuries, with exceptional delicacy. "What animals did this to you, Signor Gentile?"

"Guards, interrogators . . ."

"Bestie crudeli! Sadici! Lie back here, on the bed."

"Do you think anything's broken, Balbina?"

"Lie still. That's what I'm trying to find out."

She pulls at my arms, quite roughly. I yap like a struck dog. She tugs at both my legs, which hurts even more. I holler.

"No, they're sound," she pronounces. "Badly bruised and cut, but still in one piece."

She grasps my head firmly and turns it from side to side, then lifts it to inspect the back of my skull, tapping on it, testing it for any malleability, any unexpected dents. "This is still in one piece too, though only just."

She presses down on my chest. It's very painful. She bends forward and puts an ear to my heart, to see if it's still functioning, I suppose. Her hair, the only feature of hers that might be called attractive, feels soft and comforting. "Turn over."

When she sees the welts on my back, there's another lengthy entreaty to the Holy Mother and all the saints and to Christ and to God. And more curses at my tormentors. "How can men be so bad?" She lurches and swings to the table.

"Don't slip anything to him that you shouldn't," warns the jailer, who's not going anywhere.

She glares at him. "Did *you* do any of that?" she asks accusingly, nodding in my direction.

He lifts his hands, palms outward. "I don't do those things. I'm just a jailer. I've treated him good and all."

She snorts incredulously. She heats some mysterious liquid in a spoon over the candle and pours it onto my scars. It's excruciating, but when she's rubbed it in, kneading at me gently, the pain lessens considerably. "Now I must do the same to your front."

"What is that stuff?" I ask.

"Never you mind. I got it from an old blind witch in Pescara." She winks at me.

The jailer shudders.

When she's restored me, up to a point, with more peculiar medications, she fetches bandages.

"Uh-uh, no," tuts the jailer. "Not allowed."

"What's not allowed?"

"Any bandages or things like that."

"*In nome del Padre*, why not?"

"Strict instructions."

"Who from?"

"Can't say."

"How is he supposed to heal?"

"It's all right, Balbina, I'm better now," I say. "How are things at home?"

"Not too cheery without you around. Hostolana and Geanna are gloomy as sin. Giovanni mopes. Zinerva pretends not to worry, but she does. *Dottore* Ghiberti keeps saying he needs to get you books."

"And my father?"

"Your father's in low spirits."

"He's always in low spirits."

"Now they're lower."

"And Benvenuto? Has anyone heard from him?"

She shakes her head. "If he's written we won't know about it, unless it's something to make your father proud."

I clasp her hands tightly. "Tell everyone I'm all right, Balbina. I could be out of here soon."

She brightens. "Those scars'll come out nice in the end," she says, staring down at my blemished torso. "You'll look like *un delinquente*. Some girls like that. You've bulked up too—almost *un uomo vero*. Are those *muscles*?" She giggles.

The door is pushed open from without, and my familiar clutch of brawny guards stand there, legs slightly apart, handling their swords. Balbina looks at them in absolute terror.

"*Andiamo,*" one says, clicking his fingers.

"I'll be fine," I reassure her again, as her anxious, affectionate eyes follow me out.

33. A Meeting on the Stairs

Annibale Malipiero had felt the burdens of his profession slip from him as he'd been steered across the placid waters of the lagoon to his home on the Giudecca, and after a quick and indifferent meal with his dear wife, he had been dead to the world for a full eight hours.

Suitably refreshed, he was making his way down to Iago of Mantua's dungeon when he encountered the sweltering form of Bonifacio Colonna filling the stairwell before him.

"Thought I'd give the dog a taste of his own medicine," the giant announced. "Thought I'd give him a taste of the boot."

"Good Lord, man, did you hurt him?"

"That's the purpose of the device, is it not?" the other responded. "Howled a bit, but other than that, *niente*. He's a stubborn bastard."

Annibale Malipiero found himself shaking with rage. "Damn you!" he hissed. "Why could you not have applied the same rigor to my nephew? It was because you couldn't even touch the lout that we've had to release him! You with your blasted love of handsome boys!"

The great beast looked only mildly discomfited. The chief inquisitor calmed himself. "Can the man still walk?"

"Why should he need to walk?"

"Because when he walks, he talks."

"Why can't we just have him quartered, drawn, and hanged? Have him dangle and rot between the twin towers? The Council would approve, the Doge would approve—"

"Don't you *dare* let this get out—not to the Council, not to the Doge, *not to anyone.*"

A smile played on his associate's porcine lips.

"Oh, God, you have, haven't you?" Annibale Malipiero groaned. "Who have you told?"

"A friend or two."

"Please move back down the stairs so I can pass."

In trying to push by, the chief inquisitor now saw, over the shoulder of his prodigious adversary, the skeletal figure of Roberto Fabbri. Clutched in his desiccated talons was the bloodstained instrument of torture.

Annibale Malipiero grimaced. "Did you tell *your* friends too?"

Fabbri shook his shrunken head as energetically as he dared. Annibale Malipiero believed him; he *had* no friends.

"Damn it! Let me through!"

Bonifacio Colonna relented eventually, and he and his colleague shuffled up the stairs.

Iago of Mantua was lying on the floor of his cell, his knees pressed into his chest. His wrists had been manacled behind him, though not to the wall. The injuries to his legs and feet were hidden from view, but blood was spattered around his recumbent body.

Eyes wide, Gentile Stornello sat against the opposite wall, arms clasped tightly around his calves, emitting little squeaks of torment. His head bobbed as he did so.

The chief inquisitor eyed the trembling boy for a moment and then looked again at Iago. He went to the door, opened it, and slipped outside.

"Who shackled the man?" he hissed to the openmouthed guards. "I ordered you to take instruction from no one but myself! Give me the key."

He reentered the cell, touched the youngster's head briefly, then laid the key at Gentile Stornello's feet.

As he brushed past them like one possessed, the disquieted guards heard him mutter, or thought they did: "Let me not be mad, not mad . . ."

34. Sympathy for the Devil

I'm not much of a *conoscitore* when it comes to cruel spectacle. There's no paucity of it in Venice—especially in the Piazza di San Marco, with its daily floggings and gougings and cutting-to-bits and hangings—but I try to scurry by, averting my eyes. I'm fairly proud of my attentiveness to the many things going on around me, but I draw the line at sadism and severed limbs and gushing blood.

So I have now just witnessed what I can say with absolute certainty is the worst thing I've seen in my short life.

Iago of Mantua's leonine roars, the way he thrashed and screeched (although he never once pleaded for mercy—and he fought like a demon before the guards managed to hold him down and shackle his wrists), attested to the probability that even he had never known such pain. Although I've experienced the agony of torture myself, I still can't begin to imagine how *that* must have hurt.

They clamped the device—a kind of iron boot—around his lower leg and attached a small cylinder above the instep. There was, I soon discovered, a blade within it.

There was an enormous quantity of blood. Who would have thought that anyone could have so much in him? It spouted, like a roseate fountain—first from Iago of Mantua's left foot, and then from his right.

The fat and thin *interroganti* did not deign to look at me once during this whole procedure, and neither did they trouble to glance at me as they left the cell.

The chief inquisitor seemed almost as shocked as I was by what he saw. He left us briefly, and when he returned I felt the brush of a hand across my pate—as much consolation as he could offer me for the present—before he placed a small, shiny key at my feet.

Almost a day has passed since then. It has gone midnight now. Iago's wordless sobs have diminished, but he still jerks and quivers as he dozes. Pain reaches out to you even in sleep.

I've endeavored, with little application and no success, to talk to him.

"Is that the worst thing that's ever happened to you?" I blabbered. "It looks *bad*. You must have been wounded in the field though, in all those wars in which you fought." And: "I didn't think we did things like that here. I thought it was only the Turks. They can be absolute fiends, I've heard. They flay people alive, don't they? I expect you've seen stuff like that."

I've touched upon his childhood. "The more the body has to endure, the stronger it becomes, I think, so in a way you're probably better equipped than most to recover from injury . . . with that harsh life you've had . . . all that . . . privation when you were young."

I've pleaded with him to get better, saying (not entirely insincerely) that I miss our conversations, that I even miss our bursts of combat. "I'd still like to toughen up a bit more." I've gone so far as to suggest, in a conspiratorial whisper, that we won't have a hope of escaping unless he regains his strength. "You're right about that door. It's very flimsy. We could both ram it. If, as you said, we could overwhelm the guards, then grab their weapons . . ." I've affected defiance and disobedience in other ways too. "I should like to discuss further your idea of the world being turned upside down—it interests me greatly."

I manage to bring Desdemona into our still one-sided conversation by talking about my own love, and how being in prison and locked away from Franceschina has made me crave her all the more, and of how, once free, I shall certainly "enjoy" her—after I've killed Jacopo, of course, with his help maybe? I couldn't wait, I said, to tumble with her in a great big bed. I gabbled on, mumbling about women in general and how he, too, must miss their company, their warm caresses, their sweet breath, their heavenly touch, and all sorts of other faintly Petrarchan nonsense. "You must have had many in your time. I know so very little of the weaker sex and how to handle them . . . how to win them. Will you tell me how to do so?"

Before darkness finally fell upon us (about four hours ago, I think), I unlocked his manacles. The chief inquisitor says or does nothing without a reason. Iago of Mantua's fists barely moved as I released him. His fingers curled and stretched a little, but his hands stayed where they were, behind his back, as the cuffs clinked to the floor. There was no sign of relief or gratitude.

I scuttled away quickly, back to the position in which I'd sat all day, but my heart has gone out to him. How could it not? Can such a vulnerable, lamenting creature really be capable of immeasurable barbarism? It doesn't fit somehow.

35. A Fire at the Arsenal

A monstrous crack makes the earth itself shift. Dirt and dust and all manner of foul debris cascade onto my face. Creeping things scurry across my naked feet.

A cry beyond the door: "*Madonna mia, ma che fai? Cos'è quello?*"

Then another: "*È la fine dell' mondo!*"

Muttered prayers follow.

Now there are scuttling footsteps on the *molo*, and the barking of dogs, and the squawks of woken birds, and the flicker of torches—more and more of them. There must be hundreds of people up there. And the cry is taken up: "*L'Arsenale è in fiamme! L'Arsenale brucia!*"

The bells start to toll—first the Maleficio bell on the campanile, used to announce executions and to wake the city in an emergency—and soon it seems every bell in Venice. It's drummed into us from birth, as citizens, that if anything happens to the Arsenal, you go and help, no questions asked. If the Arsenal, our protector, is on fire, you run—not away from it but toward it, with your barrels and buckets.

"*Andiamo! È d'obligo aiutare! Andiamo! Affrettarte vi!*" Outside our cell, boots thunk upward and away.

Again the world shakes, and again. These are, I suppose, explosions. Fires at the Arsenal are not infrequent, with all that wood and tar and flaming furnaces to bend the iron, and are relatively easy to put out. But Benvenuto has warned me of explosions: "It's a powder keg in there—

one spark in the wrong spot and the whole damned place could go up, taking most of Venice with it."

A thin strip of light has appeared between the cell door and its frame, as if the bolts have shaken loose. I'm about to creep toward it when I'm grabbed, my arm twisted up behind my back, a hand clamped over my mouth.

"You will help me. If you do not, I shall kill you."

His breathing is quick, hard, determined. He's walking, in a fashion, but he's obviously finding it difficult.

I whimper through his hand.

"*Silence.* There may still be someone out there."

We're at the door.

"Open it—slowly."

He releases my arm but keeps a hand over my mouth. He stands behind me, panting, as I do so just enough for him to poke his head through.

"Good. Come."

He lets go of my mouth and buckles a little as he limps out. I follow. The antechamber is empty. The light from the four or five sconces is momentarily blinding. Once we're accustomed to it, I can see an array of weapons leaning against the wall. More quickly than seems possible for someone so crippled, he's beside them. "Here, take this and this . . ."

He throws me a small *pugnale* and a sheathed sword attached to a belt. I fail to catch either. The noise they make as they hit the floor sounds deafening.

"Damn you," he says, "you're going to have to learn fast."

Without thinking, I buckle the sword belt around my waist.

He's at the bottom of the stairs, still bent almost double, beckoning me. Then a jolt of agony passes through him and he grabs his foot. He gasps. "*God this* hurts!"

"It needs binding," I say.

"No time for that; come."

"I know where there are bandages."

"Where?"

"In my own cell, upstairs."

The news that I have had my own cell all this time doesn't seem to surprise him. "You know the way?"

"I've done the journey a thousand times."

"Is it far?"

"A couple of flights, that's it."

"Take me . . . take hold of me. Come."

I've no idea why I've suggested this. Perhaps I'm hoping that someone up there will catch us and this whole ludicrous adventure will reach a hasty conclusion. *There's no way we're going to be able to get out of here.*

I take hold of him under both arms. God, he's heavy. He can hardly move a limb. But I feel an extraordinary strength in him, a potency of will. We make it, huffing and dragging and lurching, inch by excruciating inch, to the junction in the stairs. Coming down toward us is a guard—one I've not seen before. He's young, not as heavily built and thuggish as those I've known. He stops. He's not armed. What he's doing here I don't know. He has the choice of jumping me or turning around and running. He elects to do the first and lands on my upturned *pugnale*.

I can't tell if it's entered his chest or his stomach. I hope it's the latter and that someone will come and rescue him before he breathes his last. With a horrible bark of anguish, he tumbles on top of me and therefore on top of Iago. The two of us fall backward.

We manage somehow to free ourselves and clamber on.

"Have I killed him, do you think?"

We reach the top of the stairs. The passageway leading to my cell feels ghostly in its emptiness and silence. It's better lit than usual though; more sconces glimmer on the walls.

As we get closer, I hear again the cries of the populace. *"Fretta! Fretta! Deve salvare l'Arsenale! Fa presto!"* I envy their fleetness of foot, their liberty, as I struggle with my own burden.

My jailer is nowhere to be seen, and the cell door is open. Balbina, bless her, has left her medicinal accoutrements laid neatly on the table, though not, I think, for the benefit of Venice's most heinous villain. I try to be as delicate as she is, but he doesn't have the patience for that. "Hurry up! No no! I don't need any damned potions or ointments; just bind my feet!"

So that's what I do.

"Tighter, damn it!"

"I think we should take these . . ." I pick up the *borsa* that Balbina has also left and fill it with bottles and jars, spoons and knives, and finally the candle.

"Why?"

"Because you are very badly injured, and sooner or later you're going to require proper treatment."

"Pah! Let's go. You know the way out of here?"

"Of course I don't. I'm a prisoner, like you." But I do have a faint recollection of the warren of corridors that the chief inquisitor led me through as he chortled about the impenetrability of the *prigioni*.

"Follow me," I say.

He grabs my arm. "Don't think of running off," he growls, "or I shall kill you. If I do not do it personally, I shall ensure it. I have friends, *Turkish* friends. They will hunt you down."

Some passageways are lit, though sparsely, while others simply lead into formless darkness. I feel like Theseus in the labyrinth, guided by Ariadne's thread.

"Why are you staying in the light, lad?"

"If we don't, we'll get completely lost."

Still there's nobody to prevent our halting progress. The only sounds are our shuffles, his arduous breathing, and water dripping on stone. Even the shouts from beyond the door, which I can now make out before me, seem to have faded.

The door is neither bolted nor locked.

The *riva* is deserted. Whoops of amazement, shrieks of horror, and shrill commands filter across it from the Arsenal. It's colder out here than I'd thought it would be, for the days have been stifling, at least in the *prigioni*. I feel faint at the clarity of the air.

"We must find a boat," he whispers. He's caught hold of my arm again, forcing it once more into my back, with surprising strength. He pushes me toward the jetties, clustered side by side along the rim of the *bacino*, where unmanned gondolas and skiffs and tenders and fishing smacks bob.

But not everyone's gone to the Arsenal. Out of the night, out of nowhere, half a dozen figures in cloaks and hoods fall upon us. Are these the *Signori di Notte*? No, their garb is improvised, hurriedly donned. Also, they don't appear to have any weapons.

With staggering speed, Iago has unsheathed the sword that hung at my waist and is swiping it this way and that, with both fists, roaring like a lion. They skip aside, back off a touch, but still play with him, taunting and challenging him, hopping and prancing. He's like a goaded beast. Eventually, though, the weight of the sword and the effort of handling it deflate him. He's bent forward and on his knees, head down, gasping, supporting himself on one hand, the other holding his leg just above the ankle. The sword lies beside him. One of our attackers makes to grab it.

I don't think I'll ever be able to explain, to the end of my days (and that may well be sooner rather than later), why I do what I do next. Something emboldens me. Something makes me need to save the Mantuan. My nerves jangle. I feel the rush of blood through my every sinew. I'm burning. I reach for the sword's hilt before it can be snatched away. I pick it up. In calmer circumstances, I might not have been able to even lift it. But now I have the strength of rage. In imitation of Iago of Mantua—and I'm of course nimbler than he at the moment—I whirl it up and over my head, around and around. I hear cloth ripped by iron, a cry that is more of a gurgle, and the thud of limbs on stone.

I don't dare look, and I can't anyway, because Iago has me once again by the wrist and he's pulling me closer to the water's edge.

"Find me a boat!" he demands. Our assailants have scuttled off into blackness, as fast as they came upon us—aside, that is, from the one I may have just slain.

"Have I killed him? Have I killed two people?"

"You might have. *Get me a boat!*"

A whisper. "Gentile, come quickly, over here."

Time slows for a while—as it can in moments of great shock or danger—or indeed delight . . .

Standing uneasily upon a particularly fragile-looking landing stage, holding a big bag in one hand and in the other a rope that leads to a small rowboat, is the cleverest and probably the least courageous man I know. My eyes don't stay on him for long, however, because next to him, cloaked against the chill of a morning fast approaching, is my angel, come to save me.

My sword is still in my hand. She stares at it. Her full lips widen. I sheathe it.

I return to Iago of Mantua, haul him up, and help him hobble to the creaking planks of the *imbarcadero*.

"Who are these?" he asks warily.

"This is my tutor, Dottore Baldassare Ghiberti of the University of Padua, and this," I say with a flourish of pride, "is Franceschina."

Part

III

36. Escape

Baldassare can't row; I can't row; Iago of Mantua certainly can't row at the moment. Franceschina, it turns out, *can* row. I tried, and the wobbling vessel just went around and around, going nowhere, until, with a sniff of impatience, she pushed me aside and took hold of the oars herself.

Iago is lying at the bottom of the boat, groaning, and Baldassare sits at the stern, clutching hard onto the gunwales. He looks as if he is carrying a thousand riddles in his head.

Behind him the sun is rising over the *bacino*, so for a while my tutor has a yellow halo. To his right I can see plumes of black smoke rising into the pink-tinged sky. There are no flames. The fire's been put out. Not much of the rest of Venice has been damaged, as far as I can tell. The people of *La Serenissima* have had their excitement for the night and are making their way to work. I wonder how soon the cry will go up: "*L'assassino è scappato! Il brutto è scomparso!*"

It looks like it'll be a hot, clear day. I'm seated at the bow, so Franceschina has her back to me. In the vigor of her rowing, she's allowed her cloak to slip, revealing a bare brown shoulder. Enthralled, I watch her sleek sinews contract and relax, her skin shine.

The water was like glass until stirred by the awakening lagoon traffic. We are now traveling along the great shipway that is the Giudecca Canal. Already there are cargo-heavy hulks out here, the ones that are too big for the Grand Canal. Franceschina may be a good rower, but she's not used to negotiating a tiny skiff through this assemblage of mercantile giants. Lookouts call from way above us. "*Fa attenzione! Avanti! Muoversi! Velocemente!*"

"I suggest we get out to sea as soon as possible," says Baldassare, although he doesn't look too happy at the prospect.

Franceschina is whispering something. I lean forward. She smells sweet. "Where are we supposed to be going?" she asks beneath her breath. Our own agonized cargo appears to be unconscious for the moment, sleeping off the pain.

"I've no idea," I whisper back. "Weren't you given instructions?"

She shrugs. "I was told to wait on the *molo* outside the *prigioni* and that you would be there."

I lean farther, to be absolutely certain that we're not heard by Iago. "Who told you this?"

Again her glorious shoulders rise and fall. "The *capo degli interroganti, Il Terribile*," she murmurs.

"You knew who he was?"

"He is Signor Jacopo's uncle. He has been to the palazzo before."

"When?"

"Two times—"

But now Iago roars, "Get me to *terra firma*, and be quick about it!"

"We should make for Mestre," Baldassare suggests apprehensively.

"No! No! No towns!" Iago hollers. "Go south!"

"There. Go down there . . ." I point to a narrow canal on the Giudecca that seems to head southward. As I'm not out on the lagoon much, my knowledge of its geography is hazy, to say the least. Franceschina swings the boat in that direction.

Baldassare has made the journey to and from the mainland many times. His obligations in Padua require it, although the voyage terrifies him. "Is this the right way?" I ask him.

He nods. "It can get rough once we're on the other side though. . . ."

37. Terra Firma

It was not a regular habit of Annibale Malipiero's to squat behind trees or scramble through thorny undergrowth, half bent for the most part, which was not good for his back, or to sink, sometimes up to his waist, in bogs, or to stumble and fall on jagged stones.

Worse still, this new venture had entailed travel upon water, his least favorite element. He'd never liked the journey to his villa on the Brenta, but he'd borne it because of what awaited him, and the trip to the canal's mouth at Mestre was generally short enough to be bearable. On this occasion, though, the lagoon had been, in his stout boatman Ercole's words, "angry at something, lord, and higher than I've ever known her." *Terra firma* had lived up to its name, despite its own moist uncertainty; it felt solid, fixed, positively hospitable in its reliability—at least compared to the tempestuous hour or so he'd passed in the bilge of the gondola, clinging to its sides so as not to be thrown overboard and being vigorously sick.

And the chief inquisitor had reason to feel relatively gratified with the way things had turned out so far.

The fire at the Arsenal had been successfully doused. It was a fairly minor conflagration in the history of such events. The gunpowder explosions had made it seem more portentous than it was, which had been his intention. Nobody had died—aside, that was, from the bumptious serving boy Paganello, whom he'd instructed to ignite the spark that had set the great shipyard ablaze. The brat simply hadn't run away quickly enough, which was perhaps for the best, as his silence could not have been assured.

All of Venice had sped to save the Arsenal—including those guarding Iago, after they'd been reminded of their duties to the Republic. Once he was alone, Annibale Malipiero had lit wall sconces in certain passageways in the Prigioni Ducale and extinguished others. Then he had quietly unlocked the cell door.

Gentile Stornello had proved as astute as he'd hoped, resolutely following the route laid out for him. He had also demonstrated a surprising aptitude for combat. He seemed have become a dab hand with dagger and sword, at least when under threat. Thankfully, the young guard whom Annibale Malipiero had instructed to hasten back down to the dungeon (he'd thought it best the *prigioni* did not appear to be entirely empty) had survived. So had the man he'd told, along with others, to attack Gentile Stornello and Iago on the *riva*.

He was thus more than content, especially at the sight of the incongruous foursome—the boy, the girl, the plump academic, and Venice's most-wanted criminal—still trying to get their bearings, it seemed, for they had only just disembarked from the small and deliberately unostentatious craft he'd provided on a narrow strand of mud and shingle some fifteen miles south of Mestre.

Thanks to Ercole's dexterity on the roughest of seas, he himself had landed well before them and farther north. He'd already dispatched half a dozen of his most loyal spies to the mainland. One of these had spotted the little boat being pummeled this way and that by the lofty swell and heading inexorably southward, as Iago, despite his injuries, endeavored to steer it toward the coastline. Thus Annibale Malipiero had had the time to be there shortly after the group finally beached.

Now he crouched, half sunk in the silt between the strand and the waterlogged flatland that seemed to stretch westward for miles behind him, tall grasses smacking against his face in the considerable wind, and he watched.

Iago was seated about fifty feet away, with his back to the *interro-*

gante and with his knees up to his chin. He was digging into a bag beside him and stuffing cheese and bread and sausages into his mouth. Next to him, staring out at the waves, sat Gentile Stornello.

"They had to lift him out of the boat and carry him ashore," whispered the man hunkered down beside Annibale Malipiero, "the lad and the fat bloke."

The tutor, at the shoreline itself, was squealing indistinguishable complaints and skipping to avoid the biggest rollers while dipping and flapping his hands in the water. Evidently he was trying to retrieve something from the surf.

"Says he's lost all his books and papers and quills . . ."

"The papers and quills will have to be replaced," Annibale Malipiero muttered.

Some feet away from Iago and the boy, the girl was also whining about something, squatting on her haunches, her cloak on the ground, squeezing water from her hair. She, too, was soaked through.

Suddenly she got up, turned almost directly toward the watchers—making them drop down into the reed bed—and began to stomp away along the beach.

Iago spun his head. "Where's she going? You! Girl! Come back here!"

"I need to dry off, and I'm not doing it in front of you!" She was clearly full of spirit and not frightened of much.

"Follow her!" Iago snapped to the youth, who immediately stood. "And if either of you runs, you won't get far! I have friends here on the mainland!"

Friends? the inquisitor pondered: *What friends?*

The threat made the boy pause briefly before pursuing the girl. She was heading for the only discernible building, presumably once a fisherman's shelter, now half collapsed, with a roof mostly open to the sky.

"She'll be getting naked in there, I reckon," the inquisitor's lookout chuckled quietly. "That'd be a sight to see."

"That's enough of that, thank you," said Annibale Malipiero, as the boy followed her inside.

He could not, of course, resist approaching the hut, though it involved more bending and scuttling under cover of the reeds. He had already begun to resign himself to such discomfort in the coming days or weeks, or however long it took to get to the truth.

He knew that there would be more listening, as he was doing now and had done with his ear stuck to the door of Iago's cell (more fruit-fully once the thinner one had been installed).

Hidden, he hoped, from Iago's view by rubble and weeds, he heard the clank of a bucket, and a plash of water. "Ay! Ay! Go away!" She was annoyed at having had her ablutions intruded upon.

Then the talk was clipped, urgent, and mistrustful. And *he*, initially at least, was its main subject.

Despite the girl's protests, Gentile Stornello wasn't going anywhere. "You said Jacopo's uncle had been to the palazzo two times before yesterday. Tell me about those visits."

"Why?"

"Because I need to know why we're here, Franceschina. Why you're here, why my tutor is here, why I was allowed to escape."

"Who is that man you escaped with anyway?"

"I can't say."

"Why not?"

"Because if I did you'd probably run, and I don't want you to do that. He's dangerous, that's all you need to know."

"He doesn't look dangerous. He's badly hurt. He can't walk."

"Tell me, Franceschina, when did the inquisitor come to the palazzo?"

"The first time was when he took Signor Jacopo away."

"To prison?"

"No not then. He just wanted to talk to him then."

"And the second time?"

"After Signor Jacopo had been in prison, he brought him back."

"Did he say anything to you?"

"Yes . . ." She was nervous, reluctant.

"What?"

"The first time he . . . he said the palazzo was a bad place and that I should leave it."

"With good reason," Annibale Malipiero heard the boy mutter. "And what did the *interrogante* say to you when he brought Jacopo back from prison?"

"He . . . just said he might have need of me . . . that there was something I may have to do and that I must tell no one. That is all."

"And you stayed at the palazzo after that? Even though Jacopo's uncle had told you before to leave the place?" All the anger and resentment that must have been building in Gentile Stornello could clearly be suppressed no longer. "You know Jacopo Malipiero killed Fabietto Dandolo! He must have told you, he must have boasted about it! And I have been accused of the murder! Did he not crow about that too?"

"Ay! *Basta!*" It was quite a wail, loud enough to ring across the beach. Iago heard it. Annibale Malipiero ducked.

"Scholar!" he now heard the villain bawl. "Stop floundering and flapping and come and help me!"

But within the shelter, the girl had not finished. "Why do you ask me all these questions? Are you an inquisitor too? Stop now! Where could I go anyway? And I don't care what your *interrogante* thinks. I don't care! I want to go home!"

The *interrogante* in question found himself crawling across mud and sand on his stomach, as silently as he could, around the side of the collapsed hut. If he'd stayed where he was, he'd have been spotted, because Iago was now being half dragged, half carried, in his direction by a gasping and sweating academic.

"Don't go," Annibale Malipiero heard Gentile Stornello plead, softly all of a sudden. "Please stay. Look . . . look . . . I have your handkerchief—the one you gave me to stanch the blood? Look. I've had it with me all this time. I shall keep it with me forever."

There was no audible reaction from the girl.

"This looks cozy . . ." Iago was shockingly close. "Please do not let me interrupt. Forgive me, *Signorina*, for the impertinence. I do not wish to impose."

The chief inquisitor would very much have liked to have seen the brute's face. Did it match the mannerliness of his words? Supposedly so, for the girl's voice was now a flurry of breathy reassurance.

"No . . . no . . . please." There was the scraping of what may have been a chair. "Please sit."

"Thank you, dear lady, how kind you are. You are from these parts?"

"No, no, from near Asolo—much farther north."

They might have just met at a party.

"I know it. A pretty town. What's the church there? Santa Maria di . . ."

"Breda."

"You pray there?"

"When I am in the town, but I come from the country around—"

"I think you pray a lot."

"I try to."

"I think when God looks down on you, he likes what he sees."

"Can I get you water? There's a spring."

"Thank you. You *are* kind."

"Are your feet very badly harmed?"

"Pah! It's nothing. They'll soon mend."

"They need redressing."

"Yes, they do, and by softer hands than those that dressed them first."

The girl tittered slightly. Then, in a more familiarly crusty voice, Iago said, "But in the meanwhile I've a need for a conveyance."

"Con . . . ?"

"Something to carry a person around on," Gentile Stornello explained glumly.

Suddenly the Mantuan was giving barked instructions, as a sergeant might to those awaiting his command. "This chair attached to that—the bedposts there. You! Brainbox! Dismantle that bed, break the frame, and you, lad, look for cord, from flock, or hemp, or flax, or whatever fiber you can find hereabouts, and make me a carriage!"

Annibale Malipiero had to lie on his belly for quite a time as he listened to clangings and bangings within the shelter and to Iago's occasional hisses of pain as the girl tended to his wounds. At one point he managed to haul himself far enough to peer around a corner of the dilapidated structure and saw Gentile Stornello doing as he'd been bidden, searching blankly amid the marshes behind the strand for the necessary bindings that nature might provide. The boy was too far away for the *interrogante* to give him any indication of his presence without being heard. If he'd been nearer, Annibale Malipiero might have tried to let him know he was there—if only to give the lad some reassurance.

Once Gentile Stornello had found enough grasses and rushes and other reedy plants to carry a great bale of them in his arms, he reentered the ruin. Expecting the emergence of Iago at any moment, *Il Terribile*—feeling anything but terrifying—managed to scramble, back to where the spy in his employ remained crouched. Now there were two more men there.

"There's soldiers landing," said one of them.

"Soldiers? Venetian soldiers? Where?"

"Just up the coast." The man pointed north.

So word of Iago's escape, within half a day of its occurrence, had already reached the ears of those with the authority to dispatch troops to find him. Soon these marshes would be crawling with militia.

Annibale Malipiero gazed at the unprepossessing beach. There appeared to be a single relatively solid route through the wetlands around it, via a small clump of trees to his right, leading south. "That's the only way anyone can leave here. We'll wait there, hide when they pass us, and then follow."

His other three men were already waiting in the thicket. "We will need to engineer distractions. Above all else, he *must not be caught*. Lay false scents, put down snares, create misleading trails. You know what to do. Pretend to be him, so as to confuse his pursuers. Cry out if need be, but do not, *do not*, reveal yourselves to him."

The men nodded eagerly.

"He said he had friends out here. Turks, unless I'm very much mistaken. Keep an eye out. You know their reputation."

They nodded again, though not so animatedly. One said, "Why can't we just nab him? We'd get the glory."

The chief inquisitor gave the fellow a contemptuous glare. "I did not allow him to flee so that he could just be 'nabbed,' as you put it. There are things I want to—I need to—know!" He said it with some force and with such a zealous gleam in his eye and tightening of his fists that the men around him flinched. They never fully understood the intentions of the man who paid them, but he paid them well so they were usually dependable and unquestioning. He decided nonetheless to send the one disputant out on a mission of his own. "You! Go find paper and ink and quills and a bag to carry them in."

"And where am I supposed to find those?"

"Go to Mestre and buy them if necessary. But come back quickly. I told the tubby one to write me reports, and reports he shall write."

Then, from the broken building at the other end of the beach, the Mantuan emerged, seated in a chair borne between two poles carried at either end by Gentile Stornello and Dottore Baldassare Ghiberti, both of them severely burdened. Iago, by contrast, looked jocose. The girl followed at some distance, head bowed.

It was in its way a processional. Iago had the air of a potentate, enjoying his sovereignty, glancing to right and to left, grinning from ear to ear, and issuing directions to his groaning minions.

Annibale Malipiero was uncomfortably reminded for a moment of the Doge in his own *portantina*. A new *Capo di Capi* had been elected only recently—the favorite for the post, Andrea Gritti, a seasoned soldier who by repute had no time for irresolution or ineptitude. He, the Chief Inquisitor surmised, would not be best pleased at the news that *La Serenissima*'s most famous prisoner was no longer her prisoner. And who would be held to account for the disaster? None other than he who had the ultimate responsibility for keeping criminals under lock and key.

But *Il Terribile* endeavored to remain optimistic still, reminding himself, for the umpteenth time, that all had gone well—thus far.

The bizarre little *corteo* was getting ever closer. As he'd already observed, there was no other means of leaving the beach.

"For God's sake, conceal yourselves," he whispered. His picked men were good at that.

38. Notes from an Academic

Well over a week after the first sighting on the beach south of Mestre, by which time Iago seemed farther west but no farther north or inland in any advantageous way, Annibale Malipiero and his six doughty men were crouched behind a low wall, fairly certain that the criminal was close by.

One of the number had espied, he was sure, a glistening sunburned pate popping up now and then above the rushes. The whoops and challenges of others in pursuit of the villain, growing in both quantity and noisiness by the day, resonated all around them, but they themselves had remained silent and thus had got nearer than most. There'd been no other sound, however, from Iago and his companions, nor any sign of motion.

As a result of having been in the same position for most of a morning and half an afternoon, in hot sun and then hard rain, the chief inquisitor's back was hurting profoundly. Another thunderous shower had just passed over him. With his sodden wide-brimmed hat over his ears (he hated hats, especially big ones; they made one less alert), he was feeling dejected almost to the point of abandonment.

He'd learned nothing. There had not been a single scribble from the tutor, despite new quills and ink and paper having been left, concealed only a little, beside a path down which Iago and his companions would have had no option but to travel. Perhaps the tutor had not espied his new provisions. Perhaps Iago had noticed them first. Perhaps the whole notion, of communicating with an academic—not renowned for practicality—via notes stuck between twigs or lodged into the crevices of walls, as he'd diligently instructed Baldassare Ghiberti to do before this whole adventure had commenced, was preposterous.

He was chastising himself for the haste with which he'd committed to this part of the plan when he was handed a neatly folded wad of papers. "They were in that mass of nettles," the finder whispered. "*Dio santo*, I got stung."

It wasn't so much a missive as a dissertation, with many an addendum. There was also quite a lot of Latin and some Greek. The *interrogante* had forgotten most of the Latin he'd learned at school, and still more of the Greek.

Esteemed Signors,

I trust you are well. I am not one who regularly relies on the efficacy of prayer. I am, as a humanist who once had the privilege to study under the tutelage of Pico della Mirandola, author of that fine work De Hominis Dignitate, *when he was briefly in Florence, a believer, as he was, in the power of the human will and in the idea that our individual fate lies largely in our own hands.*

However, there are instances in life when even a humanist must pray to God in the hope of being heard—or to the gods, for I am an adherent of the view held by my great mentor Pico della Mirandola that all religions, past and present, fundamentally subscribe to a Supreme Force that differs only in detail. I have made the voyage from Venice to the mainland coast frequently, for I have, as you know, regular professional obligations in Padua, where I teach grammar, rhetoric, history, poetry, and moral philosophy. Never before, though, have I endured so fearsome a crossing as I did some days ago. It rivaled those of Odysseus, I feel, as described thus by Homer, the greatest of all poets. . . .

Then came the Greek, several lines of it.

I myself called out for mercy, as Odysseus did many times, to the gods of the sky and of the deep—Zeus, Heracles, Poseidon, all his daughters . . .

Et cetera, et cetera.

. . . and it would seem my prayers were answered. We survived. I am encouraged by the inference thereby that whatever dangers my pupil and I may encounter in the days to come, we are being looked upon favorably by, as Herodotus called them, the heavenly governors of all mortal fate. I must give an account of what has occurred—as you have commanded me to do—from the moment of my first spying Gentile Stornello and the villain you call Iago of Mantua outside the Prigioni Ducale as of the Monday morning before the last one, shortly before dawn.

There was what the French call "un contretemps," in which one of the cloaked attackers was severely injured. If it is the case that the man has died from his wounds, I beg you to understand that Gentile Stornello had no choice but to act in his own defense and did so with great courage, in my humble opinion.

The serving girl was also present and remains so. I have cogitated upon the grounds for her accompanying us and must assume you are aware of Gentile Stornello's affection for her, a fondness I have endeavored to discourage—to quote his own favorite poet, Petrarch, "Youth longs only for what is dazzling"—but it is my view that you have placed her with us to give him some comfort.

The journey from Venice to the mainland was, as I have already stated, of Homeric proportions (see above).

It may be of interest to you to know that Iago has, from the moment we disembarked, declared a repeated wish to travel to Mantua—the place of his birth, I deduce—with all haste. "Haste," I fear, is not an option. There are several reasons for this. Firstly, the storm blew us farther south than calmer waters would have done, so we are reliant on foot travel solely. We are now heading north toward the Brenta Canal, with a view to stealing a boat in which we can then travel on to Padua. This brings me to the second reason for our journey being more "cyclicus," as the Ancient Romans would describe it. The terrain we must cross is marshy, rough, and uncertain. It is often difficult to know where to tread and where not to, and there are few perceptible paths. The girl, being "puella rustica," seems practiced in such circumstances, and we frequently rely on her to guide us through the uncongenial landscape.

A third impediment in our progress is the state of Iago himself. Both his feet were severely wounded, though not broken, in prison, I am supposing under torture. I presume that, as the Capo degli Interroganti, you are aware of this. As a consequence, he can walk only with great difficulty and for the most part has to be carried, either by me, with my arms beneath his shoulders or under his knees (and I am not a strong man), or by Gentile Stornello (who is far sturdier than I—indeed, he appears to have grown in strength and build recently, quite the "giovanotto solido," as Petrarch would say, or "ben proporzionato"). But it would seem that Iago prefers me to be the bearer. I have a suspicion he relishes my discomfiture, as he has often said that he despises scholars. I should mention in passing that he taunts me very often for what he calls my "braininess"—which generally I take in good part, for it is a burden we intellectuals must endure from those less advantaged with insight; as Pericles called them, οἱ πολλοί—or "the masses"—as distinct from οἱ ὀλίγοι, "the few."

He has also had us build him what one might call a palanquin, a carriage constructed of a chair set between two rods from a bed frame, and when Gentile and I convey him on this contraption, our advancement is marginally more speedy—though even then it can be perilous, as we frequently trip or slip and send our cargo toppling into bogs and mudflats. You may wish to know that Iago claims to have seen such a type of transport in Cyprus.

The fourth and final hindrance to speedy or direct travel to our intended destination, and the most thwarting, is that we are no longer alone out here. Over recent days, and with developing fervor, we are being pursued, by whom I cannot tell precisely, though I would venture from the dialect when they call out that most of our harriers are Venetian. How many of these there are, we have no way of knowing either. There could be hundreds, or there could be a handful moving about to deceive us as to their true number. We scarcely see them, and then only as the top of a head emerging above the grass or as a shape scurrying through the brush or from tree to tree.

None has yet seen us, or if they have they have not approached. Per-

*haps they do not dare, for if they know whom they are chasing, as I pre-
sume they do, they will be fearful of his reputation. But as a consequence
of their persistent presence, we must be more circumspect than we would
otherwise be, lying low during the day and traveling farther only when
darkness comes. This, too, has delayed us in our journey. To avoid the
pursuers, we have sometimes had to retrace our steps, going south, west,
east, any direction but north.*

*On occasion, however, Iago has decided to break cover. He is, we have
learned, what Plautus has called a "triconis," or "mischief-maker." He
can risk discovery, or so it seems to me, merely for the excitement he gets
from doing so. He has laughed aloud, he has even cried out to our hunt-
ers, badgering them to entrap him. He is often assisted in this trouble-
someness by the girl, who appears to find delight in the exercise. With her
"ars rustica," already referred to, she has pressed down misleading routes
through the high grass, or left delusive footprints, and has been unable to
conceal her amusement as our chasers are led into morasses and quick-
sand, clapping her hands and squealing with joy.*

*Iago claims that he has other helpers out here. These are, he says, his
"Turkish friends," who have been awaiting his escape. We have not met
them, or seen them, I think, and he has not communicated with them,
but there is undoubtedly someone other than us who is disorienting those
who are after us. Man traps are being laid, of the kind used to catch
poachers, and sham makeshift causeways have been built out of fallen
branches, which collapse when trodden on. These men too—and again I
cannot say how many of them there are—will call out, imitating Iago's
voice, making him seem "ubique atque nunquam": here at one moment,
nowhere near the next. He has also told us that were we of a mind to flee
his company, these mysterious associates of his would soon track us down
and kill us. He has described in detail the Turkish methods of treating
their captives, which are, as I am sure you know, "inhumanus" and
"cruentus." He has not spoken thus to the girl, however, as he seems not to
wish to alarm her.*

*He has become fond of the girl. Initially, Signor, I thought his liking for
her was merely due to her youth and her "pulchritudinis," or "venustas,"
as he has looked upon her with a demeanor that can only be described as*

"salax," or libidinous. But she herself is showing some sympathy for Iago and has proved skilled in tending to his injuries, with the bandages and medicaments that Gentile Stornello had the foresight, or luck, to bring with him. Iago often calls her his "sweet nurse" or his "ministering signorina"—or at moments, absurdly in my view, his "principessa ono-rata."

She has also become a provider of sustenance. We have long since run out of the supplies I brought with me from Venice, many of which ended up in the lagoon anyway, and most of the remainder of which Iago quickly commandeered for his own consumption. Again, being of rural extraction, the girl knows what is edible and what is not with regard to various forms of vegetation. She is similarly proficient at catching and skinning the smaller animals we encounter and once suggested we might roast a rabbit she had tracked to its burrow, deftly thrusting her hand into the hole and pulling it out. But Iago is—sagaciously, I daresay—insistent that on no account should a fire be lit. So we subsist on berries and leaves and grasses and weeds and whatever unprepared cereals we can find, such as oats and maize and wheat, like herbivores. There is little indication of organized cultivation or farming or husbandry in this waterlogged territory. There is evidence of the growing of rice along parts of the estuary across which we travel, but rice is not digestible unless cooked. My constitution, which has never been vigorous, is suffering accordingly. Iago, in his uncouthness, is less discriminating and will eat just about anything—lizards, snakes, rats, toads—so he receives his necessary supply of nutrition thereby, even though they are raw. He once tried to force a live frog down my throat, much to his glee, and it made the girl laugh too.

She does not of course yet know who he is, as no one has enlightened her. He has not told her, as he has indeed not told any of us, and, in line with your directive, I have been careful not to let him think I might know or to let the girl know. Gentile Stornello has also remained silent on the matter of his true identity. I am assuming, although I have not discussed this with him, that he is under similar instructions.

I have not informed Gentile Stornello that I am in contact with you, Signor, again as you directed. I am claiming, as I write this epistle, to be continuing with my treatise on Theocritus, a comprehensive and I hope definitive discourse, which I should be very pleased to send you when it is completed. Iago himself has just asked me what I am "scribbling," as he puts it, and I have told him the same. He has not, of course, heard of Theocritus.

I have been able to have no private communication with Gentile in any event, as we are never away from Iago. Even when the man appears to be asleep, I have the strong sense he isn't. Added to that, my pupil, while he displays courage and stamina (I have always recognized an inner strength in him, "a man in the making," who will someday make Plato proud), has become increasingly "miserabilis" and therefore uncharacteristically and glumly silent. He is certain, without hesitation, that he is in love with the servant girl. Many is the time that I have censured him for falling for beauty alone, and Theocritus writes that "beauty is an evil in an ivory setting." Now, I do not contend that the girl is in that sense evil, or "malefica," but her concentration, credulous as she is, seems fixed on Iago, who appears capable of a degree of "blanditia" toward her (by which I mean "charm" or "blandishments"). She responds accordingly, by attending to his injuries and listening to the stories he has to tell of his adventures as a soldier in many places and of his childhood and adolescence, which he calls "arduous" and "destitute." While he will not permit us to speak at any length, and when we say anything we must do it "sotto voce," he does not seem to apply the same constraints to himself. He will often mention, when so inclined, the deprivations of his early life, when he was, he says, of the age that Gentile Stornello and the girl are at now and indeed before, from the moment of his being brought into the world, or so he claims. The girl will only listen, enthralled, and has now and then even put a hand out to him in solicitude. Gentile Stornello, therefore, like a besotted Lycidas, pines for her notice, and I have observed him glare with some jealousy at Iago, rather as if the man were a rival in love.

Esteemed Signor, that is all that I have to report for the time being. I hope you find this manuscript and will confirm that you have by removing it and replacing it with a reply of your own, as arranged. I cannot in any case write more, for Iago has begun to look at me with "circumspicientia." He has not yet asked to read what I am writing, but I am in perpetual fear of his doing so. We are currently entrenched in a saturated, mosquito-ridden fen only a small distance from the wall in which I intend to insert this document, and I shall, when unobserved, duly do this. We are still several miles, I would estimate, from the Brenta Canal.

There was no more, which was something of a relief. Annibale Malipiero clicked his fingers and ordered, "Bring me paper and a quill and ink, now!" He scrawled:

Dottore, It may lessen the danger of your arousing suspicion if you were to be altogether less protracted. Most of what you have written I know already, as I am often close by. Please restrict your reports to what the villain SAYS. I have no interest in anything else, least of all your OPINIONS. Please do not leave further correspondence in beds of NETTLES, or any injurious plant. And, I beg you, no more Latin or Greek.

The response, left in the depths of a hawthorn bush, was short and mildly indignant.

Forgive me; as a scholar of some renown, I am not used to "brevitas." Alas, I am in no position to know what Iago has said recently, and neither is Gentile Stornello, as the man speaks only to the girl, and in a very low voice. Her response, though I know this will not interest you, is simply to sigh, and sometimes to gasp, and occasionally to titter.

The chief inquisitor replied:

Yes, you are right, the girl does not matter. In your first missive you said he had spoken of an indigent childhood and youth. CAN YOU REMEMBER THE DETAILS?

Baldassare Ghiberti wrote:

No, or rather, there are no details that he's chosen to relay directly to myself or Gentile Stornello. He speaks only in general terms, of extreme poverty as a child and of his having had to make his own way in the world since then. The vagueness of these assertions leads me to suspect they are inventions designed merely to evoke sympathy. "Non accrede dicti de nebulo."

Annibale Malipiero retorted:

Again, please no LATIN and no OPINIONS. WHERE ARE YOU NOW?

The rejoinder was speedy:

I conclude we are but a mile or two from the Brenta, though which part I do not know. The ground is firmer at last. WHERE ARE YOU?

The *interrogante* informed him:

Nearby, as usual. Never far. Try to ask him more about his nurture, or get Gentile Stornello to do so, or listen in on the girl's questions, if she has them, and his answers.

The academic jotted back:

My pupil is still moping. Iago is now ignoring me entirely, which I consider a merciful respite from his earlier gibing, so to try to engage with him would be both unsettling and suspect.

Sitting on a boulder, which itself sat on firmer ground than he'd become used to in the fortnight or so that had now passed, Annibale Malipiero kicked impatiently at the stones that lay at his feet. Darkness was descending. He missed his bed in Venice. He hated sleeping, or endeavoring to sleep, in the open. How did soldiers manage it? It was even worse when one had to do so in the day, which was his only option, as Iago and his party moved on, and so had to be followed, at night.

A sudden and tormented cry pierced the silence, sending birds chattering into the blackening heavens. There were shouts too, unmistakably from Iago, and the sound of some form of struggle in the high sedge. Then the silence returned.

The *interrogante* stumbled toward where he knew Iago was entrenched, but he was immediately pulled back by one of his men. "No, Signor, not if you value your own life."

They ventured there an hour or so later. Flattened grass gave evidence of a struggle, and he shuddered as his foot came into contact with a corpse. He lowered his torch. He crossed himself, thanking God it was not Gentile Stornello. The unfortunate stranger wore civilian clothes. He'd been stabbed in several places and his throat had been slit.

"Must be one of those *vigilanti* who are out for him" was the opinion of his loyal band. There were not only official Venetian forces scouring the mainland for the villain now; a reward had been put on his head.

Early the next morning, the *interrogante* scanned the brackish water of the Brenta Canal. The odd barge slid sleepily toward Venice or to Padua and places west. A couple of newly built villas, set in grand gardens, could be discerned in the mist. Both were far more majestic than his. One, especially showy and rather tawdry, might well have been his nephew's. He didn't know. He'd never been invited there.

Hoping that he may in his zeal have for the first time outpaced Iago, he instructed a couple of his men to find—or, rather, steal—a boat. He was about to scribble instructions to Baldassare Ghiberti when he was approached with what he presumed to be a further communication from the said academic. His heart tumbled as he saw it was a scroll rather than a folded paper. The seal bore testimony to its authority.

"Who gave you this?"

A shrug. "Some soldier, lord." So his presence here was known. That did not bode well.

The missive lacked the customarily formal preamble. It got straight to the point: *You, Messer Annibale Malipiero, citizen* (that didn't sound too promising either), *are requested to attend* (as if he had a choice) *an emergency session of the Council of Ten, in the gracious presence of His Eminence the Doge, on the morning of Friday next. . . .*

Friday next was tomorrow.

A small skiff was found. Vessels close to it were moved far enough away for it to present itself as the only immediately available means of travel. Nobody but Iago, he trusted, would be looking for a spare boat on that particular reach of the Brenta so early in the morning.

He dismissed most of his men, telling them to return to Venice, just as he was about to do. He instructed two of his most diligent followers to remain close by, to watch where the boat might go, and to follow but distantly enough never to be espied. Then he tucked a folded note into one of the boat's gunwales.

Within a mile west of here, there is a villa set closer to the water than most, notable for its modesty in comparison with those on either side. You must persuade the felon to stay there, and you and the others must do so too. Don't move until further instruction. I may be gone awhile.

39. A Villa on the Brenta

I don't dare guess who owns this place (though I have an idea), but I'm not complaining. For nearly a day I've slept the slumber of the guiltless in a bed that although not as snug as my own at home, feels to me now as one worthy of a monarch. No dreams have perturbed me.

When I emerge from this blessed oblivion, I keep my eyes closed awhile, hoping to sink back into it. It doesn't work. But the sounds I hear are benign—birds chirrup, cicadas saw, a horse neighs somewhere, the far-off clang of a church bell summons the evening. Then someone coughs beside me.

"We need to talk."

I force my eyelids open. My tutor is sitting on a straight-backed chair next to the bed, his rotund arms thrust downward between his plump thighs, fingers twiddling.

"Yes, we do," I say.

"I'm not supposed to tell you this, but I've been communicating with—"

"Shush—where is he now?"

"Talking to your Aphrodite, as usual."

"Where?"

He points glumly. "Out there."

I rise drowsily from the bed. The chamber I've been sleeping in has a pair of floor-to-ceiling casement windows that open onto a small balcony. There's a narrow terrace below it, a balustrade with unremarkable statues at each end, and a well-tended lawn beyond, which extends to the canal. And there, concealed from the water by a willow tree, Iago sits with her.

She seems to gleam, even from this distance. She's washed off the muck of the past weeks—not that she was any less glorious to me with smudges of soil and sand and silt on her nut-brown face and arms, and thorn scratches, and burrs and thistles and tendrils in her lush hair.

They are seated face-to-face and side on to me. She's cross-legged, coolly plucking at the ground; he's sprawled before her, supporting himself on an elbow, looking every bit the smitten suitor.

Baldassare rises and starts to come toward me. "No," I say. "Don't stand next to me. He might see us and he'll know we're talking."

"As I was about to tell you, I've been in touch with—"

"I know."

"How do you know?"

"Come on," I snort. "Your treatise on Theocritus?"

"Well," he blusters, "in point of fact I am endeavoring to continue with my treatise on Theocritus, even in such thwarting circumstances and despite my not having the books to hand."

"What's he said to you, the chief inquisitor?"

"That we must not attempt to make a run for it."

"Were you thinking of trying?"

"We could slip away now, head for the fields, while they're down there talking."

Of course this is an idiotic notion. Quite apart from the likelihood that we'd be stopped by Iago's Turks and have our throats cut I simply would not be able to leave *her*, and certainly not with *him*. The thought of never seeing her again is agonizing—despite her having said virtually nothing to me since our day on the beach (sometimes it's as if I don't exist).

And I, too, am expected to stick with Iago at all costs.

Baldassare knows this.

His expression changes from mild optimism to indignation. "He also says I'm too *prolix* and opinionated."

I can't help smiling. "Well, you can be."

"I'm a thinker."

"And an excellent one too."

But he's not in the mood for compliments. "Why he should make me the reporter, I don't know. You could relay it all to him yourself."

"Ah, no," I reply, "you are the one who's always insisted on facts; I am a fabricator."

I look at the couple on the lawn. He's brandishing his hands as he talks. She leans farther toward him—not as a lover might, I very much hope, but as one absorbed in what he says.

"What is it that he's telling her now?"

"How would I know? But they're evidently honeyed words, *coniglietto*."

"Yes, yes, all right."

"*Dolci parole*, or those of the devil." He's mocking me.

"Yes, all right, *yes*." I try to bury dark thoughts. "Whatever he's saying, we should be hearing it—or you should, so that you can report it."

"Whenever I try to get near them, he only insults me and tells me to leave them be."

"Me too."

"No," my tutor corrects me crisply. "You don't dare approach them."

"I don't?"

"You're a doting fathead, an infantile crackpot."

I stiffen slightly. These are strangely forthright words from my mentor. His criticism of my follies is usually more circuitous and embellished with an apposite quotation or two. "You don't want to hear what they're saying, because you're scared you might learn what you don't want to know."

"Which is . . . ?"

"That she doesn't care for you, that your love for her, as you call it, is pointless."

He's right, of course. Like a mooning dolt I've maintained my distance, watching and moping from afar—terrified that if I were to get close she might throw me one of her flaring looks, which would cut me to the quick. Or that I might overhear something between her and Iago that would do the same. I've thought of little else throughout our mad-cap journey, hardly noticed anyone or anything but her.

Like a mute, unquestioning servant, I've obeyed Iago's every whim. I've lugged him about uncomplainingly, sometimes single-handedly (although he prefers to assign that function to Baldassare, so he can scold him for his feebleness), but until recently on that makeshift *portantina*—which Franceschina found most amusing. We abandoned it on the far bank of the canal, thank the Lord. Thanks to her ministrations, he's started to walk relatively unaided now and even, when he's in the mood or thinks it best, to run. Soon he may not require us at all.

My tutor and I have protected him and provided his every comfort. We've made him beds of grass and mud, dried in the sun before he deigns to lie on them. We've scavenged to feed him, bringing him fruit and berries and even the odd crawling or slithering or hopping creature—although Franceschina is far more skilled at catching them than we are. He's compelled us to shift his painful limbs into more comfortable positions, though Franceschina is generally the only person allowed to touch him. For all our efforts to disencumber him, we earn no gratitude. I'm beginning to hate him.

"Did the inquisitor provide the boat for us?"

"Yes."

"Is this his villa?"

"I don't know. But he directed me to it."

"It was clever of you, to tell Iago that it belonged to a friend of yours and that you were certain it would be empty."

"Thank you," he says a bit smugly.

"It even looks like the home of someone who might teach at Padua."

"Except for the singular lack of books."

"That's why it could be the *interrogante*'s. I don't think he reads much." I pause. "He's Jacopo Malipiero's uncle, did you know that?"

"Yes."

"What did he say we should do here? What next?"

"He said we should stick it out."

"I doubt Iago will have the patience for that."

Suddenly Iago stands up, surprisingly nimbly. Here I am, framed in the window, and he's staring straight at me. Baldassare is still cringing behind me. The Mantuan takes a couple of halting steps, then lets out a howl of pain and grabs both of his legs below the knees. Franceschina stretches out to him and helps him to sit once more.

"Let's hope that makes him consider staying a while longer." Baldassare's tone is full of abhorrence.

"You! Gentile Stornello!" the villain hollers. "And where's that scholar? Come down and help me!"

As the two of us clatter down the stairs and out onto the lawn, I have the time to whisper to Baldassare, "I'll take him to wherever he wants to go; you stay and speak to her. Ask her what he's been talking about."

"No. You stay, I'll take him. She's more likely to tell you."

"Why is that?"

"Because you're young. I'm just a bookish old fool in her eyes, and she hasn't said a word to me yet."

"What are you two mumbling about so slyly?" Iago calls.

"We were debating the merits and demerits of Euclid's quadric surfaces," exclaims my teacher, with exceptional self-command.

"Quadric what? Pah!" Iago spits. "You! Pundit! Take me to the kitchen! I'm in need of more nourishment."

That's useful.

At least Baldassare now knows where the kitchen is. It wasn't so when we arrived. Franceschina the radiant huntress—my Diana— wanted to cook the animals she'd so resourcefully caught: a couple of trout and three rabbits that hung from a belt she'd fashioned from their skin. Having claimed to have been to the villa before, Baldassare floundered.

I ran ahead to the kitchen to help Baldassare out, and he followed (at least we both can still be quicker than Iago—physically, at least—when it's necessary). Disappointingly for all of us, the kitchen wasn't well stocked. Either the villa had not yet been used for the summer or its owner didn't require much in the way of gastronomic contentment. It made me yearn for Zinerva's realm.

There were pots and a spit and a hearth, at least, and quickly enough Franceschina had the rabbits stewing and was grilling the fish on the spit. Iago ate all the fish. Baldassare and I had to make do with what we could find in the *dispensa*, which wasn't much—a few very dry rings of *salame*, a tough cut of *pancetta*, and some moldy, rocklike *parmigiano*. By the time the *stufato* was ready, I'd gone upstairs and was asleep, so I missed it. I hope Baldassare got some.

As my struggling tutor half-lifts and half-steers Iago toward the villa, I lean toward Franceschina. "He certainly knows how to stuff himself, doesn't he?" My tone is sharp, aggrieved—maybe not the best way to start a conversation with the most beautiful girl in the world.

She sounds as petulant as I do. She's no longer cross-legged but now reclines to one side, not looking at me, supporting herself with one hand while the other plays with a strand of her wondrous hair. "He's a soldier," she declares testily, without turning. "Soldiers must eat."

"And we mustn't?"

"He's been badly hurt. He must build up his strength."

"And I haven't been badly hurt, is that it? My feet may not have been pierced, but—"

I stop. This is not the way to go about things.

But she dips her head, and with a faintly apologetic air she says, "You have suffered much too, I know."

I grab at this hint of compassion, probably making more of it than I should. I stand over her. She still doesn't look up. The hand that was toying with her hair plucks at the grass again. "He's a bad man, Franceschina," I say firmly. "He's done many, many bad things. He's a murderer. He's killed many people. He could kill us too."

She waits a little, then whispers, "How do you know he's a murderer?"

"Because . . . because I do."

"Who told you he was a murderer? The inquisitor?"

"Yes, the chief inquisitor, Jacopo's—" I sense her quake somewhat at the name, a tiny oscillation of her shoulders, or think I do, that seems to me to speak more of pleasure than revulsion. I really must stop assuming the worst from her every gesture.

"Why should he be telling the truth?"

"Because he's the chief inquisitor, Franceschina." I drop to my haunches in front of her, compelling her to glance at me, and she does. *Ma Dio*, those eyes, how they slay me! I must try to stay unruffled, forceful. "Has Iago spoken of his crimes to you?"

Her lower lip trembles. "Iago?" she says.

Cristo mio, he hasn't even told her who he is! I can see from that apprehensive face that the name means something to her, though. "Yes, Iago. He murdered my cousin, and her husband, and many others."

"Signor Jacopo's cousin also."

Of course she was going to bring that up! "Did he tell you what his crimes were?" I ask again.

She shakes her head. "He just said he was innocent of all that people are saying he did."

"Well, he would, wouldn't he?" I cry. It's too loud. It unsettles a great black crow that's been resting in the branches above us. I lower my voice. "Did you not ask him what his crimes were?"

"No."

"Now you know."

She stares at the ground. Her locks tumble over her wonderful visage. She brushes them back. She sniffs a little. Her head shakes. "He . . . cannot be that man."

"He can be. And he is."

"Yes, if you say, but . . . but if he is such an evil person, so dangerous, why are you here, and your tutor too? Why have you not run?"

This might be a question that Iago has put to her. Why is she here? Why are we three here? "Did he want to know that, Franceschina?"

"No!" And she now interrogates me. "Why did you help him flee, if he is such a bad man?" I wish I could confide in her, tell her the truth, but I say nothing. What can I say?

"He is grateful to you. He speaks well of you," she tells me.

"He does?"

"He has told me how brave you've been and . . . and strong."

I straighten at this, so that I might look taller and more generally stalwart. She raises her eyes but then glances away.

"He's spoken a lot to you, Franceschina. What else has he said?"

"You are being like the *interrogante* again."

"I'm sorry, but I have to know."

"So you can tell the *interrogante*?"

"Yes." And then—firmly, I hope—I plead, "But you must not tell Iago this, or he will kill me . . . and maybe you . . . all three of us."

The threat doesn't seem to scare her. "Ay!" She grimaces. "I don't like spies."

"Does Iago think I'm a spy?"

"No." Her tone is clipped. "He trusts you."

"He does? Has he told you so?"

She nods. "He thinks you are a good person. He thinks you didn't do what you were put in the *prigioni* for."

"I didn't."

"Then why don't you believe the same of him?" She's not just agonizingly beautiful, she's smart and vehement. Her silken cheeks flush and her black eyes blaze. "If you were unfairly arrested, perhaps he was too. Why should I believe you and not him? Why should I believe he has done all that they say he has done? He's gentle, he's kind."

I can no longer conceal my amazement. "*Gentle? Kind?* Did you see what he did to that misguided fool who found where we were hiding? He stabbed him in a thousand places, Franceschina!"

"Not a thousand," she says quietly. "He killed him to stop us from being discovered. He kills only to survive, he says."

"*What?*"

"Like any soldier, he kills to survive." She lowers her gaze once more. "He's had to fight to survive for most of his . . ."

"What? *What?*" I ask quite fiercely.

She looks up, angry now. "He had no father."

"We all have fathers at some time or other."

"His died when he was still a young boy. But not before beating him. And then his mother died too, when he was fifteen, when he was just your age." She almost chokes when she says this. Her eyes glisten. "He had to survive on his own from your age."

I feel the blood invade my cheeks. "But does that justify what he's done?"

"How do you know he did those things?" she protests again.

I've been so immersed in our exchange, so enthralled by the shapes conjured by her incomparable mouth as she speaks more volubly than ever before in my company, that I haven't noticed we're being watched. He's standing, apparently without need of support, on the terrace, chewing on some white-fleshed meat. His reluctant helper is beside him, writhing with discomposure. How long have they been there? Franceschina follows my gaze. Iago brandishes what looks like a drumstick. "Excellent bird, my girl, cooked to perfection, fit for royalty! Gentile Stornello, come try it! You haven't eaten since morning! I've found wine too! We all have need of that!"

40. *A Miserable Supper*

The table is long. I imagine the *interrogante* and his wife, if he has one, at each extremity—servants darting between them, few words passed, sharing as morose a supper as we are now. Do the memories of largely wordless meals with my father make me think this, or is it the cavernous quality of this *sala da pranzo*?

Iago is unable to stay seated for long. He's found a walking stick, cut from a single shoot of ash, curved at the top. He throws it from hand to hand and rests his weight upon it, testing its efficacy. He plants it firmly on the floor and swings around it, this way and that, to ascertain which of his legs is the better recovered. He pronounces both "sound as English oak." Soon, he says, he'll be able to walk unaided—which, he has pleasure in reminding my tutor and me, may make us "surplus to necessity." Sliding behind where Franceschina is seated, he declares, "But even a healthy man must be *fed*," and, unseen by her, throws me a revolting wink.

He lurches away from her and sits at the far end of the table, head lowered, examining his hands as he flexes his fingers. He's remembering something, and it's turned him gloomy. I glance at Franceschina. I'm gazing at her so absorbedly now, as invariably happens when I look at her for a second or so too long, that I don't notice him watching me. "You, Gentile Stornello," he sneers, "why aren't you drinking?"

I've left my cup of wine untouched.

He waves the jug beside him in Baldassare's direction. "You, scholar! Fill this from the barrel in the cellar, and bring another one too!"

"I don't much like wine," I say.

"Why? Can't take it?"

"The world is best examined without it, I think."

"Befuddles you, does it?"

"I've never drunk enough to find out. One sip is enough to make me wary."

"Then mayhap you should—loosen up some of that famed Stornello rigidity, that heart of marble."

I hear what sounds very much like a titter from Franceschina. I don't have the courage to look at her. But at least Iago and I are having what might pass for a conversation again.

"What's your god of wine called? I forget."

I'd let Baldassare enlighten him if he was around, but he's left for the cellar. "Dionysus," I mutter. "Or Bacchus, if you're an ancient Roman."

"Or the devil himself, some men have called him," he whispers mysteriously. "When the spirit of drink has the better of them, it can make a man speak *parrot*."

He rises from his end of the table and hobbles toward me, clinging to his stick. He stands behind me, just as he did behind Franceschina, his fingers drumming on the chair back. I feel the energy of his proximity. I haven't felt it for a while. It's an uncomfortable feeling.

He picks up my cup. "Hardly a mouthful you've had."

What's he going to do now? Cram the rim into my mouth? Force me to drink until I've swallowed every drop?

"Have you heard of *coraggio olandese*?"

Dutch courage? "No," I say.

"Your Dutchman is no match for your Englishman when it comes to drinking. But your Englishman drinks to be insensate, where your Dutchman drinks to fight."

"Hence the courage."

"And the loss of fear. Face an army of your Dutch and you won't live long." He leans into my ear and murmurs, "You don't have the guts to even glance at her, lad, and yet she, at this instant, is looking at you. Not at me and my ugliness, but at you. Don't stare back, because she'll only turn away. That's the custom with women." He straightens, pats my shoulders as he did hers. "Have guts, lad," he says, so that she can hear now. "Drink!"

I down the cup in one gulp. For this I earn a slap on the back from him, which sets me spluttering more than I would have done anyway, and a sweet laugh and delighted clap of the hands from her—which makes the burning in my gullet and the spinning in my head almost worthwhile. How can anybody drink more than this and stay upright or sane?

Baldassare returns, a jug in each hand.

"Replenish, man, replenish! No, more than that—to the brim!"

"Gentile's not used to wine," my teacher says, obeying nonetheless.

"Who are you, his master? His pander, that he can only take instruction from you?"

Baldassare flushes a deep crimson. "I was merely pointing out—"

"What's the purpose of your teaching, scholar?"

"To educate him to be—"

"To be a man! He'll stay no more than a boy unless he learns to drink!"

I glug down more. After all, I don't want to be thought anything less than a *man*.

He's started to sing again—in English. This time he obliges us with a summary. "A song of a lusty lass who calls herself a deer park and her lover is the deer. 'Feed where you wish,' she tells him, 'on my hills and my valleys, and if the hills that are my lips be dry, then feed lower, where the fountains are.'" He lets forth a dirty cackle.

Franceschina averts her eyes and toys with the goblet in front of her. After a moment she raises it to her heavenly lips.

"No!" Iago limps hurriedly toward her and snatches the cup. "What are you, a harlot? A wanton? A jade?"

She makes to protest, but he hastily puts a finger to her mouth. "Forgive me, *Signorina*," he pleads softly, as speedily suave as he was enraged, "but it does not suit a woman to drink. Do you wish to be thought loose? Not a virtuous lady such as yourself, surely."

She shakes her perfect head.

"So a man . . . can . . . drink . . . and a woman . . . shan't?" I stammer.

"A man must, and a woman mustn't," Iago laughs. He slips by me again, and once more proffers a hissed confidence. "Would you wish her to fall asleep on you or under you, as you lay atop her, as you *rut*?"

Baldassare, who's heard this, screws up his face. Iago has seen it of course. "What do you know of what passes between men and women, scholar?" he snarls. "Tell me about your friend."

"My . . . friend?"

"Your friend, he whom you say owns this house."

"Oh, him . . ."

"Do you share more than your intellectual chatter? Are you playfellows too?"

"I don't quite—"

"Do you dance between the sheets, man?"

"Um . . . certainly not." He squirms and turns crimson under the force of Iago's unblinking examination.

"Is he as clever as you?"

"Cleverer, I would estimate."

"He, too, is an outstanding instructor, is he?"

"One of the best." Baldassare is visibly pleased to be talking of matters cerebral once more.

"What does he instruct?"

"As I do—history, grammar, rhetoric, poetry, and moral philosophy."

"What is moral philosophy?"

"Some call it ethics. As first posited by Aristotle, it has to do with notions of what is good and what is bad. What is right and what is wrong."

"And that you teach, do you?"

"Indeed I do."

"Pah. I've not had need of a teacher to know what is good and what is bad."

"I imagine," says Baldassare, rather bravely, "you have learned such things from life." For all the peril of his present situation, he's beginning to enjoy the exchange.

"Life's university," says Iago brightly. "Or what I call the school of hard knocks." He glances at Franceschina, who's smiling again, seemingly enthralled. My tutor also permits himself a grin. He's interested in the phrase. He's going to store it away. I wish *my* brain was able to store anything at this moment. I feel giddy and sick. My queasiness is not helped by another thump between my shoulder blades.

"Ha! Who needs Padua?" Iago exclaims. "What's he called?" He's returned to Baldassare's imaginary colleague.

"My . . . friend?" There's the tiniest hesitation before my mentor says, with faltering confidence, "Pico della Mirandola."

I try not to react visibly. This is a former professor of his, and a great one, his idol, a humanist famed among recent thinkers. He's also dead. I hope that Iago's knowledge of modern philosophers is not expansive.

"This Pico from wherever he comes from—a learned bugger, is he?"

Baldassare recoils mildly at the distasteful appellation. "Extremely."

"And yet this learned friend of yours has no books?"

Ah. Now my beloved sage had better think of something very sharp indeed.

"My talented fellow theorist does not require books! What is written and thought of he already knows. It's in his head."

"That must be a big head, then, to carry so much in it." Iago taps Baldassare's own thinning pate. "Do you lug so much about in yours?"

"Not nearly so much," Baldassare replies tremulously. "Compared to Pico, I'm a dunce."

"I think you are a dunce anyway."

"I'm sure that nothing I can say will convince you otherwise."

Iago keeps tapping. "I've a mind to open this up," he says. "To see for myself what cleverness is hiding therein." His other hand is narrowing around the handle of his walking stick.

"You wish to be Galen, then," my tutor says, standing his ground, incredibly.

"What? Who?"

"A physician and thinker."

"Another of your gifted friends?"

"No. He died over a thousand years ago. He was Greek."

"Still another of your accursed old-time Greeks? What was so very clever about him?"

"He dissected the brain—not of humans but of animals. He was among the first to posit that intelligence and thought might lie within the brain, something that we now take for granted. Unfortunately, he found nothing within the structure of the brain to give him any obvious indication of the possibility, or none that subsequent scholars have considered satisfactory. There's still work being done on this in Padua, as it happens. But I think as a commonly held tenet there's not much to gain from opening up the brain in order to find the secret of what makes one man cleverer than another."

"How do you then conclude what makes one man cleverer than another?"

"By what he thinks or says."

"Or writes?"

"Yes, logically, that also."

"So show me."

"Show you?"

Iago thuds the stick on the floor with impatience. "Your writings, fool, the tract you've been scribbling."

"My treatise on Theocritus?"

"Yes! Show it to me!"

That's it. We're done for. Although the thought occurs to me that most, if not all, of what Baldassare has been writing must be in the hands of the *interrogante*, this is now very perilous indeed. Has he scrawled any more today, not yet delivered? How's he going to explain away having nothing to show? Or what if he has written something more and is forced to produce it?

"I . . . I . . . I . . . I . . . I . . ." He looks quite defeated.

I manage to conquer the derangement of my own faculties and say, "He's very modest about letting anyone read his work until it's finished to his satisfaction. Aren't you, *Dottore*?"

"Yes, I feel it's not quite ready—"

"*Show it to me!*"

"I . . . I cannot."

Iago's stick is now swinging out and upward and is about to crack down, I'm certain of it.

"He's destroyed it!" I blurt.

Iago sways in my direction. He looks as if he might be about to smash *my* skull to bits.

"Forgive him, but he's . . . he's such a perfectionist. This afternoon he burned the whole thing."

"Yes, yes, yes." Baldassare breathes in obvious relief and gratitude. "I . . . I feel I must rewrite it, from the very beginning."

Iago thrusts his face once more into my tutor's. Baldassare, inevitably, cringes. "Do I repel you, scholar?"

"No."

"I do, I do. I'm a scurvy featherbrain and you, a fine academician, you scorn me."

"Not at all."

"You think me a savage. I can see it in your eyes, hear it in your smarmy superiority. Am I a low sort, a beast, a mere *animal*?"

He swings away and makes for Franceschina. She looks fearful herself, now. He's still brandishing the stick. Is he going to hit her? Surely not. Though he remains determined to crack someone about the skull, I'm sure.

"Do you think me a beast, lady?" he asks of her.

She shakes her head.

"Am I then worthy of your regard, *Signorina*?"

She nods.

"What, though I speak like an uneducated brute?"

"You speak very well," she whispers.

"Yes, you do," I concur.

"There now, scholar," Iago says, brushing past the back of my chair again and facing Baldassare once more. "These young sweethearts, these pretty chicklets, think I speak well."

"I never suggested you didn't."

"I knew a fellow once, highborn and educated, and a soldier, and handsome too." The Mantuan's eyes are still fixed on my tutor's, though he is addressing the three of us. "A handsome, scholarly soldier, who spoke well. You, my lady, would have thought him a fine buck. But he angered me." His fingers grip the handle of his stick more tightly. "I'll confess to jealousy. And beware jealousy, Gentile Stornello; it can mock you. He affected a high opinion of me, called me brave and honest. We would carouse together. We were the closest of comrades, at least by outward appearance. But I knew better. One can denigrate by voice and demeanor, and so he did with me. There was many a time when I wished to beat him around that comely, clever head of his. It's a pity I never had the option. Would you oblige me, Professor of Philosophy, by being that fellow now? You are by no stretch as easy on the eye as he was, but . . ."

I watch the walking stick rise, rotate violently, like a branch caught in a wild wind, and descend. Blood spurts from the instantly gaping chasm in the middle of my teacher's skull as he sinks without even a whimper to the floor. He's dead, I'm convinced of it. More blood pours onto the boards, rivers of the stuff.

I pass out too, partly from the drink, mostly because of what I've just seen. The last thing I hear is Franceschina's scream.

41. A Rough Awakening

Some thinkers have it that dreams predict the future; if that's the case, I should be the happiest person alive. As I jolt into wakefulness, what I remember from the dream I just had is a lot of falling around with *her* and her laughter—not mocking but happy and excited. In my dream, she said with absolute sincerity that I was a fine, accomplished lover—quite the buck—and I was rewarded for my proficiency with a flurry of well-placed kisses.

But I'm now conscious of a presence at the foot of my bed—and it certainly isn't her. A sniff alerts me to it. The bed itself is soaked with sweat, as am I. My hose and shirt cling to me. I haven't undressed. How did I get here? Which room is this? I recollect Baldassare's head being cracked apart and a cascade of blood.

"Happy slumbers?" Iago croaks. He has his back to me. "You were lashing about, lad."

"You killed my tutor, the cleverest man I know."

"I should have warned you, lad, that wine will provoke the desire, but it can compromise the performance. You fell asleep! Where's the pleasure for a woman in that?"

"I did not fall asleep. I fainted, because you killed my tutor."

"Pah! You were drunk; you thought you saw more than you did. From your own experience of a split head, you must know by now that it looks worse than it is. He bled, but he's not dead. I have even bandaged him."

"Where is he now?"

I detect a shrug in the gloom. "Where I left him, I'd surmise. I helped him on the way by filling him with wine."

"Why did you strike him so soundly?"

"He needs that scholarly pride clouted out of him."

"Like the man you spoke of who angered you?"

There's a short silence. His shoulders rise and fall. "There are those who think that all of life's lessons can be reaped from reading. I despise them."

"Despise them?"

"What a man does with his brain is his concern, not mine. Just do not let him think he's a better man for it. That angers me."

"He was one such?"

"You might say so."

"And you were jealous of him?"

Another silence. I could be risking a clout myself. But he turns to me, slides a little closer. "Why don't you go and make love to your girl? She'll have found a feathery bed, the best in the house. Women have a nose for luxury. Why not seek her out and join her?"

I realize I'm in a smaller room than the one in which I spent most of yesterday asleep. "Go rouse her with kisses. But I'd wash first." He waves a hand before his nose and grimaces. "Though some women like a man with the stench of the night."

I try to sit up. The world whirls and I feel a stabbing between my eyes. I shall never take another drop of wine again.

He guffaws.

"I heard her scream," I say.

He grins. "She'll recover, as she did when she watched you being given a hiding. Go make love."

"Perhaps she doesn't think you so kind and gentle now."

He looks surprised. "She said I'm kind and gentle?"

"She described you so to me."

His chest swells. "What else does she say of me?"

I'd not thought him vain until now.

"That you are misjudged."

"That I am, lad; that I am. Do you think I'm misjudged?"

"I was once ready to give you the benefit of the doubt. I'm not too sure now."

"I have my rages. When I'm crossed, I strike. Does that make me a thoroughgoing villain? I bound his head, did I not? Would a villain do that?"

"You showed no mercy to the poor wretch who found us on the marshes."

"He deserved all he got. He was a snitch and a profiteer."

"You ran after him. You stabbed him again and again."

"I'll give a soldier a fair chance, sword to sword." He's sounding gruffer now, less relaxed. "But a squealer who'll betray me for profit— that I'll not stomach."

"But he was only trying to put money in his purse." I seem to remember him using this phrase.

His eyes narrow. "You ask a lot of questions of me, Gentile Stornello." Then he smiles and slaps the sheet again. "Go pleasure her. She's in need of delight."

"Can I be certain you won't kill him, then—Baldassare, I mean—or me, or Franceschina?"

"I'm no promise maker. But your fates are in your own hands."

"How is that?"

"Don't vex me and you'll live—as will he, as will she. That's all I require. Now go play with her. Strum her strings."

"I'm not sure I know how."

"It's simple. You touch her here, you touch her there. Gently, mind. Then she'll dance to your tune. There's no finer act than to wake a woman in the morning with your caress."

I've got to admit it's a sweet prospect. Dawn has arrived. A silvery light is tiptoeing into this small room through its only casement. It's so very peaceful, so unthreatening—and outside the birds are caroling. Where is she? In that great snug bed in which I slept yesterday? I could creep down.

But I've never touched a woman "here" or "there" before. I could get it terribly wrong. I feel such a baby. And, appropriately enough, he's now gazing down at me in a fatherly way, without menace as far as I can make out. But do I have the courage to ask him, risking his derision?

He stands up, a little shakily, and shuffles toward the window. "I wouldn't leave it too long, Gentile Stornello," he says, staring out. "We can't stay here forever."

The brutal truths of our situation momentarily invade the idyll, but I'm still concentrating only on a picture of her, sprawled perhaps, naked perhaps, on that big bed downstairs, so within reach. *Carpe diem*, I'm thinking, *quam minimum credula postero*. And who *knows* what the future holds?

"When you say *here* and *there*—what do you mean by that, pre- cisely?"

"Am I supposed to show you, to go down with you and point?" he chortles, then smiles indulgently. "There's symmetry in the act. Where you most want to touch a woman is where she most wants to be touched. Go with your desires. Don't think too much."

I stand up—too quickly, as it happens. I reel and wobble, have to sit down again. It's not just the hangover. There's still the fear of disen- chantment; I couldn't bear it if she were to laugh at me. I'd die. "What if I fail?" I'm frozen like a field creature in a lantern's beam.

"Come." He catches me by the back of the neck and marches me down to the *primo piano* of the villa. He knows exactly where to find her. Did he take her there last night? "I'm not going to allow you to flee," he whispers. "No running off now, lad."

The door is unlatched, so I push it open. "The chagrin of an empty chamber, so recently deserted," Iago murmurs. The bed has been slept on. Indeed, the coverlets and bolsters have been cast off and the silk sheets are rumpled.

The windows that lead onto the balcony are open.

We approach the bed. He picks up a sheet and sniffs it. "The scent of a woman . . ." He pushes it fairly roughly toward my nose.

There's a fruity aroma, a hint of lemon, but I can also smell flowers and spices—lavender and what seems like the fragrance of cloves.

"Orchid," he breathes. "She found some on the way here. I saw her crush them to a paste, which she applied most generously. My, she knows how to entrap a man. But it seems, Gentile Stornello, you are too late. I told you not to dawdle. Unless . . . unless . . . ." He propels me toward the windows. There she is, seated with her back to us, in the shade of the willow tree. "Unless you want to despoil her out there on the grass. I wouldn't stop you."

She's wearing no more than her white shift, which hangs by thin strands of linen from her incredible shoulders, so that I can see the hollow between the blades. She also has her arms raised, arranging her luxuriant hair atop her head.

"You see, lad, she still perfects herself, like one not yet fully aware of her advantage. Mayhap she's only just noticed how slender her neck is, and so now she'll show it to the world."

"It is amazing, isn't it?"

He squeezes my neck. "Go tell her how *amazing* she is. It may be that no one has let her know that as yet. Go be the first."

"You think I am the first?"

"You think not?" He affects absentmindedness for a moment, then: "You speak of him? The scoundrel you believe has her heart? Put him out of your mind, lad. Where is he now? Not here that I can see. You are anxious that when you tup her she will be thinking of him?"

"Please don't use that word. I want her to be . . . to be mine alone."

"Such sentimental drivel, Gentile."

Is that the first time he's addressed me solely by my first name? I think it is. He's loosened his grip.

"Yes," I say quite forcefully. "I love her, and I don't care that you don't believe in love; I do, and I love her, and that's the end of it."

He grins. "The idiocy of the young and what they glean from books, to imagine they are in love when all they want is to sate their itch for copulation."

"Baldassare says much the same thing, except in more poetic terms, and he doesn't deny the existence of love altogether."

"He wouldn't. Because he's in love, or so he thinks it, with *you*."

I stiffen and stare directly at him. He's grinning; his teeth, jagged and filthy though they are, seem to glint in the rising light of the morning. All I can say is, "What nonsense. He cares for me, but only as my educator."

"He's inclined to educate you with more than just literature." Iago's lips curl, and he gives me another of those winks that I don't much like. "But let's not talk of your galling teacher; there are fish you can frolic with more freely—that is, unless you, too, have a preference for your own gender. Look now at the bed she slept in. Isn't that a signal to you, Gentile, of a girl who needs tupping? Envisage what a restless night she's had, with no redress."

Oh, I've envisaged it, all right.

"Does it matter whom she's been wanting? Is it not enough that she wants?"

I stare at him. "I want her to be mine."

"Then we must leave this place," he murmurs slyly. "For she did speak of him—your rival—only yesterday. I did not wish to make you fret over it. He resides not too far from here when the summer comes, or he flits back and forth, as all rich Venetians do."

"She told you this?"

"Yes."

"How near?"

"Near enough to see it as we rowed here. She's been there many times. She is a servant of the household, or do I need to remind you? Are all the houses on this stretch Malipiero homes?" He at last stops clasping my neck and lays an arm across my shoulders. "If so, it would be best for all if we moved on, do you not think? Let's put the good-looking brute behind us and move on . . ."

Utterly oblivious to us, Franceschina is plucking daisies that are opening up to the morning. Iago mutters, "I'll tell you then, as a friend. I must be honest with those I think of as friends, and so I think of you—for we have shared much, have we not? Are we friends, Gentile Stornello?"

I nod distractedly. I can't possibly consider him a friend, but he seems to accept my affirmation.

"Then from now on, Gentile, I shall tell you all that she says to me, though it may cause hurt at times."

"Yes, tell me," I urge breathlessly.

"I shall expect you, as a friend, to return the favor—to always be honest with me."

"Yes, yes," I gasp.

"I asked what ailed her. As you've observed yourself, she's been pre-occupied since we arrived here, sorrowful. She was not forthcoming. But I have earned her confidence, and so in a while she told me."

"Told you what?"

"That on our way here we had passed the summer home of someone she knew well. I pretended to know nothing of whom she spoke. I questioned her then on who he was and what she . . . thought of him."

"And?"

"This will hurt."

"Go on."

"She said he was the handsomest boy she'd ever known and that she thought she was—sorry, Gentile—in thrall to him."

I swallow hard. "*In thrall*? She used those words?"

"Yes, they surprised me too. A very educated way of talking for a servant girl. Mayhap she learned them from him? Or from you? Have you told her you're in thrall to her?"

"No, of course not. Oh, God, I'm in hell."

"Hell does not exist, except of our own making. Hell can be dismantled if you have the power for it. Go down there now; make love to her."

Despite the counsel, he's preventing me from moving an inch. His arm has snaked about my neck again.

"How can I?" I pant. "When she's in thrall?"

"You did not listen to me well, Gentile. She said she *thought* she was in thrall. She is not certain of it. You might persuade her otherwise."

"I want to die."

"Come, now."

"I want to run down there and throw myself into the canal."

"Nobody's yet died for love, and you are not about to be the first to do so."

Why's he grasping me like this? It reminds me of the dark time when he tried to kill me, when I was certain I *would* die. His mouth is very close to my ear. "But before you do anything," he mutters, "before you plow her or try to kill yourself, or both, it is time for your side of the bargain."

I'm suddenly very frightened. "What's that?"

"As . . ."

"Yes?"

"As an *honest* friend, Gentile Stornello, I have a suspicion that you've not been wholly honest with me."

These are almost the very words used by one of the inquisitors in the *sala degli interroganti.* But now, instead of facing that blubbery monster and his skeletal associate, I'm in an armhold so very muscular that I can scarcely exhale, let alone speak. Much like the inquisitors, he doesn't seem overly interested in what I might reveal in any case. He does the talking, and Franceschina seems to vanish like a specter, as does Jacopo Malipiero, because what I'm hearing now is far more troubling even than the news that I'm not loved and never will be.

"You must be well enough acquainted with me by this time to know I'm no idiot," he whispers. "Your tutor is himself an idiot for thinking so. This house does not belong to any friend of his, though it does belong to someone he knows, and you know this person too. His name is Annibale Malipiero. Do you think I idle my time away in prison, like most men? No, I do not. I find things out. He is the chief inquisitor. The others—the fat fool who did this to my feet and his silent thin companion—don't have the power. Only Annibale Malipiero, *Il Terribile*, has the power. I know he has a villa on the Brenta, and this is it. Why has he brought us here? We are part of a strategy, Gentile Stornello. Don't refute it. From the moment of our escape I've known it, and everything in our adventure up to now has but borne it out. How else could we have got so far? I am a villain wanted by Venice. How is it that the full might of the cursed *Serenissima* has not yet entrapped me? I'm a wily rogue, some say, who can make himself invisible for a good while, and I can hold men at bay and fight my corner, but I'm not *that* sly. And here we are, in the villa of the *Capo degli Interroganti*, and still he has not pounced. He has even stopped other pursuers from catching us, I think. Why is that? What does he wish for us? It's more than a noose around our necks, I'll be bound, or a cutting open on the campanile so that the blood-hungry people of Venice can crow." He continues, as if to substantiate our criminal alliance: "You must know you are no more than a pawn in a game over which you have no mastery. We are but puppets, Gentile Stornello, and he is our puppeteer." Then he mutters, "I am of a mind to regret ever opening my mouth to you, after such a long silence." He grasps me tightly by the back of my head and yanks it around so that my eyes meet his. Gray-green and bright with interest, they seem to eat into my soul.

He wants me to confirm his suspicions. I ask, "If you know all this, why haven't you killed us?" Which, in a way, is a confirmation.

He appears to consider this, with a small, broken-toothed grin. "Oh, I shall do so eventually, I think. As I told you, I don't like being crossed." He gives me a squeeze of the throat, to push the point home. "Regrettably, for the present, I need you, you and your pederast tutor. And the girl is far too pretty to kill yet." He looks out to the lawn again, at her. He hasn't let go of my neck. "And should you not have her, Gentile, before you die, if just the once? I owe you that at least."

She's still there, tugging at daisies. She's making a chain of them, carefully slicing their stems with a fingernail.

Then he says, "And aside from that, "I've begun to like you."

"You have?"

He ruffles my hair. "Yes, even though you're a clever little spook."

"I'm a spook?"

"In England it means *spy*. England is full of *spies* . . ."

The acknowledgment of it makes me feel slightly . . . what's the word? Shifty? Grubby? She called me a spy too, with distaste in her voice.

"But for all that," he says, "we have much in common. We've both been heinously accused of crimes we did not commit. So let's fight them off a while longer, shall we, Gentile? Let's be as one in whatsoever awaits us!" He's almost shouting now. He doesn't care who hears. Franceschina turns in surprise and looks up at us. He waves. "We're going to fight, my lady," he calls. "To save our names!"

She smiles. I expect her to clap and cry out, "Bravo!"

"If I am to be honest with you," I ask, "will you always be honest with me?"

"Indeed," he says. "From today we wear our hearts upon our sleeves."

"You are Iago of Mantua, are you not?" It's the first time I've had the nerve to be so direct in my questioning.

"Of course I am. Who else did you think I could be?"

"No one. But I needed it confirmed."

"So there you have it, lad."

"Did you kill my cousin Desdemona?"

There's but the hint of a pause before he says very quietly, "No, I did not kill your cousin . . . Desdemona." I detect the smallest catch in his voice.

"Did you kill her husband, the Governor of Cyprus?"

"No, I did not."

"Who killed them, then?"

"The plague did, haven't you heard?"

"Nobody believes that anymore."

"And rightly so," he says. "He killed his own wife and then himself."

That's news to me, big news—and would be, I dare say, to most of Venice. Who else knows that, if it's true? The *interrogante*? He must. Ah, but then, he said there were things he remained unsure of. He has to be told this. Is Baldassare listening somewhere, ear to the door behind me, as he's been instructed to do?

"Did you kill Jacopo Malipiero's cousin Roderigo?"

He seems to have to think about that one. "Roderigo? Oh, now I remember Roderigo Malipiero—I had not made the connection. Yes, I killed him, because he crossed me. He was a dog, Gentile, a worthless, vainglorious whey-face. You would have wished the same fate on him."

So that's Roderigo Malipiero dealt with. I suppose someday I am going to have to learn if there was some more specific reason why he had to die, if I care much about any Malipiero.

"Did you kill your own wife?"

Again he pauses, jerks his head back in some surprise. "So they are saying that too, are they? No, I did not. Why should a man kill his wife—unless another man performs his office between their sheets and he learns of it?" He turns to me again with that grinding gaze. "Why are you asking me such questions, lad? *Il Terribile* does not need to know such things. He knows them already."

"I think *he* wants to know why . . ." I begin.

But he's not listening. He stiffens, as if he's seen something. And he has—beyond her, on the far canal bank, among the pines and tamarisk trees. He can spot things as a bird of prey might. He catches hold of my arm and twists it up into my back. I can't make anything out at all. "We're being watched," he says through clenched teeth. "Do you know who's watching us? Is it he?"

"I . . . I . . . I don't know." I gasp once more. And I really don't. "Could it be your Turkish friends?"

"No. They're too canny to reveal themselves." Then he says, with some decisiveness, "We'll leave now. We'll go to Padua. We won't take the boat. We'll walk. We need somewhere to lose ourselves. Look for more weaponry. Your inquisitor friend is bound to have weapons here." And he finishes with a chuckle: "Let's give him a run for his money."

42. *Doge Gritti*

Il Terribile was barred from entering the *sala degli interroganti*. "Sorry it's our orders." Some guards stayed deferential. Others curled their lips.

Bonifacio Colonna ranted from within.

"Is *he* in charge now?"

There were dispirited nods.

"Good luck with *that*," said Annibale Malipiero.

At the altogether more ornate door of the *Sala del Consiglio dei Dieci*, there was no "Signor," no "lord," no *"Capo degli Investigatori Notevole."* Just "You'll have to go around the front way, like everyone else."

So he was of the many now, no longer of the few.

As he traced his way back through the labyrinth that was the Prigioni Ducale, Annibale Malipiero considered going home. He had been delivered directly to the prison dock by Ercole. He had not seen his wife for more than a fortnight, but apparently Doge Gritti, unlike his senile predecessor Grimani, was a stickler for punctuality. He had better face the great man now, even though his cloak was soaked, his beard unclipped, and he probably smelled to high heaven.

The *riva,* once he'd reached it, was as busy as ever at such a time of day. As one of the many, he hurried unnoticed along the *molo,* into the piazza, and toward the great, florid *porta* of the Palazzo Ducale. Something of the patrician must have remained in his bearing, if not in his shaggy appearance, because here at least he was let by.

The *cortile* of the palazzo was abustle. He could barely move for senators, all of them perspiring copiously in the heat. Taking a deep breath, he climbed the wide and very public stairway, overlooked by the fine statue of Doge Foscari, humble before the Lion of St. Mark.

The huge bearpit that was the *Sala del Maggior Consiglio* was crammed to its sumptuous rafters, so that the fine paintings and tapestries that adorned its ample walls could barely be seen.

He had long considered it nothing more than a gargantuan shouting-house, where nothing of importance ever occurred. Every noble citizen of Venice was a member of the Great Council, after all, so there was never any serious debate—only excessive name-calling and mutual loathing and no shortage of fighting either. Today was no exception.

"Hang the traitor!"

"Let's see the Malipiero turncoat between the pillars of the Piazzetta!"

"Tear him to pieces!"

Much of this opprobrium was initiated by the Stornelli, of course, but the other illustrious lineages—the Dandoli, the Contarinis, the Mocenigi, the Grimanis, the Vendramins, the Loredans, all of them—soon joined in. Was the fury against him so very great that he alone had succeeded in uniting the warring families of Venice?

Guards arrived to escort him through, thus sparing him from physical violence, though not from further indictment.

"Hope they torture the truth out of you, Malipiero vermin, so that you and the Mantuan can both be brought to justice!"

"Hiding him somewhere still, are you?"

"Working for the Turks, are you now?"

The last visage to thrust itself to the front of the horde, just before he was manhandled out of there, was that of Fabrizio Stornello. "Where's my son? What have you done with my boy?"

In the comparative quiet of a corridor just outside the Great Chamber, he was at least allowed to brush himself down and rearrange his clothes. Thus, maintaining as straight a back as he could, he arrived at a door that he knew to be the other—the *authorized*—way into the *Sala dei Consiglio dei Dieci*.

In the antechamber in which litigants, betrayers, pleaders, the accusing and the accused, their notaries and counsel, were made to await summons before the Ten, he saw only one other person: his houseguest, Graziano Stornello, looking untypically sheepish.

"Good morning, Captain-General."

"Good morning to you." The old sailor gave the smallest of coughs and turned a wide-brimmed hat between his fingers. His eyes darted everywhere but into Annibale Malipiero's own.

"So you've decided to break cover, have you?"

"It seemed best . . . in the circumstances."

"I see. How's my wife?"

Another cough. "She's well."

"And to what circumstances, precisely, are you referring?"

There was no chance of a reply, as the door was now opened, and Annibale Malipiero and Graziano Stornello were ushered into the prestigious presence of the Ten.

In his previous meetings with them, the chief inquisitor had always spoken first, and he did so now. "Is His Eminence not here?"

"He will join us in due course," said Councillor Cristoforo Stornello. The other nine sat impassively alongside him. One of these, Annibale Malipiero noted, had quills and ink and papers and was already scribbling furiously at the end of the long table.

"But the summons specifically mentioned"—Annibale Malipiero pulled the scroll from beneath his cloak—"*In the gracious presence of His Eminence the Doge.*"

"He will join us in due course," Councillor Tommaso Stornello echoed.

"We should be grateful if you would answer some questions," said Cristoforo Stornello, with icy courtesy. The Ten were not, on the whole, good at interrogation. That was why they had the *interroganti* to do the job for them; they could mete out the final judgment, yet sleep untroubled.

"I cannot possibly answer any questions until His Eminence is with us." Annibale Malipiero adopted the tactic used to considerable effect by the worst villain he'd yet encountered. He would remain silent until he had his way.

"You may not be aware of what has been happening in Venice and in

Cyprus during your *unauthorized* absence. There have been distur-
bances here in the city. Many Turks, going about their daily transactions,
have been attacked. Three have been killed. Also, most distressingly, the
tomb of my brother . . . *our* brother"—Cristoforo Stornello nodded to
his right and then before him—"in the church of San Rocco, has been
defaced, desecrated, by some members of your own family, Messer
Malipiero, with the words, *May All the Stornelli soon lie in such a place*."
A tremor of condemnation passed through the row of patricians. "The
flowers and messages of condolence that have been placed at our brother's
tomb, in memory of our niece Desdemona, have regularly been tram-
pled into the ground."

Annibale Malipiero remained aloof but did ponder the no doubt
certain role in all this of his dreadful nephew Jacopo, free to roam the
streets again with his disgusting band.

Cristoforo Stornello's lofty peroration moved then to recent events in
Cyprus. "You may also be unaware that the governor has been murdered."

Annibale Malipiero thought, *Everybody knows that.* Then he grasped
that it wasn't the Moor who was being talked of but his successor,
Lodovico Stornello.

"We learned of this tragedy only last night. He was assassinated in
the citadel in Famagusta by a band of insurgents who had infiltrated the
garrison as kitchen staff. They stabbed him in a hundred places as he was
sleeping, then cut his throat. They cried out the name of Iago as they did
so. They persisted in that revolting call even as they were eviscerated and
hanged for their insidious crime."

Annibale Malipiero glanced at Graziano Stornello then. The stolid old
warrior had bowed his head.

"You are right, brother, to be distressed by these regretful tidings,"
said Cristoforo Stornello. "And how would you like to justify your
actions in this whole sorry episode?" Before allowing a response, he
added, "You will have noticed I no longer continue to address you as
Captain-General, as we, the Council of Ten, have decided to deprive
you of that post forthwith." He snapped a glance at the *interrogante*.
"Just as we must deprive Messer Malipiero of his."

Aside from a slight drooping of his broad shoulders, the former captain-general stood unmoving, then raised himself to his full and still impressive height. In a measured and impassive tone he said, "I was wrong to have left Cyprus under the sole charge of our brother; he had no experience of leadership."

"Yes, yes," Cristoforo Stornello interjected, "but what of your part in the capture and traitorous concealment of Iago, followed by his escape?"

Graziano Stornello let the question hang in the air.

"As Signor Malipiero will concur, I had nothing to do with the escape of Iago of Mantua from the Prigioni Ducale."

He stared straight in front of him. Annibale Malipiero did likewise. He wasn't going to concur with or dispute anything—not until he was in front of the Doge.

"It was my idea to convey the villain in secret to Venice," Graziano Stornello continued, "and mine alone. Nobody knew of it except a few men in my charge. It was what you'd call a spur-of-the-moment decision, as one might make in the heat of battle—"

"Wait . . . *Wait!*" Tommaso Stornello slammed a fist on the table.

"No, no, *no* . . ." Cristoforo Stornello groaned, and shook his head.

The others stayed dumb but gaping.

"I say only what is true, Signors. I trust you would not want me to speak falsely."

"You had correspondence, you cannot deny that, you and Messer Malipiero here!" Tommaso Stornello squeaked.

"I'll deny nothing. Yes, we wrote to each other, but again at my instigation."

Annibale Malipiero had an inclination to step over and hug the big man. He remained resolutely straight-backed however, though something like a smile flitted across his lips.

Tommaso Stornello perhaps noted this. "You!" he spat, directing his full ire at Annibale Malipiero. "Confess that this was all your doing from the very start!"

There were nods and mutterings along the table.

Cristoforo Stornello laid an authoritative hand on Tommaso Stornello's arm to quiet him and continued to address his other brother:

"You are aware, I take it, of the severe penalties we can impose on those who endeavor to mislead us. Messer Malipiero will certainly be cognizant of them."

Tommaso Stornello, far from silenced, said to Graziano Stornello with a scowl, "You do realize you're declaring yourself a traitor?"

The soldier remained unbending to the last. "Do with me as you will," he said. "I've never lied in my life and I'm not going to start now. Unlike those in this room who have also *colluded* in the concealment of—"

He wasn't allowed to finish. "That's enough treachery!" Cristoforo Stornello spluttered. The other nine darted their heads at one another and gobbled and squawked like a flock of disturbed chickens. Annibale Malipiero wanted to decapitate them one by one and then watch them scuttle about and die.

But in a fluster of nervousness and doffing of hats, they suddenly all stood up. From behind Annibale Malipiero came a voice, gruffer and more imperious even than Graziano Stornello's. *"Treachery? Who's a traitor?"*

Annibale Malipiero turned. From where had His Eminence Doge Andrea Gritti, Supreme Prince of *La Serenissima*, appeared? Aside from the rustle of a capacious gold and red cloak, there had been no announcement of his arrival.

Annibale Malipero had never met Doge Gritti before, or not in his new capacity as Doge, and had certainly never been this close to him. The elderly ruler was still comparatively spry for a Doge and assuredly more so than the previous incumbent. Tall and broad-shouldered, if quite rotund in the belly, he had big watchful eyes and a white beard that was thicker than Annibale Malipiero's own, though cropped more roundly about his jaw. Annibale Malipiero trusted that impressive facial hair was not the only thing they had in common.

Doge Gritti was a soldier through and through, with many years of military experience, and like a true fighting man he was renowned for his forthrightness. He still required an answer to his question, so he repeated it, staring in turn at the two Stornello councillors. "Are there traitors here? Hmm?"

Cristoforo Stornello simply looked down at his hands. Tommaso

Stornello could say nothing either but pointed at Annibale Malipiero, then falteringly at Graziano Stornello, and then more firmly still at Annibale Malipiero once again.

"Are you accusing your own brother of treason, Signor? That would be a first, would it not, for a Stornello to be indicted for so dire a crime—or any misdemeanor at all, come to think of it?" Annibale Malipiero thought he heard a chortle from somewhere beneath that generous beard.

Now the estimable prince was more spirited in his tone. "I'll leave the business of who's a traitor and who isn't in your very *capable* hands, Councillors," he declared, "but at this juncture I think there are more relevant-topics to be discussed." He peered at Annibale Malipiero closely. "Would you not say so, Signor?"

It was an intrusive gaze, Annibale Malipiero thought, but also seemed encouragingly conspiratorial. "Yes, I think there are."

"The crucial question is where this Iago of Mantua might be now, is it not?"

"Unarguably," Annibale Malipiero replied.

"Because the villain must be caught, after all."

"He must indeed."

"And who better," Doge Gritti exclaimed, turning once more to the array of statues behind the table, "to help us in this mission than the man—no, no," he corrected himself, "than the two men"—with a wave of a multi-ringed hand, he included Graziano Stornello—"who might be said to have come to know the odious fellow best? Hmm?"

There were murmurings of accord from the other councillors now, though not from the two Stornelli.

"The summoning of these Signors has caused nothing but unnecessary prevarication, in my opinion," the Doge declared, "I was also not aware of it until just now. I should be grateful if in the future you would not issue directives in my name without asking me first."

"But . . . but . . . we are the Ten," Cristoforo Stornello blurted.

Doge Andrea Gritti tapped a heavily bejeweled finger upon his own imposing chest. "And I would remind you, and not for the first time, that I am the Doge, elected by the people of Venice *over your heads*." He let this assertion sink in, then swung around to Annibale Malipiero again, adopting quite an informal tone. "Where do you think this Iago fellow is now?"

"I cannot be certain as to his specific whereabouts. He's a slippery beast." Annibale Malipiero thought it best to make no mention of the villa on the Brenta.

The Doge looked mildly disappointed. "Has anyone actually spotted him?"

"Not as such, Your Eminence. He's been heard rather than seen."

"Heard?"

"He makes a habit of causing alarums and laying false trails."

"Hmm, a slippery sort indeed. Perhaps he's not within our borders at all; have you considered that?"

"It has crossed my mind, yes."

"He must have friends and supporters hereabouts, just as he did in Cyprus. Perhaps it is they who are causing these . . . these distractions."

"That also has occurred to me."

The Doge appeared pensive. "Isn't there some theory among you *interroganti*, something about criminals returning to the scene of the crime?"

Now the ex-inquisitor knew precisely where this little inquest had been heading. "If you mean that he may have gone back to Cyprus . . ."

Doge Gritti nodded. "My thoughts exactly!" He turned to the councillors, and to Cristoforo Stornello in particular. "Is anyone out looking for him in Cyprus?"

Cristoforo Stornello floundered. "I . . . I would imagine so."

"You don't know?" the supreme leader snorted. "The sooner there are some proper military men on the Council of Ten, the better!" He looked directly at Graziano Stornello.

The veteran was still standing stiff-backed and with a blank gaze, like a trooper at an inspection, but Annibale Malipiero was sure he could make out a thin smile of agreement on that weathered face.

Doge Gritti then began to strut about, as a commander might before a battle, issuing terse instructions. It was an odd sight, as the weight of his sumptuous attire was not conducive to any sort of hurried movement.

"Let's throw all we've got at finding him in Cyprus. We'll cut down on the forces out looking for him on the mainland. We might as well withdraw them altogether. They're not having much success are they? The perfidious creature perhaps had unfinished business in Cyprus, yes? Turkish business. Must be tempting for him to . . . carry on. The rebels there will be pleased to see him. Perhaps his return prompted their assassination of the governor." He stopped his striding for a moment to ask of Cristoforo Stornello: "What are the arrangements for the funeral, by the way?"

The councillor choked at the abruptness of the question. "His body . . . will of course be shipped back to Venice . . . and he will be buried with all the ceremony . . . and majesty . . . he deserves."

"I daresay he will," said the Doge. "But don't expect the state to pay a ducat for it. The Stornello millions, I'm sure, can bear all the necessary expense. Hmm?" His tone was amused, almost mocking. Then he faced the impassively upstanding Graziano Stornello. "Cyprus has need of firmer governance than your brother provided, Captain-General," he said. "Would you take the job?"

There were gasps of astonishment along the table, and Tommaso Stornello piped, "He's no longer—" The words "Captain-General" faded on his lips.

"Thank you for thinking me worthy of the position," said Graziano Stornello quickly. "But while I've grown fond of Cyprus and am tempted to revisit that land, I no longer seek office of any kind, anywhere in the world."

Doge Andrea Gritti tipped his head to one side and gave the old fighter's shoulder a gentle squeeze. "Now," said the great man, still without so much as a glance behind him, "I should like to have a conversation alone with these two Signors, if I might."

"But . . . but they're in our charge!" Cristoforo Stornello exclaimed.

"The inquiry has not been concluded," said Tommaso Stornello. "Sentences still have to be decided upon."

Doge Gritti rotated to face the table once more. His thickly hirsute visage was scarlet. "I have already given you my opinion of this so-called inquiry of yours, Signor." He then addressed the full array of quaking men before him. "I have made a decision. You will abide by it. You will ratify it, as is your function." He put a hand on Annibale Malipiero's shoulder. "I am sending Signor Malipiero here to Cyprus, where he will continue the search for Iago and will assuredly find him. I had hoped that he might be accompanied by the exceptional soldier who stands alongside him, whose qualities you have so impertinently snubbed. It is not his wish to take up the governorship of Cyprus, and for that I respect him, but I still require his advice. That is why I wish to speak to these two men alone, now, and here. So I would be obliged if you would leave us to do just that."

"But this is quite against official policy! Nobody is permitted to have private discussions in the *Sala del Consiglio dei Dieci*! At least four members of the Ten must be present at all times, and all conversations must be witnessed and recorded!" In affirmation of this dictum, Cristoforo Stornello pointed in the direction of the still scribbling councillor.

"Is that so?" Doge Gritti retorted. "And what of the secret rooms off this famous chamber? I've heard that many unrecorded little chats have been held there—some of them *without* the required quorum."

That silenced Cristoforo Stornello quickly enough. The particular "little chat" to which the Doge obliquely referred could be none other than that hurriedly convened shortly after Iago's arrival in Venice—the very meeting that Graziano Stornello had begun to allude to earlier.

The Doge wagged a finger at both Stornello councillors and said, with barely concealed glee, "Judge not lest ye be judged, Signors. Now," he snapped, "in the name of San Marco, leave us! If you value your offices and preference and advancement, go, all of you!"

Most scuttled out swiftly. Finally, Cristoforo Stornello, after a momentary glower of indignation, pulled his cloak about his shoulders and left the great room also.

Unusually for a dignitary of such high office, Doge Andrea Gritti himself shut the big double doors behind them and even drew the bolt. "Come," he said to the two men who remained in the chamber, and moved to the table. He dropped into a chair with something of a groan. "They'll be listening out there, I don't doubt." He removed his horned hat and scratched a thinning pate. "Sit . . . sit!" he commanded, though not too imperiously. The former Captain-General and the former *Capo degli Interroganti* sat.

The Doge turned to Graziano Stornello. "I'm sorry I had to be so brusque with those brothers of yours."

"It's of no consequence, Eminence; they can be very—"

"What angered me most was their condescending attitude toward you, my friend. The nerve of it! Are you sure you don't want your old job back? I'm inclined to give it to you just to annoy them."

"The matter of appointments is rather more complex than that, Eminence."

"Graziano, I was joking!" Doge Gritti put a hand on the soldier's own. He looked at Annibale Malipiero and sighed. "I had to be in this post for only a few days to realize how little actual power I have! You wouldn't believe it—the bureaucracy, the paperwork."

"I experienced a fair amount of officialdom myself as an inquisitor," said the ex-inquisitor, beginning to feel a bit left out.

"I daresay, I daresay," said the Doge, without seeming too interested. He pointed to the bolted door. "They're probably debating among themselves right now as to whether or not I have the authority to send you to Cyprus."

Annibale Malipiero said, a touch nervously, "It is possible, Eminence, that I may apprehend the villain without venturing personally to Cyprus."

The Doge's expression hardened. "For all our sakes, I sincerely hope you're right." Then, he chuckled. "Did you seriously imagine I was going to send you to Cyprus, when I know well enough that Iago is not there?"

Annibale Malipiero felt outsmarted, a circumstance he never liked. "I suspect there is much else that you know besides," he said quite coldly.

"Oh, I know everything," said the Doge. "Or everything that Graziano here knows."

Graziano Stornello looked only mildly apologetic.

The illustrious one stood up, rearranging his red and gold cloak over his bulky frame. "But," he announced firmly, "as far as everyone else is going to know, especially those out there"—he didn't need to point—

"you *have* gone to Cyprus, and by the next available ship." He turned briefly to the erstwhile Captain-General of the Sea. "You can still arrange all that, hmm? Spread the necessary rumors and so on?"

"And am I to . . . evaporate?" Annibale Malipiero inquired.

"I'm tempted to ask," said the potentate, "where Iago is right now, as I'm sure you do know where he is, but . . ." He put a finger to his lips. "It is up to you now, Signor Malipiero." He became crisp, resolute, again the no-nonsense commander in chief. He spread his hands and said, "I shall indulge you, though not for long. Graziano has explained to me that you have this curious desire to discover what makes a villain tick. We all know what he did, don't we?"

"Though perhaps not quite yet how he did it," Annibale Malipiero said.

The former sea captain stared at him in some astonishment. "You do not believe he made the Moor kill my niece and then himself?"

The investigator looked relatively contrite. "Forgive me, Signor, but even your Florentine friend—"

"God rest him." Graziano Stornello hastily made a sign of the cross.

"Indeed, indeed. But even he could only surmise. He did not see it happen."

"He *heard* it, and he certainly saw the consequences."

"Yes, yes," Doge Andrea Gritti said testily. "A murderer is a murderer as far as I'm concerned." His tone mellowed but only marginally, as he stared once more at Annibale Malipiero. "According to my good friend here, you are less interested in the nature of a crime than in its motive. Is that right?"

"Nature and motive are often connected, but, yes, you are correct, Eminence."

"You wish to know what demons lurk within his dark soul, or something of the sort. I don't understand it myself, but as Graziano seems to be of the same inclination—this Iago must be a fascinating fellow indeed—I shall allow you to pursue your odd little venture for . . . shall we say a fortnight? For my part, the only thing I must know is his association with the Ottoman." He paused. "Do I make myself clear?"

"Abundantly," said Annibale Malipiero.

"Once you feel you know all there is to know, you can call on the might of Venice to take him and to return him—alive, I hope, and in chains. Until such a time, Venice cannot help you. It will be put about that you've lost yourself in the Cyprus mountains and possibly, in due course, that you're dead." Doge Andrea Gritti's gaze became more steely. "Which you most certainly will be, should you fail in your endeavor."

43. Padua

This play that I'm in, this *commedia*, is becoming more peculiar, more *comedic*, by the day.

Right now we're monks—or friars, to be more precise, mendicant friars. All four of us, in the full garb—cloaks, scapulars, cowls covering our faces, rope belts around our waists. Even Franceschina is now a little friar—and a very fetching one she makes. She thinks the camouflage great fun. She giggles a lot, which isn't very monkish, particularly since we're supposed to be mute. Iago has insisted we should all pretend to have taken a vow of silence.

Curiously, ever since having his head half shattered (and he still wears the bandage to prove it) Baldassare has become more argumentative with Iago, not less. He says that if we're supposed to be Augustinians—and it was from four Augustinians innocently plodding toward Padua that we stole these clothes, leaving them all but naked and tied to trees by the wayside—then we cannot be silent. The followers of Saint Augustine are not a silent order. In fact, no mendicants are silent. The mute orders don't go meandering about the countryside; they tend to stay locked away in their monasteries. "That's the whole point," said my tutor. "They're not supposed to mix with the world."

Iago told him to shut up or he'd earn another crack.

They've been bickering like a couple of old market women ever since—when there's nobody around to hear them. I don't think Iago will strike Baldassare again though. I suspect he's beginning to enjoy their spats.

So far his strategy has worked. I know from previous visits that Padua's not the easiest of cities to enter or to survive in once through her massively fortified and extremely well-guarded gates. She's a dangerous place, despite being the greatest center of learning in the world; the students have made her so. When not studying, they're getting drunk and beating up one another or anyone else who happens to be around, and such behavior encourages the dregs of Italy and beyond to congregate here. Nobody with any sense walks about Padua after sunset. Baldassare, who's here often, knows this better than anyone, having been at the receiving end of many a cudgeling on these streets. He, of all people, should be grateful that he's now a monk.

We weren't stopped at the gates or called to identify ourselves or frisked for weaponry (which was lucky, as we're bristling with it beneath our fustian). And up to now nobody's assaulted us or challenged us in any way.

I do get a curious thrill whenever I come to this town. The risk might have something to do with it, but mostly it's the sense of being at the very heart of some great, effervescent, intellectual mass. In Venice, the talk one overhears is either gossip or haggling and not much else. In Padua it's proper debate, in every portico or dark corner, with sometimes bloody conclusions. "A thousand of the cleverest minds in the world fighting for mastery in a snake pit" is how Baldassare has described this defiantly clever city. He loves Padua too, for all the pain he has suffered here.

There aren't many students around at the moment, as it's high summer. The place seems to be crawling with soldiers, even after sunset. They must be here because we're now in a war zone, or on the edge of one. I hope it's for that reason and not because some of them are looking for us.

"Did you note how your girl stopped and trembled?" Iago murmured to me, as a drunken band of them went roaring past us (we arrived here not much before midnight).

"Yes, they frighten her."

"No, lad, that's lust." He turned to Baldassare. "Where are your lodgings? We'll stay there."

"That would not be wise," said Baldassare snootily. "When in Padua I stay in the dormitory of the Monastero di Santi Filippo e Giacomo. It's run by *Augustinians.*"

We were tired. We'd walked without stopping all day. We were also very hungry, having eaten nothing since early morning, when we snatched a meager breakfast of moldy bread and even staler cheese and some leftover bits of leathery chicken at the villa on the Brenta. But it appears that a mendicant friar has not long to wait for the offer of food and lodging, for soon enough an innkeeper was calling from the door of his small and rather dilapidated-looking hostelry. "*Benvenuti, frati santi!*"

We sit opposite him now—with our backs to a wall on a bench that can barely accommodate the four of us. Perhaps fortunately, the only light in here comes from a very weak fire. He is drunk, and therefore morose. "Forgive me for the many sins I have committed, I ask your penitence, your absolution."

We must listen to his rambling confessions as we wolf down watery soup and gristly sausages and stringy *agnello arrosto*. His wife's left him, he cries, because he was adulterous with three other women, *un marito infidele all'estremo*, and he's now a desperate *peccatore solitario*, with no friends. "I have no one in the world! I have no *clienti! Guarda! Osserva!*" He waves at the thankfully empty room. I already have no doubt that the dire quality of his food and the vinegary nature of his wine (one sip for me and no more) has kept people away.

All I can think of for the moment is how I'm jammed up against Franceschina. It's the first time, I realize, that I've ever been so close to her (she's on my left and Baldassare is pressed against me to my right, with Iago beyond him). She's so extraordinarily warm. I can feel her breathe and quiver with amusement at our wailing host. She never raises her face from beneath her cowl. Once, a long time ago, I caught a bird, a house swift, that had flown through the casement of my bedroom. I took it in my palms before carrying it to the window and letting it go. It wasn't frightened. It trusted me. I was enthralled by the pulsing ferment within that fragile body. Franceschina's frissons remind me of that minute, accepting creature now.

The *locandiere* howls on, revealing a toothless mouth, and beats his forehead with a filthy fist. His children have been snatched from him too—his *bambini belli*. There's nothing worse in the world, he cries, than a father parted from his children. But he deserves all this, he groans. "Such is the cost of *una vita peccaminosa*! You, *fratelli santi*, you are men who have lived *una vita virtuosa*! Grant me God's pardon! *Assolva me, assolva me!*"

So we absolve him, as best we can, with signs of the cross—or three of us do; Iago sits motionless, like some grim specter at the feast. Of course we can't say anything. The blubbering man blinks at us, confused by our muteness. He wants a spoken absolution, obviously. Now he's even mumbling the words to himself: "*Dominus noster, Jesus Christus . . .*" and as he does so he grabs at the sleeve of Iago's habit, tearing at it, somehow sensing his authority despite his not having moved a muscle. "*Padre spirituale! Rimetti a me i miei debiti!*"

There's a low snarl from beneath Iago's cowl. Frantically, I tap the innkeeper on the shoulder and mime an explanation, passing my hand across my mouth.

"Oh," he slurs, "*un ordine silenzioso.*" He drops his head into his hands and promptly falls asleep, facedown on the table.

Iago stands up and pulls back his hood and tries to rid himself of his friar's attire. For a while he's a flailing, cursing whirl of limbs and wool and linen. His weaponry clanks beneath his clothes.

"No! No!" Franceschina whispers, her own hood falling. "You will wake him."

Iago obeys her, or perhaps the effort of tugging all that heavy fabric up and over his head is too much for him. He lets out a tirade against all clerics, without exception; the "dissemblers and swindlers," the "thieves and spongers in the guise of pious men" who use their supposed innocence and devoutness to "bleed dry the rest of us."

Baldassare—many of whose colleagues, of course, are of the cloth themselves—is still in a quarrelsome mood and takes immediate offense.

"How dare you speak of some of the brightest minds in the world in such a way?"

Iago leans toward him. He doesn't hit him but goes further in his excoriations. Now he's condemning the holy orders not only for their scrounging and general deviousness but for their wantonness too. He's calling them "fornicators" and "pederasts" and "wenchers," "every man jack of them filled with Epicurism and lust." He calls them "idle ruttish roosters" and "rampant goats," who exploit their duplicitous piety to engage in all manner of filthy sins.

It's decidedly odd, almost droll, to hear such scabrous fulminations coming from the mouth of a man dressed as a monk. Baldassare continues to splutter objections. Franceschina sits upright and stiff-backed. Her lovely fingers open and close just a touch on her lap, and sometimes there's the smallest intake and exhalation of breath. But although her mouth and eyes are more open than normal, her face remains surprisingly expressionless, as if she's taking it all in but quite calmly.

Iago now tells us of how he has visited monasteries on his travels, in Italy and abroad, where the monks are no more than procurers, "where, if you pay enough, a godly fellow will find you a nun who will give herself most accommodatingly." He adds to the indecency by talking of "pricking priests" and "brides of Christ with their habits about their faces." Then he tells us of a particular abbey in Cyprus where the friars, "known as the white friars, as they dress in hypocritical white," take many wives for themselves, "the prettiest girls on the island," and then sell them for congress, "as the whores and sluts that they are."

"Ay!" Franceschina finally cries out, *"Basta! Basta!"* A hand flies to her mouth.

"That's outrageous!" Baldassare yells. "Most holy houses are pure and devout places, dedicated only to prayer and good works and—"

"You would not know a dirty monk if his cock was up and crowing for all to see."

"Ay! Ay! Ay!"

In an instant Iago is kneeling before her, an entirely different being, prostrate and full of contrition. He takes that jolted hand of hers in both of his and lowers it, very delicately, onto her lap. I don't feel her shy away. Still clasping it, he says with extraordinarily credible earnestness, "*Mi dispiace*, my lady, for my commonness. It is my way. I am rough. I am a *soldier*."

It occurs to me that this whole filthy tirade of his has not simply been to enrage Baldassare but to gauge Franceschina's reaction too, to see how much she'll take, to throw her away from him by disgusting her and then, as he is doing now, to win her back. It seems to me like some twisted form of courtship. To confirm that he has been in some way duplicitous, he looks at me now and winks.

Now our landlord stirs, snorting like a pig in a trough. Quickly, Iago takes Franceschina's cowl and pulls it over her face, then does the same with his own. The man raises his head from the table. If he's surprised to see one member of our silent order kneeling before another, he doesn't show it. Iago's lurid talk must have invaded his dreams, for he, too, now mutters about "lechery, yes, lechery" and "fornication and copulation, yes," and then he howls, "I shall go to hell, *fratelli onesti e virtuosi*, if I am not absolved, for I am a dirty, *dirty* sinner!" Again he demands, "*Assolva me!*"

Iago stands and hovers behind him, digging beneath his cloak. For a second or two I think that the innkeeper will be rewarded for his interminable requests for forgiveness with a slice to the throat. Once more I come to the wailing idiot's rescue and perform another little mime— this time putting my hands to the side of my face, palms together, as I make a snoring sound and briefly close my eyes.

"Yes, you must sleep—it is late. Allow me to show you where, *monaci buoni*." Our host rises shakily and, with much obsequious gesticulating, ushers us toward a narrow staircase.

There's but the one room and in the middle of it the one bed—or, rather, a straw-filled expanse of fustian, sufficient for four friars if they were comfortably acquainted with one another. We consider our options.

Iago whispers to Franceschina, "You will sleep there. We will find other means of repose."

After some not very convincing dissent, Franceschina acquiesces and lies down. She removes only her mud-caked shoes. Her graceful brown feet poke out from the underside of her cloak. Within no time, she's asleep.

Minutes pass before Iago says, "She's away from us. Where's the harm?" And with that he's lying next to her, but with decorum: a few inches away from touching, and with his back to hers.

Baldassare yawns mightily, then he, too, makes for our sole means of respite and lies adjacent to Iago. I concede to my own exhaustion and settle down, as best I can, alongside my teacher.

"Mind he doesn't molest you, lad," Iago advises with a chuckle.

Baldassare is too tired to emit more than a sniff of umbrage.

Slumber doesn't come easily. Iago decides to keep the talk going for his own amusement if not for ours. "So monks are a brainy lot, are they?" It sounds strangely conciliatory, though I'm sure some belligerent purpose lies behind it.

Baldassare is not of a mind to answer for a while, but eventually he mumbles, "Some monks are the cleverest men I know."

"How is it you're no monk yourself," Iago asks, "if you think them all so damned smart?"

Baldassare has never been one to resist the opportunity of cataloguing his scholarly achievements. "In point of fact," he says, "I took the novitiate at the Monastero di Santi Filippo e Giacomo, and the abbot there was keen that I should enter the order; he was most impressed by a treatise I wrote on—"

"But in the end they wouldn't have you, is that it?" Iago brusquely interjects. "Why was that? Because you couldn't keep your hands off the *coristi*?"

Baldassare starts to wobble again with outrage. "I'll have you know—"

I quickly interpose. "There were some differences of doctrine, were there not?" Of course my tutor has told me all this before, on more than one occasion.

He grunts in affirmation. "And it was my choice, not theirs."

"What differences?" Iago sounds mildly disappointed.

"Mere nuances, subtleties of definition, really."

"Blast your high-flown language. What differences?"

"I thought myself somewhat too secular to become a man of God, in the full sense."

"Secular! Ha! So you're an infidel then, an unbeliever!"

"Not at all," says Baldassare.

"Who'd have thought it? Dottore Baldassare Ghiberti of the University of Padua is a heathen. What does your virtuous family make of that, Gentile Stornello, that you are the student of so godless a teacher? Or do they know?"

"I am not godless."

"He's a humanist," I say, not that I imagine such a vindication will help in any way.

"What's that? More highbrow gibberish? More of your university piffle?"

"It's a philosophy adhered to by some of the finest minds alive today," my mentor explains in a clipped voice. "We believe in a divinity, yes—but we query the notion of a single all-powerful God who shapes our ends. Ours is a doctrine of education, whereby we instruct men to believe in their own will, the mastery of their own fates, through the reading of philosophy and rhetoric and poetry. One might say that study is the proper making of a man. As Aristotle himself said, a proper man can be judged by . . ."

He stops, because Iago has started to snore, dead to what he has no doubt considered to be inconsequential ramblings. And I'm dozing off too, having heard it all many times previously, and at greater length.

Before falling—thankfully—into the realms of Morpheus myself, I look up at what I can make out of the inn's rafters above me, which isn't much. I ponder beyond them, up far higher than the night, and try to conceive what God might think of us now—four fugitives from justice imitating pious men (one of whom is not by any stretch a man), in the full accoutrements of blessedness and inviolability, on a makeshift mattress in the smartest city in Italy. I doubt he'd approve, although he might be amused.

I wake, I don't know how many hours later. I know it's morning from the light that pierces my aching eyes through a small window somewhere in the gloom. It's enough to see that between a still-dormant Iago and me, there's nothing.

Oh, Dio mio, *he's run.*

As noiselessly as possible, I rise. Yes, Baldassare has slipped away. He may of course have simply snuck downstairs. I make for the door. Before descending though, I glance back in the direction of Iago and Franceschina. I don't want to, but I can't prevent myself.

He has his arm about her waist. For a horrible moment I imagine them to be lovers, in a nonchalant converging of bodies, as if they've known each other for years. I once entered, as a child, my father and mother's bedchamber. I don't know why. I had many a sleepless night then, but it was usually Zinerva who consoled me. On that night, I saw my parents thus; I saw it as a sign that they loved each other deeply (and they did). I gazed upon them in a kind of wonderment. But now I'm disgusted.

How could he, how could *he?* I protest inwardly as I plummet down the stairs. By the time I've reached the bottom, I've resolved to have nothing more to do with Iago. I'll escape his clutches finally and forever, as Baldassare has done. But there's no sign of my tutor anywhere.

I move a few yards down the street, and soon enough the innkeeper is at my side. "I hope, *fratello generoso,* that you will pay *un poco qualche cosa* for my hospitality?" So much for his bounteousness.

"The friar who remains upstairs will pay."

The innkeeper doesn't seem too surprised by this sudden breach of my vows.

I haven't gone far before another voice snarls in my ear. "Where's your teacher?"

"He's . . . he's . . ."

While I falter so, I see Franceschina alongside him. *Still* he has his arm around her, but no longer with any sign of easeful acquaintance. There's something powerful, feline, about her as she starts to struggle. He grasps her more firmly.

"He'll have gone to where he teaches, I suspect," I say, before I can stop myself.

"Take me there."

So the three of us set off for the Chiesa di Santi Filippo e Giacomo

and the monastery to which it is attached. It takes time to find, as I'm
not that cognizant of the byways of Padua. But finally the great building
stands before us, with its rather plain ochre façade and its imposing
campanile, taller than any other in the city. I know the route now, and
skirting a great number of friars of various orders bustling this way and
that, I lead the way around the side of the church to the cloisters. "He'll
probably be in the library," I suggest, as we face a door carved with the
figures of studying ecclesiastics. As I'd supposed, Iago is rather daunted
by the prospect of entering such a place, with his mistrust of scholars
and books. He pauses long enough for me to slip in alone.

What am I hoping for now? To disappear into this silent throng,
most of them in habits of various sorts, hoodless heads bent in study?
There are tables and tables of them. Aside from the occasional clearing
of a throat, there's not a sound.

If Baldassare thinks of anywhere in Padua as home, it's this huge
learned room. On the way here I've pictured him trudging toward Venice and freedom. I've even bade him *vai con Dio!* Now, though, I think
of those Turks that Iago is always ready to remind us of, who will prevent us from escaping too far. So I'm really quite grateful as I see my
plump and ever-serious friend, tucked into a dark corner at a table of
his own, writing away frenetically by the light of a single candle, with
(as cover, I presume) a copy of Theocritus's *Idylls* open beside him.

I turn quickly in the direction of the door. Iago doesn't seem to have
dared to cross the threshold yet. I slip silently through a throng of heads
bent in study.

"What in God's name are you doing?"

"I'm carrying on with my treatise." It's all very *sotto voce.*

"No, you're not; you're writing to the *interrogante.* Have you seen him?"

He shakes his head.

"How do you know where to put what you've written?"

Covering the information with a cough or two, he murmurs, "There
were two men outside the inn. They've been watching us all this while.
I'm to leave my report here for them."

"*Madonna mia*, Baldassare, this is dangerous—"

And now Iago has spotted us. He's slouching toward us, still holding on to Franceschina, by her wrist now, as a senior friar might a novice. Baldassare makes a move to hide the papers under the book of poems, but not quickly enough.

"Forgive me," he mumbles, "but I had to take the opportunity to—"

Iago raises a finger to his lips, reminding us again that ours is supposed to be a silent order. Then he pushes the Theocritus aside, picks up one of the sheaves of paper, and begins to read.

Baldassare groans. Franceschina senses something's very wrong indeed and releases an all-too-feminine gasp, but nobody raises a head.

I think of running there and then. I'm sure Baldassare's of the same mind. I glance in the direction of the door, hastily mapping the fastest route between the tables and benches and studying clerics. I think Iago's sight might not be too good, because he's lifting the paper close to his eyes and squinting. I don't note any change of expression. If anything, there's increasing absorption. He's reading our death warrant.

He's taking his time about it. He's making us *squirm.*

He moves toward the center of the great room, where there's more light, taking the sheaf with him and still apparently engrossed. He beckons to us to follow, which we do, like lambs bound for slaughter. Without raising his head, he clicks his fingers in the direction of two spare places at a table. Franceschina and I sit, with diligent bookworms to our right and left. The four of us are the only ones with our hoods up. Still Iago reads on, as he guides Baldassare—not roughly but with some purpose—toward another table, at some distance from ours (although I can see them both out of the corner of an eye). He doesn't wish us all to seem too associated with one another.

He continues to pore over Baldassare's jottings leaf by leaf, turning them over now and then, reinvestigating a particular passage, and sometimes seeming to either nod with approval or shake his head dismissively, as if he were the instructor and Baldassare his uneasy student.

After agonizing minutes of this, he puts the papers down and taps them into a neat pile. He pushes them aside and turns to Baldassare, who is frozen with terror by now. Then, astonishingly, Iago pats him on the back—reassuringly, even appreciatively. I realize that this show of interest in Baldassare's writings is just that—a charade.

I hear his voice in my head, his railing against books and bookishness and bookish people . . . Then I realize.

I feel a wave of pity for him. Not because he can't read. I know many people who can't read: Zinerva, Balbina, all the servants at home. And Franceschina too, I now see. The book she's snatched in a busy pretense at studiousness, licking at a delectable finger to turn the pages, is upside down.

No, I feel sorrow for Iago because he needs to feign that he can. It seems so unnecessary somehow, and wretched.

Now, incredibly, Baldassare has started to scribble again. He has obviously come to the same conclusion. But Iago does not seem to care. That's a brave thing my tutor is doing, nonetheless.

Franceschina can sense my relief, I think. She raises her eyes beneath her cowl to look up at me. There's still some anxiety there, a need for reassurance. I smile at her. She returns the smile, and it's dazzling. Our legs are almost touching under the table. I push mine closer to hers so that they do touch.

A cloak sweeps past us, brushing against mine. I hear whispers of respectful recognition all around me. Who's this, then?

His vestments and regalia denote someone of considerably higher status than that of a mere monk. He's wearing a white and gold miter, a bejeweled cope, again mainly of gold, and he's carrying a gleaming black and gold crosier: He's the man in charge around here. I've seen him on my previous visits to Padua; Baldassare has pointed him out to me, with some awe. But I don't remember his name. He's an Augustinian—and he's making his way directly toward Iago and Baldassare.

"Good morning, *frati santi*. I don't believe I've had the pleasure . . ."

I don't suppose the abbot of the Monastero di Santi Filippo e Giacomo is much used to being met with complete silence. He appears bemused and then affronted, as do the acolytes in his train—boys, mainly, in spotless white surplices. A priest snaps, "*Il Padre Eminente* is addressing you. Stand up!"

This they do, though they remain resolutely mute. Baldassare looks as if he's trying to make himself smaller or to disappear altogether, his chin in his chest, his arms hugging his tubby frame.

The abbot tries to peer beneath my tutor's hood, then pulls it off. "Dottore Ghiberti, are you a brother now? I did not know you were in Padua." His stupefied gaze moves from Baldassare's grimacing face to his bandaged skull. "What has happened to your head?"

The priest tries to do the same to Iago and receives a swift blow to the stomach.

With remarkable speed, Iago grabs Baldassare's arm and scuttles toward the main door. He also manages to snatch at Franceschina on the way, causing her to lurch backward over the bench on which she's been sitting. And now *her* hood falls back, and her hair tumbles everywhere, and she also lets out a very high-pitched scream, in pure soprano. There are cries of *Madre Santa di Dio!* and such, and many signs of the cross over pious breasts, and someone howls, "A woman! A woman in the *Monastero Consacrato!*"

Iago doesn't let go of either of them. All three have reached the door. Everyone in the library remains too stunned to give any kind of chase. His hood is still up. I hear mutterings of *"Un demonio, un maligno, il diavolo in persona!"* Then there's a great rush to the entrance—monks and friars and scholars stumbling and clambering over one another in an uproar of shouts and continued invocations to God and all the saints. I've no choice but to join the hue and cry. I lower my own cowl at last. Nobody, I imagine, will recognize me.

By the time I've managed to push my way through the throng and into the gardens that surround the Church and Monastery of Santi Filippo e Giacomo, it's not only those who were in the library who are doing the pursuing. It seems to be most of Padua, and that includes a lot of soldiers. There are more students now, too, the ones who've stayed in town for the summer, for whom it's still far too early in the day to do any work but who've been woken by the clamor, flexing and swaggering and readying themselves for bloodshed. I don't think anyone knows who or what everybody's supposed to be looking for, but Padua, I daresay, just like Venice, does love to hunt down a villain.

There are cries of "He's over there" and "No, he isn't, he's there" and "They're heading for *il centro della città!*" and "No, they're not, they're making for the walls." With them I rush hither and thither, tagging along with one group, then another. I find I'm as desperate to find the prey as any hunter, though for different reasons.

I crash against a soldier, nearly trip, and spin around, muttering, "Sorry, sorry."

He's not accepting the apology. Maybe he suspects who I am. There must be some kind of warrant out for my arrest, like those they pin up on doors, with a description of the criminal being sought and sometimes the offer of a reward. There are probably such notices all over the Veneto. What does mine say? *Ricercato morto o vivo, un complice del diavolo?* He seizes me by the shoulder, examines me, stares into my face. His breath is foul and full of drink. He doesn't arrest me. Instead, he gives me a punch to the abdomen, which sends me sprawling. "Watch where you're going, *rammollito*," he growls, and shuffles off, taking care to spit on me as he passes.

The street I'm in is empty. The horde has moved on, sending echoes of the manhunt to every corner of Padua. A mightily strong hand catches me beneath each arm. Iago grins widely with those broken teeth of his. Baldassare shrinks back into the shadows of the portico under which I presume they've been hiding. Franceschina, however, runs forward. She's flushed, gleaming, with moist skin, panting with the thrill of it all. She smiles at me uncertainly, but with what I hope is a kind of breathless concern.

"It's time we left this erudite city," says the Mantuan.

44. The Euganean Hills

At last we've reached a part of the Veneto that everyone concurs is beautiful. Everywhere before this has been flat, relentlessly so, and, because it's August, invasively sultry. I know that we Venetians like our villas along the Brenta, but the true lovers of *Il Pastorale* go just that bit farther west of Padua to bathe their weary limbs in babbling rivulets, to breathe in the balmy air, like proper *campagnoli*. The spring water has curative qualities, they say. The divine Petrarch himself spent his last years within this sylvan landscape, finding peace among the olives and the vines, "frail of body but tranquil of mind."

I have an uncle who now chooses to spend most of his time in these parts—the only one of the forbidding bunch whom I actually like, the only one indeed who deigns to acknowledge that I exist: my uncle Ubaldo, with whose sons Liborio and Maurizio I used to attend the seminary. He has a villa here, though I don't know precisely where. The last time I saw him was at my uncle Brabantio's funeral. I remember his amiable but solicitous face as he wandered among the mourners.

We're at the top of what I think is called Monte Rosso. It's not the highest in this range of hills, but it was a struggle to get up here. Iago cursed us for our lassitude, our puniness, as Baldassare and I had to stop many times to recover.

"I'm sorry," I puffed. "I've never been up a mountain before."

"This is no mountain! I could show you mountains!"

The chase through Padua has energized him. He scrabbled over rocks and ledges, bounded up precipitous footpaths, strode across brooks, almost without pausing for breath, and yelled, triumphantly down to us. I think his feet have healed, or he's found some cure not available to most men, some power of mind over body that can subsume all affliction.

Franceschina more than matched him in dexterity and stamina, and when he scolded us she'd laugh. She's supple as a sylph, fearless as the goats one sees here that scamper up vertiginous escarpments. She even challenged Iago to pursue her at times, daring *him* to be so intrepid. She was barefoot. She had tucked her robe up around her waist so that her legs were bare too. They glistened with exertion. She was an Amazon; she was Penthesilea; she was Antiope.

"Isn't she the most heavenly being you have ever seen?" I asked Baldassare. He was either reluctant to agree or too winded to speak. "Go on," I persisted, "admit it. How could any poet not worship so marvelous a creature? If Petrarch were here now, he'd be . . . dumbstruck!"

"Petrarch was never dumbstruck," said Baldassare. But his eyes never shifted from Iago, who at that moment was negotiating the crossing of a hazardous crevice many feet above us and therefore well out of earshot. "I don't believe in the forces of darkness, as you know, but if I did, I'd say he was the devil."

"He certainly seems more than human sometimes," I concurred.

"If we were up there with him now, and we . . . pushed him off that rock, what would happen? Do you think he might fly?" Baldassare looked downward, as if to calculate the distance the man would plummet if he didn't.

"He'd fall, but then he'd pick himself up. And then he'd kill us."

"We could try to make a dash for it," Baldassare suggested halfheartedly.

"We'd probably trip and die in the descent. In any case, we can't. We've been *instructed*, remember?"

"And you'd have to leave behind your *innamorata,* your Artemis, your virginal goddess of the wilderness."

I was short of breath once more. "Doesn't she look like a celestial huntress?"

"Though I'm not sure about the 'virginal' analogy."

That earned him a thump on the arm. He looked at me in surprise. I'd never struck my tutor before.

But then, as if searching for something, he glanced around and down at the plain that stretched to the city we'd just fled, no longer the absentminded academic. "Where is our instructor anyway? He wrote to me he was 'never far.' I asked the men outside the inn where he was; they would not say. Perhaps he's abandoned us." He scanned the seemingly deserted landscape awhile longer. "And where, come to think of it, are these Turks that are apparently following us everywhere?"

Now I sit atop the hill. Iago sits beside me. He's sent Baldassare to gather firewood, while Franceschina, my slim and nimble divinity of the chase, my heavenly daughter of Zeus and sister of Apollo, darts among the outcrops and hollows at some distance below us. Her long neck twitches from side to side like an ever-alert deer, but she's the seeker, not the prey. Sometimes she crouches like a young lioness, poised to strike. Iago has lent her his dagger. He's told her to try to catch and kill a goat for our supper.

The outlook in every direction is breathtaking. South of us are more prominences in this range, which is named the *Colli Euganei*, after some long-extinct tribe that used to live here. To the north, the fertile Paduan plain spreads to the foothills of the Dolomiti, which even Iago, I think, would call mountains. The day is so clear that I can make out the silhouettes of yet higher, still-snow-clad pinnacles beyond them. Padua herself looks positively hospitable from here, with her dun-colored cupolas and ochre campanile. East of her the line of trees that masks the Brenta snakes its way to the lagoon and Venice herself, a glittering gemstone of a hundred hues.

Iago is staring westwards where a lush terrain of gentle slopes and valleys undulates to a hazy horizon. Somewhere down there is the border with Lombardy. Beyond what we can see are Verona and Milan, and Mantua. I can make out Vicenza—I've been there with my father on business trips—and a handful of scattered villages and farmsteads. I can hear the gurgling of innumerable brooks and becks and, farther off, the roar of a waterfall. And, echoing across the vast expanse with such clarity that they could be close at hand, the bark of a dog, the lowing of cattle and the jingle of the bells around their necks. It all looks, and sounds, so restful, so unassailable, so empty.

"Are you looking for Mantua?" I ask.

"Don't be a dunce, lad. Mantua's still many miles off."

"How many would you say?"

He shrugs. "Over a hundred." He snatches at a blade of high grass and puts it in his mouth, twirling it in his teeth like *un contadino vero*.

"But we're still headed there?"

He nods. All the athleticism, the liveliness, he showed just a short time ago has abandoned him. His features are drawn, pale even for someone so weather-burned. He reaches down to grip his feet, to squeeze them gently, as if trying to wring from them whatever vestiges of pain remain. He took his boots and bandages off earlier to wash his feet in a stream. I look at the wounds, the first time I've dared to. They're clean but each instep has a deep crevice in it, about two inches in length, startlingly pink against the leathery brownness of the skin around them. These slits are beginning to close. I've become increasingly amazed by the body's ability to mend itself, but I know he must have suffered greatly.

He gives a hiss of annoyance and looks down at Franceschina, still squatting and hopping and darting about among the crags, enjoying her role as divine poacher. He sighs. I've heard him sigh before, but this is different. His chest heaves three or four times, like one who's trying to void not only the physical torment within him but some profound melancholy of the soul. To underscore the sadness, he stares once again in the direction of what I think must be Mantua.

"You probably can't wait to get there," I say. He doesn't react. "To Mantua, I mean. Personally, I can't think of anything better than to be back in Venice." I'm telling the truth. I long for my bed, the comforts of home. "One always misses the place where one was born, doesn't one?"

"Does *one*?" His emphasis mocks my use of the word. "Does one indeed? I don't."

"You don't miss Mantua?"

"Mantua, yes. The place of my birth, no."

"You weren't born in Mantua?"

He gives me a disdainful glance.

"Where exactly were you born, then?" I'm quite hoping Baldassare's nearby, though he's supposed to be collecting wood. Anything Iago might now reveal will have to be noted and delivered.

Iago answers my query with terrible succinctness. "In hell," he says. "I was born in hell."

I can't help but recoil a little. Is he about to declare that he is, after all, the devil? Although in truth the devil wasn't born in hell, if one wants to be pedantic; he was thrown there.

He lets the horrific possibility hover awhile before putting out a palm and clasping my upper leg quite tenderly. He's grinning. "You think I am Satan?"

"It's crossed my mind more than once that you might be."

He laughs, or rather cackles, quite loudly, like some stage villain, so that Franceschina looks up from her hunting. He bares his teeth at her, growling. Predictably, she recoils too and freezes in momentary dread. He curls his fingers inward so that his hands are claws and strikes at the air. She giggles uncertainly. "You and all the world," he says to me. He hauls himself up with some distress, holding on to his thighs as he does so. "Let it be known, then, that I am not," he murmurs. "Does the devil bleed like a man? Does he know pain like a man?"

Then he roars, as if not caring who hears, to all the world in fact, so that his bellows reverberate about the hills and valleys: "I am not the devil. I am a man!" Whereupon the hands that were claws become fists, and he beats his breast. "I am a man! I am *a man!*"

Franceschina applauds with both relief and excitement, as if he were a thespian whom she's always admired and who has delivered a particularly thrilling oration.

He sits again, breathing heavily.

"This hell you speak of: I presume you aren't referring to hell as such, by which I mean most men's perception of hell, as a place of eternal damnation and of fire and brimstone and such things—"

"Pah, lad," he snaps, "you begin to sound like your tutor. Too many words, too many words."

Temerity has indeed made me overly loquacious, so I inquire directly, "Where were you born, then, if not in literal hell?"

"It was a hell on earth. That's all you need to know."

"And where is this place?"

He's gazing westward again.

"Over there somewhere?"

He nods. "Just south of Milan."

"So why are you known as the Mantuan?"

His sturdy shoulders lift and subside. "That's to be answered by those who call me so."

"And what of Iago? It's not a name I've heard before."

"My mother was Spanish."

"So it is a Spanish name . . ."

His mouth tightens. His eyes narrow. He's closing up. I remember Franceschina telling me that his mother had died when he was my age. I wonder if I dare mention it. I decide it's worth the risk. "I understand your mother passed away when you were only a boy."

He stiffens. "Who told you that?"

I tell him. He looks down for Franceschina, but she seems to have vanished for the moment behind some jutting escarpment, although we can still hear her scuffs and skips and little gasps of exertion as she goes on with her hunting. He's scowling now. I feel I may have betrayed her and she could suffer for it.

But I continue: "Do you miss her?"

If I was expecting some affirmation, I'm not going to get it. He still stares ahead without moving a muscle.

"I only ask," I say, "because I rather miss mine." Maybe I'm hoping for some bond of shared sorrow between us. I'm not going to get that either.

He turns to me again. His expression is cold. "Mothers are mothers," he says.

Is it my imagination, or do I detect moistness around the edges of his adamantine gray-green eyes? "We need horses," he suddenly announces, and once more looks out over the abundant countryside to the west. The late afternoon sun is almost blinding us now. "We need horses to get to Mantua." His tone is urgent. "No more of this traipsing and trudging and dodging." Yes, he's had enough of the chase.

"I've an idea where we might find some," I blurt, really without thinking.

"Where?"

"I'm not sure precisely, as I've never visited the place, but I have an uncle who owns a villa somewhere around here. He breeds them— horses, I mean."

Astonishingly, Iago says, "I know." Then, more incredibly still, he informs me, "I have been there."

This is turning into quite a day of revelations. I stammer, "You . . . you know my uncle Ubaldo?"

He stands up. It's a less effortful rise than previously. He's again full of that purpose that takes away the pain. "You forget, Gentile Stornello, that I was a friend of the family."

I don't remember him ever saying such a thing in so many words. Of course he knew the Moor and Desdemona—and probably killed them, though he's denied it. I struggle to recollect some mention of greater familiarity with my clan. "You've never told me that."

"Now you know," he says.

After a skirmish of some kind among the boulders and crags and clefts in the vertiginous hillside immediately below us, we hear the startled squeals of a captured goat. Finally Franceschina appears, with the slain animal over one shoulder and Iago's dagger glistening in her hand. She gleams with the sweat of conquest. Her bosom heaves with victory.

"Is there no limit," says Iago, gazing down on her, "to the skills of your pretty darling?" Then he mutters through the side of his mouth, "You see how she pants? You see how she wants you? She is like a kitten, bringing home prey to her master."

I whisper back, "She doesn't want me, she wants . . ."

He waits for me to continue.

But for some reason I can't. To go on would be an admission of a kind—as if we were both suitors for her hand and I was conceding that in any contest he would win. I'm not thinking of Jacopo as my rival anymore. It's *him*. I can see it in her wide effulgent eyes, craving his approval. She's not even looking at me.

Once more he reads my thoughts. "I'll not say she wouldn't wish me to plow her furrow and scatter my seed, but as you know, lad, I've a taste for fillies of higher stock, while you—"

"Yes, yes," I interrupt irritably. "You've said all this before."

"Then why the pother? Take her, she's yours. Watch how she breathes. That's lust. That's concupiscence. And last night she said to me she was growing in her liking for you. She quaked as she told me so."

"When last night? At the inn?"

"When we were *abed*, yes. You should have felt how she trembled at the mere utterance of your name. And you, foolish pup, were asleep."

"Did you . . . ?"

He waits for me to finish, but I can't.

"Your uncle's villa is near Luvigliano," he continues blithely, "not too far from here. A most cordial place, as I remember, where a man might easily while away a summer among the terraces and the vines or a lad might lie with his beloved in the flower-strewn meadows." He sounds almost Petrarchan. "Yes, we shall call on your hospitable uncle."

"Is that wise? He might let it be known where you are."

"We shall have to ensure that he doesn't," says Iago, rather chillingly. "As I remember, he has few servants. We will bring him that fine animal as a gift." He nods in Franceschina's direction. She's struggling up the scree toward us, with the goat now clasped around her neck, its stiffening legs straddling her glowing shoulders. "We shall have a meal fit for a king," Iago announces, "and drink the wine from your uncle Ubaldo's vineyards. Then we shall all *go to bed*." He gives me one of his salacious sidelong glances. "And in the morning we shall ride to Mantua."

45. *Murder, Love, and Jealousy*

The report left by *Dottore* Baldassare Ghiberti of the University of Padua in the library of the seminary attached to the Monastero di Santi Filippo e Giacomo extended to seven or eight pages of meticulous but spidery script. Annibale Malipiero had groaned inwardly when it was handed to him, but as he read it for the first time, he grew more indulgent toward his informant. There was little Latin and no Greek and no irritating deflection from the facts. There was still no shortage of opinion, but it was less arbitrary, less solipsistic, than before. Some of it had even been quite acute. But perhaps the most intriguing revelation of all was the very last the tutor had scribbled.

To my considerable disquiet, he has just examined much of what I have so far written here, but despite my apprehension he has neither broken open my skull again nor put me to the sword. I am of the view, therefore, that he is illiterate.

Annibale Malipiero sat within the shade of a cypress halfway between Padua and Vicenza. He was alone, apart from a horse he had obtained now tethered to a fence and chomping at the roadside vegetation. It had proved to be a skittish beast, rather too large and powerful for his liking. The man who provided it had proudly informed him that it was a courser, the best of its kind, born and reared in Mantua by none other than Marquis Federico Gonzaga. It was therefore expensive too.

Annibale Malipiero had chosen it in the perhaps unscientific hope that if it was Mantuan, it might instinctively know the shortest route to that city. He was now wishing that he'd picked a less volatile animal, even if the journey became longer as a consequence. As far as he knew from his two remaining spies, who'd been observing Iago's every move (from a cautious distance, except when they had moved too close to the villa on the Brenta), the felon had not yet elected to proceed by any method other than foot.

Annibale Malipiero turned once more to the document in his hand, starting with its opening.

You should be aware, Signor, that Gentile Stornello now knows that I am writing to you. I did not have to tell him. He worked it out for himself.

Well, that was no bad thing. Perhaps he should have known all along.

In the first instance, as I have already informed you, Iago chose to speak at any length only to the girl. Since then, Gentile Stornello has managed to glean from her some of what Iago told her. In doing so, however, he revealed to her Iago's identity, which she did not previously know, and something of his transgressions, which she chooses to believe are fabrications, as Iago still refutes them, at least within my hearing or to the girl. With regard to any affirmation on Iago's part of the specific manner in which he murdered anyone in Cyprus, I am unable to enlighten you as yet. He did have a conversation with Gentile while at your villa on the Brenta, but regrettably I was unable to hear anything that was spoken of on that occasion, as I was still recovering from a severe head wound administered by Iago, from which I continue to suffer. Since then, my pupil and I have been unable to communicate with each other privately.

That might be thought a pity, but, as Doge Andrea Gritti had already pointed out to him, the specifics of the killings did not matter to Annibale Malipiero as much as the cause—the root, the spring, the source of Iago's malevolence.

The man had indeed had a destitute upbringing, or at least one without sound parentage—a lack of moral guidance, therefore. His father had died when he was still a small boy. He had also been beaten by his father. That was not too much of a shock. Fathers beat their children every day, at least in poorer, more backward households, cursed with the stresses of indigence. His mother had also died when he was fifteen, though the manner of her dying had not yet been found out.

Annibale Malipiero imagined the boy thrown onto the streets. He'd interviewed scores of such urchins during his time as an inquisitor— sniveling louts, all of them. The prognosis for most of them was not good. But that such misfortune should lead to Iago's horrific wrong-doings was still quite a leap.

The academic's report went on to complain not only that he was still being subjected to Iago's gibes *against scholars and monks and books* but that the brute had become increasingly vulgar: *using language I shall not transcribe verbatim, Signor, but shall only remark that it is aimed as much at the girl as it is at Gentile and myself, and in a very sordid and dare I say forward manner. He is also, I believe, encouraging my pupil toward lechery with her, while at the same time behaving as if he might wish to do the same. He speaks often of your nephew too, so as to induce envy in the poor youth—*"

All of a sudden, behind him, or it may have been in front of him, or to the left or the right, or way above him, from the heavens themselves, Annibale Malipiero heard a shout. It was so unexpected, so disturbing in the tranquillity of the late afternoon, that he found himself on his feet within a second. His equine companion let out a whinny that also echoed about the hills. Somewhere far away, an awakened dog barked angrily.

"That," said the patrician to himself, "was a voice that I know to my bones." But what had he shouted? As if in reply, the words were repeated, as clear and sonorous as a lone church bell. *"I am not the devil!"* Iago cried. *"I am a man!"*

Without stopping to think, Annibale Malipiero strode quickly to the base of the hill that still held the echo of Iago's reverberant hollering and began to climb.

Scaling the scree and sliding back down it in almost equal measure, he found himself muttering, "I know you are a man, Iago of Mantua, I have always known that. It is others who think of you as the devil, or a superhuman beast, but not I."

He allowed himself the liberty to stop whenever he could find a securely embedded boulder on which to rest, not because he wanted to but because he felt that if he didn't he would die for absence of breath. *He knows who you are and that you follow us,* Dottore Ghiberti had written, *or, if not you, then those under your guidance. He has called us "pawns in your game." He has said to Gentile, "Let us give your inquisitor a run for his money."*

Annibale Malipiero pondered the notion that if he came face-to-face with Iago at last on the hilltop, he might well be killed. Thanks to the Doge, he was entirely alone. After they had delivered to him the *Dottore's* latest missive in Padua, he had told his two remaining spies to go home. That was how he'd wished it to be—but now he felt very solitary indeed. Iago would have many weapons. In another part of his report, the tutor had written: *We have raided your armory, Signor, having found it in your cellar.*

But still he climbed. Scrambling and slithering, he felt in his doublet for the small bundle of love letters that had been found on the felon's person when he was finally apprehended in Cyprus. Annibale Malipiero had carried them with him from the moment he'd set out on this hunt. He resolved that he wouldn't let Iago kill him too speedily. "Tell me about these!" he'd cry. "Tell me who they're from." He might just be obliged with an answer before having a sword plunged into his heart. And although there was so much more he needed to know, he would die with that riddle solved at least.

No wonder, thought the ex-inquisitor, scrabbling through barbs and spiky branches that tore at his clothes—no wonder Iago had never replied to her endearments and her pleas, sending her into a tumult of remorse and eventual recrimination. He could not reply because he could not read them and could not write.

Oh, was that a pang of sympathy for the man? The agony of being unable to know what she was writing to him, and the humiliation of being unable to respond! The mortification! The blows to his pride!

And yet he'd kept those letters, tying them up in a neat little packet and taking them with him wherever he went, close to his heart, though he had no idea what they contained. Listening outside Iago's cell, Annibale Malipiero had heard him denounce love as a fiction: "We are but beasts in nature, and like beasts we must have our concupiscence."

Was such detraction mere bluster, then? Surely his devotion to the persistent but indecipherable flirtations of a besotted girl was a sign, if not of love, then something close to it?

Could one kill the person one loved? Of course one could—*un crimine appassionato.* The ex-*interrogante* had examined countless such cases—jealous husbands, jealous lovers . . . Was it possible that Iago, as well as being in love, had been jealous?

Iago certainly knew about jealousy. He was a master of it. He'd filled the Moor with it. In Graziano Stornello's very first letter from Cyprus, Annibale Malipiero had read of . . . how had it been put? He could not recall precisely, but he remembered some mention of a poisonous suggestion that was like a malady or a plague—yes, now he had it, or something resembling what had been written: *a pestilence that can creep unnoticed into the blood and kill a man before he knows he is sick.*

It was then that the struggling, sweating Signor realized why he was ascending that mountain so hurriedly, or as hurriedly as he could, even at risk of death at the hands of Iago, and it made him more purposeful still. He was going to rescue Gentile Stornello, that inexperienced lovelorn boy, from the creature into whose poisonous presence he, *Il Terribile*, had delivered him.

The criminal had said that they were pawns in Annibale Malipiero's game. But it was the other way around. Iago was the game player.

In a moment of certainty, accompanied by a degree of contentment as to the virtuous nature of what he was about to do, Annibale Malipiero decided, uncharacteristically, that all his inquisitorial efforts to delve deeper into Iago's soul could go hang, if it meant that he might at least rescue an innocent being from further confusion and darkness and probable death—for he had no doubt now that Gentile Stornello was in serious danger.

He had reached the summit. He was still enclosed by thistly foliage—it bit into his face, filled his hair and copious beard. Once he'd thrust his way sufficiently through the clumps of stinging vegetation to get a glimpse of the small but open space (with clear views in every direction) where he'd supposed Iago and his companions might be, he was quite on his own.

But the ground had been recently trodden. Some fresh kindling had been gathered in a tidy pyramid, although it had not been lit. Amid the arrangement he noticed another hastily scribbled missive from the good *dottore*.

If hell exists at all, he says, it is here on earth. He was born, he says, in hell, which is not Mantua, as we thought, but south of Milan. So Iago of Mantua—nominetinus, or "so-called"—is not Mantuan at all. Mantua, however, remains our destination.

Gentile has just asked him the derivation of his given name. It is Spanish, as I had always suspected. His mother was from Spain.

Now he has said we need horses. He has resolved to get quickly to Mantua. Oh

Oh . . . ? *Oh, what?* Annibale Malipiero fumbled among the twigs of the unlit fire. Nothing. He moved to the edge of the clearing where the four had so recently been, and he sat looking westward. Where in the immensity that lay beneath him—its fertile dales and fells, its glinting streams and compact farmsteads—had they disappeared to now?

He had no choice but to make his way back down. He searched for a path and found one. He had not gone far when he saw another hastily scrawled note, placed in the roots of a sapling, in danger of being blown away by the breeze.

Gone . . . Signor Ubaldo Stornello . . . villa near Luvigliano . . . horse breeder . . . Casa dei Fiori . . . know him . . . very clever man . . . Iago there before . . . with Moor and Desdemona, we think.

46. A Brief Idyll

Baldassare once defined for me what he considered to be perfect happiness here on earth: to be in the company of like minds, after a good meal, with just enough imbibed to ensure that the conversation flowed. It might be only the most fleeting of moments, destroyed in an instant by some foolish interjection or overindulgence. But for the time it was there, you knew it for what it was, and it was sublime.

Well for me, I think, transcendent happiness is where I am now: sitting in a flower-sparkling meadow on a temperate summer evening, with the loveliest girl in the long history of existence at my side. It, too, could be all too transient.

My uncle Ubaldo was of course astonished to see us—but also delighted. "I say," he said, "what a very pleasant surprise. Well, well now, Gentile, you've grown a bit, haven't you? Filling out at last, I see. Is your family well? And Dottore Baldassare Ghiberti, if I'm not mistaken . . . Well, well, I say, I say, what brings you to these out-of-the-way parts? And who is this pretty maid? Is that a goat around your neck by any chance, young lady?"

"This is Franceschina," I said. She blushed and curtsied, as daintily as she could with a goat for a collar. I added, perhaps unnecessarily, "We've brought it as a gift."

"A gift? I say, how kind." He didn't appear to recognize Iago, which was odd, although I suppose he might have changed a bit since he was last here. Maybe he was paler, less weather-roughened. Maybe he had hair. "And you are, Signor . . . ?"

Iago chose not to reply, staring grimly ahead of him, so I thought it best to respond on his behalf.

"This is . . . this is . . ." I began, and then for some reason decided to make up a name. The heady scent of herbs in Uncle Ubaldo's vegetable garden—which was where we'd found him, plucking big fat tomatoes— lent me inspiration. "This is Basilio . . ." I started, then glimpsed the surrounding hills, ". . . Montagna. This is Basilio Montagna, a good friend of mine."

Neither did my uncle display any amazement that this taciturn "good friend" with a decidedly aristocratic name looked like a robust but common soldier nearly three times my age. He did, however, notice the swords and daggers hanging at our waists. "You do seem well armed . . ."

"We've been traveling by night," I said. "You know, robbers and such."

"Yes, yes, one can't be too careful. Well, I say," he went on, "you are most welcome to my humble *casa rustica*, Gentile and Dottore Ghiberti, and you sweet lady, and you, Signor . . . *Basilio Montagna*. Most welcome, yes. I've been rather alone of late, so it is always nice to see some new faces. I'm sorry that Liborio and Maurizio are not here to greet you, Gentile, and you, *Dottore*. They are my sons, Signor Montagna, and were once pupils, as Gentile is, of the good *dottore* here. I'm afraid they are both away at their respective universities—Bologna and . . . and Padua."

"We've just come from Padua," Franceschina announced brightly.

"Really? Well, well, and why did you not call on Liborio, Gentile?"

"I do not know where he lodges, and I thought as it was August he would not be there."

"Oh, Liborio is there whenever he can be. He's a most hardworking boy, Signor Montagna, although not quite as clever as Gentile here."

Baldassare, who'd so far not uttered a word, replied, "Yes, Liborio is a painstaking student certainly—"

"We need horses," Iago interjected gruffly, also speaking for the first time.

"Horses?" my uncle inquired, startled a little. He put his fingers to his chin. "I do have a few of those. They're not here, unfortunately; they're at my stables in the town—only a twenty-minute walk away. Do you want them now?"

"No," Iago briskly declared. "We must wash, and eat, and sleep."

"On all three I hope I can satisfy you, Signor Montagna. It will be an honor to offer you my hospitality, although I'm quite servantless at present. They've disappeared for the month—all but four, that is—and my cook, I'm afraid, is visiting her daughter in Sabbioneta."

"I can roast this goat," said Franceschina, with a radiant smile.

So after showing us around his profuse vegetable plot, and encouraging Franceschina to pick anything she wished—plump *melanzane*, rich green zucchini, bulbous *cavoli*, shiny *peperoni* of red and yellow, and *limone* and *limette*, to say nothing of a host of different wafting herbs—my uncle Ubaldo took us to the kitchen of what he called his "modest *casa*" but which was actually a three-storey *villa grande della campagna* set solidly within statue-bedecked terraces, its walls covered and windows almost hidden by a riot of climbing plants—vibrantly scarlet bougainvillea, blue and white campanula, and others I don't know the names of. It looked like some huge rectangular piece of foliage in itself, a defiant assertion of vegetation over architecture, or like a colorfully decorated oblong cake.

There were three near-comatose servants in the commodious kitchen—a boy and two men; none of them weaklings, I noticed. My uncle shouted at them to rouse themselves. He told the boy to start filling baths and basins and the two men to help Franceschina prepare supper. "Whatever she commands, you will do," he snapped. "She is our *capo-cuoco* for the evening!" Surly though they were for a moment or two, the sight of a pretty girl revitalized them quickly, and within minutes they were slicing vegetables, peeling fruit, setting the goat on a spit over the faltering fire, throwing more wood onto the embers.

With the goat roasting and the side dishes bubbling away, we sit, Franceschina and I, in a meadow full of flowers, just above and behind the Casa dei Fiori, as it's appositely named. She has bathed, I have bathed (not together, you will understand), Iago has bathed, and so has Baldassare. My tutor is now in my uncle Ubaldo's library. Iago is with my uncle.

"Go," he said to me. "Find some field in which to make love to your sweetheart, or do it under a shady tree, like a poet. I must talk to your hospitable kinsman."

"What about?" I asked anxiously.

"This and that. He does not remember me."

"So I noticed."

His crooked teeth flared into a grin. "I like the name you gave me. If I live, I shall henceforth be known as Basilio Montagna." Then he was serious. "I do not know if I believe him. I must see if he's bluffing."

I was still concerned. "You will treat him kindly, won't you? He's just a gentle, generous old man. He's the only uncle I like."

He clasped my shoulder, I hope with reassurance. "Go," he said again. "Rut with her on a bed of grass and flowers; then we shall eat and you can rut again, on a real bed. Have you seen the beds here? Most accommodating."

Franceschina has found fresh clothes—a *camicia* of light green, a robe of dark-brown velvet with threads of gold silk woven into it. They belonged to my uncle's wife, my aunt Lorenza, who died less than a year ago. I recall her as a slim, handsome woman. Her garments fit Franceschina almost as if they were made for her. My uncle remarked on it, with a gasped *Madonna mia* and a slight choke. I think he loved his wife very much.

They're rather revealing. The bodice of the robe is cut wide and quite low. It's almost slipping off her russet shoulders. The *camicia* droops a little loosely too, and I've noticed (how could I not?) that she's knotted the laces at the front somewhat hastily but pulled them tightly around her minuscule waist. The effect is . . . dramatic. I am reminded of the finery that Jacopo Malipiero sometimes made her wear as he preened with her in the Campo Sant'Angelo.

She knows the names of every flower that encircles us—*ranuncoli, denti di leone, girasoli, calendole, lysimachie, digitali, margherite* (I know those; they're daisies), and one tiny blue one with an iridescent amber stigma at its center, which she calls something I don't catch at first. *Notiscordame?* No. She pronounces it more slowly, syllable by syllable. *"Non-ti-scordar-di-me."*

"How might I ever forget you, Franceschina?" I reply, endeavoring to be courtly. I very nearly take her hand.

"It's just the name of a flower," she says.

I tell her to make a crown of the ones she's gracefully described as *viole del pensiero*—"thoughtful" flowers, neat little beauties of purple and orange-yellow. "As I watched you do with daisies at the villa on the Brenta," I remind her. She frowns a bit, not knowing she'd been spied upon.

But she doesn't seem too annoyed. "You make it," she says, and teaches me how to craft a chain—slicing through one stem with a fingernail and then sliding another through it. Easy enough. "No, no, more gently—you with your rough hands, you'll split it."

As I work away, she announces, "Iago says you're a poet." I'm taken aback, by the abruptness of the statement, by the thought of his having had yet more private conversations with her, but mostly by the informal way she's called him simply "Iago," for the first time in my hearing.

"I'm no poet," I say. "Just because I write the odd sonnet doesn't mean I'm a poet."

"What's a sonnet?"

I do my best to explain—its fourteen lines, its quatrains and its tercets, its meter and its rhyme schemes. I don't get far.

"Recite me one," she says.

Instead of picking something from Dante, or Cavalcanti, or Petrarch, I foolishly try to remember one of my own immeasurably inferior efforts—one of those I composed for her, in fact, when mooning about Venice like a bedraggled dog, when the thought of ever getting this close to her was something of which I could scarcely dream. "Can I deign to look in your eyes like stars . . ." I begin, then recollect how Baldassare blanched when he heard it. "I speak only silently of your glowing—" No. "I speak in silence of your shining charms, As there's no uttered language can convey . . ." And then I can't come up with any more of that one either. "I'm sorry," I say weakly. "I can't remember any of the ones I wrote to you."

Her eyes widen. "You wrote sonnets to *me*?"

Oh, how I want to kiss her. "Quite a few actually, but I'm afraid they've all gone from my mind—probably because they're so very bad."

"They sounded . . . nice," she says, and softly, without any sort of awkward preamble, she slips an arm through mine.

I can't speak.

She looks around her, at the flowers blanketing the sloping field, at the verdant woods that surround it on three sides, at the villa below us with its tumult of vegetation, and then up at the sky, pinkish blue still, even though the sun has set. She spots something at the top of the hill. "Is that a castle?"

"Where? Oh, there." It is indeed a castle, just visible behind the trees, but it's not a very big one, or it doesn't seem so from here. There's no sign of activity.

"Is it full of soldiers?" she asks, trembling. I can't tell if it's with fear or some kind of overcurious fervor.

"It looks pretty closed up to me."

She lays her head on my shoulder and murmurs, "Isn't it beautiful here?"

"Staggeringly so," I manage to gasp. I mean her, of course, and not the lush environment.

She giggles. "*Staggeringly*—you with your long words, Gentile Stornello." I've finished making the chain of *viole del pensiero*—the blooms of thought. It sits on my lap, in a completed circle, the last stem in the last stem. I say to her, "Wear this."

She says, "You put it on me." She raises her head from my shoulder, rearranges herself before me on her knees with her legs and feet tucked under her.

So I do, letting the crown of purple and yellow on her glossy chestnut tresses, freely caressing her exceptional face, and say, "You're incomparable, you're inimitable, you're flawless, you're perfection." But I still can't kiss her.

So she does it for me. She puts her silken hands to my cheeks and leans forward. Our breaths seem to embrace. Her lips jut and she presses them against mine. Her eyes are closed, and mine close too. Her lips, however, remain open. Her tongue taps at my mouth, forcing it open too. She's like a *snake*.

"Supper time!" Of course he's been watching. It's almost night by now. I hadn't noticed.

We head toward the torch he's carrying on a terrace at the rear of the Casa dei Fiori. "Run along now, *piccolina*," he says. "It's time to serve up." He pats her behind with casual impertinence as she passes.

"Well?" he quickly asks me.

"Well what?" I reply, trying to affect a detachment of my own.

"What took place?"

"She kissed me," I say.

"Is that all? I know she kissed you, lad. I told her to." He suddenly seems to be like some lubricious brothel-keeper, some drooling procurer.

"I don't think that's what made her do it," I say proudly, remembering her head on my shoulder, the tremor of her heart as she nestled against me.

He still prevents me from moving toward the house. "You must know I've had to deal with the servants."

That frightens me. "Deal with . . . ?"

"Not kill them—although I was tempted, truculent oafs. I've locked them in a closet in the kitchens. I've had to see to your uncle also."

"See to?" My brain is afire with ghastly possibilities.

"I have not slain him either. Would I do that to the only uncle you like? I've had to"—he pauses—"tie him up."

"*Tie him up? Why?*"

"Because of course he knows exactly who I am, and told me so. The servants know too." He releases me. "Worry not," he declares cheerily. "Your benevolent Uncle Ubaldo will still eat with us."

47. The House of Flowers

He'd thought it wise to leave his decidedly quarrelsome animal at some distance from the villa itself. The little town of Luvigliano was a slumberous place, even well after siesta time. There was not much to get up for, Annibale Malipiero presumed, in the middle of August. The grapes were plumping up nicely but weren't ready for harvesting. The olives in their ancient groves would not be ripe until November.

The place had an ancient feel to it too. No new stones had been laid here for at least a century, maybe more—apart, that was, from the Villa Stornello, which sat halfway up the hill. On the summit stood a somewhat neglected castle, built by Venice in the days when *borgi* at the edge of the Veneto needed keeping in hand; as Luvigliano had long since resigned itself to the yoke, that was no longer required.

There were residues of recalcitrance, however, among the very few people Annibale Malipiero encountered, who would grunt incomprehensibly, faces lowered, when he asked them the way to the Casa dei Fiori. Or perhaps it seemed to them a stupid question. Wasn't it obvious? You only had to look up and there it was, the sole example of relative wealth and ostentation in the vicinity.

It reminded him of the flower stalls in the Rialto, of the *mazzi* of blooms sold there for special occasions. You could hardly make out the walls of the boxlike structure for the cornucopia of vegetation that clung to them. Ubaldo Stornello had built himself a massive oblong *vaso per fiori* and had called it a *casa*. Annibale Malipiero had often thought of brightening up his own dwelling with some form of climber—a bougainvillea perhaps, or a *caprifoglio*, nothing too brash. Unfortunately, his dear wife had what the family physician called an *allergia* to pollen. Flowers made her sneeze.

An unruly tumult of every imaginable hue poked up through the long grasses of the meadow, which rested like a bedspread on the side of the hill, behind and above the villa itself. The primary cause of his astonishment was, however, the presence, at its very center, of a boy and a girl. She was wearing a gown of brown velvet and gold with puffed sleeves—and was resting her head on the youth's shoulder. He was in a loose white shirt and hose only, seated cross-legged, and seemed to be gazing up at the sky with an expression of absolute bliss.

The ex-inquisitor had not seen Gentile Stornello for weeks but in that short time he seemed to have become sturdier, broader, more straight-backed. There was an assurance in the way he sat. He also appeared to be doing most of the talking. And the more he held forth, the more she seemed to like it.

Annibale Malipiero was reminded of the rather pagan paintings that were becoming fashionable in Venice, of gods and young goddesses gamboling against pastoral backgrounds or of piping shepherds and their nymphs, with some town in the distance, not unlike Luvigliano now, with its crumbling rust-colored houses and its slender campanile against the darkening sky. It was a congenial tableau, and for a while he was happy for them.

Then he thought he heard shouting from within the villa—two raised male voices, a few barks and growls. It was over as quickly as it had started, but it was enough to lower Annibale Malipiero's temporarily uplifted spirits. A few minutes later he caught sight of a figure moving onto the rear terrace of the house. It was Iago, of course, who scuttled toward the statue of some scantily clad dryad, behind which he hid and from which he popped his shining bullet head to peer at the girl and boy.

The ex-*interrogante* heartily wished he could get a better view. He could tell a great deal from faces, even stubbornly silent ones, and yet more from those that did not know they were being observed. Was he grinning lewdly, like some *guardone volgare*, salivating over what he was witnessing? Or was his mouth open in wonder at such a spectacle of unguarded tenderness? Was he capable of knowing love when he saw it? He professed not to believe in love. So were his intentions lubricious or simply vicious? Both, conceivably. With one hand he was absentmindedly caressing the near-naked statue; in the other he held what looked, in the shadows, like a club.

Annibale Malipiero remembered the tutor's last message: *Iago there before . . . with Moor and Desdemona, we think.* Was he recollecting, as he gazed on these young lovers, happier times of his own?

Now Gentile was placing a crown of pansies on the girl's head, as she squatted on her knees before him. Next she took his face between her hands and pressed her lips to his—quite forthrightly, Annibale Malipiero thought for a lass who'd seemed so demure on the few occasions he'd encountered her.

It was getting dark. There was little sign of illumination within the villa, and he could no longer tell if Iago was still lurking in the gloom. Then he saw a flare of flame; it wasn't a club the villain had been holding but a torch.

48. *Food and Death*

A stranger happening upon the scene would have thought it none other than a companionable occasion. The fare was plentiful and being devoured voraciously, with grunts of approval. Judging by the four large flagons on the table, so was the wine—indeed, the host of the evening was now singing its praises. "From my own Nebbiolo grapes, an excellent year 1512, still plenty of room to mature, a fine nose—note, if you will, the clear flavor of *prugne*, with the merest suggestion of *tartufo*."

He then turned to congratulate the young woman sitting to his left: "Well, well, I must say that this is a most excellent repast. The goat . . ." He put his fingertips to his mouth and snapped them outward, "Simply superb, cooked to perfection, *ottimo, ottimo*." He raised a cup to her, and she, if slightly gauchely, raised hers, and they clinked.

"It was the servants who did it, mostly," she said coyly.

"But that, my dear, is the mark of a great cook, *una cuoca magnifica*": "making others do the work." He looked about him. "Where are the servants, by the by . . . ?"

There was no sign of them in the walnut-paneled *sala da pranzo* of the Casa dei Fiori, which was hung heavily with tapestries (of hunting scenes, as far as the secret watcher could make out).

"They're still down in the kitchen, I think," the girl said. "Shall I go and get them?"

Iago, seated at the far end of the table, stiffened visibly but stayed silent.

Picking up on this perhaps, the venerable Signor patted her forearm. "No, no, don't trouble yourself. Who needs servants, anyway? We indolent *nobiluomini* have far too many of them. Why can't a man just help himself?" He leaned forward and plunged a knife into the gleaming carcass that lay on the platter some way down the table.

Annibale Malipiero noted that it required some effort on his part to rise from his seat at all. Unlike most of his brothers, Ubaldo Stornello was a healthy-looking fellow for his years, portly but robustly built, with a heavily lined mahogany-colored face and a clipped black beard, a fine head of black hair, and bushy black eyebrows. But he appeared to be less than supple from the waist down, as if something was holding him to the chair.

Annibale Malipiero felt less than supple himself, and it didn't help that in order to look through the small mullioned window of the *sala da pranzo* he had to stand on his toes. Soon he might just sit on the ground, rest his weary bones, and listen, since the casement was open to the night.

As it was, Iago had to turn his head only a little to the right to spot him. Between Iago and Ubaldo Stornello were the boy and the girl, with their backs to the window, sitting a bit too closely for formality; the academic was opposite them. He would merely have to raise his eyes to notice the slightest movement of the foliage beyond the window for there was absolutely no wind. Fortunately, he didn't seem interested in gazing anywhere but down, as he plucked hungrily at the victuals on his plate or refilled his goblet. He appeared determined to get drunk—which surprised Annibale Malipiero. He had known Dottore Baldassare Ghiberti to be a sober sort of fellow when he'd taught his own son.

As the best hosts do, Ubaldo Stornello was jovially ensuring that no one felt excluded. To the girl, he said, "You look like *una ninfa di bosco,* my dear, with your pretty crown of flowers."

"What's that?"

"A sweet woodland spirit! And seeing you there, dressed as my late wife was dressed, in her very clothes, brings back pleasant memories. There's her picture, do you see?"

Annibale Malipiero did his best to peer through the leaves. Behind the lolling head of the *dottore* there was a portrait—the only canvas in the room, as far as could be made out—of a young woman with startlingly golden hair. It must have been done a while ago. Beside her stood the smiling figure of her husband.

"Oh, but she's beautiful!"

"Thank you. Messer Cariani certainly thought her so, although why he should have insisted that a fat old chap like me should be included in the *ritratto*, I really can't imagine."

"Do you miss her very much?" the girl inquired.

"Dreadfully. But, I say, we mustn't dwell on the past, not now!" He lifted his cup again. *"Mangia bene!"* he cried. *"Beve! Beve bene!* Happy memories only from now on!"

Next he asked of his nephew, "And how is your father? And your brother? And your studies, are they going well?"

Gentile Stornello answered these inquiries respectfully, if distractedly, for most of his mind must still have been on the pleasant time he'd spent in the meadow. Yes, his father was well. He hoped his brother was well, although he always worried about him, as he was away fighting. Yes, his studies were going well, although they'd been somewhat interrupted of late.

"And why is that?" Ubaldo Stornello's brows arched.

The spectator behind the vines could not help but notice that he threw a sidelong glance in Iago's direction as he asked this. Iago didn't look up.

"We've been . . . traveling. I . . . I decided I should see a bit more of the country."

"Well, well, good for you!" declared his uncle. *"Il viaggiare estende la ragione!"* Wouldn't you say so, *Dottore*?"

"Absholutely . . . no queshtun about it," the scholar agreed.

An increasingly abstruse discussion followed between the genial *nobiluomo* and the man who had been tutor to his sons—mainly about the books that Baldassare Ghiberti had been perusing in the library of the Casa dei Fiori. As the pain in his spine got worse by the second, Annibale Malipiero was grateful that it didn't go on too long.

No doubt mindful of Baldassare Ghiberti's unusual lack of clarity,

Ubaldo Stornello at last directed his amiable attention to Iago. "And you, Signor, does my simple country home conjure up pleasant memories in you?" A stranger might have thought it an affable sort of query, but Iago stared at him, stopped chewing, and remained mute.

"Oh," said the girl, "so you have been here before?" Her careless naïveté might prove useful in the coming minutes, thought Annibale Malipiero.

"Two times—or was it more?" asked Ubaldo Stornello.

"I've been sheveral more timesh than that . . . shix or sheven at leasht," Baldassare Ghiberti interposed helpfully, though by now he was patently very drunk.

"Yes, but not when Signor Iago was here."

"Twice," said Iago crisply.

"I thought he was Signor Basilio now," the girl trilled.

Ubaldo Stornello gave a round, bold, warmhearted guffaw. "Oh, that, oh, how very funny. Oh, yes, that was some invention of Gentile's here. Yes, very funny. No, no, my dear, Signor Iago and I have known each other for a year now—since last summer."

The girl tapped Gentile Stornello on his arm. "Then why did you introduce him as Signor Basilio M-m-m . . . whatever?"

She earned a sharp poke to the ribs from the boy's elbow, after which Gentile Stornello remained as unbending as a sculpture.

Ubaldo Stornello raised a hand. "I've no doubt your reasons for wishing to protect your friend's identity were noble, as is everything you do, dear boy."

The expectant silence that followed wasn't quickly filled.

The convivial owner of the Casa dei Fiori was the first to do so. "What a fine summer we had of it last year . . ."

Annibale Malipiero slid downward, hoping not to make too much noise as he did so. He even risked grabbing at a few grapes on his way. He chomped at them greedily. They were heavy and deep purple and sweet, with an herby tang. As Ubaldo Stornello continued, he plucked at more.

"Was it not, sir, an excellent summer?" There was no reply. "Better than this one, which has been too dry, too hot. We've had no rain to speak of since March. The Nebbiolo needs moisture in June and July to grow and a dry autumn to flourish. I've a feeling the rains will come in August—too late, too late. This year, I predict, will not be a good vintage. As for my olives, they're already shriveling. So a bad yield all around . . ."

Annibale Malipiero hoped that this homily wouldn't go on for much longer.

"But nature is God's will and there's nothing to be done," Ubaldo Stornello pronounced with welcome finality. "And last summer, as I said, will amply make up for my losses this year. What a summer it was! And not only for the harvest, isn't that so, sir?" He'd dropped the mildly mischievous formality of the "Signor." There was no audible response from Iago. Now the good-humored patrician dropped his voice a touch, as if sharing a confidence with those closer to him. "I've not known so pleasant a one in a long, long time and there never will be such a one again—for me at least." He had become momentarily melancholic.

The girl asked, "What was so special about it?"

"My wife lived, for one thing, my dear."

"Oh . . . yes."

"But for her too, I think, it was the perfect summer. Her final summer on earth was at least a happy one. So many people—*happy* people. The Casa dei Fiori is made for people. It's no place for a single lonely soul. And such pretty, attractive people. I do like pretty people, don't you?"

"Oh, yes," the girl concurred.

"My fields, my meadows, the house itself, were awash with them, young lady, for those two or three months. It was *una scena . . . una scena . . .* what's the word, Gentile, for those pictures one sees of shepherds and their lasses frolicking in the woods?"

"Bucolic?" suggested Gentile Stornello, rather tautly.

"*Una scena bucolica, assolutamente! Una . . . Una . . .* Arcadia! Is that the right name for the land where everything is always happy, *Dottore*?"

"Arcadia'sh ackshally a real plaish, in Greesh."

"*Una* Arcadia *veramente!* With many a comely nymph and lusty swain!"

The girl giggled.

"So many beauties, my dear, to warm an old man's heart! Your cousins were here, Gentile, and some young acquaintances of theirs. Your uncle Brabantio's daughters, dear boy—Rosalia, with her handsome new husband, and dainty Severina, with her delightful school friends, and Caterina—such a beautiful woman she's becoming—and of course..." He paused briefly, his breezy tone vanishing, "and of course Desdemona."

"Desde—" The inquisitive girl didn't complete the name; perhaps she'd just received another nudge from Gentile Stornello. Maybe, thought the former inquisitor, it was time to heave himself up and look through the window once more.

"Now that I think of it," Ubaldo Stornello continued sadly, "it was a last happy summer not only for my dear wife. Your uncle was also here, my boy, *che riposi in pace.* He didn't have a country retreat of his own. He thought two homes an unnecessary extravagance. And your own wife was also here, was she not, sir? *Ma senz' altro* she was. She was Desdemona's personal servant, was she not?"

There was still no reply.

"And your commander too, the Moor. *O Dio mio,* as if it was— *Madonna santa—predestinato*! There was just the slightest pause. "Ah, so much *bellezza,* so cruelly cut down."

Annibale Malipiero thought it was definitely time to get up and take another peek.

Iago had not raised his head one inch. Utterly motionless, he was staring down at his now-empty plate, on either side of which his strong hands lay, palms on the table.

The girl said, in a somewhat injured tone: "You're married?"

"Was, young lady. He was married. Unfortunately, she also... perished, did she not, sir? You must mourn her passing."

"Oh..."

"Has Signor Iago not told you the whole story?" Ubaldo Stornello inquired of her.

"He's told me of his childhood, which was sad, and of his bravery in battle."

"I wouldn't know anything of his childhood, and I'm sure he's one of the most courageous men alive. But did he not talk of his great leader, his great captain, the Moor—the finest *condottiere* of the age, some say—he who was my niece Desdemona's husband?"

"No, he never mentioned him."

"He was here also. You might say that it was here they first fell in love. Many have loved and been loved in my modest abode. Is that not so, sir?" He tried another tack. "Would you not agree, sir, that the Moor was an exceptional soldier?"

Was that the smallest hint of a shrug from Iago?

"Ah, the adventures they had together, my dear—over most of the world—they spoke of them much last summer. How the girls clung to their every word, and Desdemona most of all! She liked to hear of battles and bravery. But how we all did! How we listened in wonder at their exploits! Where was it you went, sir? As far south as a man can go, and east to the lands of the Ottoman, fighting all the way, and west, and north to . . . to England! Can you imagine, my dear, a country where if you don't wear an animal's fur all year round you'll die from frost and snow?"

Iago coughed. "He did not travel with me to England."

"Ah! I say, no, of course not! You went there with . . . with . . . who was the first *condottiere* you worked for? Oh, how could I forget? Francesco Gonzaga, Marquis of Mantua! He went with the Marquis of Mantua to the court of the King of England himself, young lady! Oh, Signor Iago has supped with royalty! Where did you meet the Moor then, sir? In one of those skirmishes to the west of here, wasn't it? During the first wars with the French?"

"Marignano." Iago gave it a weight that left them in no doubt he would not have called it a mere skirmish.

"They fought on different sides—the Moor for the Duke of Milan, and Signor Iago here for Francesco Gonzaga, as I said, who was then working for the King of France. Am I right, sir? The French king wanted Milan, do you see? They always do, the French; they've always wanted a bit of Italy and will go on doing so, I daresay. Old King Louis did, and now King Francis still does. I think they like our grapes and olives. The Moor and Signor Iago fought hand-to-hand, did you not, sir? And the Moor was so impressed by his opponent's skills that he hired him there and then, snatching him from under Francesco Gonzaga's big beaked nose!" He snorted with mirth, then quickly put his hands to his own nose to stop himself.

There was a short hiatus, Iago still looking at his plate, Gentile Stornello as stiff as an iron pole, and the tutor by now (or so it appeared) asleep, his head on his folded arms. The girl, her head turning between the hero of the story and the storyteller, had perhaps not been able to follow the narrative in every detail, for she asked, "Why do you call him 'the Moor'?"

"Because of his skin, child—which was black *come asso di picche!*"

"Oh."

"Did you ever see him, Gentile?"

"Once, when they left for Cyprus."

"Did you meet him then?"

"No, he was on the prow of his galley."

"And what a picture he must have been! *Un magnifico vero e proprio!* I never go to Venice much myself nowadays, so I miss all these spectacles. At my age it's funerals mostly. But when he arrived here! Ah, *ma sinceramente*, a sight to behold! In his colorful robes and with his booming voice—my wife, you know, called him *come un leone terribile*. Is that not true, sir? And your cousins and their friends, Gentile, how they trembled. Who would blame them for it, as they had never before seen anyone so black!"

"Why was he so black?" asked the girl, trembling a bit herself.

"Because they all are in Africa, my dear! Isn't that the case, sir?"

"Have you been to Africa?" the girl asked of Iago. He shook his head. She seemed a little disappointed. Then she announced, "I've seen some black men, but they are servants."

"Was he not once *un schiavo*, sir? I think he said he was, but he also said he was a prince, *un persona di prestigio*, did he not?"

"He was a prince in his own kingdom," Iago said. "And sold into slavery."

"Ah, *ma vero*, that's it! And then he was given his freedom by the King of . . . the King of somewhere or other."

"Portugal," said Iago.

"Portugal, that's it! I say, it's all coming back. You see, the Moor, too, had been with kings! The King of Portugal plucked him from his retinue, freed him, then reemployed him as a soldier! What good fortune! What a warrior he must have been, to have risen as fast as he did! What a story, isn't it? From prince, to slave, to soldier, to one of the most distinguished captains of men in the world! Well, can you imagine, dear girl, how we marveled as he spoke of his turbulent life, from boy to man. He talked, you see, of Africa too—a frightful place it sounds, where men eat one another."

The girl shivered. "Did he eat men himself?"

"Oh, no, young lady, he was a decent soul, was ... was—" Ubaldo Stornello stopped, then he said, "Do you know, we always knew him as the Moor, but he did have a name, did he not, sir? I can't for the life of me remember what it was—an African name, I presume, very odd. Ogello, Orello ... ?"

"Otello," Iago mumbled.

"Ah, indeed, *Otello il Moro.*"

Then the girl, by now entirely entranced, in dread and fascination by turns, asked, "Was he handsome too, this Otello?"

Ubaldo Stornello seemed to splutter slightly at the query. "I say, I wouldn't know how to describe him. I've never really thought about that. Intriguing, yes; amiable, certainly; unusual; alluring—all the women found him so, and Desdemona more than most. He was a splendid fellow in many ways. Your uncle Brabantio, dear boy, even thought him so for a time, but handsome? Would you have called him handsome, sir?"

Annibale Malipiero, still at the window, was also enthralled by this time. In fact, the pain in his lower back was gone, or he'd simply forgotten about it. Iago still wasn't saying much, but those thick scarred fingers were bunched into fists and he was glaring at his questioner unflinchingly. The gaze was being returned, with equal resolution. To their concealed spectator, the two men seemed like pugilists readying for a match, or like those gladiators he'd read about as a boy, waiting for the first strike.

Iago said, with quiet self-control, "Can we talk of something other than the Moor?"

"Of course, of course!" Ubaldo Stornello exclaimed breezily. "It must be grievous for you, sir, to be reminded of so superb a commander, whom you must have admired greatly—well, I saw it, when you were both here last, and saw his respect for you as well—and now dead, in tragic circumstances, I gather. I know nothing of what occurred in Cyprus, as I don't get out much. I hear the odd rumor, even out here in the wilds, but I've never trusted gossip. But enough of him—*Dio si prenda cura della sua anima.* He was a noble creature and God *will* take care of his soul, and that's the end of it!" He turned to the girl. "What shall we talk about, young lady? Pretty maidens and their handsome suitors?"

"Yes, please," she said, with a flutter of relief.

But the impish man did not indulge her just yet. He stared at Iago and scratched his neat beard. "Talking of suitors, there was one quite repulsive cove you brought with you on one of your visits, sir—what was his name? A Malipiero, I believe. Not handsome at all. What happened to him?"

There was no response of any kind from Iago.

With another flap of a hand, Ubaldo Stornello leaned confidentially toward the girl. "We don't want to talk of ugly people, do we?"

She shook her head.

"Then I'll tell you of a *very* good-looking fellow who was here—also, as it happens, with an odd name. I'm sure you remember who I mean, sir."

If it was possible for Iago's clenched fists to tighten further, they did. Annibale Malipiero had to admire his fellow patrician's determination. If he was still the chief inquisitor, he thought, he'd have signed up Ubaldo Stornello on the spot.

"Michele was his first name, I remember that, but the second was almost Latin, like one of those conspirators who murdered Julius Caesar—one of those democrats, you know. I think he was quite a democrat himself, which isn't surprising, as he came from Florence, I seem to remember. Clever fellow, too, if a bit too full of theory for my liking."

The mention of an ancient language shook the tutor momentarily from his inebriated stupor. "Brutush? Cassiush? Cashca?"

"He went with you to Cyprus, didn't he? Of course he did, because he was also in the Moor's service." He slapped a palm to his brow, almost too theatrically. "Yes, I recall it now. It was on your second visit. He was a soldier too, and an excellent one, or so the Moor told me. He praised him to the heights, in fact."

There could be no question that the villain was now very incensed indeed. Every muscle vibrated in his solid, sinewy body. His already swarthy face was darkening yet more, to an intense purple.

"Now, he, this Florentine," said Ubaldo Stornello to the girl, while still not taking his eyes from Iago's for a second, "was a charmer—quite the *uomo di mondo*—and young too." He didn't stop there in his listing of the Florentine's attributes:

"Well-favored, strong of limb, finely dressed, with a first-rate singing voice, as I remember, good with a lute too, and something of a poet as well, Gentile. Or he knew of poets, and he'd recite them melodiously. Easy on the ear and on the eye, my dear late wife called him, *come un vero corteggiatore*. Desdemona was most taken with him, as she was by far the best read of my brother Brabantio's daughters. Do you know"— here again the patrician lowered his voice, though he could be heard well enough—"I do believe Otello was the tiniest bit jealous?"

"Because the Florentine was the center of attention?" the girl asked.

"Always, my dear. Or he'd become so, as the Moor had been before. There are, I'm sure you know, certain people, men or women, who— how did my wife put it?—*illuminano la stanza*, just by being who they are. He was one such. Or what was it *your* wife described him as, sir? A young god, wasn't it? *Un dio amoroso mandato dal paradiso per deliziarci noi.* She had a fine way with words too, did Emilia."

"How old was he?"

"Young enough to be good-looking, old enough to know how to enchant."

"Enough!" Iago swept a hand across the tabletop so that plates and bowls and food and goblets and jugs went flying. Everybody jumped— the girl with a yelp of alarm, Ubaldo Stornello rather stiffly and without much evidence of surprise, Gentile Stornello with a swift wrench of the neck in Iago's direction, Baldassare Ghiberti with an upward jolt of his head, looking about him as if wondering where he was.

The observer behind the window had also jumped. Thankfully, the noise of breaking crockery was so loud that nobody would have heard anything else. Where were those servants? Why had no one come running?

Then Iago posed a question that Annibale Malipiero himself had been pondering. "Why are you doing this?" he asked through clenched teeth.

"Why am I doing what?" the venerable patrician replied. "I was merely reminiscing, sir."

"Pah! Enough," said Iago again. "We're going. You, Gentile, get horses. Take her with you, as she claims she can ride. You, drunken oaf"—he was addressing the tutor—"go with them."

"I . . . I don't know where they're kept," the boy said haplessly.

"You!" Iago pointed to Ubaldo Stornello. "Show us to your stables."

"You'll have to untie my legs from this chair first," said the still surprisingly calm and good-humored host.

"Oh!" squeaked the girl.

"I could get a servant to show you."

"Your servants, Signor, are locked in a closet in the kitchen."

"I wondered where they could have got to," said Ubaldo Stornello offhandedly. Then, in a more solemn tone: "Not *all* of them, in truth."

Iago stood stock still, moving only his eyes in the direction of the door leading to the kitchen.

"Knowing who you were at once, sir, and of the foul deeds you have perpetrated since I last met you—we had *un piccolo contrattempo* about it earlier, didn't we, before this pleasant meal?—I instructed some of them to hide. I've sent a couple of my most *fedele* retainers to alert the authorities. They don't have far to go. Did you notice the little castle atop the hill behind my house? It looks empty, abandoned. It isn't. It's full of Venetians readying for war. I'd say they will be here at any moment."

Annibale Malipiero groaned—that was the very last thing he wanted to hear, that the hills roundabout might be crawling with soldiery. The groan was rather too perceptible. Iago turned to the window. His watcher did not dare cower back, for fear of disturbing the vine and thereby making his presence more obvious. But the man's eyes, despite glimmers of rage and hatred, were leaden.

"Go," he charged the others again. "Find the stables. Bring the horses to the gate. I'll meet you there. *Go!*" Then: "Don't forget your weapons!"

They scrabbled in a corner of the room at an assortment of swords, daggers, halberds, axes—all the gory requisites of battle that they must have collected on their journey. The boy took most of them, the girl snatched at a couple of *pugnali,* and the lumbering academic picked up a blade that was far too heavy for him.

"No! I'll take that," said Iago, grabbing the weapon—an especially savage-looking implement with a long, thin double-edged blade and a chunky hilt.

"You're not going to—" Gentile Stornello began to ask nervously.

"Go!"

They went.

Iago tapped at his palm with the longsword's blade. He approached the entrapped but harmless Signor as if he was some longtime enemy snared at last. Ubaldo Stornello still didn't seem the least bit fearful.

"You have angered me," said Iago.

"I know," said Ubaldo Stornello.

"Why?"

"Because I'm a sad and lonely old chap who wants to die," said the Signor simply. "My wife's gone, and with her my life. I've had a good life; now it's time to end it. I would have done it myself before this, but there's always the difficulty of how and of the servants rushing in to stop you. So in a way you're my savior, my *salvatore opportuno.* You can do it for me. I only ask that you make it as quick and painless as possible—none of your usual savagery, if you'd be so kind. And I suggest you don't linger on it too long or we *will* be invaded."

"I could behead you," Iago said.

"That's best; that would be speedy."

"You will not feel a thing."

"I say," Ubaldo Stornello chuckled, "I feel like one of those ancient Romans. You know, they believed that all of life was a preparation for a good death."

"The readiness is all."

"That's a fine way of putting it. Shall I lay my head here?"

"As you wish."

"Perhaps you could loosen my shirt, just at the top here; that's how it's done, is it not?"

"That's how it's done."

"But before you do kill me, could I ask a few questions?"

Iago sighed. "As you reminded me, I don't have much time."

"Did you kill my niece?"

"So you wish me to confess, is that it?"

"Why not? I won't tell anybody." Ubaldo Stornello chuckled at his little joke.

"No, the Moor killed her."

"Did you kill the Moor?"

"No, he killed himself."

"But I think you had a part in it all, did you not? I saw you play them here—the Moor, and that man Michele . . . Michele . . ."

"Cassio."

"That was it. Stupid name, As if he were some great senator. You hated him, did you not?"

"Yes."

"Why? Because he was beautiful?"

There was no answer.

"Did you hate the Moor too?"

"Yes."

"Did you hate my niece?"

There was the smallest silence, then Iago said, "No."

"Did you love her?"

Iago didn't answer that one either. He was facing away from Annibale Malipiero at this point, sword lifted. How the ex-*interrogante* wished he might see the creature's expression at that moment. Ubaldo Stornello already had his head down on the table.

"Did you kill your wife?"

"Yes."

"Did you love *her*?"

"No."

"You married her only to find your way into Desdemona's confidence."

"Of course."

"And Michele Cassio—did you kill him too?"

"I had him killed."

"Thank you," said Ubaldo Stornello. "I like to tie things up. I'm all set now."

Iago tested his aim, lowering the longsword onto the neck but not touching it.

"Oh, one more thing: Did you bed my wife?"

"No," Iago said. "She would not let me."

The jovial and benign Ubaldo Stornello's end was as swift and trouble free as he'd wished it to be, as befitted his simple and largely contented life.

49. *Godlessness and Savagery*

We had no idea where the stables might be. I'd thought it a simple enough task—to be guided by the sound of neighing or the scuffing of hooves. It's not a big town, after all, and it was deathly silent. But horses, Franceschina informed me, don't actually neigh much, and only when they're unhappy. "Or when they're in love," she added with a grin.

We did see a horse on our way out of my uncle's villa, tethered to the main gate. It was whinnying and restless. Franceschina's touch calmed it. "You're a fine-looking beast, there, there . . ." she said. I suppose it was fine-looking, insofar as horses can be. But then, I don't know much about horses. It was definitely big, and strapping, and almost wholly white. Franceschina suggested we should steal it. I said we shouldn't, as it probably was a special sort of horse, belonging to my uncle. I now know that it belongs to the chief inquisitor, because he had it with him when he found us looking for the stables. He was holding it by the reins and it was bucking all over the place. It seemed desperate to be off somewhere. So did he.

He addressed the three of us crisply. "You'll be tempted to flee, and I wouldn't blame you, but you mustn't. I instruct you not to do so. I saw and heard everything that went on in the villa—"

"Is my uncle all right?"

"Your uncle is fine. But, listen, I shall be following you closely from now on. There's no need for you to write me any more notes, *Dottore*, as I shall always be nearby. Do not on any account, if you see me or hear me, give any sign that you've done so. Above all, stick with him. You're doing very well so far. *Buona fortuna!*"

As Baldassare and Franceschina turned away to continue their search, he held me by the wrist and whispered urgently, "I almost pulled you out of this, up in the hills. But you'd gone." He looked me up and down, assessing me by the light of his torch, as if I was a horse perhaps and he an exacting purchaser. "I think you can handle whatever may happen next. But you must continue to get him to talk of his childhood and his youth. Also, I think he was in love—"

"With Desdemona? He didn't kill her, did you know that? The Moor killed her and then killed himself. He says he didn't kill his wife, but he did admit to killing your nephew Roderigo Malipiero."

He gripped me still more tightly and murmured, "Concentrate only on what we need to know. Listen to nothing else. He's like a poison, Gentile, his words are dangerous, pestilential, so you must be cautious."

He was gone. It was the strangest thing, to be visited so briefly by the person who's had such sway over my every move and all that has happened to me—over my very being, in fact—and then for him to vanish again, rather as if God himself had dropped in for a minute to check on how I was doing. Actually he didn't disappear that quickly. He had some trouble mounting his very lively steed.

We finally found the stables—or Franceschina did. She doesn't only seem to know all there is to know about horses, she has a nose for them, literally. She smelled her way through the town, her pretty nostrils twitching, and there they were. She picked the largest and strongest, of course: a glossy black creature with big watchful eyes, *un stallone vigoroso—non castrato*, she told me, with another of her meaningful glances. "You must have *una cavalla*," she said, and chose a fairly placid-seeming, and much smaller, mare.

I didn't argue. For Iago she selected another male, though not as obviously formidable as her own. Baldassare, who has become increasingly cantankerous, insisted on a quite spirited young colt, against Franceschina's advice. "I can ride, you know," he grumbled. He travels by horse quite often, between the universities of Padua and Bologna. Although he cuts a rather comical figure, and it took some effort to get his foot into a stirrup and to heave him onto the saddle, in our travels thus far he hasn't fallen off once, even at a gallop. I've done so twice—to Franceschina's tinkling glee and Baldassare's disdain.

Iago was waiting for us at the gate of the villa. He was breathing heavily, and his eyes were bloodshot and darkly ringed, as if he'd undergone some supreme physical undertaking or some test of his resolve and had emerged from it completely drained. I didn't dare ask what he might have done, and still haven't.

Franceschina is amazing on a horse. Because she loves them so, they love her back and will do anything she wants them to do. She tugs here and tugs there and they do her bidding. "*Andiamo!*" she cried, as we rode. "*Vai! Vai! Presto! Presto forte! Lentamente adesso! No, cessa! Fermo! Buona bestia, buona buona.*" She looked so authoritative. Yesterday, in the meadow, she was the sweet dryad—*una ninfa di bosco*, my uncle called her—but now she's become the goddess of the chase once more.

Iago's not a bad equestrian either, but then, you'd expect that of a battle-hardened soldier. "We will ride nonstop to Mantua!" he announced as we set off. "No breaks, no sleep, and no complaining, scholar!"

But horses, I've learned, don't like rain. More specifically, they don't like galloping, or cantering, or even trotting through it. But they're relatively placid when they've got some trees that they can shelter under, which is what they're doing now, chomping contentedly at the wet grass.

So we rode through most of the night, but now we've had to stop. It's mid-morning and it's bucketing. The late summer deluges my uncle feared (which will probably ruin his grapes and olives still further) may have come even sooner than anticipated.

We've found refuge from the elements in a small church—or half of a church, to be precise, as it's a ruin. Most of the roof is open to the teeming sky. Iago believes that it was destroyed only recently, that it hasn't stood here abandoned for years and crumbled naturally. The charred timbers under which we huddle may testify to this. But who'd set fire to a church? No Christian surely. Iago hasn't referred to his

Turkish friends lately. And we haven't been pursued by hordes of Venetian militia either.

"Do you think my uncle was lying when he said that castle was full of soldiers?"

"Never trust a Stornello" comes the terse reply. He's looking at Franceschina, who is kneeling some distance away from us, like a supplicant, head bowed and covered by her shawl, before a round-arched niche in which there must once have been a statue or a painting of Christ on the cross or the Madonna. She mumbles scarcely audible imprecations; her delectable hands move up and down and across over and over again. No longer a goddess of nature, she's a simple God-fearing maid once more.

"She has much to be contrite for. Let us hope her prayers are answered," Iago whispers.

"She does?"

"You believe that because she is lovely, she must be virtuous. But she's no saint and you know it. Would a saint kiss you on the mouth as she did?"

"You told her to kiss me."

"She didn't have to do my bidding. Did she show unwillingness? Was she cool? A reluctant one keeps her lips closed—did she? Who taught her to kiss so well?"

"You?"

He throws me a sharp, astonished glance. "Me? You have a storm of jealousy in that young head of yours. I warned you to beware jealousy. You think I have kissed her?"

"It's crossed my mind."

He gives me a soft clout on the back of my head. He even ruffles my hair. "I repulse her. I'm old; she's young. She craves youth, she craves vigor, she craves—they have a saying for it in Mantua—*la bella figura*."

I must be looking very morose indeed. He tips his face closer to mine. "Do you still mope about that boy in Venice, that bully?" I don't even nod.

"Pah! All women have a liking for brutes, though they'll seldom divulge it. But look at her—*look* at her."

I've been doing nothing else.

"Watch how she breathes, even in prayer, how she palpitates. She's full of game . . . She's ripe . . . She yearns for pleasure . . . Her body requires it. And her eye must be fed. 'Oh, yes,' she panted to your uncle, 'I love pretty people.' And she needs more than just the one, Gentile Stornello."

"I wouldn't describe myself as pretty, I don't think."

"Come, you do yourself down. In some lights you resemble a sweet blushing maid yourself." He chuckles, then stares at her again. "Is she praying or only contemplating aloud?"

"Contemplating? Contemplating what?"

"Whom do I like most? Whom do I want most? My thug of a master, who is handsome to be sure but who's in Venice? Or my *pretty* Gentile, who's here?"

"Could we maybe talk about something else?" Or preferably not talk at all. But now I'm thinking of the chief inquisitor's last instruction. Facts, simply facts . . .

"Franceschina trembled a bit when my uncle talked of the Moor too." I feel quite clever.

But from the stiffening of his frame, I've a feeling I shouldn't have mentioned Desdemona's husband.

He says, "Women like brutes, as I've told you."

"The Moor was a brute?"

"He was an *African*."

"And that makes him a brute? I thought he was a prince, or a king, or some such."

"You!" He calls to Franceschina, who's still mumbling away and crossing herself incessantly. "You, girl"—no more "my lady" or "sweet lady" or *"signorina"*—"who are you praying to? There's nobody there! Look!" he shouts. "No statue, no picture, nothing!"

"L'anima is still here," she says softly.

"Spirit? Whose spirit?"

"Of the Blessed Virgin."

"Pah!" he spits. Then again: "There's no one there! There never was!" He walks out into the rain, which is lessening now, and thrusts a fore-

finger at the overcast sky. "There's no one there either!" He jabs downward at the muddy ground. "Or there! No Blessed Virgin, no God, no
Christ! No hell! No devil!" Franceschina has turned to him, openmouthed. He strides over to Baldassare, who's crumpled and sleeping
against a small moss-covered tomb. He kicks him awake. Baldassare
lets out a little shriek of pain. "You! Brainbox! Do you believe there's
anyone up there?"

"Up where? Oh, there. Yes, I do, in point of fact. As I've said, I'm a
humanist and therefore don't credit the efficacy of prayer myself, but I
do subscribe to the"—he coughs—"concept that somewhere 'up there,'
as you put, someone is looking down on us."

"Why?"

"Why?" That stumps my tutor somewhat. Maybe his drink-sodden
mind needs a bit more time to analyze the question. "Because there
must be?" he ventures.

"Why must there be? Because you have been told there must? Or has
your scholarly brain worked it out for itself? No, you have read it, so it
must be true. And who writes these books that say what we must
believe? Our lords and our masters, who want to hold us in check. We
must bow and scrape and suffer because there is a God. Well, I say there
is no God. No gods either, if that's your fancy."

"Who made the world, then, and all the things in it?" asks Franceschina simply.

He swings toward her and stares at her with such virulence that it
makes her flinch. "*You* did," he says. He points to me, then Baldassare,
then himself. "Just as he did, and he did, and I did."

She crinkles her delightful nose. What crazily godless notion is he
going to come up with now? He approaches her. She looks uncompre-
hendingly up at him.

He taps his temple. "The world and all the things in it are in here,
girl, nowhere else." He puts out a rough hand, and with surprising delicacy runs it through her hair. "Even in your beautiful head." He drops
to his haunches before her. "Close your eyes."

She does so, not too willingly.

"What do you see? Nothing. Cover your ears. What do you hear, apart from the throb of your pretty young heart? Nothing. When your hearts stops, when you die, that will be all there will be. Nothing. No heaven, no choirs of angels, no life after death, nothing. When you stop, the world stops." He clicks his fingers, like *un mago* making something disappear. "*Pffffft!!*" He blows whatever it was away.

Franceschina is a welter of puzzlement and irritation. Either she doesn't understand a word he's saying or she does and doesn't like it. She beats at her brow with her dainty fists, shaking her head so that her fabulous tresses fly this way and that. She drums her delectable feet on the ground. "Ay, Ay, Ay!" she cries. He reaches out for her. She pushes him away. She's strong, of course. He almost falls backward. *"Brutto! Brutto!"* she howls.

He's stronger. He grabs her, holds her, pushes her into his shoulder and again strokes her hair, cooing, "Shush now, shush. Do you not see, Franceschina? Do you not see it's a good thing, it's a *good* thing?"

"What's good about it?" she snuffles.

"Because the world is in your head; you own it. The world is what we make of it. We are gods ourselves. We are each a god in our own world." He takes her face in his hands. He's smiling. He tips his own head to one side. "Do you see?"

She doesn't. Without getting up, he shuffles toward me, his hands flat on either side of him, like some hideous, demonic beast. He grasps one of my arms before I can scuttle away myself. His eyes are wide and fiery with enthusiasm. "Once you know the world is of your own making, Gentile, you can do with it, and those in it, what you will. *You* then are the world's master, no one else."

I simply stare back at him, in blank, unforthcoming amazement. It's perilous talk, after all, spectacularly heretical. And it's as demented as the ramblings of *un pazzo* in *un manicomio*. He's spoken before, much to my disquiet, of the world being turned upside down. Now I realize he wants to do that very thing *single-handedly.*

His eyes go dead, as if someone within that world in there has doused the lamps. He emits a short growl and spits on the ground. He thinks I'm a fool too. He turns to Baldassare, whose lips are gaping even more widely than mine. "Scholar, do you have a conscience?"

"A . . . a conscience? Yes, I have a conscience. Don't we all?"

"Get rid of it. Then you, *Dottore* Baldassare Ghiberti, can be master of the world. It is only conscience that makes us cowards."

Thinking of the rain that has delayed our progress to Mantua, which can't be too far away now, and to which he said we should ride nonstop, I say rather impertinently, "Do you have control over the weather too?"

He glares at me.

But amazingly, only a few moments after I've said this, the downpour ceases. There's only the plink of droplets on the stones of the destroyed church, coming from the half-tumbled roof above us, as if the tired old ruin were shaking itself dry. More incredibly still, a spear of sunlight pierces the gray-black clouds and plants a yellow circle on the wet grass not far from us. Then there are further shafts, cascading across the hills around us.

Iago spreads out his arms. "What do you think?" he declares. "What do you *think*?"

He doesn't seem dangerous anymore, or even mad. With his arms still outstretched, he's turning in circles, doing a little dance, kicking and crossing his feet. "This is called a jig," he announces. "I learned it in England, from the king himself."

Franceschina, still sniffing a bit but glad to put all the talk of nothingness and godlessness behind her, begins to clap along.

Baldassare creeps toward me. "In point of fact," he whispers, "he's an Epicurean, were he but to know it. Epicurus believed that once you were dead that was it, so you had to make the most of life."

Somewhere not far off, behind the crest of a slight incline in this generally level environment, a dog barks. It all seems peaceful enough until we realize it's more a call of distress than a warning. Other dogs pick it up and start to yelp too. Suddenly there's a chorus of clucking and crowing and frantic squawking, from hens and cocks and geese. Our horses, sensing nearby jeopardy, let out strident whinnies, and they rear and kick, trying to pull themselves from the branches to which they've been tethered. Then we hear men shouting, and a woman scream—an echoing ululation of pain and terror. Smoke is rising from over there—not the friendly white smoke of an ordinary fire, but gulping black puffs.

Iago runs, not from the sounds and the smoke but in their direction, up the hill and away from us. In his impatience to see what's going on, he sometimes stumbles, falls, and curses. Franceschina follows him, in a kind of trance. As he reaches the ridge, he drops to his knees. He turns, scuttles back to her, and stops her from going any farther. Whatever horrible things are happening down there, he doesn't want her to witness them. He creeps on all fours back to the crest. Resolute as always, she does the same, ignoring his command. The shouting and screaming have stopped. Now it's only the dogs and shrieking geese.

When I reach the top of the slope, Franceschina has her hand to her mouth, retching silently. Below us is a scene that would silence even the most stoic of philosophers. Close enough for us to discern its every detail is a farmstead—or the remains of one. Five or six buildings are crackling and smoking. Some are still aflame, but the rain has prevented the fire from catching properly. In the central yard, where the disturbed farm birds continue to scamper and screech and cackle, and the dogs on their leashes leap and growl, are the scattered bodies of six unfortunate souls, freshly slain, lying in still-growing pools of blood. One has had his arms chopped off; two have been decapitated. Another is still twitching, coughing scarlet phlegm.

"Your Turkish friends?" I whisper to Iago.

"Look," he says. Scrambling up another hill to my right are a dozen or so men, waving swords and daggers, swaying and stumbling. Their raucous laughter fills the valley. They're too sated, or drunk, to notice us, even if they did care to glance back upon the scene of their recently inflicted savagery.

"Who are they?"

"Soldiers; yours, no doubt, marauding Venetians on their way home from war. Or deserters," he adds with disgust. "Whatever battle they've been in, their spoils of victory must have been meager. Their lust for slaughter and pillage is still up."

Baldassare has been brave enough to follow us. He stands ashen-faced. He, too, is trying not to be sick. Then he falls forward and vomits prodigiously. "Oh, God," he groans. "Oh, *miserere* . . . oh, *miserere*."

Miserere indeed. *Lasciate ogne speranza, voi ch'intrate.*

"So now you pray," Iago observes, "to a God who can permit such cruelty."

Baldassare is wiping his messy mouth with the back of his hand, and because I feel so very sorry for my long-suffering teacher at that moment, I instinctively reach into a pocket and take out a handkerchief. I realize that it's Franceschina's, with the stitched "F" in the corner, now crumpled and wet. I wonder if I should show it to her, to remind her that she, at one time a long while ago, felt sorry enough for me to offer it as a token or at least to ease my own agony. But I give it to Baldassare.

"It's time to inspect your cruel God's handiwork," Iago mumbles. He takes Franceschina's hand, and although he tried to prevent her from seeing the carnage earlier, he now slithers with her down the slope into its very center. Baldassare and I slither too.

We stand at the edge of the farmyard, scarcely able to look, as Iago picks his way through the corpses (the twitcher has stopped twitching), examining each with considerable meticulousness, lifting an arm here or a leg there with his foot, and occasionally dropping to the ground to scrutinize the damage even more closely. He does not do so with any relish; it's more clinical than that, like an army physician, I'd imagine, on a recently vacated battlefield. He's checking on the precise nature of the slashes and severances. "Bad killers," he mutters. "Amateurs," he tuts. "These fellows have been a long time dying." And as he stands up again, he says, "They prayed, I don't doubt, to your unheeding God. They had to believe in the hope of a better world to come. Much good will it do them."

He quickly turns his head. He's heard something—something other than the dogs and the poultry. We hear it too. It's coming from a smoldering building that I think is the main house, a one-storey structure that may once have been a pretty home. Now it has no roof. Whoever remains in there is alive, if barely. A woman's moans soon turn into keening wails.

Franceschina moves instinctively toward the house. Iago grasps her arm. Just as he does so, a man emerges, having to duck under the low door. He's fat, grizzled, pockmarked, sweating. I can tell he's a soldier by his surcoat, although I don't recognize the livery. It's not the Venetian lion anyway. He's tucking his shirt into his hose. He's tottering slightly. He's drunk.

He blinks in surprise at seeing us. Then, in his bleary eyes, there's a sign of vague recognition, which becomes clearer as he waves a finger at Iago and blurts, "Hey! I know you, you're . . . you're . . ."

Keeping a firm hold on Franceschina, because she's still struggling to get into the house, Iago approaches the gruff soldier. "I don't think you do," he says.

"I'm sure I do. We fought together at Ravenna, and Novara, Marignano too. You were the bloke who went off with the black captain, what's-his-name . . ."

"Who've you been fighting for now?" Iago asks.

"Gonzaga, like you did, before you . . . before the blackamoor employed you. Seen much action since?"

"Enough," says Iago.

"Well, to each his own. Me, I'm a Mantuan through and through. Couldn't work for anybody else." The man is relaxed, unthreatened. He's too drunk to notice Iago's coldness and thinks he's come across a fellow warrior who might wish to share a few gory memories. "Now, there was a dustup, Marignano, eh?"

"How far is Mantua?"

"From here? Only ten miles or thereabouts."

"What are you doing on this side of Mantua? Why aren't you at the wars?"

"Bit of fun, just a bit of fun," the soldier slurs defensively. "Are you my captain all of a sudden? I'll go back there in a while. Followed some Venetians going home. Not many pickings hereabouts, unlike the old days, eh?" He chortles and leans forward, taps the side of his scarred nose. "Speaking of which, there's a farmer's wife and her daughter inside that house. I've had the wife—so did some of the others—but I'm spent. You can have the daughter; she's a cute little filly, fresh as a daisy, can't be older than fourteen. I found her; the others missed her. She was hiding in a chest. I pulled her out and made her watch me and her mother. That was something. Never done that before." Now he turns his inebriated gaze on Franceschina. "Who's this beauty?" he leers.

Franceschina lets loose a scream of outrage, and with the sheer strength of her anger she frees herself from Iago's clutches and runs toward the house. Within seconds, Iago has both his hands around the extremely surprised lecher's throat. "Now you must die," he says simply, "for that if for nothing else."

"For calling your girlfriend a beauty?" gasps the soldier, still incapable of understanding that he really is about to die.

"No, for what you did in there. You made the girl *watch*?"

I can't bear to witness more bloodshed, so I follow Franceschina into the house, even though I know I will loathe what I find there. In one corner of what I suppose was the kitchen floor, a woman sits, her hair tumbling over her downturned face. Her legs are spread, twisted outward. There's something wrong about the angle at which they protrude. Are they broken? Her skirts are ruffled around her waist. She's stopped wailing, but she's still sobbing—great exhalations of humiliation and pain. In another corner, being comforted by Franceschina, is a girl, no more than a child, staring ahead, eyes locked wide in confusion and terror, opening and closing her mouth but unable to emit a single sound.

"There, there," Franceschina coos, as she tries to caress the fear from the trembling mite's body. "*Cara bambina*, don't be afraid, *piccola fanciulla . . .* it's over, it's over . . ."

I can hear the yells of the revolting old soldier, Iago's onetime comrade-in-arms, as he's punched and kicked and stabbed in a thousand places. After quite a while there's utter, dreadful silence.

"No! No, don't come near her! *Bestia! Diavolo!*" Franceschina cries as Iago enters the awful stillness, pushing Baldassare aside. He's covered from head to toe in blood. He's still clasping his dagger, its blade dripping. His chest heaves. His wild glare takes in the picture before him—the woman, then her daughter. "No!" Franceschina shouts again, pulling the child closer to her still. "Don't even dare to touch them! *Brutto! Assassino!*"

As he looks at the frozen girl, his stare mellows. His gray-green eyes stop flaring. There's something I've not seen in them before—pity, the sort you can't hide. His shoulders droop. The dagger clatters to the floor.

"What makes you think I would touch them?" he asks softly. "I've just killed their abuser, have I not? For what he did to them?"

She relents a touch. He approaches her and the girl and crouches before them. Carefully, he extends a hand, so that the poor thing doesn't flinch too much, and he strokes the girl's hair with extraordinary tenderness. "He won't come back now," he whispers. "They won't come back. They'll never come back."

"Papà?" she asks faintly. "Where's Papà?"

Is that a sob I hear from him? After a moment he says, "Your *papà* has gone away, but you still have your *mamma* here."

He's brusque again, but he raises his voice only a little as he gives us instructions. I am to fetch water so that he can wash away the blood that covers him. Franceschina must see to the woman. Franceschina asks Iago if we can take the girl with us, and he says, no, of course we can't. She has her mother, and nobody can tend a child better than a mother. Baldassare is told to pile up the corpses in the yard and burn them.

"B-b-burn them?"

Iago hisses in his ear, "Yes, to a cinder. The child thinks her father has gone away. Make him *go away*."

Franceschina sets about her task, dully, mechanically. I watch her, try to smile at her, but she's removed, separate. I hear Iago shout, "No, fool, not him! The others! Over there! I need to check this villain for loot—he's bound to have some."

"You did say 'bodies,'" Baldassare splutters, "so I presumed you meant all of them."

"Silence! Get to it! We must be in Mantua by nightfall!"

50. Mantua

The lakes that encircle Mantua make it appear to hover slightly above the lush meadows and pastures that also surround it—or like two cities, one of them upside down. Not as sprawling and colorful as Venice, it's nonetheless eye-catching, assertive, even daunting, which was presumably the intention of the militaristic Gonzagas who designed it and who rule it still.

"It can be hellish cold in winter," Iago says, and even now, despite the August sunshine, there's a distinct chill. "It's the wind from the Mincio." The Mincio, I gather, is the river from which the lakes have formed. It flows into the Po, which in its turn winds toward the sea, near where we first set out on this journey.

As all cities on the mainland must be, it's heavily fortified, locked into unscalable walls. But we have no trouble entering it, and we don't have to pretend to be silent monks. Iago found some old clothes in the decimated farmstead and now looks every bit the toiling countryman. Franceschina has exchanged my uncle Ubaldo's late wife's finery for a simple shift from the farmer's widow. Baldassare never needs to change to look unthreatening. I'm still wearing my filthy shirt and hose, but I'm probably hardly noticeable anyway. We're without our horses too; we left them tethered to a couple of trees in a field at some distance from the city gate. We also hid our weapons there—although Iago has no doubt concealed a dagger somewhere about him.

I have the sense that he's somehow shedding things—the accoutrements of the chase, if you like. This visit to Mantua has the feeling of a homecoming, even though he's told us it wasn't his birthplace. He strides through its wide streets with a swagger, not caring who sees him. He shows us around almost as if he owns it.

He's enjoying himself hugely. "To your right, the duomo; to your left, the Palazzo Ducale, the home of the Marquis of Mantua, Federico Gonzaga, and his mother, the Marchioness Isabella d'Este Gonzaga, whom I have met personally many times." The building in question stretches before us like a never-ending fortress.

Baldassare, who's also never been to Mantua—he sticks to "seats of learning"—says, "It's assuredly big."

"Bigger than any palazzo in the whole of Italy," Iago proudly declares. I'm not sure he's right about that. The Palazzo Ducale in Venice is surely larger and definitely more elaborate, with its marble and its tracery and gilt.

Mantua is a very neat city. Its many grand houses, the exteriors of which are as unadorned as the great palazzo itself, all seem scrubbed. Its spacious streets, its *corsi* and *viale*, are ordered, straight, geometrical. Iago says that the Gonzaga wanted it built that way, to a rigid plan, from which no one is permitted to stray. I prefer the confusion of Venice—a city that took shape over a thousand years.

We can't sightsee for long. Night is descending. We need to find a hostelry, which we do quite easily because Iago now has money, as he'd hoped, from the plundering soldier's purse. We have gold to spend.

So we dine on the finest gastronomy Mantua has to offer—or, if not the finest, which I suspect is reserved for the grand houses, then the best that a modest though roomy and comfortable inn can provide. There's very little meat. It's mainly fish, which I'm not thrilled about, despite being a citizen of the greatest seafaring nation in the world. I hate all the bones. But I'm starving, so I pick at *pesce con* this and *pesce in* that as the *locandiere* bobs about us, keen to know what we think. Zinerva would loathe him. "*Buffone arrogante!* With his *arie di superiorita! Cretino ipocrito!* Let him eat his own *escremento!*" How I miss her *cucina della casa!* Her food is meant be eaten, not admired from a distance.

Franceschina usually crams whatever's to hand into her lovely mouth, letting it dribble from her full lips, licking it from her slender fingers, allowing it to drip onto her skin and clothes. Now she doesn't raise even a morsel from her plate and for long periods stares into the distance.

I've seen so many of her moods, but never this drawn, shadowy melancholy. She hung back as we rode from the farmstead, no longer the galloping goddess. "Come, girl, don't linger!" Iago called. But ever since, she's seemed lost, a slim pale spirit wandering in some grim world of her own.

I try to engage her in small talk. "This is Virgil's city, you know." She gives no sign of even having heard me. "Publius Vergilius Maro—he was born near here, the greatest of the Roman poets."

"That's debatable," Baldassare mumbles through a mouthful of bones and fish flesh.

"Baldassare, tell Franceschina about Virgil."

She stands and leaves the room.

"She's seen more than any girl should ever have to see," I say.

Nobody says much after that, not even Iago. She's silenced us all.

Fortunately, we don't all have to sleep in one room or crammed together on a single mattress, as we did in Padua. We each have a bedchamber. Hers is next to mine. A rickety wall of latticed worm-eaten wood and flaking clay is all that separates us. *Where's the harm in a bit of comfort?* I think, as I slide from my bed and tiptoe to her door. I could just sit with her, put my arms about her shoulders, and let her weep, if that's what she needs to do.

I whisper her name. I knock nervously. There's not a sound within. I knock less tentatively. I put my ear to the thin door. I think I can hear her breathing. Yes, I can—it sounds like the sea, a friendly sea, advancing and retreating on a peaceful shore. *Where's the harm,* I'm now thinking, *in entering and watching her sleep?* I reach for the handle. It's bolted from the inside.

He asks in the morning, "Did you try?" He's standing at the end of my bed. He's shaken me awake. "You did, I know you did; I heard you creeping."

I can't answer immediately, because he's transformed himself. What is he wearing? A multitude of colors. His already broad shoulders seem even broader under a slash-sleeved green-and-yellow doublet of velvet, over which there's a black-and-gold full-length low-cut jerkin with a flaring skirt. On top of that there's a purple cloak, which reaches only to his knees, trimmed with white fur. His high-ruffed shirt is a virulent blue. His hose is reddish-brown. His calf-length boots are of shiny black leather but rather effeminate, narrowing to a stilettolike taper at the toes. Most incredible of all, though, is his hat: a great floppy crimson thing, with an upturned brim. It sports several silver buttons around its rim and a flapping peacock feather of green, white, black, and yellow. Beneath all this flamboyance somewhere is Iago—scrubbed to a polish. His dark rough skin gleams.

"Did you make sweet love?" he persists, ignoring my amazement.

"Her door was locked," I inform him gruffly.

"Ah. Poor Gentile. When will he ever mount his mare?" He contemplates me, scratching his chin. Are those rings he's wearing?

"Did you kill the man you stole those clothes from?"

He steps back, affronted. "I do not need to kill for clothes! Neither do I need to steal!" He jiggles the purse dangling from his waist. From the same belt, I notice, hangs his dagger. "I bought them from an Englishman. We were carousing in the small hours, while you were slinking about up here. He was reluctant at first, but when he saw the gold . . ." With arms outstretched, he twirls almost, inviting my opinion. "What do you think? Do I not look like a king? Like the King of England?"

"I wouldn't know," I say. "I've never met him."

"I have," he reminds me. "I've met the King of England, and now I look as he looks!"

"How much gold do we have left?"

"Not much, but no matter—we will all be rich soon. Come. There's someone I want you to meet!" He thumps on Franceschina's door, and on Baldassare's. "Wake up, girl; wake up, scholar. There's someone I want you to meet!"

Who can this person be? Some benefactor, some Mantuan-dwelling

Croesus who will take him in, protect him? Is this, then, why we're in Mantua? He seems very jovial and carefree this morning. Perhaps he hopes that in these new (and quite ridiculous) English garments he won't be recognized. Though he'll certainly be noticed.

He preens as he marches, flouncy-hatted head held high, through the broad, already sunlit avenues. People skip aside with mouths agape as he cuts through the throng like a flag-festooned galleon. We follow like chicks in a row but doing our best not to seem too close to him. Even sad Franceschina smiles a little at his outlandishness.

We skirt the Palazzo Ducale. I think for a moment that we might be going there, but he leads us on to a fairly deserted *calle* and bids us wait. The sun has not yet hit this place. He approaches an arch that leads through an inner courtyard to a comparatively modest palazzo with a simple orange façade and small barred windows. Iago pounds on the gate. He waits, a confident hand on his hip, his legs slightly splayed, like *un corteggiatore*, like *un uomo di mondo pittoresco*.

"He looks mad!" I whisper.

"Yes, he does," says Franceschina. They're the first words she's spoken in a whole day.

Nobody answers for an age. An elderly retainer finally appears. Words are exchanged, which we cannot hear. The retainer shuffles off. Again we wait. Iago turns to us, smiles a self-confident smile, and even waves to us, his peacock feather bobbing. The gatekeeper returns. More words pass. On Iago's part they become loud, persistent. We still can't hear what's being said. The old man leaves. Iago rattles the gate, cursing to himself. He kicks at the iron bars.

He tramps along the front of the palazzo and disappears down a dark and narrow side alley. He's bent double now, creeping, scuttling, stealthy in the dim light.

"This doesn't look good," Baldassare says.

We hear banging and the rattle of a door. "I demand to see *la contessa*! I demand to be taken to *la padrona della casa*!"

So this Croesus of his is female, and an aristocratic female too—though she doesn't appear to be especially benevolent at the moment.

"You can't! She won't see you!" someone squeaks.

There's a crash, the metallic scream of torn hinges. *"No! No! Non passa! Ah, villano maleducato, cattivo incolto!"*

"That won't please him, to be called those things," Baldassare opines.

Almost immediately, from the only lit window above us, comes an intake of breath and the outraged cry of a woman. If she's the *contessa*, I'm calculating, then there must be a *conte* somewhere, but there aren't any notably male voices aside from the low rumble of Iago's own. The servants, if they're up there too, have stopped their protests. There's an air of hushed expectancy—as much from the three of us watching below as from within the palazzo. We strain to hear Iago's words and hers in return, but I'm aware only of a plaintive tone to his voice that we've never known before. He seems to be pleading with her. Her sharp retorts, by contrast, are stiff, frigid, haughty.

Now they're shouting. He's hurling ferocious accusations at her, and she's screaming back with a dangerous clarity. "It's too late! It's too late! Stupid, *stupid* man!"

And from him there's a great, shattering roar of hurt and grief.

"Let's get the hell out of here," I whisper to Baldassare and Franceschina. I can't bring myself to witness his distress.

"A most sensible idea," says Baldassare. "And *not* before time . . ."

But our way back up the *calle* is now blocked. The all-too-familiar figure of Annibale Malipiero, *Il Terribile, Il Capo degli Interroganti*, is silhouetted against the bright sunlight at its end. As he gets closer, he waves a finger from side to side, making it abundantly clear that we must stay where we are. He raises the finger to his bushy mouth and looks upward, toward the window. We look up again too.

We watch a kind of show, un *spettacolo di marionette,* but the puppets are almost black against the flickering light behind them—shadow puppets. One of the figures is wispy and delicate, with long hair, flashing gold sometimes as it flails. The other is stocky, belligerent, with no hair at all. A host of lesser specters bounces about these two, trying to separate them, though without success. The squat one suddenly has its thick fingers around the fragile one's slender neck. We hear a gasp, a loud retch, followed by another scream. The thin puppet drops out of the frame. The other stands alone for a while, chest heaving, looking down.

A chorus of shrieks and moans echoes through the palazzo. *"Ah, ma Dio! La signora, la signora e morte! Dio e gli angeli salvate noi, la contessa è passata di vita, è perduta!"*

The thickset shadow has a dagger in his fist, which from this distance looks no bigger than a pin. Briefly we see the shape of his victim again, rising up into the picture, head thrown back, hands tearing at her assailant, beating him on the chest, but with increasing powerlessness. He raises the glinting pin and punches down with it—down and up and down and down again.

We're speechless. So, for the moment, are those in the house.

Franceschina trembles beside me, her mouth opening and closing in silent horror. Instinctively, I take her hand, hold it fast. I turn to look at the inquisitor. I want to say to him, "Can we go *now*?"

But Annibale Malipiero is no longer there. Of course he isn't. The watcher always, never the doer. And Baldassare's also vanished. He's probably followed the *interrogante* to safety. I'm not too displeased about that. He should have escaped days ago. It's just Franceschina and me now.

A servant—only a boy—comes scampering from the passageway, briefly puncturing the grim silence with high-pitched cries of *"La contessa! Il mostro l'ha massacrata!"* Oddly, his shouts don't get much beyond the end of the *calle*, and all is once again deathly still.

I don't have time to think why the boy's yelling has been so hastily extinguished, because Iago now emerges. He looks terrifying. The clothes he wore so proudly only a while ago are caked in blood. One sleeve of his fine English doublet hangs forlornly from a wrist. The dagger he still holds is crimson and dripping. Through rivulets of scarlet on his face, his eyes are filled with the rage of slaughter. He's like some creature from the worst depiction of hell—*un mostro*, indeed, *sanguinoso e pietrificante*.

He approaches us. Franceschina gives a whimper.

I ask: "Who *was* she?"

He gazes at me. His blazing, hate-fueled eyes seem to soften. There are tears there as well as blood. His mouth turns down a little. Then he swings away from us and bends at the waist, one arm across his face, the other thumping at his breast. The dagger drops with a clatter onto the ground. He stumbles forward, racked with sobs, moving, as if ashamed to be seen thus, into the darkness of the alley once more.

Whoever she was, I'm thinking, *he loved her. He loved her and now he's killed her.* One can kill those one loves.

"Gentile Stornello!" calls a sneering and all-too-recognizable voice. "Finally we find you, louse!"

"Signor Jacopo!" Franceschina gasps.

My nemesis struts toward us. He's hatless. His chestnut curls swing. His infuriatingly broad shoulders ripple. He's not wearing a cloak or a jerkin, just an open leather doublet and an unlaced shirt, in a casual though somehow deliberate *disordine—un bravaccio bello ma arruffato.* He's not alone—he has a handful of his toadying cronies with him. I spot his squirt of a younger brother, Nicolo, among them.

He told me once that he'd dispatch me in some dim, anonymous place. So is this the way it's been ordained, that I should finally be killed in a now sunless side street in Mantua? Will Franceschina just stand by, as she did in the Campo Sant'Angelo? There were *some* signs of concern on her part then. Will she show such compassion again?

Jacopo Malipiero takes hold of her wrist and yanks her away from me. "I've missed you, *tesora bellina.* It's time to come home, *mia piccola principessa.*" She appears to resist, if only minimally, and she looks at me. Even the slightest defiance is enough to incense him. He hits her with stinging force across her right cheek. She yelps in shock. There's a great wheal on her cheek. He snarls, "Don't run from me again, do you hear? Don't *ever—*"

I'm upon him. I can't stop myself. I've never been so angry in my life. I've got him by the throat with my right arm. I lug him away from her, but he's clasping her so firmly that she lurches after him. "Leave her be! *Let go of her!*"

He's stronger than I am, of course. Nevertheless, the fact that I've had the nerve to attack disorients him for a few seconds. Eventually, with a heave of his shoulders, he shrugs me off, with such strength that I find myself sprawling on the ground, and there he is, towering over and scowling down at me, and we're back to our more customary configuration. "Why, is she yours now?" He unsheathes his bejeweled *pugnale*. "I don't think so."

There's something about his lip-curling vanity—the inbred presumption that the world and all that's in it is his to pick and choose from—that emboldens me now. With an accuracy of aim that surprises me, and with an instinctive force that amazes me still more, I bend my knee and kick out, hitting the dagger absolutely where it should be struck and sending it spinning out of his grasp.

I don't wait to see his reaction. Astonishment, I suspect. I hope so. I'm on my feet again and I throw myself at him. My sinews feel tight and ready for anything. I punch, I flail blindly, I roar. With immense joy, I feel my blows land. The *potency* of it! The thunk of my knuckles against his flawless flesh! Now, incredibly, it's Jacopo who's on the ground. He's just as I was when I was the blubbering recipient of his perfect fists. I slam down with both of mine, again and again. His fine hands are at his face. "Help me!" he's coughing through a mouthful of blood. "Nicolo, Piero, Tommaso, Beniamino, Flavio, Rafaele—help me!"

But they're not moving. They're in a circle around us, as awed as I am, I very much trust, by my sudden tremendous *mightiness*. Now they're backing away. From the corner of my eye, I see Iago's knife and reach for it. The blood caked on its handle sticks to my palm.

"*Dio mio, no!* You wouldn't kill me, would you?" Jacopo Malipiero burbles, his hazel eyes—those that so seduce the girls of Venice—ablaze with uncomely terror.

Why not? That's what I'm thinking. *Why not?* He undoubtedly deserves it. He should have gone down for the slaying of Fabietto Dandolo, for which I was incarcerated, with all that has followed. *Why not?* He's a killer and should be killed. I glance in the direction where I last saw Franceschina. She's still there, wide-eyed, her hands to her mouth.

I bestride Jacopo Malipiero like a Colossus. I feel the delicious vigor of revenge. I have turned him, at least, upside down. If I'm not actually a god, I'm *un uomo potente, formidabile*! I raise the blade.

There's a throbbing, tautly muscled arm around my gullet and a gravel-voiced whisper in my ear. "Would you put yourself in the mire, lad? I'm there. You're not." My dagger—*his* dagger—is snatched from me.

The cohorts saw him before I did. Now they're scattering, bolting along the side street, every single one of Jacopo's evil acolytes not so loyal anymore. Nicolo is the last of them, squealing like a piglet. The domestics of the *palazzo*, or some of them, have congregated by the entrance to the alley. They've stopped in their tracks, dumbstruck.

Much as Jacopo might have done in the days when he ruled my existence, Iago flings me aside. I'm a puppet again. It's Franceschina who stops me from falling. She steadies me. A soft arm slips into mine. She's shivering but warm. Then she murmurs, so very faintly that I'm not sure if I've heard it right, "*Giovanotto pericoloso.*" Whether she means me or Jacopo, I cannot tell.

There are noises from the main street—the rapid but rhythmical tread of heels on cobbles, the unmistakable tenor of official intrusion. Then, of course, the voice of the inquisitor. "No, not down there, they went *that* way!" The sound passes on and diminishes. Our watcher wants this little *scena* to be played out to the end.

Iago is insensible to any distractions. With one hand alone, he reaches down and picks the flailing Jacopo up by the neck and carries him thus, past the quivering servants, into the gloom of the alleyway.

Franceschina grips me more tightly.

Iago materializes some moments later, like a hound surfacing from the blackest depths of Hades. He looks even bloodier than before as he makes his way toward us. He's running, full of energy. He grabs my arm and tugs me from her grip. He snarls at her, "Go to your master, strumpet."

"She's no strumpet!" I yelp. "Don't you dare call her a strumpet!"

"All women are strumpets. Leave her be. Forget her. Come."

He's hauling me toward the main street. Again I summon the strength that I didn't until recently know I possessed. I wrench myself away from him and run back to her. If this is the last I'm ever to see of my angel, then there's something I must say. "I love you, Franceschina. I've loved you from the moment I first saw you!"

He's got me again, his blade up and under my chin. If he pushes any harder, that'll be the end of me. And still I cry, "I've sat in wind and rain and hot sun, night and day, Franceschina, just to catch a glimpse of you.

I love you—I love you more than anyone has ever loved you or could ever love you!"

"Don't . . . don't hurt him!" is the last thing I hear from her as he drags me into the main street.

There, under the unclouded sun and among an apparently indifferent populace, stands the *interrogante*. He seems surprised to see us. I don't think he'd expected our emergence to be quite so quick. Next to him, quaking and sweating, is my tutor.

"So we meet again," says Annibale Malipiero—a bit theatrically, I think. Iago doesn't bother to throw him even the slightest glance.

"I'm sorry about my revolting nephew," Annibale Malipiero announces, with a disquieting nonchalance. "Wholly unexpected. Did you"—he starts to finger his beard—"kill him, by any chance?" I don't know if the question is aimed at Iago or me. I've the feeling that an affirmation from either of us would please him.

But Iago remains of a mind to say nothing. He backs off, with his dagger still pressing at my neck, as Annibale Malipiero simply watches. There's no pursuit, no command to arrest us. The *interrogante* is allowing us to vanish into the throng of the industrious city. Beside him, Baldassare mouths, I think, my name—or if not my given name, the one by which he's always affectionately known me, his *coniglietto*.

Some passersby gape at us, but none seems inclined to get too close to a raging madman in multicolored, bloodied English clothes, holding a knife to the throat of a trembling, disheveled, and blood-soaked boy.

"*Did* you kill him?" I splutter.

"There are some in the world who deserve to live and others who should never have been born," he says.

He lowers his blade at last but still holds on to my arm. "There's a favor you owe me," he murmurs.

We've entered an enormous ornamental garden, removed from the rest of a bustling Mantua but still within it. There are exotic trees and great flowering bushes that I've never seen before, and wouldn't know the names of even if I had, and a lake with clusters of colorful swimming birds and carefully organized streams with little bridges over them. There are small dome-topped pavilions dotted about and strategically placed mounds of rock and earth with dark entrances. There are no gardens like this in Venice. There's no room for them. It all seems a bit well behaved for my taste. It's nature, but it's not natural. It's peaceful though. There are a few people here—couples mainly, finely dressed, mostly quite young, far too absorbed in themselves to notice us.

The garden is bordered at one end by the city wall. He pulls me toward it.

"Where are we going now?" I pant. "And why are you taking me?" I stagger after him, irrevocably connected. "Can't you just leave me here? Why do you need me anymore?"

"I never did," he says.

"Then go. I won't say where you've gone. I must be a burden to you—"

There's a cry behind me. "Gentile!"

She's running, stumbling, tripping through the manicured grounds. She seems to be covered in mud. She looks like a disheveled street girl—but no strumpet. Those in her path step neatly aside, thinking her just that. She doesn't notice them. She's heading for *me*.

At this precise point in history (a late morning in the closing days of August some fifteen hundred and twenty or so years after Christ, I think), I'm the most deliriously contented *giovanotto* (and not in the least bit *pericoloso*) in the whole of the great world.

Iago, I'm guessing, doesn't share my untrammeled joy.

51. *Isabella d'Este Gonzaga*

"Iago . . . Iago . . . yes, I remember him, indistinctly, principally for his name. It does have a Spanish air to it." As she mused, the Marchioness of Mantua stroked a dog that lay to the left of the thronelike chair she sat in—a wolfhound, she'd called it, from somewhere in the frozen north. It was lean and covered in long silvery hairs. It was also extremely big but hadn't yet snarled at him, as dogs were disposed to do. "Oh, wait . . ." She laid a heavily manicured finger upon a painted lower lip. "I *do* recall him—a boy, he was just a boy! And a *bad* boy at that!"

"In what way a *bad* boy, your . . . your . . . ?" He wasn't sure of the correct way to address a marchioness, never having been in the presence of one before. So he called her *"Marchesa,"* adding an *"onorevole"* and hoped that would suffice.

"This is Signor Tiziano's latest portrait of me; do you like it?" She indicated, again with that skeletal finger, a painting on an easel to the right of her, as yet unframed. The question, he instantly realized, was going to be difficult to answer, because the accuracy of the depiction was startling—and therein lay the problem.

"I'm not sure," he said. "It seems to me . . . a touch . . ."

She leaned forward. "Erroneous—is that what you were going to say?"

"Yes indeed," he replied with relief.

"It makes me look so old," she said with a sigh.

"And you are not old, Marchesa."

A thickly rouged mouth curled into a satisfied smile. "I shall send it back to Signor Tiziano and ask him to correct it. It's simply not good enough!"

"You said, if I might remind you, that he was a 'bad boy'?"

"Who? Signor Tiziano? I never knew him as a boy—although his work can be somewhat *risqué,* as the French put it."

"I was thinking more of Iago," he said patiently.

"Iago," she echoed ruminatively. "Iago, yes—a very bad youth. You see, we don't allow that sort of thing in Mantua."

"What sort of thing, if you don't mind my asking?"

"I've always encouraged a healthy liberality in my court, as did my late husband. I don't see why people shouldn't enjoy themselves. Are you familiar with the teachings of Epicurus?" She was off again.

"Alas not."

"Have you *heard* of Epicurus?"

"Vaguely," he lied.

A narrow black eyebrow was raised. "Are you an educated man, Signor . . . Signor . . . ?"

"Malipiero," said Annibale Malipiero. "Not as educated as you, Marchesa, I'm sure."

"What is it that you do?"

She did have a way of flummoxing a man. "*Do?* I am an inquisitor." He considered adding "or was" but decided not to make things more complicated than they needed to be.

"And what is it that inquisitors do?"

Perhaps they had no need of his profession in Mantua.

"They . . . they endeavor to discover the truth."

She sniffed. "By torturing people?"

So it *had* been a leading question. He swallowed hard. "Personally, I favor more productive methods."

"Such as?"

"I prefer to . . . dig into a criminal's soul."

He was rather pleased with the phrase, and so it seemed was she. "And it is into this Iago's soul that you wish to dig?"

"I'm trying to, yes. There are things I must know."

She suddenly tilted her head upward, and he followed her gaze. Above them was what he initially took for an ornate vaulted ceiling, but after some time realized was simply one huge, room-length painting, executed in pin-sharp detail. The most audacious feature of all was directly overhead: The ceiling appeared to be open to the sky through a circular balustrade, upon which sat a number of chubby, naked, winged boys; intermingled with them were various courtly women, smiling down at him. Beyond these figures there was—nothing; just sky and clouds. That disturbed him. If this was a depiction of heaven, then why did it not contain any holy figures—Christ, or the Blessed Virgin, or God?

"Epicurus," said the Marchioness of Mantua, and as she was a marchioness and he was a mere inquisitor (or ex-inquisitor) he did not feel he could stop her, "Epicurus, as you may or may not remember, was of the view that when we die we are dust, that death is the end of everything for us, that there is nothing after it."

"Ah . . ." Something was ringing a bell.

"Many may think that the idea of becoming nothing when we die is rather depressing, but Epicurus embraced it. Why be afraid of nothing? When we die, he said, we will feel nothing, no pain, no pleasure. Why be afraid of that? Understandably, Signor, one thinks more and more of matters of this nature the"—she coughed slightly—"older one gets." She couldn't have been yet fifty, but she did seem frail. "So he advocated a full life, that we should make the most of it, because this life of ours is all we have."

Annibale Malipiero must have looked uncomfortable. She took it as boredom, or even censure. "You do not much approve of our Mantuan ways, do you, Signor?"

"Whether I disapprove or approve is not relevant to the—"

"You think us wastrels, idlers, licentious immoralists, even depraved—all you Venetians do. You think that because my court promotes an Epicurean way of living it also encourages immoderateness without limits. It does not, and neither did Epicurus. True pleasure requires discipline, restraint—otherwise, where would we be? Happiness, he said, is the avoidance of pain."

He was going to have to stop her. "Marchesa . . . Marchesa"—he

struggled for some suitably flattering adjective and found three—
"*illustre . . . conosciuta . . . incomparabile . . .* I am only endeavoring to
investigate a murderer, the like of which the world has never known, an
incalculably cruel man who, may I remind you, has just slaughtered, in
an especially vicious fashion, a member of your court."

The dog beside her growled. It really was a very big dog. He chose
not to meet its eyes.

She, however, adopted a soft, rather wistful tone. "Poor Maddalena.
She was a good girl, intelligent, but flighty—and she married too young.
I know you Venetians like to marry your girls off early, but here in
Mantua we prefer to see a girl properly educated and ready for the
world before she gets a husband. But the Conte di Asti would have her,
and he is unconscionably rich, so . . ." She paused. "There. There he is."

She indicated yet another painting, some distance from where she
sat. It was one of many hundreds—for the chamber was very broad and
long—so he could not make out what, or whom, it depicted.

"Come," she said. "I'll show you. You will have to help me, Signor
Malipiero."

The process of standing was lengthy and complex. The retainers in
the room rushed forward, but she irritably waved all fifteen or so of
them away. "No, no this *nobiluomo* will take me."

Annibale Malipiero felt suddenly quite honored.

"My stick—where's my stick?"

"Here, Marchesa."

"You will have to catch me if I fall. I have a habit of tumbling."

He made certain she didn't tumble or even trip. It took some minutes to get to the work of art in question.

"This was done by some Bellini or other, I forget which. Anyway,
here they stand." Her scarlet lips pouted. "Men! So proud—as always.
So full of themselves."

The half dozen or so men in the picture, and even the one boy present, did indeed look arrogant, and well fed and immensely prosperous,
with their chins raised, their hands tucked into their sword belts, and
their preciously colorful clothes, their silks and furs and chains and
rings and brooches. She guided him through the assemblage. "There's

the *conte*, Maddalena's husband, you see? Fat, would you say? I would. There, next to him, is my late husband, Francesco Gonzaga." She seemed to catch her breath.

"He's handsome," said Annibale Malipiero, he hoped consolingly.

"No, he wasn't. He was an ugly brute, really, but he was fun." She emitted a snigger, quite infantile and rather wicked. She wagged a finger. "But let nobody dispute that he was the best soldier in Italy; let no one argue with that."

"I wouldn't presume."

The marchioness pressed lightly on the arm to which she was clinging. "There's my son, Federico, the present marquis, he was only . . . what . . . thirteen, perhaps, then? But he has the Gonzaga bearing, don't you agree?"

"Assuredly."

"He *is* handsome. Though a mother must always think that of her son. But let's not talk of these personages, who can, even in a painting, speak for themselves. Let's turn our attention to *him*." At this she extracted her arm from his and jabbed at the canvas so that it wobbled. "The Bellini responsible was most insistent that he should be included, I recall, perhaps as a symbolization of deference. As we were speaking of him, I remembered. Here he is . . ."

Annibale Malipiero felt a small frisson of excitement. He even gasped. "Ha!"

Iago was probably not yet twenty years old in the picture—slimmer therefore, but there were already signs of a burgeoning solidity, and there was that now-familiar cropped head. His skin was dark, probably from the sun, but not lined or weather-beaten. He wore a doublet and jerkin of brown leather, black hose, and knee-length boots. His outfit was modest in contrast to the flamboyance around him. But if he was supposed to be "a symbolization of deference," it hadn't worked. He displayed no esteem for his superiors, and the painter had been careful to depict this. Entirely undaunted, he stood upright and seemingly self-satisfied, as if in emulation of the dignitaries he was alongside. His instantly recognizable gray-green eyes were blessed with the brightness of youth, but they were already piercing, defiant. As he leaned closer to the canvas, Annibale Malipiero thought he detected a hard maturity in them, way beyond his years.

"And he was bad, you said."

"Very bad. He broke the rules, do you see?"

"The rules of Epicurus?"

"Yes, the rules of pleasure and pain—and of my court. One simply doesn't go around raping women."

"He *raped* women?"

"Two, at least, as far as I know."

"And Maddalena—she was one of them?"

"No, no, *no*," said the grand lady impatiently. "One can't be said to rape a girl who wants it! No, they were servants merely. A kitchen girl, I think, the other a chambermaid. But one doesn't go raping even servants—not in my court." She pondered further, then said, "Not that he was too successful in his efforts, or so I've heard."

"Not successful?"

She tapped her beaky nose. "He was—to use a French expression—*toute la bouche et pas des pantalons.*"

Annibale Malipiero had no French but nonetheless muttered, "I see."

"That, however, did not stop the poor dears bawling their eyes out and telling all and sundry. So he had to go."

"Go? Go where?"

"To the wars, with my husband. It was my husband who had hired him in the first place. Maddalena, poor lamb, was most distraught."

"So they were already . . ."

"Sleeping together, yes." She smiled at him, relishing her own bluntness and his discomfiture.

"And was she married by this time?"

"Oh, yes, to the fat *conte*. But then she had *un penchant* for young fighting men—or slimmer ones, at least." Her eyes sparkled alarmingly. "As did I, when I was a slip of a thing." She examined the painting once more. "A not unprepossessing young man, in a rough fashion, and she was very, very pretty."

"And she was blond."

She blinked up at him. "How did you know that?"

"I've just seen her corpse."

"Oh, dear . . . oh, dear, oh, dear, yes." The playfulness in her voice was gone in an instant. "Yes, unusually blond," she murmured sorrowfully. Either a sadness of memory or simply the fact that she'd been standing for quite a while made her wobble slightly, and she reached out for a smallish chair with a curved seat and arms.

He put his arms out. "Would you like to sit down?"

"I think that would be best."

It was time, he decided, to show her something—or two things, to be precise. First he extracted from inside his doublet the lock of hair that he'd carried with him from the moment of his having received it, which he'd foolishly suspected, until only yesterday, to be Desdemona's. "Might this be hers?" he asked.

She squinted at it, then nodded. "We called her our *astra luccicanta*, because of her hair and how it made her stand out. Dear, foolish, *importunate* girl."

Annibale Malipiero dug once more into his doublet. "And might these be from her? There appear to be about thirty of them, sent to Iago, I think, over a period of several months."

She couldn't hide her excitement. "Letters! You have letters!" She snatched at them like a greedy collector in the presence of some priceless and long-anticipated treasure. She tugged at the ribbon.

"She was evidently not aware of the fact that he couldn't read," he said.

She snapped at him, as if to an especially stupid pupil. "Of course he couldn't! He was a street boy! An urchin!"

"He's very well spoken, on occasion."

"Anyone who spends a year in my court will emerge from it well spoken. I make sure of it. I shall need my *occhiali*. You!" She shouted across the vast, echoing space.

A servant brought her spectacles and balanced them obsequiously on her nose.

"I hate these things," she grumbled. "Another of the burdens of decrepitude."

But she was sprightly enough when reading. She devoured the contents of the letters, page after page.

"That is her hand, I take it."

"Yes, yes, it's her sweet, careful hand. How fascinating!" She didn't appear shocked by what she was so avidly perusing, as he once had been. "Oh, dear, dear," she'd frequently mouth, or, "My, oh, my," or, "Well, well." Once she even said, "Naughty, naughty!"

"She was . . . quite the *minx*, it would seem."

"Minx?" She didn't like the word. "Do you disapprove of her, is that it?"

He wavered. "Well, Marchesa, her behavior was quite . . ."

Her eyes—regarding him over the bulky wooden frames—were amused rather than stern. "You are a most censorious Venetian, aren't you, Signor Malipiero?"

"If you mean that I don't condone adultery, then you are correct."

She looked quizzical. "Do you believe, then, that women are not permitted the pleasures that men enjoy?"

"Not outside a marriage."

"And if a husband strays, as husbands do, is the wife not allowed to also?" He couldn't answer that one, or not quickly enough, because she went on: "Men have a way of excusing their lusts. They say they can't help it. They call it a frailty. Don't women have frailties likewise? Don't they have sight, smell, palates, affections . . . desires?"

"I suppose they—"

"The Conte di Asti strayed rather a lot, despite his girth; he still does. My husband strayed—and he died from his straying. He caught the French disease. My son's going the same way. All men stray. Do you want their wives to remain locked up and chaste while they go out and play, is that it?"

"I don't stray," said Annibale Malipiero.

"You don't?"

"And I've been married to the same woman for over twenty years."

The marchioness looked absolutely astonished. "Then you are a most uncommon husband, Signor Malipiero."

"Is your court in the habit of bringing in poor young men from the streets, Marchesa?"

She gave him one of her haughtiest stares. "We are not snobs, Signor, if that's what you mean. Talent or wit or some manner of accomplishment are the passports to entrance here."

"Iago had accomplishments, did he?"

"I don't remember him that much, in truth."

"Try to." Some of Annibale Malipiero's old inquisitorial flare returned to him as he regarded her through narrowed lids.

"My husband admired his 'way of combat,' as he expressed it. He'd seen him fighting with other young wastrels in one of the less wholesome parts of our city—we do have them. I think he may have been some part of a *street gang*, as I think they're called, or even the leader of such a band of ruffians. So my husband engaged him. Francesco was always munificent in that respect, seeing potential in the less privileged. As far as I remember, the boy had no parents or anywhere to live. Originally from the country, I think. Abandoned, therefore. That alone made him interesting. And I recall he was also clever and learned the ways of the court remarkably quickly."

"The ways of the court?"

The Marchioness of Mantua sensed disapproval. "Yes, Signor—the necessary proficiencies of any courtier: singing, dancing, the mastery of an instrument or two, but most importantly the art of conversation. He was quite the charmer—although, now that I think of it, there was another thing . . ."

"And what was that?"

She tapped her roseate lower lip once more. "There remained something of the child about him. Yes, that was it: He was like a child, entertaining in the way only a child can be—smiling, chuckling, innocent, wide-eyed, delightfully confused, really, by . . . by all this." She waved a scaly hand around the huge gilt and marble and pictured and frescoed and luxuriously ceilinged chamber. "Maddalena's was not the only fluttering heart."

"So he was a like a pet, a toy," Annibale Malipiero heard himself murmur.

"I'm sorry?"

He coughed. "She loved him, you claim. And yet only yesterday she wouldn't let him into her house."

"It was a long time ago that she loved him, Signor. Love does die, you know."

"But he loved her; he truly did love her. That's why he came back."

She became prickly again. "But she has children now, she has responsibilities, a mother's obligations." She paused. She mellowed. "Do you have children, Signor? If you do, I'd imagine you're a good father, aware of your own duties toward them, that they should be brought up decently."

"I had a son," said Annibale Malipiero. "He died."

"Oh, I'm sorry. As a baby?"

"He was fifteen. Beyond the dangerous age. He died inexplicably, quickly, of no known disease."

"I'm so very sorry." She stretched out a hand to pat him, quite consolingly, on his forearm.

"I think the notion that death is nothing, and therefore not painful, affords little comfort to those who survive."

The Marchioness of Mantua appeared to have no answer to that.

He became brusque, professional. "I shall need troops."

"Troops? For what?"

"To catch Iago. Fifteen or twenty of your best men should do it."

"*My* best men? They're not my men, Signor Malipiero; they're my son's. The provision of men is his department, not mine. I am merely a *woman.*"

He raised an eyebrow. He knew, as all of Italy knew, that the Marchioness of Mantua had once commanded armies herself. "Is he here?"

"No, he's . . . I have no idea where he is. At the wars, very possibly. That's his job, to fight wars." She sighed. "Men and their need to fight wars—I've never understood that."

"Marchesa," he said firmly, "I am sure you have it in your power to provide me with fifteen to twenty men. Do you not wish this brute brought to justice? He murdered a lady of your court. He did not just murder her, he beat her, he stabbed her. Do you suppose *she* did not feel pain as she died? There is evidence of a lengthy struggle."

"Yes, yes, *please*," the illustrious woman protested. "Don't you have men yourself, as an inquisitor of Venice in pursuit of a dangerous felon?"

"I could, if necessary, summon the forces of Venice in an instant," he lied. "But would it not be best for the murderer of a Mantuan *nobildonna* to be apprehended by Mantuans and returned to Mantua for his deserts?"

He remembered then that she was a Ferraran by birth, not a Mantuan, but it worked. Of course she loved Mantua. It was where she'd thrived. It was her realm, her hospitable hearth, her playground.

Still affecting some disinclination, because that was her way, she said, "I shall see what I can do."

"Thank you kindly, Marchesa *straordinaria*. I have learned here today much that I didn't know before."

"That's good," she said simply.

He made for the door through which he'd been ushered into her presence, a good fifty yards away.

"Are you going?"

He turned back. Perhaps one had to be dismissed. But she didn't look imperious in the least, only sad, her eyes beseeching over those ridiculous spectacles.

"I have a job to do."

"Go, then," she commanded. "Catch the monster and bring him back."

As he reached the door, she called, "And do *cheer up!*"

With that piece of Epicurean advice ringing his ears, he left the august company of Isabella d'Este Gonzaga.

52. The Wasteland

On the way here, he had to show us Marignano.

It's half a day's ride east of where we are now. I have to say I was disappointed. What did I expect to see, fields full of skeletons and battered skulls? It was peaceful—a few working farms, a slumberous little village with a church. So it is, I realized, that combat crashes through a place and is then gone, and life does its best to return to normal, and the dead and their cries are forgotten.

He strode about the vanished battleground, trying to summon up the ghosts of clashing armies, describing the horrors in a suitably blood-curdling tone—pointing here and there, talking of tens of thousands of men being slaughtered within two hours of darkness and of cannons blasting them to pieces. It seemed somehow unimportant to me—ghastly, yes, but of another time, like the wars that Baldassare has forced me to read about in Thucydides and Herodotus.

I didn't even ask him about the Moor, although it was there that the two men first met, or so my uncle Ubaldo said. The Moor and even Desdemona and whatever may have happened in Cyprus now seem of no consequence either—bits of history themselves, hazy and remote, like characters in a fiction.

We sit, Franceschina and I, on a decomposing tree trunk, watching him. I've a feeling we're not alone in doing this. Behind us there's a hill, topped with a few clusters of trees. It's the only elevation for about two miles in any direction. If anybody's watching us, it'll be from up there.

He picks and prods through the rubble of the house where he was born. Mostly it's just weeds—prickly, stinging ones—covering everything. That doesn't stop him from pulling them away with his bare hands. Slowly, he reveals a few stones, the remnants of a wall, the odd rotten post. If these are the foundations of what was once his home, it was a small one—probably no more than a single-room hut.

There are some broken fences, and some pasturage, and what might have been a pen for livestock. Similarly crumbling and deserted smallholdings dot the barren landscape under an obdurately blank sky. The air is thick and hot and moist. The soil at our feet is hard and cracked, but in places there are pools of stagnant water, above each of which is a haze of flying things. Insects—fat, sluggish beetles, oversize hornets, bloodthirsty midges and mosquitoes—are the only living creatures here, it seems, apart from us and our horses. These three poor beasts (we had to steal them, as the ones we rode to Mantua had fled or been stolen themselves) are tethered to the remnants of a fence, flicking their tails, stomping and snorting, trying to tear some sustenance from the unhelpful earth as the bloodsucking pests gorge on them. Nothing much grows here. Nothing, I think, ever really did.

Franceschina has spoken hardly a word since we left Mantua. She wasn't interested in Iago's stories of Marignano either—even less so than me, and only a few days ago she had an unquenchable appetite for tales of soldiery and bravado. Now she just stares at him, entirely absorbed. Her silken brow is crumpled, her lips tight.

He picks up a rusty old cooking pot, full of holes, and gazes into it. I think he hoped to find more here. I already know, though not in any detail, that his childhood was a grim one. Today he seems to be surveying its complete obliteration. He continues to poke among the rubble, kicking the stones away, cursing quietly. Sometimes he drops to his haunches and peers intently downward, for minutes on end. And still she examines him.

"What are you thinking about?"

She makes a face but still doesn't look at me. "Ay!" she gasps. "To kill someone you love—*orribile, orribile, non e possibile.*"

"You think he loved her?"

"Of course. Do you think not?"

"I'm *sure* he loved her."

"And perhaps she loved him also, once."

"Maybe . . . maybe if you are in love with someone and that person does not return your love, it's better . . . it's better for them not to exist at all."

"Ay! *Non capisco!*" She does that stamping thing with her feet that she does when she's perplexed and annoyed with herself for being so. And yet she goes on staring. He's tugging more weeds away. I think he's looking for something in particular.

"Do you continue to feel sorry for him?" It's a question I aim as much at myself as at her.

"A little. It must be sad to be in love and not be loved in return." She still doesn't take her eyes off him. It's as if she's spellbound. He's cast another spell. "He doesn't look dangerous today," she says, almost tenderly. "He just looks sad."

He stands again, a hand to his chin, turning right and left as his eyes sweep the ground. His hefty shoulders droop. She's right. There's no menace there at the moment. If anything, he appears irresolute, defenseless, frail.

"He lost his younger sister to the *mal aria*," she suddenly reveals. "That must have been here, I think."

She notices, as if for the first time, a blood-plump mosquito crawl up her arm and start to feast on her brown skin. She slaps it dead, leaving a crimson smear.

"You didn't tell me that," I say. "Is there anything else he told you about himself that you haven't told me?"

She shrugs. "Does it matter?"

"Maybe not to you, but it does to me."

"Why?"

"I want to know where all his hatred comes from."

"Is that what Signor Malipiero wants to know too?" She flicks her head briefly back in the direction of the hill behind us. She also suspects he's up there, watching this play out.

"Did Signor Malipiero tell you to follow me in Mantua?"

"No!" she protests. I believe her.

It's been a bit too loud, I think. I quickly look at Iago. He's still oblivious to us. He's wandering about the remains of his former home, picking up more stones and pieces of wood, then throwing them aside.

And then I ask an even stupider question: "Are you sad that Jacopo is dead?"

There's only the smallest pause before she announces, "I don't understand why people need to know everything about other people. *Does* he hate everyone? He doesn't seem to hate us."

Iago picks up a long piece of wood. He uses it to dig beneath the obstinate soil.

"I lost my father too," she says.

"I'm sorry, I didn't know."

She twists her shoulders. "Why would you want to know?"

"Because I love you."

She sighs wistfully. "I have a mother. Also three sisters and a brother, all younger than me."

"All still in Asolo?"

She nods. She's thinking of home. I'm thinking of home too. I want to be there. I want to take her with me, away from this festering, forbidding wasteland.

Her eyes begin to glisten. "A child must have a father." She rests her head on my shoulder. I can scarcely breathe.

Iago has his back to us now. Soil is flying up and over him. Sometimes he stops, drops to his knees, and thrusts his hands into the trench he's making. What's he found? Buried treasure? He's burrowing like a dog for a bone.

"Where *does* his hatred come from?" she asks.

"I don't imagine being born somewhere like this, with nothing, can make you like the world very much."

"I was born with nothing," she announces simply. "And I don't hate the world."

Ah, I think, *but you are the most beautiful thing in it.* "But you have certain other advantages."

"What are those?" she asks.

"Did you have a father who beat you?"

"My father loved me."

"As everyone who knows you must," I say.

She gives a small cry.

Iago has unearthed a weapon. He's now holding it in both hands, aimed straight at us. I've never seen any sort of gun before, but Benvenuto has told me a bit about these small cannon that don't have to be pushed about on wheels—which a man can actually carry, as Iago is doing now, though with some effort. He must be forty feet from us, and yet he could, if he was so minded, blow us both to smithereens.

I'm on my feet in an instant. "Run! Take a horse!" I whisper to Franceschina. "I'll distract him."

He doesn't lower that horrible barrel as I approach him; its portentous black muzzle is pointing directly at my breast. It moves as I move.

"I knew I'd buried it somewhere," he says.

"When you were a child?"

"Pah! No, lad. When I passed by a few years back, on the way from Agnadello."

I assume this is yet another battle.

"I had to slice a man's throat for it, and not just any man—one of the *Bande Nere.* Have you heard of the *Bande Nere*?"

"I have not," I readily admit. Did he honestly expect that I had?

"Best fighters in all of Italy. Called so because they dress all in black."

"So you hid it here in the event of needing it in an emergency?"

"You might say that."

"Such as now?"

"Such as now."

At close quarters, the weapon looks still more ferociously lethal than it did at a distance, even though it's rusty and covered in soil. The barrel is about four feet long, a good six inches in diameter, and curves to a thick wooden handle, where there is some kind of firing mechanism. It's a sort of loop with a small lever in it; it's over the lever that Iago has his finger.

The barrel of the gun shifts, as he shifts, to my right temple, against which I now feel cold metal, juddering minimally.

"I could blast you to nothingness in an instant," he says. "And then you would see if there's a heaven or a hell."

As I anticipate my extinction, I have the oddest thought. Sometime during this frenetic journey, I had my birthday. I don't know when exactly, but on the twenty-third day of July sixteen years ago I was born in a velvety bed, as Iago has sneeringly described it, to a mother who loved me very much, I think, and who now, of course, is dead, as I'm about to be.

"You haven't flinched once."

"Oh, I think I have, just a little . . ."

"Some weeks ago you'd have been cowering, blubbing, begging. Have I made a man of you, Gentile Stornello?"

He lets the barrel tip brush my cheek and then lowers it. He slumps on the residue of a wall of his former home and lowers the threatening device onto his knees. "You don't know much about guns, do you?"

"I know absolutely nothing about guns."

"If you did, you would know that even so potent an instrument of death as this needs fire to make it work." He kicks at a small clasped box at his feet. "I have the shot and the powder; I have the *archibugio*; but I need fire."

I've been trying to recall what Benvenuto called these grisly things.

"Make one," Iago instructs me. "Make me a fire."

"So you can kill me?"

"Mayhap, and your whore of a girl, and your *interrogante* friend who's watching us."

I look back. Franceschina has gone. I feel a surge of happiness for her, even though there's a hole where my heart should be. I glance toward the horses. There are still three of them, grazing dispiritedly. I glance at the summit of the hill.

"Did you tell her that she might find safety up there? I doubt she has. What my Turkish friends might do to a pretty Italian whore does not bear contemplation. And as for what they've already done to Annibale Malipiero . . ."

With no care if he tries to stop me or how he might choose to do it, I turn and run toward the hill.

"Don't be foolish, lad," he cries. "They'll skin you alive!"

I pause for a moment, then dart on. But my hesitation has allowed him to catch up. God, he can be fast! He has his arms around my chest, crushing the breath out of me. Now he's carrying me, legs kicking, back to where we were. He dumps me on the merciless ground. Before I can even raise myself onto my elbows, he's grabbed the gun, and he's clasping the barrel with both hands and holding it over me, like a massive club. There's immense power in those wrists. "You may have grown in strength, lad," he growls, "but I could still pound you to dust." Then: "Make a fire."

"Why don't you just batter me to death with that thing? Why do you have to shoot me?"

"Because I want to see if this blasted contraption still works. Make a fire."

There's plenty of wood around here, most of it very dead. I gather it as best I can and start to form a neat enough pile. I'm reminded of when I used to help Zinerva as a boy. She taught me how to pack the logs and kindling beneath her cooking pots, not too tight.

He's sitting again, the gun across his lap. "What will the great *Capo degli Interroganti* think," he ponders, "when he sees his boy, his pawn, having his head blown off? All that effort come to nothing. And what will your harlot think?"

"I doubt he'll be thrilled," I say miserably. "But please stop calling her a harlot and a whore."

"What shall I call her, then? Your angel?" His tone is gentler. "That's enough wood. I only enough need flame to ignite this weapon. We're not going to sit around it chatting. Light it. You know how to light a fire, do you?"

I do. Zinerva taught me that too—how to strike flint against iron over tinder and watch the sparks catch and flare. I look for stones with sharp edges and sticks and decayed leaves that aren't too moist.

"What do you make of my place of birth?" he suddenly asks, and in a mockingly highfalutin tone: "Rather different from yours, would you not say, Signor, *what, what*?"

"It's horrible," I reply. "And very sad."

"I don't require your pity, Gentile Stornello," he says crisply. "I'm a murderer, remember, and I'm about to murder you."

But then he begins to reminisce—quietly at first. As he speaks, he sometimes lets his gaze roam about the pestilential, portentously vacant wilderness. "There were thirty or forty crofts here when I was a lad. Each had its scrap of land and an animal or two. We had a pig and a cow and chickens and a sickly old mule, nothing else. We grew what we could in the good years, though it was always hard to sow and reap. But when the droughts came, there was nothing—yearlong droughts.

"We did not own our land. We were in thrall to a grasping bastard of a Milanese count, a Sforza, who had all the countryside between here and the city. When the earth yielded nothing, he paid us nothing. All the Sforzas, who ruled Milan then, were pitiless miserly pigs, who spent money only on themselves. Pah! They're gone now. Good riddance. And to everyone else who tried to force a living here. There can't have been much point in staying after he'd left. Or perhaps the *mal aria* reaped its final harvest. Do you know what the *mal aria* is, boy?"

"It's a dreadful disease, I've heard."

"It thrives in places like this. One minute you're in an inferno, the next in ice. You shake so much you have to be held down. Your bones bend and go brittle. You can't walk or in the end move anything. You go blind. And then you die." He chokes and shudders. "Have you found anything to light that damned fire?"

"Yes, some stones and—"

"Then light it."

I struggle to do so, scraping and blowing. Nothing much comes forth—hardly a spark from stone on stone.

"I tried to kill that Sforza hound," he murmurs.

I stop the scraping. "You did?"

"Tried to poison him." His eyes scan the ground at his feet. "There are thousands of scorpions in these parts. You snap off their tails—" He rubs his grubby fingers together. "You crush them, and you put them into food or drink." He looks northward, into the distance, then sees my shock. "He raped my mother. He considered it his right as a thieving *nobiluomo.* I could not stomach that. He liked his wine, so I put the powdered scorpion tails into his cup." He adds bitterly, "It didn't work in his case." Then: "My father was not so lucky."

I'm stiff with horror. I can't move a muscle. "Your father? You . . . you poisoned your father?"

"My first slaying." His apparent detachment chills me to the bone. "He beat me, he beat my mother, he beat my sister—all of us, day after day, unceasingly, half to death. When my sister died—of the *mal aria*, yes, but too weakened by his thrashings to fight it, I killed him. You would have killed your father, Gentile, if he'd been like mine."

I manage to splutter, "I might have wished it, but I don't think I'd have done it."

"There, then," he snaps. He examines a jet-black beetle crawling toward him along the top of the stones on which he's sitting. "That's the difference between you and me." He picks the insect up, allows it to struggle for a while, then lets it fall into his open palm. He closes his fist and squashes it.

It occurs to me now that this creature who murdered his own father (how old can he have been?) might also have slain his mother. No, he could not have. He loved her. Every time he's spoken of her, there's been that slight catch in his voice. But then, he has sent those he's loved to their deaths—at least two of them.

"Did your mother die of the *mal aria* as well?" I ask.

"Light that fire!"

"I'm trying, I'm seriously trying," I whimper. At last there's enough of a glimmer to get the tinder going.

I watch the flames flicker and expand as I hear, or think I hear, "She was murdered. In Mantua."

"*O Madonna santa!*" I turn back to him. "Murdered? Who by . . . ?"

His big hands are clasped before him. His gleaming brown head is lowered. An already engorged mosquito, almost as big as a hornet, attacks his neck. Without thinking, he slaps it against his skin. Blood seeps through his curled fingers. "By another fat slug of a *nobiluomo,*" he snarls quietly. "By a craven snake of a Mantuan."

"But why? Why did he murder her?"

He looks up at me from beneath a pair of leaden lids. His eyes are dulled, seemingly soulless. "Must you always fathom a reason for the things men do?"

"Yes," I gasp. "I fear I must."

He sighs. "He killed her because he could, lad. He killed her because he was . . ." He pauses. "He was rich and he was her . . . *customer.*"

I can barely speak. "She was . . ."

"A whore, yes. A paid whore. When they troubled to pay, that is. *Una puttana scrofulosa. Una prostituta ripugnante!* What else could a woman with no money in Mantua do?" He suddenly drives a clenched fist into my chest. "I killed him though. I followed him into the street and I tore the dog's heart from his breast with my knife."

I struggle for breath. "You saw her murdered?"

"I saw everything—all that there was to see. I was made to."

"M-Made to?"

"I was forced by filthy perverts to watch them use my mother. There was added payment in it. There were *increments—*"

"Stop! Please!" I stumble unseeingly away.

He doesn't follow me. "Well, you did ask."

I can't turn around for the moment. I listen to the crackle of his feet on dead vegetation. The footsteps aren't getting any closer. Perhaps he's raised the gun and is aiming at me, so I must get ready for my end. But there's only silence now, aside from the snap and hiss of the fire.

So eventually, I look at him.

The fire's doing its best to burn. Iago's sitting cross-legged, warming his sizable hands, palms open, or trying to. "Go!" he calls to me, without glancing up.

"Go?"

"Go to your girl."

"But . . . what about the Turks?"

"There are no Turks," he declares simply. "Or not in these parts, I trust." He runs a hand over his skull. "I hate the Turks. I always have. I hate them even more than any Christian."

"But you . . . you fought for their cause in Cyprus!"

"Their cause?" He cackles. "I've never fought for a cause in my life!"

"But . . . but men have died there, scores of them, in your name!"

He shrugs, somehow smugly: "We must each do our part to turn the world . . ." He turns his head away. "Go!"

As I scramble up the hill, revolting visions swim within my damnable imagination—of leering men, of an appalled boy observing from some corner . . . I fight off any picture of the woman in all this, because I can only conjure up a likeness of my own dear dead mother.

As I reach the crest, I look back down at him. He's still before the fire and looks as if he has no intention of going anywhere.

It seems I'm completely alone up here. No Franceschina, no inquisitor, and certainly no Turks.

The plateau is more spacious than I'd expected. A few copses of wind-bent pines are impenetrable through an undergrowth of ferns. There's some evidence of color at least, a few flowers that have somehow managed to bloom—*ranuncoli, digitali, viole del pensiero* . . .

The sun comes out, almost shockingly, and warms my back a little. I hear what sounds like thunder—a roar, not too far off, somewhere to the south. I daresay this barren environment will welcome a good downpour.

Then, emerging like a dryad from a thicket, with burrs and brambles and brushwood in her hair and on her clothes, she runs toward me.

53. *Love and War*

"You're shaking—like you've seen a ghost."

"I thought the Turks—"

"Ay! *Orribile*, the Turks—"

"I should have warned you; I should have stopped you. I'm so sorry."

"But they are not here, Gentile. Look, there's no one."

"I know that now. He doesn't like the Turks. There were never any Turks. What about Jacopo's uncle, the *interrogante*?"

"No, there's nobody. No Turks, no Signor Malipiero. Just you and me."

"Did you look in those trees?"

"Too overgrown—*cardi e pruni e ortice e spine*. Nobody could go in there."

"I love you, Franceschina. I've always loved you, from the moment I—"

"Hush. You said."

"I need to say it over and over again, until you believe me."

"I believe you. Quiet now. You're still trembling. Lie down. There, lie now."

She produces a handkerchief to wipe my brow. It's hers, with the "F" in the corner. Baldassare must have given it back to her.

"He is not a good man, but he has endured so much," I say.

"I know."

"Can you imagine, being made to watch your . . . ?"

She kisses me. It's little more than a soft peck on my brow, but it's the best feeling I've ever known. Then she puts her mouth to mine, probably to stop me talking.

To state the obvious, I'm no great lover; I'm no kind of lover at all. Well, I am only fifteen years old—no, sixteen now. I've not known, as you might call it, *the touch of a woman* before, or not this sort of touch. I remember being enfolded in my mother's arms, when frightened of something as a child, and her warm, consoling kisses—on a cheek, or on the top of my head. Zinerva has done that too, when I was much younger, rocking me and singing me to sleep. Balbina has touched me, of course, when soothing and dressing some injury or other. Once, I remember, I tried to snatch a kiss from Hostolana, the prettier of our two housemaids (encouraged to do so by Benvenuto, I might add), for which I was rewarded with a slap and a squeal of indignation—or possibly disgust. But I've never been touched so by a woman, not until now, and definitely not with such determination or at such length. And what follows is utterly new to me too.

Like any boy with no experience in these things, I was always a little fearful of what might have to go where, and who exactly was meant to do this or that and to what. Now I realize, and pretty quickly, that all my worries have been groundless. Perhaps I'm luckier than most. Not all novices, after all, have a Franceschina to tutor them. She seems to know *precisely* what's required and *when* it's required—for her own contentment, I hope, as well as mine. Can someone so proficient in these things genuinely be unaware of her own loveliness? To be honest, I don't care.

I want to please her, nothing more. From the sounds she's making, some of which I've never heard from anyone, I manage to convince myself that I am.

"Life would be so much simpler, wouldn't it," I whisper eventually, "if one didn't have think too hard."

She didn't hear me or understand me, I think. I'm lying over her, nose-to-nose and mouth-to-mouth, drowning myself in her eyes, still unable to believe quite how beautiful she is or quite what we've just done. She turns her eyes, and her head, away from me. She looks suddenly sad.

"Where will you go, Franceschina?"

"Go? When?"

"Back to Venice?" It's a brave question, in that I fear the answer.

"There is nothing for me there. I should go to Asolo. My mother and my sisters and brother need me."

"Yes, of course." The thunder is getting louder. And it's starting to sound like something other than thunder.

She freezes.

"Gentile, lad, come see this!"

Of course he's followed me. How long has he been here? Has he seen everything, watched it all through salacious eyes? Again, I don't care. But I don't move. She's struggling to extract herself from beneath me. I feel a need to keep her where she is.

"Get up, boy, there's something you must see!"

He's facing away from us, at the southernmost edge of the hilltop, gazing out at whatever is producing that relentless roar. He's straight-backed, no longer cowed or exhausted, quite the stalwart man-at-arms once more. Mercifully, he hasn't brought his gun with him. He probably couldn't have hauled it up here anyway. He does have a sword though, unsheathed and in his right hand.

I have to see what he's looking at. I grab Franceschina by a slender, trembling wrist. She stops wriggling when she sees what lies before and below us. And in my own amazement I release her.

"I'll wager you've never witnessed anything like *that* in your life, eh, lad?"

Spread out on a vast flat basin through which two rivers course and flicker, under brilliant sunlight now, thousands upon thousands of men are fighting, although from this viewpoint they seem more like an infinite collection of tiny vivid pinheads, swirling and intermingling, a great reptilian mass speckled with myriad glints of steel, and the snap and flash of scores of guns reverberating loudly even at such a distance. Beyond this mêlée, still farther south, there's a walled town—not as grand as Mantua or Padua, and I don't know its name—being battered by cannon fire.

"A siege," Iago explains. "And someone's trying to lift it."

"The French? The Germans?"

He shrugs. "I don't know who's fighting for what anymore, but they have a lot of *archibugii*, I see. Damn it, I should have brought mine." His fingers curl around the hilt of his sword. His stocky body twitches, as if he's coiled for flight. "It's quite a sight, is it not, Signor?"

"Yes, it is," an immediately distinctive voice concurs.

Iago hasn't even had to turn around to know that it's no longer just the three of us atop this hill. But I must do so now.

Annibale Malipiero is a few feet away. Because he's making valiant efforts to hide it, his embarrassment gives him a briefly comical quality, as does the dishevelment of his clothes and his hair and his great white beard. He starts to pluck off bits of foliage with as much nonchalance as he can muster. He also seems to be in some pain, with a hand to his back, trying to stop himself from bending forward. He must have been hunkered down in some particularly meddlesome stretch of under-growth for hours.

"You are encircled, sir," he says. "I have forty soldiers, provided by the Marchioness of Mantua. They are stationed all around this summit."

"I can't see them," Iago growls.

"You will soon enough, if you try to run."

"So I'm to be taken at last. You've taken your time about it."

"I've had my reasons. Come, sir, give yourself up. You cannot possibly escape."

"We'll see about that," says Iago. "For the present I'm of a mind to take a closer look at this battle." He grabs my arm with his swordless hand and runs down the slope; I stumble alongside him. He whirls the sword over his head and whoops.

Now from behind every shrub and every gnarled tree, it seems, soldiers at last emerge, popping up like startled rabbits, and give us chase.

54. *What You Know You Know*

'm slowing him down; one or two of our pursuers are even drawing level with us. They're a nimble lot. He seems heavy, lumbering, by comparison—an old lion harried by cubs.

I suggest that I might be something of a hindrance. "Why don't you let me go?" I pant. "I won't run off, I promise."

"Because you're my trump card, lad." He suddenly halts, draws breath, and turns to face them. As I'm so firmly in his grasp, I have to do so too. Some scamper on past, most stop with us. They must be awaiting orders, I presume from the *interrogante*. He's still making his way down the hill, puffing, mopping his brow and cheeks, beet-hued beneath his beard. Franceschina is following him. *Dio mio*, she looks so gloriously unkempt. For a time, I can see no one but her or think of anything but her sweet warmth.

"Look behind us," Iago snaps. "Tell me what's going on."

"About ten of them are ahead of us now. They're not moving in though. I think we're being surrounded."

"Not *them*," he snarls. "Tell me about the battle. Describe it to me: what arms, what colors?"

I've never been asked to describe a battle before; I've never seen a battle before. This one is still at some distance, in the center of the plain at the very bottom of the hill, about half a mile away. But what I can see is more than I ever want to see again.

All that Baldassare has insisted I read about ancient wars has not prepared me for this. How should I describe it? In every gruesome detail? Iago knows all about that already, I'd say—the hacking, the slicing, the arms and legs flying and heads being chopped from torsos and men falling to their knees and choking blood and howling and others on rearing horses swinging their reddened swords about their heads and down into the bodies of those below them and horses themselves being slaughtered and dust and mud and smoke. He can hear it anyway; it's so loud now, an evil cacophony of bangs and screams and roars. It's such an incredible *mess.* How can anybody tell who anybody is?

"What colors, lad?" he persists.

Colors, yes. What I see mainly is the color of blood, in many shades—scarlet, ruby, the red of wine, some so dark it's almost black. "A whole host of colors," I say.

"*Landsknechts?* Do you see *landsknechts?*"

"I don't know what a *landsknecht* looks like."

"They dress like peacocks."

"Yes, there are quite a few of those. Who are *they* fighting for?"

"For whoever pays best. And Swiss, do you see Swiss? They'll be in slashed blue and yellow."

"Yes."

"How many?"

"Thousands."

"Then whoever has employed *them* will win. And what weapons do you see?"

"Oh, swords, pikes, lances, axes, clubs, and guns."

"How many guns?"

"At least a hundred."

"Who carries the guns? Are they clothed all in black?"

"Yes."

"That'll be the *Bande Nere,* then, of Giovanni de' Medici. I had the chance to work for him once. I should have taken it. Things might have turned out differently."

I can't watch any longer. I turn away. I feel his hand tighten around my forearm. "Stay away from battles, lad," he advises, his mouth brushing my ear. "They are not for you."

"I intend to," I reply.

There's a crisp barked instruction. It isn't the *interrogante*. It's haughty, sneering. "Iago of Mantua, lay down that sword! You are under arrest for the murder of the Contessa Maddalena di Asti!"

Iago sniffs. "You have my name wrong, sir. I am no Mantuan. And you are . . . ?"

A puffed-up, expensively dressed young man has the temerity to walk to within a few feet of him—so close, in fact, that he could have his head struck off by Iago's sword in a second. I have to admire his courage—or his youthful bravado. "I am Giulio Gonzaga, nephew to the Marquis of Mantua, second cousin to the *contessa*. You will obey my order now!"

"Never heard of you," says Iago. "And I will take no orders from you or any gutless *Mantuan*." He spits. The other soldiers bridle, clearly Mantuans to a man.

"Then perhaps you will take one from me." Annibale Malipiero has finally reached us and seems rather annoyed himself by the youngster's intrusion. Franceschina, wisely, is hanging back.

I can feel Iago's labored breathing as he chuckles. "I've an idea, Signor . . ."

"And what might that be?"

"That you and I should fight, man to man, right here."

"I don't *do* fighting, I'm afraid."

"You've never held a sword in your life, have you?"

"Never. I hope I never shall."

"You are a coward, then."

"You are right in your opinion of me, sir. I'm a dreadful coward."

"You are the worst type of coward, for you still send men to their deaths."

"Strictly speaking, it is not I who sends them. I can only recommend."

"What would you recommend for me?"

"A ghastly fate, I'm sure. Do you want me to go into the specifics?"

"No trial, then?"

"Trial?" Annibale Malipiero blinks in astonishment. "Do you

seriously think that the people of Venice, or Mantua—or the whole world, for that matter—want you *tried*? They wish you to be broken apart and hanged, as soon and as gruesomely as possible."

The soldiers flourish their swords in chorused agreement or bang them against their shields, crying, "Yes, string the beast up! Tear him to pieces!"

Iago wrenches me still closer. "It would do you some benefit too, Signor, would it not," he growls, "to bring me back in chains to Venice?"

The inquisitor shrugs. "Venice . . . Mantua . . . that still has to be discussed."

"No, it doesn't!" the eager young Gonzaga exclaims, approaching us again. "He's coming back to Mantua with me!"

Now Iago's sword is at my neck, as I've suspected it would be eventually. I hear a whimper from Franceschina.

The *interrogante* reaches out a hand—a beckoning, quite propitiatory gesture, palm upward, fingers curling inward. "Come," he says. "At the very least give me the boy. He was only doing what he was told to do. Then we can talk."

"No," Iago snaps. "No more talking."

He hauls me off with that extraordinary strength he can summon in an instant. *Where's he taking me now?* He grabs me around the throat and brandishes his weapon, defying all comers. They back off, terrified and dumbfounded, as I've seen so many do before. The circle breaks.

In front of us is a river. It's wide; it looks deep; it's fast-flowing, rushing over and around glistening black boulders. Once more the sword is pressing on my gullet. "It's time for a leave-taking, Gentile Stornello," he rasps.

With a fist in my back, he forces me nearer to the water's edge. It's quite a drop—at least a man's height beneath us. I stare into the bubbling maelstrom. He knows I can't swim, that I once almost drowned in a canal . . .

"Say goodbye at least, boy," he grunts.

"Goodbye, Iago," I sob, and close my eyes.

"Come, don't blub now, be a *man*. You've proved you can be."

From behind us, there's a sound more distinctive than the general cacophony of battle. It's deafening nonetheless, and it's getting nearer—the reverberation of hooves on earth. I open my eyes to see him step toward the very edge of the bank. I hear him mutter, "Good luck, lad; you've so far had more of it than I ever had."

He's about to plunge into the flood himself. He stretches out his arms in readiness, bends his knees . . .

But his leap is stopped by a longsword, thrown with remarkable accuracy, piercing his upper torso and entering it directly between his shoulder blades, up to the hilt.

At exactly the same moment, a horse, a great white muscled charger, snorting and braying, rears onto its hind legs, almost above the two of us, as its rider pulls hard on its reins and calls out, in a voice I'm sure I recognize, "Whoa! *Cessa!* There, boy! *Cessa! Calma!*" It's a good thing he did, or he and his beast would have gone tumbling into the current themselves.

Iago swings around, the sword sticking out of his chest, blood spraying along and around the blade. His mouth opens as he gapes at this mysterious and entirely unexpected assailant. He looks affronted. Then, with the weapon still in him, his flinty gray-green eyes lock briefly with mine before they turn blank and his legs buckle and he topples backward into the river.

His cannonball head hits a rock. I watch his once-robust body become a slack collection of limbs, knocked from stone to stone by the potency of rushing water, until it sinks.

"You've killed him!" I hear Annibale Malipiero cry out in fury. "*I did not wish him killed!*"

"Steady on," says my rescuer. "*He* was about to kill my little brother. I couldn't let him do that now, could I?"

"I don't think he was . . ." I mumble.

At last I glance up at him. Astride his still gnashing and stamping stallion, he looks every bit as he should—a knight in shining armor, *un cavaliere senza macchia*, without a stain, as a poet might put it, gleaming, brilliantly metallic. On his white jerkin over all that glistening protection there is a coat-of-arms depicting the double-headed eagle of the German emperor.

I can't see his face, but after some fiddling with various clasps and hinges, he pushes his visor up and there it is, as open and uncomplicated and beautifully unimaginative as ever. It scrunches up. "What are you doing here of all godforsaken places?" Benvenuto asks. "And why aren't you in Venice? And what's going on? And who *was* that fellow?"

"That was Iago," I say. The name, of course, means nothing to him, and further explanation would be fruitless, I imagine.

I drop to the ground and I'm allowed to sit there for a while, my knees scraping my chin. I weep tears of exhaustion, finality, and loss.

55. The World Turned Upside Down

I don't return to Venice much these days. Even though I'll always consider her the greatest of cities, impossibly beautiful and complex and enthralling, my memories have made her a dark realm—a place of sinister dealings, brutality and punishment, and pain, sorrow, and death.

When I got back there all those years ago, I attended two funerals in quick succession. The first was my uncle Ubaldo's. I'm sure he would rather have been buried somewhere in the rich Euganean Hills, but the clan insisted he should be entombed in the Frari, alongside ex-doges and ex-soldiers and ex-Stornelli. The fact that, in our obsequies, we had to file past a closed rather than an open coffin caused a fair deal of speculation as to *how* exactly he had met his end.

A couple of weeks later, another of my uncles was interred at the Frari. The corpse of Lodovico Stornello, shipped from Cyprus, boasted a sarcophagus far grander than that of Uncle Ubaldo, and his funeral occasioned far greater pomp. But there was no fudging as to how *he* had died. He'd been murdered by Cypriot rebels, in the cause, it was said, of the Ottoman. There was much baying for Cypriot and Turkish blood from the crowds during that ceremony.

The talk among the extended family on that occasion had little to do, however, with the dignitary being laid to rest—it was of the recent news that a third uncle, Graziano Stornello no less, once Captain-General of the Sea, had fallen to his death from a mountaintop, also in

Cyprus, to which he'd retired, and where he had become betrothed to a woman who had once been (this was whispered in especially hushed voices among the younger members of our tribe) a prostitute. He'd taken up walking in the hills, apparently, and was visiting a fortress where the notorious felon Iago had once—briefly—been incarcerated. The drop from this particularly precipitous peak was some three thousand feet.

I learned too, that after the murder of Lodovico Stornello, a new governor had been appointed, by the name of Bonifacio Colonna. If I'd never previously given much thought to the inhabitants of that unfortunate land, I definitely didn't envy them then.

At these funerals I looked for Annibale Malipiero—for most of Venice, as is the custom, dutifully turned up for them, burying, along with the bodies, all familial differences for the occasion. But I didn't see him and in fact had not since we spoke on that battlefield south of Milan. I hope I told him what he wanted to know—or as much as I could remember, at least.

Oddly, for all the tribulations he and I had been through, he didn't seem to listen to me much. I stared at him, and it seemed as if—how should I best put this?—as if his cogitations had moved beyond and above such things.

"He's dead too," Baldassare, who had been tutor to his son, announced to me. "He killed himself." Baldassare, by the way, has become far less discursive than he once was. He speaks *pat*, to the crux. Which is no bad thing.

"Killed himself? When? How?"

A shrug. "Sitting in his garden on the Giudecca, said to his wife, 'What's the point of anything?' or words to that effect, sent her in to prepare dinner, next he's being dragged out of the canal."

There's always a reason . . . That, at the very least, is what Annibale Malipiero has taught me.

"He never really got over the death of Carlo."

"Carlo?"

"Yes, the boy I taught. Died of some illness they've never been able to fathom, when he was around your age."

Little wonder that I think of Venice as a town of mourning.

But that was then—five years ago, in fact—and this is now. Bad memories and ghosts don't matter anymore. What matters these days is what I can grasp.

The world has turned—though not as yet entirely upside down. Padua's not quite as violent as she used to be. There are still the roaring students, but thankfully there aren't so many soldiers, as the wars are effectively over, or so I've heard. I still have no interest in war and who's won or lost what, but even I know that the French king was booted out of Italy—finally and irrevocably, we all hope—more than two years ago. There's some trouble in Rome, I gather. According to the worst reports, *La Città Eterna*, as it likes to call itself, is being ransacked by marauding Germans in the name of some new ascetic form of Christianity, led by firebrands denouncing the pope for being a meretricious anti-Christ. But Rome is four hundred miles south of here, and a kind of peace has descended on this northern conglomeration of bits of Italy for the present.

Somewhere even farther off, way out east, Venice still holds the Ottoman at bay, but the Ottoman, as usual, aren't giving up.

I'm a teacher in Padua now. But my subjects are not, you may be surprised to learn, poetry, or philosophy, or history, or anything in truth that has much to do with what's written down, except by men like Hippocrates and Galen. Yes, my study is medicine or, more specifically, the human body. I've become enthralled by the way it works and quite often doesn't, or not as well as it might. I'm hoping that my research will do more actual good, will serve humanity better, than any amount of fictitious meanderings or even the airy musings of the great thinkers or the sometimes misleading maze of the imagination. Baldassare disagrees with me, but I'd expect him to.

My lodgings are in a not very salubrious part of town. I can afford nothing else, not on a lecturer's salary. Sometimes my father sends me the odd stipend, but it pains him to do so, not because he's still cold to me—when I returned home all that time ago he greeted me like a long-lost, if wayward, son—but because he has very little income himself. Benvenuto, who inevitably remains his favorite, is the main breadwinner in the Palazzo Stornello Piccolo. I'm sure he's going to be very rich indeed someday—he's quite the *condottiere illustro*. He, too, sends me a few ducats now and then.

It's raining, as it frequently does here in the depths of winter. I warm myself in front of a fairly measly fire after another day of rambunctious argument with my students. Baldassare is snoring. He's always here, when he isn't teaching. A book (Theocritus, inevitably; he still hasn't completed his treatise) has fallen open at his feet. He's getting even fatter. Balbina feeds him more than she should. She's preparing something weighty and filling right now, following some guarded recipe of Zinerva's to the letter, in what we call "the kitchen" but is in truth a tiny corner of this one cramped downstairs room.

Balbina was insistent she should accompany me as soon as I said I was leaving Venice forever. She wept and pleaded with Zinerva, who let her go with gruff reluctance. "She'll never feed you like I've fed you, *ragazzo risoluto ma insensato*," I was warned. But from the pleasant aromas drifting over from a pot she's stirring now, I can tell that Balbina's doing just fine.

Zinerva also rebuked me for having the idiocy to leave at all. "Who will you find to marry in a place like Padua?" she sniffed.

"Who will want to marry *me*?" I replied.

Well—and like an actor who's been rather fine in a play, I think I deserve *some* acclamation, hands together, *gli spettatori*, if you please— the sole possessor of my heart sits opposite me. She, too, has a book— and it's the right way up. I'm teaching her to read. She's struggling a bit, but there's a creased determination to her brow. She looks up and smiles, like the sun on a very good day.

There's a crash and a cry from upstairs. Franceschina fears the worst. So do I. "Ay, Ubaldo!" my wife cries.

We're up the narrow staircase in an instant. Balbina hobbles after us. She adores the boy as much as we do.

But Ubaldo is all right. He's been playing (when, as his mother firmly reminds him, he should have been asleep) and simply tripped over something. He's a tough little mite—four years old now, with curly chestnut hair and stocky; dark of hue, but with bright blue eyes. He stares up at us with some boldness, but also fears rebuke. "Sorry, Mamma, sorry, Papà."

Children are everything, I think—an assurance against oblivion, a guarantee that there is something, some continuance, beyond death.